Avalon: TimeFall

STEPHEN JENSEN

Avalon Books, LLC

AVALON BOOKS, LLC
SALT LAKE CITY

Copyright © 2023 by Stephen Jensen

Printed in the United States of America by Avalon Books, LLC

The AVALON CLOCK colophon is a trademark of Avalon Books, LLC. Registration pending

avalonseriesbooks.com

Paperback ISBN 978-1-960860-01-9

Hardback ISBN 978-1-960860-00-2

Ebook ISBN 978-1-960860-02-6

First Edition

Cover art by Byron Pixton and Stephen Jensen and Lincoln Writes

Photo by Ralph Jensen

Book design by Stephen Jensen

Maps created by Stephen Jensen

Interior art by Stephen Jensen

In loving memory
Of
Carol

BERMUDA TRIANGLE AND COLONIAL AMERICA 1692-1697

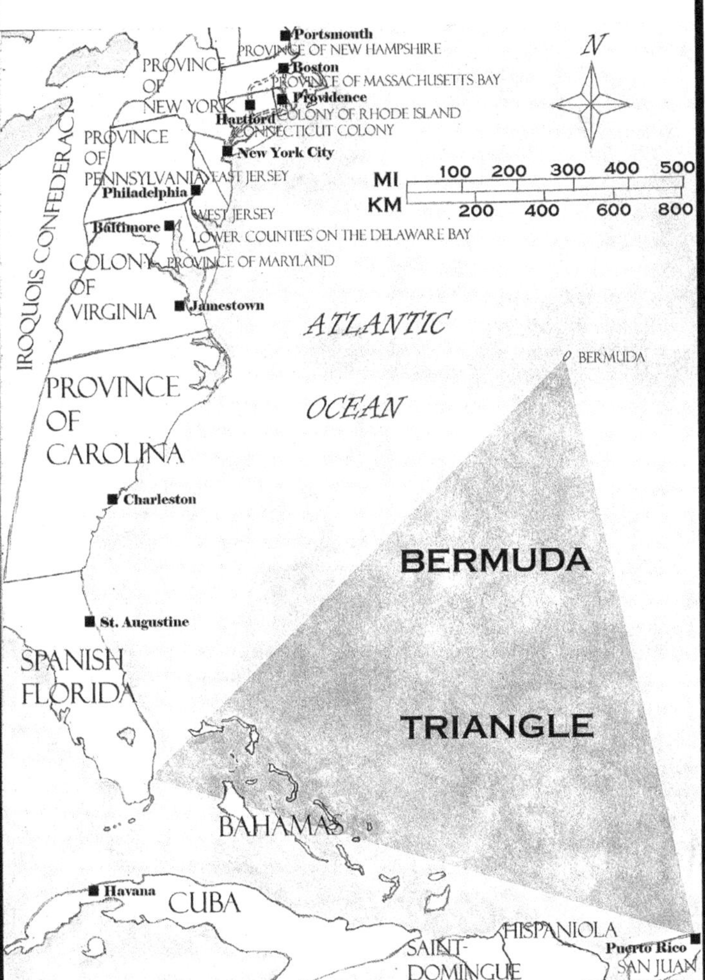

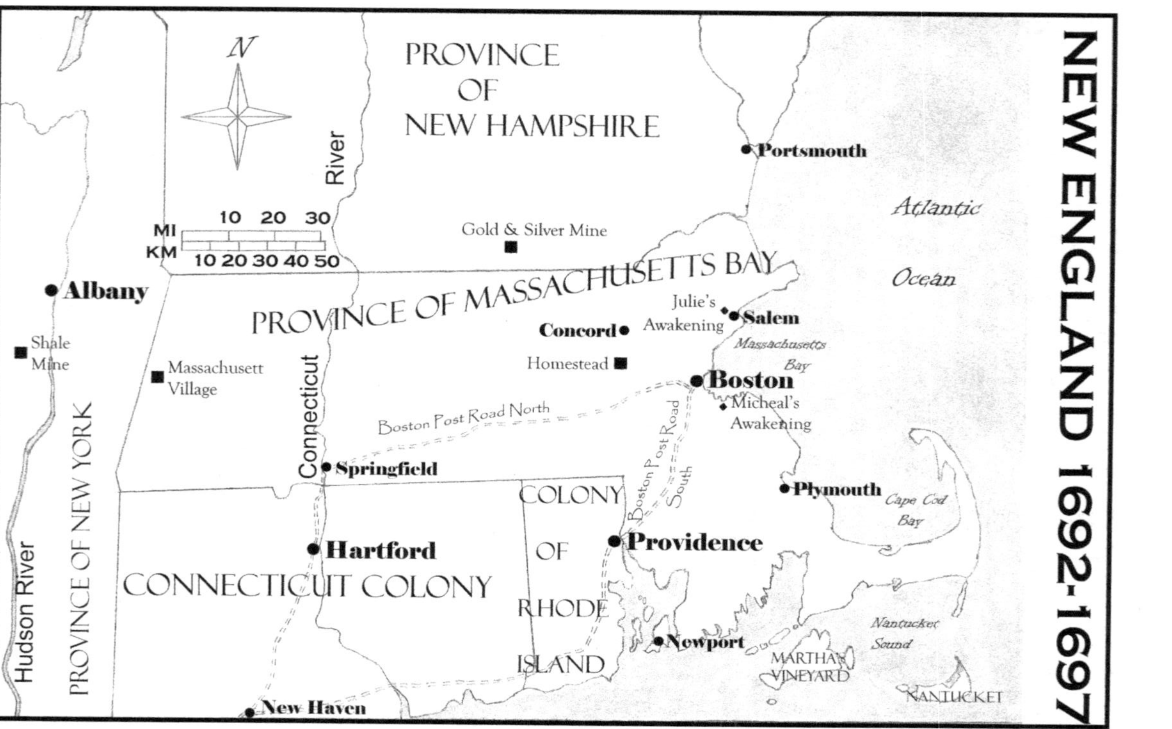

NEW ENGLAND 1692-1697
N
River
PROVINCE OF NEW HAMPSHIRE
Portsmouth
Atlantic
Ocean
MI
10 20 30
KM
10 20 30 40 50
Gold & Silver Mine
Albany
PROVINCE OF MASSACHUSETTS BAY
Julie's Awakening
Salem
Concord
Massachusetts Bay
Shale Mine
Homestead
Boston
Massachusett Village
Connecticut
Micheal's Awakening
Boston Post Road North
Boston Post Road South
Springfield
Plymouth
Cape Cod Bay
COLONY OF RHODE ISLAND
Hartford
Providence
CONNECTICUT COLONY
Hudson River
PROVINCE OF NEW YORK
Newport
Nantucket Sound
MARTHA'S VINEYARD
NANTUCKET
New Haven

BOSTON AREA 1692-1697

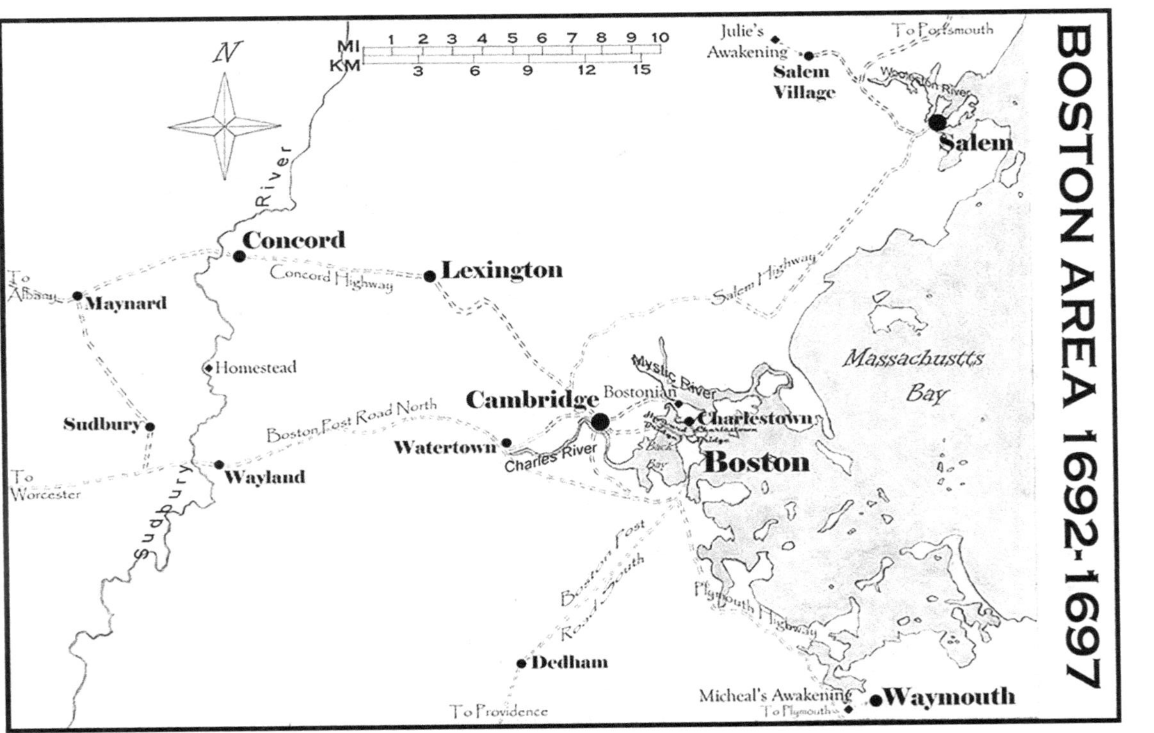

BOSTONIAN PALACE

Contents

28°-19'-12" N, 80°-14'-24" W

CAITLIN'S EYE WAS CAUGHT by a glow off the side of the boat, stopping her in her tracks. As she stared into the deep abyss of fading twilight, an eerie green glow lurked below the surface. She blinked, and it was gone. She shook her head and looked again, but there was nothing.

As Caitlin continued forward, she couldn't shake the feeling of dread.

"Of course there's no cell service out here," Caitlin heard Ashley say. Her parents were celebrating something to do with their business. Her mom's friend, José, had bought a big boat. She heard them call it a yacht. As she approached the front of the ship, she spotted Ashley with her friends.

Caitlin interrupted. "Ashley, can I—?"

"Caitlin! Get out of here! Go hang out with Darrin." Ashley pointed toward the back of the boat.

"He doesn't want me around."

"Then go bug mom—"

"But Ashley!"

"Go!!!"

Caitlin walked along the side of the boat. The sun was setting. She thought it looked so pretty. Ashley was her big sister. She always said Caitlin was too young to hang out with her and her friends. Caitlin was eleven and a half, almost twelve, which was old enough. Ashley was only sixteen. And her brother Darrin never wanted Caitlin around either.

"Karen, are you going to retire also?" Marcus asked as Caitlin approached the rear deck. "Jasmine and I are planning to have a yacht of our own so we can enjoy our retirement."

"Karen? I don't think so. She's too in love with work," her dad replied.

"That's definitely true," Karen agreed. "Besides, David, how else are you gonna afford all of your safaris?"

"Oh yeah, you love working with animals, don't you, Dave?" José asked.

"Yeah! He's a regular Steve Irwin," added Marcus.

"Mom," Caitlin cut in. "Ashley won't let me hang out with her."

"Caitlin, the grown-ups are talking."

"But Mom!"

"Caitlin, listen to your mother. Go watch a movie or something," her dad said.

Caitlin walked around for a few minutes, trying to find something to do. She climbed the stairs to the top deck. As she approached the bridge, Captain Yamaguchi smiled and said, "Come to see how the boat works?"

"Ok!"

"These are called throttles, the right and the left. Go ahead and push them forward," the captain instructed.

When she pushed the throttles forward, the boat sped up.

"Ok, pull it back a little," the captain said.

When she pulled the throttles back, the boat slowed down.

"Now, this is the wheel. Take over 'Captain Anderson'." He placed his hat on her head when she grabbed the wheel.

Caitlin gazed out of the window with a new sense of freedom. All she could see was open ocean ahead of her.

A few minutes later, she turned the wheel to the left. As the twilight horizon came into view, everything went dark. The boat stopped.

"What's going on?" The feeling of dread returned.

"Step back, Miss Anderson," the captain instructed.

Caitlin stepped aside and watched the captain mess around with the controls. Her tummy tickled.

Mr. Patel, the engineer, ran past her. "Captain, what's going on?"

"It just stopped. I can't figure out–" Everything turned back on.

The lights flickered around them. "The engines are still dead."

"I'm trying to— What is that?" Mr. Patel pointed at something outside.

Caitlin stepped up on the tips of her toes to see the green glow had returned, coming up out of the water.

Captain Yamaguchi grabbed the radio. "Mayday, Mayday, Mayday. This is the *Esperanza*. Our last know coordinates are 28 degrees 19 minutes 12 seconds north latitude. 80 degrees 14 minutes 24 seconds west longitude. This is a power super yacht, thirty meters. Color white. Seventeen people are on board. We've lost power. Our instruments have malfunctioned–"

The green light turned into green mist.

"Oh my, we are being surrounded by a green mist. Have lost location and bearing. Require immediate assistance. Over."

Night suddenly turned into day. There was an island straight ahead.

How could that be? Caitlin thought. Just moments earlier there was nothing but open sea. The sky was a luminous purple. The water was a silvery green. She stared in shock as the light faded to black. Once again, it was night.

Fear gripped her. Caitlin hurried down to the second deck where people were running around screaming. The darkness made it impossible to see.

She turned right, heading toward the front of the boat, when the sky changed from dark to light, then back again. She was blinded for a moment. As her eyes came back into focus, Darrin ran right at her. The collision knocked them overboard.

Caitlin went under. She fought to break the surface. When she broke through, she was surrounded by thick green fog. She spotted the faint outline of the boat some distance away. Only it was too far away. She couldn't get back to it.

PETTY OFFICER ANTHONY JACKSON had commanded a medium response boat for the coast guard out of Cape Canaveral for about six months. They were on patrol, about twenty miles north of the Cape, when they received a distress call from a yacht called the *Esperanza* about five miles due east. They headed off at full steam to help.

He'd heard stories from other officers about the crazy things they'd seen. Things they would never put in an official report. He supposed it was part of the deal when you worked in the Bermuda Triangle.

Jackson gathered his crew to brief them on the situation. Within minutes, he spotted the ship on the horizon. It was enveloped in an eerie green mist. As they approached, the ship blinked in and out of sight, flickering like a hologram. When they were one hundred yards away, there came a sudden flash of light.

The ship had disappeared.

They searched the area and found one survivor. A little girl.

The men searched for days. There was no trace of any ship.

In the end, like those before and after him, Jackson had his own story to tell and left out the extraordinary details from the official report.

Who would believe him anyway?

PART ONE: PRESENT TENSE

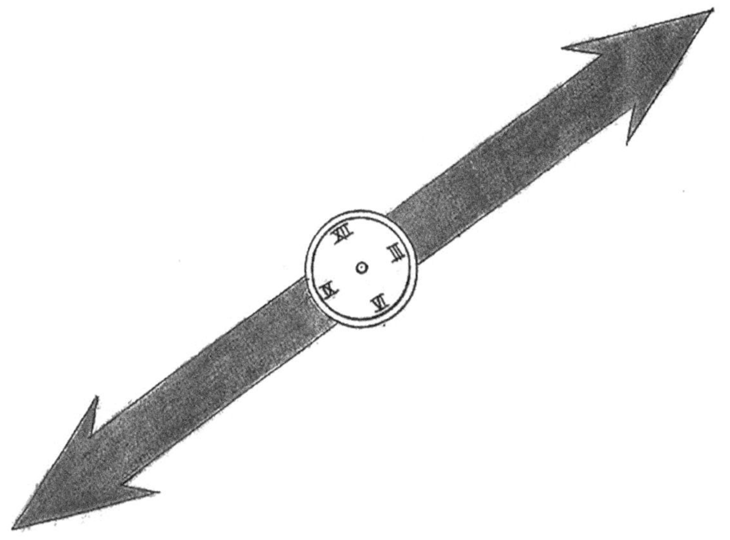

CHAPTER 1:
JULIE ALEXANDRA BUCKINGHAM

I: Christmas 2009

JULIE LOOKED AT HER childhood home with a feeling of longing and foreboding, like this might be the last time she'd ever see it. It was strange coming home to Virginia now. There was an empty space in the house, one that could never be filled, ever since her older sister Jessica died.

Her husband, Aiden, grabbed her hand, snapping her out of her daze. "Are ye ready?" His sweet Irish accent soothed her.

She nodded. They walked up the path to the front door. Before they could reach it, her parents emerged.

"Julie!" Her mom threw her arms around her.

"Merry Christmas, Mom," Julie replied with a smile. "Dad!" She hugged him next.

"Sorry we're late." Aiden nodded his head.

"It's no trouble," said her mom. "How are you?"

Before he could answer, her dad yelled, "Hey everybody! Julie and Aiden are here!"

They were already in the middle of one of their family traditions, storytime. They'd each take turns telling one of their favorite family Christmas stories. Her brother Jason's wife was in the middle of hers.

"—Dad did his best impression of Clark Griswold. He thought it was a good idea to cut down our own Christmas tree from the forest. But he had a procrastination problem. Three days before Christmas, we finally went into the forest to cut down a tree. After decorating, we discovered the candy canes had been gnawed on. We looked and looked, but we couldn't figure out why it kept happening. On Christmas Eve, while Dad was reading *A Christmas Carol*, the culprit behind the Candy Cane Caper appeared. A squirrel jumped onto the mantle from the tree. Everyone freaked out. The tree was knocked over and the living room was trashed. It was the most memorable Christmas. But we never cut down our own tree again." Amy finished her story to the sound of everyone laughing.

Aiden took his turn telling a heartwarming story about the time he played Santa to a bunch of kids at an orphanage in his hometown of Dublin. Then it was Julie's turn.

"It was Christmas 1992. Jessica had an idea to play bad Santa. Now I had known Santa wasn't real since I was five. I learned—"

Jason cut in. "You mean Santa Claus isn't real?!"

Julie glanced around the room to make sure no kids were present.

"—I'd learned that the fastest anything could go in the universe was the speed of light. I calculated that even if Santa could move that fast, it still wouldn't be fast enough. So there was no way Santa Claus could be real. But I digress. Jessica thought it would be funny to make Jason and Jennifer think they were on Santa's naughty list. A couple of days before Christmas, we wrapped a bunch of fake presents filled with coal. Mom and Dad went to sleep after putting out the presents. We snuck down and changed out Jason and Jennifer's real presents for the fake ones. Their reactions were priceless. Jessica and I couldn't stop laughing. We were both grounded for a month after that, but it was totally worth it."

The room filled with laughter.

Jennifer shook her head in disbelief. "I couldn't believe Santa thought I had been naughty."

"I expected to be on his naughty list, but I always got everything I asked for. I didn't think Santa would ever punish me. Then he did," Jason added.

"We knew immediately what had happened," her mom said. "It had Jessica written all over it. Jessica and Julie were like twins, born three years apart. We were so mad at you both."

"What do you mean they were like twins?" Jennifer's boyfriend, Hunter, asked.

"Well, first the obvious. They looked nearly identical," Her dad began.

Her mom leaned into Hunter and whispered, "Jennifer doesn't like to talk about Jessica."

"They were both tall and slender. Jess wasn't quite Julie's height. She was five foot ten, just a couple of inches shorter—"

—And Jess had platinum blond hair compared to mine—

"—And Jess had platinum blonde hair, compared to Julie's dark-brown hair. Sometimes we would joke that Julie was the night and Jessica the day—"

Julie's cheeks flushed with embarrassment because of the focus on her. Her dad couldn't help it. Jessica left a big hole in his heart. It was almost automatic for him—

"—Yeah, yeah. My eyes are turquoise like the sea and Jessica's are light blue, like the sky. Come on, Dad, that's enough."

"A lot of people said they should be models—" her dad continued.

"Dad!" Julie snapped and regretted it immediately. A look of pain crossed her dad's eyes—the look of a father who was still waiting for his little girl to come home.

"She's embarrassed. He can't help but go on and on about those two," her mom whispered to Hunter.

"I'm sorry, honey. I got carried away." Her dad managed a smile. "It's okay, Dad. I miss her too." Julie reached out to hold his hand. He held it tight.

"Now, I think it's Jennifer's turn," Jason interjected.

As the night went on, Jennifer and Hunter lightened the mood and lifted the family's spirit with tales of rubber masks, Modge Podge, and buckets of confetti.

Conversations continued. Good times were had. Mostly by Aiden, in the form of eggnog. He was certainly the life of the party.

When they retired to her old bedroom, Julie said. "Now, Aiden,

I know we've missed each other the last few months. Have you been practicing?"

They had finally invited Aiden to sing with her, Jason, Jennifer, Amy, and Hunter at the Christmas Eve performance at St. Patrick's Church in downtown Richmond. It was another family tradition.

"Not really, but don't worry."

She looked at him skeptically. "Sing 'O holy night'."

He began. "Oh holy..." His voice broke. He cleared his throat and tried again. "Oh holy ni..." His voice broke again. "I dunno what the problem is."

"I think you're drunk. Maybe you should sit this one out."

The next day, following brunch and family pictures, they met at the church to get ready for the concert.

Julie was preparing to sing lead for the concert. She had been in the choir when she was young and would sing in the Christmas Concert whenever she came home for the holiday.

When the concert was supposed to begin, the choir director's assistant informed her there was a problem. Mikk the male vocal lead, canceled last minute due to illness. She would have to go on alone.

As the curtains lifted, the melody stepped in, and she began singing "The Christmas Song", a traditional start to the concert.

She continued with "Have Yourself a Merry Little Christmas".

As she was coming to the end of her verse, her mind filled with anxiety about having to do a duet alone. Suddenly, a new distraction came into view. Aiden stood in the wings, on cue to Mikk's mark. When the male vocal began, Aiden was right on tune. Her knight in shining armor.

He sang lead alongside Julie for the rest of the concert, finishing with 'O Holy Night'. To the delight of the entire audience.

Aiden and Julie were surrounded by family immediately after the curtains went down.

"Aiden! My goodness! That was amazing!" Jennifer said.

"Yeah, Aiden. You really knocked it outta the park!" added Amy.

Aiden turned to Julie. "It looked like you needed help out there."

"You always take care of me. How did you convince Angela to let you sing?"

"Well, after my voice went aresways on me last night, I thought I let you down. I overheard Angela in a panic and offered my services. I sang a little bit for her. I suppose she liked what she heard."

Later that evening, Aiden sat down next to Julie at the dinner table.

"Nuttin' says Christmas like crab cakes," Aiden joked.

"It says Christmas to me," Julie said.

She always loved their nontraditional seafood dinner on Christmas Eve. Along with the crab cakes, which were homemade, the dinner included oysters, calamari, and shrimp.

"It's been a tradition for generations, ever since my great-great-grandfather settled in Virginia," her dad commented to Hunter.

"I call this one 'Julie's White Christmas,'" Julie presented this year's sushi roll creation. Rolling sushi was always her favorite part of dinner.

"It has white crab meat, calamari, bean sprouts, and water chestnuts. I used a light drizzle of Japanese white sauce."

"That sounds great," her mother said. "Jason, would you say grace?"

"Of course."

As Jason concluded his recitation of grace, Julie couldn't help but glare at him for his next statement.

"And, dear lord, please protect us from Julie's latest sushi concoction, for we would very much like to make it to midnight mass alive."

"Jason!" Her mom cut in.

A round of laughter filled the room as dinner began.

As plates were being cleared, Julie announced. "I have a special gift for each of you."

With Aiden's help, she retrieved some canvas on which she had created individual family portraits in oil.

"This looks amazing!" Jennifer said, receiving hers.

"It's like a classical painting." Her mother ran her fingers over the brushwork.

"How much do you think it will fetch on eBay?"

"Jason!" Amy chided her brother. "It will look beautiful above our mantel,"

"I made this one especially for you." Julie presented a portrait of Jessica to her father.

"Oh, honey." Her dad's eyes welled up as he hugged her.

Later that night, everyone went to midnight mass. Except for Julie. She hadn't been to midnight mass since Jessica's death. She blamed herself for not being able to save Jessica. She also blamed God.

Instead, Julie's midnight mass was spent alone at Jessica's grave. It was snowing at the cemetery as she made her way through the graveyard. The sight of the angel gravestone brought her back to that day at Lake Anna in the summer of '95. As she stood over Jessica's grave, she closed her eyes and fell into a memory.

"So how's Harvard? Meet any cute guys?" Jess turned the steering wheel and pulled into the state park.

"Ha ha I'm fifteen. Besides, I'm not there to make friends. I'm going to Harvard to get PHDs, Jess. Not STDs."

Jessica laughed. "Good one!"

"I just wanna focus on graduating in the next two years."

"Three doctorates in two years, not three?"

"Well, I figured I would just take it easy," Julie replied. They both laughed as they got out of the car.

They gathered their gear and set off to find a spot at the southeast end of the beach.

"It's gonna be nice for you to be so close to home next year."

"No, I'm not going to Duke anymore. I'm going to Stanford."

"What? But that's on the other side of the country."

"Yeah, I thought it would be nice to have a little space."

"From Mom and Dad, or from Caleb?"

"A little of both, if you know what I mean."

Julie knew what was going through Jessica's mind. She settled into her chair and caught Jess looking out to Goodwin's Point. Her blond hair was swaying behind her. Jessica was too much of a free spirit to want to settle down. She wished she could be like that.

Jessica turned her head and caught Julie's reflective gaze.

"What's up, Jules?"

"Oh, nothing. Just looking at Jett's Island behind you."

Jessica turned toward the island, then back. "So no one's caught your eye? I mean, guys must be all over you."

"I get hit on a lot. A quick one-liner from a cute guy is sometimes nice, but it gets pretty annoying."

"Gotta beat 'em off with a stick, eh?"

"Obviously they're all too old."

"And I'm guessing that high school would be awkward?"

"Yeah...well, there is this one man..."

"Man? Jules, what are you talking about?"

"So he's Scottish and from a big family. A clan, actually. He has curly red hair and is tall and has just the right amount of facial hair."

"Who is it?"

"His name is Jamie Frazier, and he's a character in this book I'm reading. I told you, Jess. PHDs. Not STDs."

Julie saw Jessica's face change from concerned mother to semi-amused best friend.

"Whatevs... come on. Race ya to the buoy and back."

Jess led the way. They stopped short of the waves reaching their knees. She looked at Julie and gave a determined smile.

"Same bet?"

Julie looked at her sister for a second before returning the same smile. "Same bet."

They dove at the same time, and the race was on.

Julie knew she was going to win and already knew what she wanted as her reward. It had been the same for three years. Breakfast in bed for a whole week.

Julie took the lead. The gap between them grew bigger and bigger as they approached the cordon. She was in her own world.

When she reached the marker, she began her trip back and soon passed Jess, who had not yet made the turn.

Her focus was broken when Jessica's voice called out for her. "Julie!"

She paused and looked back. There was nothing. Jessica was gone.

Julie froze for what seemed to be a lifetime. She didn't know what to do. Then Jessica emerged from the water, arms flailing.

"Julie!" Jessica yelled. "I'm cramping! Help!" With that last call, Jessica went under again.

"Jessica!" Julie screamed. Her body was already in motion, making its way toward Jessica. She was fifty feet away and closing in fast.

Jessica had been under for a while before Julie began her dive.

Each time she dove into the murky depths, she came up empty-handed. Her desperation grew. Minutes felt like hours. When she began to lose hope, her hand touched flesh. Her fingers wrapped around Jessica's ankle. Julie began kicking hard toward the surface.

They were met by a lifeguard who drew Jessica back to shore and onto dry land. She yelled for space and began CPR.

Julie had no choice but to watch from the sidelines. Watch a stranger try to breathe life back into her sister. Time began to slow. The rescuer's palms sunk deep into Jessica's chest over and over. Slower each time. A crowd gathered with blank faces. Mere forms like the silhouette of a skyline in front of a full moon. Forms that were irrelevant. She was now part of that scene. There, but unable to do anything.

The crowd split when two people in uniforms made their way through. Julie turned to the only thing she could do. She clenched her hands and pulled them to her chest as if she held Jessica's very soul in them, not wanting to let go. With her head bowing and her gaze locked on Jessica, Julie began to pray. She called out to God to keep this from happening. To help her now more than ever. To not take away her sister.

She prayed for her mother and her father, for their love to help keep Jessica from leaving them. She prayed for every dream her sister shared with her. For every dream she had still to live out. She prayed for the promises made to one another. To see each other grow old and happy. To see Jessica smile again.

But it was all in vain. God was not there for her that day. All her hopes and dreams for Jessica came crashing down as the lifeguard cease her efforts. Her heart dropped, and her body lost the will to keep herself up. She fell to her knees in agony. Tears cascaded down her cheeks. She screamed Jessica's name and held her sister's body close.

Jessica was gone.

———⋈———

"You okay, Miss?"

Julie snapped out of her trance. She was on her knees. Her face soaked with tears. She wiped her face and tried to muster up the words that she was okay. She turned to an old man standing behind her.

"Yes. Thank you. Just missing someone."

"Ah, yes. Holidays have a way of reminding one of what's been lost. Just remember, time heals. Take care, my lady." The man was odd. He wore a black hooded robe and had a long gray beard.

"Thank you."

She waited until he was a good distance away before standing up. She didn't know why, but she didn't want him to see her move. Not while she was so vulnerable.

"Jessica," her voice cracked. She looked up as pigeons flew up into the air from behind the gravestone. "I'm sorry," Her voice lowered. "Why did we go to the lake that day?" It was her fault. She was responsible for her sister's safety and failed her. This was her cross to bear.

"I know you wouldn't want me to blame myself for what happened. But the lake was my idea. I always think there was something more I could have done. I know I could have...I still don't understand why God didn't help us that day. I'm so sorry..." Her brows furrowed. Her head began to shake slowly as anger took hold. More tears came as she stewed in her resentment towards God. Julie's eyes landed on the plaque at the base of the angel. It read, "Jessica Buckingham." A sense of warm calm washed over her.

Jessica was there.

Julie rose to her feet. She brushed the snow off her pants, secured her coat, and dried her cheeks from the new tears of relief. The angel again came into her perspective. It reminded her of Aiden. A voice like an angel.

"Aiden came to my rescue today. Singing together at the concert was such a joy..." her face grew brighter.

"Everything is great between us, except for the past couple of months when we've barely seen each other. We'll make up for it this weekend... Oh! Can you believe my show is almost five years old? I love it... It gives me a reason to talk to Mom every night and if I'm lucky, Dad chimes in if he's still awake. They miss you. I miss you... On a different note, I studied physical chemistry at Columbia. Now I've moved on to computer sciences. It gives me the mental workout I need. I know you wouldn't want me to let my 269 IQ go to waste. You were the only one who didn't think I was wasting my genius on business. Mom and Dad wanted me to be the next Einstein... I try to make sure to notice the good things. To 'focus on the green'. Like you taught me..."

As more tears came, joy turned back to grief. Her smile faded. A prelude to her hardest goodbye.

"I miss you so much. It's been so hard without you. I love you, Jess. Until next time." She stood in silence. Her tears streamed while the snow fell. She closed her eyes and felt she could feel Jessica's comforting presence there with her.

II: Bull Markets

JULIE began her first show of the new year. 2009 saw her highest ratings yet. Perhaps in 2010 she could become the queen of cable business news.

"I'm Julie Buckingham. Today is Monday, January 4, 2010, and this is *Bull Markets*. Our bulls today are for the year ahead. The NASDAQ: all equity markets were up last year, but the tech-heavy NASDAQ outperformed. It was up forty-four percent for the year and seventy-nine percent since the March 9 lows. It will remain the strongest of the markets. We will see a gain of around fifteen to twenty percent this year. I have a target of 2700 points by year's end. Our commodity bull is oil. West Texas Intermediate was up seventy-eight percent in 2009. The growth will slow down, but it will still end the year up about twenty-five percent. My year-end target is around one hundred dollars per barrel. Our treasury bull is the thirty-year bond. The yield rose last year by forty-seven percent. As equities continue to rebound, the flight to safety is coming to an end. If you want to be in the bond market this year, the thirty-year will fall the least, probably no more than five percent, and it will remain flat with a year-end target yield of four-point-five percent. And you can ride those bulls all the way to the bank. Now let's bring in Lindsay for a market update." She tossed to Lindsay and took a deep breath.

The show progressed and Julie relaxed into the familiar format, discussing the new year with various experts in different areas of business. She was in her last studio interview with Mark Barton, a business acquaintance and an expert in currencies.

"We have a target of a dollar-thirty-four for the Euro by year's end. But we think the Yen will be the strongest this year. We are looking for around eighty-five to the dollar." Mark said.

"Thank you, Mark. That was Mark Barton, Barton Capital Investments. And we will be back, in the China Shop," she said, closing out the segment.

"It was a great pleasure!" Mark said as he rose from the glass table.

"Pleasure was all mine. Thank you, Mark." Julie walked to her final cue mark.

"In three... two..." Rachel cued her.

"Okay, so there have been many bulls in the shop this past year, but usually you wouldn't open the door for them. Just before Christmas, Green Haven Financial was concerned Chief Investment Officer Jerry Carlisle would leave and take a large portion of their analysts with him. So what was their brilliant strategy to prevent this from happening? They sent him packing. And what did he take with him in his briefcase? Oh, about half of their top analysts and fund managers. And now Carlisle is setting up a competing firm. They were so concerned this might happen, they decided to guarantee that it would. Talk about opening the door for that bull. That's our first show for the year. Now get out there and grab the bull by the horns."

"And we're clear," Rachel nodded.

Julie walked off the set, heading down the hall towards their offices, and Rachel came with her.

"Rachel, I'm going to move my flight to Monday. Aidan is going to close the deal in Napa earlier than expected, so he will be in town this weekend. I think we need some quality time together. You'll fill in on Monday and Tuesday?"

"Of course. You and Aiden haven't been able to see much of each other lately."

"I know it's short notice..."

"Don't even worry about it."

"Are you sure?"

"I would love to. You enjoy the weekend. I'm sure Aidan will."

"Rachel!"

"You'll have to give me the details next week."

"Thanks Rach!"

As she continued down the hallway, Julie's mind went to the last time she and Aiden had been intimate. Their schedules had them missing each other since Thanksgiving. Aiden was back and forth from California on a couple of major deals his real estate firm had been working on. She'd had some unforeseen obligations come up in relation to her investment firm. The only nights they had been together since were during Christmas at her parents. They had tried to find a private moment, but with so many people in the house that had proved impossible, so she planned to make the most of this weekend.

"Nikki, can you move my flight to Monday evening?" She asked as she entered her office.

"Of course. I'll get you a revised itinerary as soon as possible. Oh, the man from the Journal called again. He wanted to know if you'd reconsider his request for the interview."

"He's persistent. That's what? Three requests in the last week alone?"

"Four. I gave him the same response as last time. Also, this came for you," Nikki said, indicating a large bouquet of calla lilies on her desk, her favorite.

Julie read the card. "My precious jewel, I can't wait for the weekend. Love, Aiden."

III: The Weekend

The weekend couldn't come soon enough.

As Friday night approached, Aiden mentioned a special surprise he arranged for the two of them the following day. Julie, surprised to hear Aiden's request for an early night, resolved that whatever he had planned would be worth it if only they spent time together after all the lonely months apart.

Julie awoke the next morning to find Aiden fully dressed. He had laid out a dress for her. The notion was romantic.

"Now that we're all dressed up, where are we going?"

"Let's take a walk," Aiden suggested.

They walked through the park. It was perfect with just the two of them. Just the way she wanted it.

"We got all dressed up for a walk in the park?"

"Aye, it's a lovely day for it, no?"

"It's beautiful."

She'd run or take walks in the park nearly every day since they had moved into 15 Central Park West, one of the most exclusive buildings in Manhattan. They'd lived there since they got married.

The snow-covered Sheep Meadow. It sparkled like a field of diamonds in the morning light.

As they approached the fountain, she realized where they were headed.

"Bring back any memories?" Aiden gently prodded.

She paused when he pulled her in to kiss her.

"How about now?"

"How could I forget after such a demonstration?"

Bethesda Fountain was the first place they had kissed on the night they met following the Met Gala. They left the crowds behind and went for a walk in the park. They were sitting by the fountain talking when he suddenly leaned in and kissed her. Despite her surprise, she couldn't help but kiss him back. They'd been introduced by a business associate and had had almost instant chemistry.

She might have suspected their destination had she recognized the dress sooner. She'd been too excited to spend time with Aiden that she hadn't realized the dress he laid out for her was the one she wore the night they met. It was her first time being invited to the Met Gala. The theme was 'In the House of Chanel' and she had worn a thin strap low cut black dress with firework sparkles on it. It was vintage from the late thirties.

As they continued walking, she said, "So we're going to the Met. Isn't it a little early?"

"It's been arranged. I've missed ya these past few months, so I wanted to do something special."

As they climbed the steps, they were greeted by the museum director.

"Thomas, how are ya?" Aiden asked pleasantly.

"Mr. O'Leary, Mrs. Buckingham, we're happy to accommodate you this morning. Everything is as you requested."

"Very much appreciated, and thanks for all your trouble." Aiden touched his shoulder.

"No trouble at all. We greatly appreciate your generous support."

Aiden led her to the Petrie Sculpture Court. As they entered, a string quartet began playing, and they were greeted by a man in a tuxedo who led them to a table.

"Wow, you really planned this out, didn't you?"

"Oh, just a few phone calls. No big deal."

They were served a gourmet breakfast and had a chance to just relax in each other's company.

Following their meal, Aiden rose from his seat, reached out his hand, and said, "Would ya like to dance?"

Enchanted by the gesture, Julie extended her hand and placed it in Aiden's. They made their way to an open section of the gallery and began to dance. Julie fell upon another pleasant surprise. The band started playing their song. "Forever In Love" by Kenny G.

"This is exactly what I needed," she sighed, sliding her hands behind his neck as they swayed to the melody.

"I felt like we were losing our connection. That I was losing you." He held her a little tighter.

"You'll never lose me."

They swayed in each other's arms for what seemed like only moments when Julie remembered something Jessica had told her once.

"Put your hand on a hot pan and a minute can seem like an hour. Put your hand in the hand of the one you love, and an hour can seem like a minute. Everything is relative, Julie." With that thought, she held Aiden even closer.

Julie laid her head on his chest and closed her eyes. She was taken back to the magic of the night when she knew she'd met the one with whom she would spend the rest of her life.

When the music was over and the spell of the moment faded away, Julie and Aiden left the museum. A carriage was waiting outside to take them home. The rest of the day was spent making up for lost time.

On Sunday they went to a preview of *Time Stands Still* by Donald Margulies starring Laura Linney and Alicia Silverstone on Broadway at the Friedman Theater.

The discussion of the play continued as they entered their penthouse.

"I love how the relationship evolved between Sarah and James.

And Mandy was the perfect comic relief." Julie said.

"Oh, aye. Sarah and James made me think of us."

"How so?"

"How their relationship had to change. I've been thinking good and long about it. I'm going to scale back my involvement in so many deals."

"You can't do that. You love it too much."

"I love you more. I want to spend more time with you. You're the most important thing to me."

"You're the only thing that matters to me. I can quit the show—"

"I would never let that happen. I've spent so many years doing deals. I'm ready to be a husband... and father."

"I can't... father?"

"Aye, I would love to have some children around the house."

Julie knew he meant it.

She took his hand in hers. "I would love to have children with you."

"Want to start now?" He pulled her to him.

There was a look of surprise on Aiden's face as she pushed him to the bed. Not wanting to wait one more moment, she made her way on top of him and kissed his neck. She bit him a little, then met his lips with hers.

Aiden's hands undid her bra just as she got him on his back. He slid it off as they rolled over, and he was now on top. Julie finished unbuttoning Aiden's shirt. He threw it on the floor and resumed his kiss. She gave in to the touch of her husband. Gave him the freedom to explore her body as he had the first time they'd made love.

Aiden took her in his hands. As he moved from Julie's soft neck down to her collar, she shivered with pleasure and urged Aiden for more. He continued to move his lips down her chest. As he reached her delicate navel, he slipped her panties off with his hands and began kissing her further down...

CHAPTER 2: MICHEAL WILLIAM HALL

I: New Year's Eve

MICHEAL'S FRIEND TC DID his best Kramer impression as he entered his apartment and grabbed a soda from the fridge.

"Mike, you gonna come to the party with me? There's gonna be so many hotties there. I'll hook you up."

"I don't think so."

"You don't have to drink. Come on, we'll find someone to kiss you at midnight," TC tried to convince him.

Micheal rolled his eyes. "Yeah right."

"Why do you always do that?"

"Do what?"

"Put yourself down like that."

"No woman at a college party is going to kiss a chubby behemoth like me," he replied with a derisive laugh.

"Most of them are in med school. They're not undergrads. You're the smartest person I know by a long shot. They'll like that."

TC was in his last year of specialty training to become a neurosurgeon. The two had met in kindergarten, when TC still went by Tyler Collinsworth, and they had been friends ever since. TC was pretty much Micheal's only friend. They were like brothers.

"I don't know how to talk to women. I'm a high school dropout.

They'll think I'm a loser."

"You don't think I'm insecure about my height? I'm five foot six. What I wouldn't give for a few of those inches your six-foot-four ass is wasting."

"You seem to be doing just fine. What did they call you in high school? Black Velvet?" Micheal snorted.

"I... don't know what you're talking about. That doesn't sound like me." They both chuckled.

"You could smooth talk your way out of anything, or *into* anything, right?"

"You could too if you would actually try."

"I'd rather not embarrass myself."

"Whatever. I wish you saw your own potential. Catch you later," TC said as he walked out the door.

Micheal decided that instead of celebrating the new year with a bunch of other people, he would watch the mini-marathon of the Lords of Avalon on the History Channel. He settled into his favorite corner of the couch and turned on the TV.

"For centuries, treasure hunters have scoured the globe for the lost Treasure of Avalon. During the four-hundred-year reign of the Lords of Avalon, they spent only about one-third of that time in England. Where were they the rest of the time? Those missing years led people to refer to them as the enigmatic 'Lords of Avalon'...". The phone rang just as the show began. He muted the TV and considered not answering, but changed his mind.

"Hi Mom."

"Micheal, are you coming tonight?"

"Um... I don't know?"

"Brandon and Rachel are here with the kids. So are Kim and Mark, and Vanessa and Tom will be here soon."

He sighed in defeat. "Okay Mom, I'll be there as soon as I can."

"That's great, love you." She hung up before he had the chance to change his mind.

The Lords would have to wait. He stepped out the door and gaged the temperature on his skin. It felt warm, a little below freezing. The previous days dusting of snow sparkled in the fading sunlight. Perfect weather for a new year. He doubted this one would be better than the last. But his family awaited.

As he entered his parents' house, his mother came to greet him. "Micheal!"

The family was gathered around the coffee table playing Uno.

"Deal him in," his mother instructed as they found their places.

As they began their third game, his sister Vanessa and her family arrived.

"Uncle Mike!" his niece and nephew screamed.

"Come play with us."

The kids dragged him away from the table.

"What are we doing first?"

The other nieces and nephews joined in. They played all kinds of games and played with various toys. There was a lot of rough-housing as they tended to climb all over him. He enjoyed playing with them.

From Micheal's first moment, his perfect memory had put him on a lifelong quest for knowledge. It made him feel like he never really had a childhood. His awkward, shy nature made him an outcast and a target from his first day of school. He'd only had one friend his whole life. As his depression sank deeper, he ballooned into a behemoth. He knew that, combined with his social ignorance, made him repulsive to women. So he'd never have children of his own. This was the closest he would ever have to feeling like a father. When they had all tired out, he went to get a soda.

"So Brandon, what happened against BYU?" he teased his brother about the football game. Brandon was a University of Utah fan. BYU's archrival.

"They got lucky. We came back from down twenty to six in the fourth quarter to force overtime," Brandon argued.

"Hall to George, boom, walk-off in overtime," Micheal chuckled.

"Yeah, whatever. At least they both won their bowl games."

They discussed BYU and Utah for a little while longer, which transitioned to other bowl games.

"So who do you like in the championship game?" he asked Brandon.

"I think Texas has a real shot. I mean, Utah beat Alabama in the Sugar Bowl last year."

"Yeah, but Saban was only in his second season and Alabama's hitting their stride. I'll put my money on Saban."

"Okay guys, enough football talk. It's a few minutes till midnight," Vanessa said, ending the debate.

Micheal's family were devout in The Church of Jesus Christ of Latter-day Saints, most people call them Mormons. His rational mind found it challenging to have faith. He studied every major religion when he was young. None of them were convincing. Not long after his eighth birthday, he fell away from the church.

No one in his family drank, so they shared a sparkling cider toast at midnight. They used confetti poppers and noisemakers. Micheal knew it was much tamer than the party TC invited him to. One time, a few years ago, TC talked him into going to a New Year's party. He was the only one not drinking. Most of the time, he'd sit in the corner by himself. While it was entertaining to watch a bunch of college kids make fools of themselves, he had more fun spending time with his family.

"What about you?" Kim asked.

He shook his head. "No. I never make resolutions. They're lame."

"Party pooper," Rachel said.

"Micheal, when are you going to get married?" his mom asked.

"Here we go." He shook his head.

"What? You're such a great guy! Plenty of women would love to be with you."

"When are you going to go to college?" His dad chimed in. "You have so much potential. You'd be great at whatever you decide to do if you'd put in a little effort."

Micheal put his hand over his face and let out a deep sigh. This always happened when he visited his parents. A barrage of questions.

All he had to do was look in the mirror. He knew the chances of him getting married were as good as finding a warm place in deep space: absolute zero. He weighed three hundred and fifty pounds. Why would any woman give him the time of day?

Micheal always had trouble motivating himself, especially going to school. He never had a problem succeeding. He had an eidetic, photographic, and photo-autobiographical memory. He literally couldn't forget anything he saw or read. But his ever-growing knowledge meant that in thirteen years of *education,* he learned nothing new. School was pointless.

That experience told him the chances of learning anything new at university were small. Why would he waste the time and money to get a stupid piece of paper that said he was smart? He already knew that, and it was the only positive thing he had going for him.

The problem was that he'd spent most of his life gathering knowledge from other people. While he was full of many grandiose ideas himself, he'd never made a real effort to see if he could turn any of them into reality. Now he was about to turn twenty-seven and done nothing with his life. What if he and everyone else were wrong about his potential?

Whenever he feels particularly low, he tries to convince himself he's a modern-day Leonardo da Vinci.

Da Vinci claimed a similar memory capability to his own experiences. His mind conceived of things no one else could fathom, as well as nearly instant understanding of the way things worked.

Micheal didn't believe in role models. But if he did, the closest one he'd ever found was Leonardo da Vinci. The biggest difference was that Da Vinci turned his thoughts into real-world results. He'd have inspiration and, in a matter of days, there would be a working prototype. But Micheal had never tested any of the ideas running around in his mind.

He liked to pretend he feared nothing, but, if he was honest, he'd admit his only fear was failure. If he tried and failed, it would prove his genius was all a fantasy, and what would be left? At that point, he might as well end it all. But if you never try, you never fail. It would then remain a mystery if he were truly that smart.

As thoughts ran through his head, he robotically replied to the same old string of questions with the now canned answers. Did they hear themselves repeating the same questions? He wondered if they really heard him. With the interrogation over and the party winding down, he said his goodbyes. He hugged his father. Kissed his mother. Then headed home.

As he got in the car, he checked the time on his phone. It was 3 AM and TC had left a message.

"Hey dude! You missed one hell of a party. This one chick and her boyfriend got into a huge fight. She went crazy! She downed half a bottle of vodka and ended up passing out on the couch. Another guy was yelling, 'I've never been more sober...' then crashed through the beer pong table. It was some crazy, funny shit. Oh, and remember Veronica? Yeah dude, she came home with me. Well, happy New Year's. Next time, right? Later, dude."

"Yeah, sure," he said. He made the right decision not to go.

II: Appointed Rounds

"Hey, Mike. I heard you have next week off." Rick said as MICHEAL entered the post office.

"Yes."

"The holidays just ended and you're already taking a week off? Sounds like you need a holiday from your holidays," Rick laughed.

"It's my birthday."

"Oh, all week? Just kidding. What are you doing for your birthday?"

"Going to Florida."

"Florida? Cool. Well, have a good time. It's the best time to go. Get out of the snow and cold, catch some rays, and pick up some hotties in bikinis," Rick said with a wink and a smile.

"Absolutely," he feigned agreement.

"I want to hear all about it when you get back."

"Sure."

"Later," Rick walked off.

"It's about time," he mumbled. He's become a mail carrier for the solitude and didn't care much for social interaction. Rick was new. He didn't know. He'd eventually realize Micheal wasn't worth talking to.

It was Saturday, his flight was in the afternoon the next day. He'd never flown before and was about to turn twenty-seven. Growing up in poverty would do that. No one in his family flew when he was young. But things changed.

Micheal moved out at seventeen after he dropped out of high school. Rather than waste time, he'd research anything that caught his interest. He'd been stuck in the rut of his daily routine ever since. Then, about a year ago, he watched a documentary about the top ten most famous lost treasures in history. The number two spot was held by The Treasure of Avalon. The treasure was compiled over the centuries by the Lords of Avalon, who were supposed to be the descendants of King Arthur. Their actual family name was Whitaker, his mother's maiden name, so it piqued his interest.

When he was seven, his grandma told him the story about the family being descended from King Arthur. She even gave him a ring. It was the ring of destiny, or so she claimed, and was passed down from King Arthur himself. At the time, he thought it was all bull crap, a family fish story.

His interest in the story was renewed after watching the documentary. After making a few inquiries, his mother pointed Micheal in the direction of her father.

With a practice he referred to as total recall, he could close his eyes and think of a day or person and relive any event of his life.

While on his lunch break, he sat in his truck and focused on Grandpa Whitaker. He was in the memory from that day over a year ago.

"Hey Grandpa, Mom said I should ask you about the Lords of Avalon," Micheal said.

His grandpa laughed. "Why yes, your Highness! Prince Micheal." His grandpa said in jest. "You're the long-lost heir to King Arthur. They're drawing up the papers and declaring you've inherited the lost Treasure of Avalon."

"So, there's no truth to it?"

His grandpa sobered up. "You're serious, Micheal?"

"I was just curious," he said.

"Actually, your grandmother was the one who put more stock into it than I ever did," his grandpa admitted.

"She told me the story of Guinevere."

"We've been trying to quell the rumor within the family, but I suppose it's not possible. I will tell you what my father told me just before he left to fight in World War II. He told me my grandpa was the younger brother of the last Lord of Avalon. The noble line officially ended in the eighteenth century in England. But some of the non-title-holding younger brothers of the Lords moved to America to continue the legacy. That was who my great uncle supposedly was. He died in World War I. With his death, my father and his other siblings decided it was time to put an end to this 'Lords of Avalon' nonsense. I don't know anything definitively. But it is possible. We didn't want everyone running off on a treasure quest," his grandpa finished.

Micheal came out of the memory and instinctively placed his hand over his shirt pocket. After a second of relief from finding the object still there, he took out the ring his grandmother had given him.

He'd done some research on the inscription engraved on the inner band of the ring. It was in Roman Latin and translated to 'A God on Earth. A King in Heaven'.

He was distracted in contemplation when a voice snapped him to the moment.

"A Deo, et in Terra, Rex in Caelis," a woman said in Latin.

She was exotic and beautiful with black hair framing upturned green eyes. She wore a low-cut dress, wrapped in a white hooded cloak.

"The words of Avalon."

"Quis es? Et quid scis quod?" Micheal asked.

"Good luck, my lord." She flipped the hood over her head and melted into the heavy snow.

"Wait! Who are you?!" Micheal exited his mail truck, but she had already vanished.

An odd chill ran down his spine. Who was she? What did she have to do with Avalon?

He'd avoided directly researching the Lords of Avalon. He knew how his mind worked. Too much information about the Lords might muddy the waters. Moving his mind's speculations in the wrong directions. Besides, everyone else's research led to the popular suspects. He didn't need to do it anyways. None of the popular speculated locations of the treasure had struck him as very likely. He decided to trust his instincts. So he had thought to himself. *If I were the Lords, where would I hide it?* An island made the most sense. He spent a year researching islands all over the world for anything unusual.

He narrowed it down to five. They were spread out all over the world—from India to the Philippines and French Polynesia to Argentina. The last one was closer, near the Bahamas. He decided to start there. He didn't think anyone else suspected any of the five islands. But there were many people looking for the treasure. Now he was going to try to see if he was right, but would he be too late?

As he walked the neighborhoods making his rounds, he thought about his future possibilities.

Occasionally, he'd think, *"if only I had the means I would be able to make all kinds of world-changing inventions"*. If he was right about the treasure of Avalon, which was rumored to be in the trillions, he'd be able to change the world. But doubt and pessimism crept back in.

What was he thinking? He wasn't going to find the treasure. His trip was booked, so he was going, but it would end in failure like everything else he tried. After watching the latest documentary on the lost treasure, he was still sure no one suspected the location he'd found. But it was filmed months ago. There was still a chance someone would beat him to it. That would be typical. Similar outcomes had occurred many times in his life. He had the worst luck in the world.

III: Great Potential?

Sunday came and MICHEAL sat at the airport gate waiting to take his first flight. He'd been in a small Cessna while earning his Aviation Merit Badge, but it never left the ground. He arrived early, just to be sure. With some time to kill, he did what he normally did in these situations. He went inside his head. He began analyzing one thing that the new year always brings to the forefront. His potential. Everyone around him tended to focus on his intelligence. But if that genius was born into a fat loser with no personality, whose bad luck was his real superpower, then that was no potential at all.

Micheal felt like a mutant from the X-Men. He had his 'special power', but no one understand how it could affect him.

His 'gift' hadn't helped him lose weight. He tried every diet and exercise routine on the planet. He'd try one plan for a few months and nothing, so he'd move on to another. The last one he'd tried was P90X, over a year ago. Three months of dynamic diet and exercise produced no result. It had been the final straw. It marked ten years of effort. He was doomed to be fat forever.

Then there were the musical instruments he'd learned to play. After years of practice, he still wasn't good with any of them. For someone who could remember everything he'd ever seen or read, what had he accomplished? Nothing. Everyone was right about his potential. It was wasted on him.

The ten years since his ultimate failure had been nothing but 'unrealized potential'. But how much did he truly have?

Micheal knew he was different from most people. The most obvious was his memory. He eventually coined a term for his condition: total recall. He realized it wasn't normal when his family regularly forgot things. At first, it didn't make any sense. How could they forget? He did what he always did. He researched it.

Micheal's mother had taught him to read when he was one. The first thing she gave him was a comprehensive dictionary.

"Now Micheal, this is the most important book you'll read. It will inform your understanding of all the other books."

He momentarily drifted into the memory.

His mom had always encouraged his thirst for knowledge. He was never sure if she recognized his ability. Through Micheal's interactions with his schoolmates, he discovered how rare it was. None of them seemed to remember even a fraction of what he did.

His research found only one person who claimed to share his gift. Leonardo da Vinci. The Renaissance genius had claimed memories all the way back to the womb. While Micheal didn't quite remember that, he did recall his moment of birth. With that, he was back to his first memory.

Micheal was trapped. He couldn't move his arms. There was force from all sides. In one moment, the pressure released. A sudden chill came over his body.

He felt himself rise and there was noise all around him. He didn't understand it at the time, but it was a mixture of people talking and medical equipment.

There were blurry, moving blobs surrounding him. Then one of them did something to his mouth.

Micheal took his first breath, tasted something foul, and could suddenly smell a mixture of different odors. The cold was replaced by warmth when something wrapped around him.

He began to cry. One scent rose above the rest. It became stronger as he was passed from one figure to another.

The pleasantly familiar aroma and comforting embrace settled him. He stopped crying, relaxed, and fell asleep.

Micheal came back to the present with that fond memory of his mother's arms.

In his early years, he had avoided that memory. But after he learned no one else could remember their first moments in this world, he had become curious enough to go back a few times over the years to study his unique experience.

This detail led Micheal to wonder if he was anything like Da Vinci. Who was the definition of a Renaissance Man. He studied Da Vinci's life. The more he read, the more daunting the prospect felt.

In one documentary about geniuses of the past, they had a list of the highest projected IQs in history. The top three, in ascending order, were Nicola Tesla approaching 300, Isaac Newton at over 300, and, of course, Leonardo de Vinci at upwards of 400.

Micheal thought if his shared capability of 'total recall' meant he had a similar level of intelligence, how could he possibly live up to it? Even if they shared the same mind, de Vinci seemed to possess an extroverted personality that served his social interactions. Micheal enjoyed no such advantage. He was a black hole of charisma. His presence seemed to be repellant to people.

The Renaissance genius had dreamed up things five hundred years ahead of his time. Clearly the greatest mind of all time.

Micheal could never imagine himself on the same level as De Vinci. The most glaring example of his inadequacy was his failure to solve the only problem that ever truly mattered. And that had cost his family everything.

He became consumed, dwelling in the past.

Beginning with his interactions on the first day of kindergarten, it was clear something was wrong with him. Nearly everyone he met there treated him poorly.

And with that Micheal drifted back to August 1988.

By recess, none of the other kids had talked to him while he sat in the back of the class. When he went to the playground, no one would let him play with them. So he went and sat on the curb in the corner of the yard and began observing a colony of ants coming and going from a crack.

"Hey, Fatso! What's the matter? You don't have any friends?" Four older kids approached.

"Leave me alone."

Micheal got hit in the face with a spitball. He wiped the saliva off his cheek and tried to walk away.

"Where are you going, chubby?" They followed him.

"I didn't do anything to you." Micheal tried to run, but they surrounded him and were so much bigger he had no escape.

"Are you going to cry now, piggy?"

"Maybe he'll oink for us."

"I think we should make him squeal."

"Yeah! Squeal for us, little piggy!"

They pushed him around between them. When the bell rang, they pushed him to the ground and ran away.

Micheal sat there crying and knew they were right. He was fat, which was clearly a bad thing. That must be why no one liked him.

Micheal came back to the current day. He stared at his rotund self. The feeling of worthlessness washed over him as it had that day. He was bullied throughout his time in school. The only positive that came out of this was he'd learned to defend himself. He researched every major martial art. And while his family couldn't afford professional instruction, he utilized the concepts to become a competent street fighter. That was the only way he'd survived school.

By the time he was in the third grade, he was more isolated than ever before. He'd stay with his normal class at the beginning and ending of the day, as well as for physical ed. The rest of the time, he'd move from one room to the other.

Micheal would go to one sixth-grade class for math and science, the other for reading and language arts. And finally, he would go to a fifth-grade class for social studies and music.

As a result, he was around kids who were much older than him. This led to more bullying. He was ostracized by his normal peers because he was 'special'.

There was only one kid who was ever nice to him. His only friend, TC. Sometimes Micheal still wondered why.

Aside from his family, TC was the only one who knew about his 'total recall'. On occasion, his friend and family would talk about how great it would be to remember everything. But Micheal knew better. Remembering everything was a curse, not a gift.

Micheal sat there and relived every bad thing he'd ever done in his head. While other people could escape their failings with the passage of time, he'd never forget.

With the mountain of contemptible evidence of his nature staring him in the face, he understood why everyone said negative things about him. He was obviously a bad person.

The more he learned about his unfortunate aspects, the more he tried to make up for it with his only good quality. His intellect.

Micheal studied anything and everything. He lived in libraries. He read college textbooks on every scientific discipline, and regularly read science journals to keep up on the latest research. He read about different periods of history and worked to nurture his artistic side.

Da Vinci was a famous painter. But Micheal had always had melodies dancing in his head. He learned to read and write music and began learning how to play multiple instruments. His mom gave him piano lessons from a young age on her grandmother's upright. He learned the guitar and violin on some apparatuses he handcrafted as part of different scout projects.

This thought brought him back to his twelfth birthday in 1995.

Micheal sat with his guitar in a treehouse he had built with his dad a couple of years earlier. Like every other birthday, he knew he wouldn't be receiving any gifts.

His parents spent any money they could save on Christmas for the family. There wasn't anything left for his birthday just a couple of weeks later.

With that in mind, he'd come up with his own tradition. He made this day for him to do whatever he wanted. He had been allowed to stay home from school, beginning in kindergarten. Today was a Thursday and, instead of wasting time in class, he was about to attempt what he had decided to give himself. He was going to write his first song.

Micheal strummed out the melody that played in his head the longest. It was his favorite. The tune was best in adagio, with a melodic tone most reminiscent of an '80s rock ballad.

He listened to the sound coming off the strings and added a few more changes to the score. Satisfied with the tune, he focused on the lyrics next.

Micheal crafted a solemn poem about living in dreams that he set to the beats of the music. He closed his eyes and created the sensation of the song in his head.

When he opened his eyes, he thought of a name. He translated his title into Latin and said, "In Somnis."

Micheal opened his eyes to find the terminal. He'd been humming the tune.

His time in the Boy Scouts gave him real-world experience. With the poverty of his family, he'd never had access to the necessary resources for a hands-on experience for everything he'd studied. It was only through the generous donations of his church who offered help to the troop.

Micheal was able to build his tools for music, which enabled his musical expression. He also built a truck engine from scratch and constructed a small cabin in the woods, all by himself, with just a few simple tools.

This access had motivated him to be active in scouts and, on average, he earned a merit badge a week. In just two and a half years, he'd earned all one-hundred thirty-seven badges.

Micheal prepared to do his Eagle Project early in the summer of '95 when his classic bad luck reared its ugly head.

Due to various circumstances, he hadn't been to a Court of Honor for scouts in more than a year. His scoutmaster called him in to inform him they had lost his records and he would have to redo all the merit badges that had yet to be presented to him. That would mean repeating eighty-one badges.

Micheal quit instead. What was the point?

This was just one more sign from the universe that no matter how much work he put in, he was destined to fail.

A couple of months later, his move to junior high was a disaster, compounding the message.

Micheal's new school said his advanced instruction at the elementary didn't count because it was elementary. He'd not only have to redo most of his classes, but he'd also have to regress in several of them.

The most frustrating change was math. They placed him in pre-algebra, a subject he'd already studied in fourth grade. He had already repeated algebra in both fifth and sixth.

Outside of school, Micheal already mastered trigonometry and calculus, and moved on to statistics and theory.

The double setback had destroyed any motivation he had to go to that 'institute of learning'. It was a pointless waste of time. Looking back now, if he'd been able to go to some kind of special school, maybe his life would be different. But it's not like his parents could afford something like that. And even when two of his fourth-grade classmates got skipped straight to sixth, he went with his parents to ask if he could do the same. The school rejected the request and never explained why.

This only accelerated his downward spiral, and he withdrew further into himself. To his friends and family, he pretended everything was fine. Why should he be any more trouble to them than he already was? His façade of normality had become quite effective. It's not like anyone could understand his plight anyway.

Micheal started skipping classes. It took a few months, but his mother caught him. He explained all of the challenges, and in response, she brought him to the community college.

He took the entrance exam. They said he'd earned the highest score in their history. 99 was the highest possible score, and he achieved that in all four subjects. But his parents couldn't afford $8000 a year. And after attempting to apply for some form of financial aid, they found that his father's tax situation was such a mess he couldn't qualify.

With Micheal's life in misery, he saw the end of the road. His mind went back to that dark moment.

Micheal's sister Vanessa tried to cheer him up. They went for one of their hikes on Mount Olympus, East of Salt Lake City. They were nearing the summit when the trail ran next to a cliff. He let her walk up ahead.

Micheal peered over the edge.

...how easy it would be to just step off...

He could close his eyes and feel the rush of falling, then his nightmare would be over.

As his toe reached the edge, a couple of stones tumbled over. He tracked their hundred-foot flight to the bottom.

...what about Vanessa? Would she blame herself? ...

...would the family be relieved to not have the burden of him? ...

Right when he was about to make his choice, Vanessa touched his shoulder.

"Micheal? ...are you alright?"

"Just enjoying the view."

"Come on...we're almost at the top."

As they continued toward the summit, he thought about everything. His best argument against suicide was that while he may be the worst person in the world, at least he was smarter than everyone else.

Micheal got up and walked to the window. While looking at the airplane, he considered how close he came that day to ending it all.

He was thirteen years old and had already failed at life. What he didn't know was that his biggest failure has yet to come.

Micheal languished over the next few months. Then everything changed.

A medical emergency in the family motivated him to put his so-called genius toward one purpose. It was four years of medical research. He studied every possible solution. By the end, he probably knew more about medicine than the most highly educated surgeon, but it wasn't enough. Death is a merciless enemy. In the misery that followed, only one thought festered in his mind. If he had exchanged places with Da Vinci, the Renaissance Man would have found the cure for cancer.

Micheal's futile efforts found him back on a cliff's edge.

Micheal climbed to the pinnacle of Mount Olympus. He waited until he had the mountain to himself. He gazed out over the valley and reflected on his life.

His 'superpower', seventeen years of gathering knowledge, and four years of non-stop effort ended in failure. With his only good quality in tatters, there was nowhere left for his true self to hide.

Micheal stepped to the edge, closed his eyes, and felt the wind on his face. He took a deep breath. He was ready.

"I'm sorry." He stepped forward.

"Micheal, stop!" A woman's voice froze him in his tracks.

He spun on his heel and found the peak empty. He closed his eyes and replayed the moment. He had clearly heard the voice.

As Micheal tried to regather his resolve, the cool breeze was replaced by a warm calm. An odd peace came over him and a tear streamed down his cheek.

The moment passed. He knew she was there with him.

This memory had sustained him as time went forward. As he wondered about what really happened that day, the final boarding call was announced for his flight. He headed off to test himself once again.

CHAPTR 3: ORLANDO

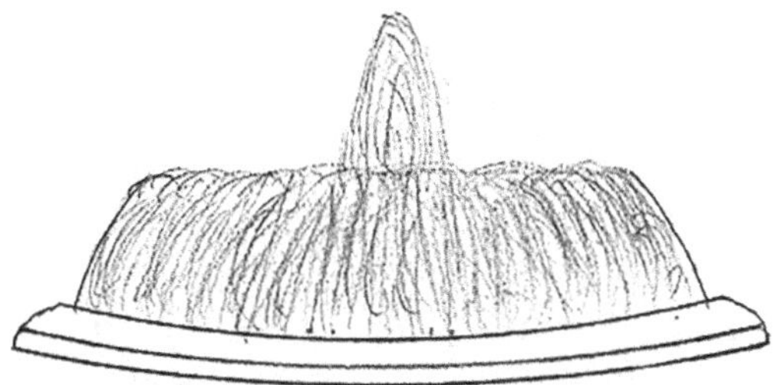

MICHEAL EXPERIENCED A TERRIBLE layover at New York's JFK Airport. His original connecting flight was delayed, so they offered him a seat on a different flight that was later canceled. By the time he tried to switch back, the first one had already left. Now he was finally on a flight to Orlando.

"Ladies and gentlemen, this is the captain speaking. We seem to be having a malfunction with the landing gear. We're going to have to go back to the gate. We apologize for any inconvenience this may cause."

Micheal wasn't surprised. It figured the first flight of his life would be beset by so many problems.

As he sat in the gate area, wondering if he would get on another flight that night, he heard his name. "Micheal Hall? Micheal Hall? Please come to gate C 69."

He approached the counter at the gate, hoping for good news.

"I'm sorry, there are no available seats until tomorrow at the earliest," she said.

"I see. Are hotel vouchers available?" he asked.

"Unfortunately, we ran out. I can give you some extra food vouchers," she offered. "Hold on one second... I have some bad news. Apparently, there was a mix-up. Your bag was sent to Seattle."

He put his hand over his face and shook his head. With a heavy sigh, he said, "I'll take the vouchers."

"Once again, I'm terribly sorry for all the trouble. We'll have you on the first plane out in the morning."

Micheal had his doubts.

As he lay on the floor near gate C 69, he wondered if the universe was telling him something. Maybe he was being told not to search for the treasure. Then again, this kind of thing always happened to him.

Micheal's nightmare flight only got worse the next day. To his disappointment, but not to his surprise, 'The first flight out' became the second and now the third. This was on top of the four attempts the previous day.

"The flight is full. You're going to have to take a later flight," the gate agent said.

"Please? Is there anything you can do? I've already delayed more than a day. This is my seventh attempt to get on a flight, since yesterday." He pleaded.

She offered him a sympathetic look. "Let me make a call."

"Thank you!"

After a moment, the agent came back with what Micheal thought would be worse news.

"You're booked on another airline. It's in terminal eight, gate 12. They will have your ticket at the gate, but you must hurry."

"Thank you so much!" He hurried off.

Micheal arrived at the gate in time. They held the plane for him. "Thank you! You have no idea," he said with a sigh of relief.

"Hold on, there's a problem," the gate agent said. "This is saying that this seat is already taken."

An odd image came to mind. Tom Hanks, stuck at an airport for days on end. He supposed he could learn to live there just like that movie. "I think I'm starting to like it here. It's beginning to feel like home," he said aloud, shaking his head, chuckling.

"Okay, we're putting you in first class, you're in 1B." The gate agent said with some amusement after hearing his comment.

As Micheal approached his seat, he stopped dead in his tracks. The woman in the seat next to his was easily the most beautiful woman he'd ever seen. Her almost black hair hung just past her shoulders and her deep-sea turquoise eyes were like windows to heaven. He had to remind himself to breathe. She'd caught him by such surprise he hoped he hadn't revealed his amazement. He'd spent years trying to hide his interest in women. He was repulsive enough as it was. He didn't want to creep them out even more. Micheal realized who she was. She was Julie Buckingham of *Bull*

Markets. He had watched her show from the beginning. She was the most beautiful woman in the world. He knew she wouldn't want to talk to him, but he couldn't stop himself.

JULIE saw a very large man board the plane. She hoped he wouldn't recognize her. That would probably lead to a conversation, and that was the last thing she wanted.

"You're Julie Buckingham, right?"

Dammit, Julie thought.

"I am."

"I love your show. I watch it almost every day."

"Thank you. I always like meeting fans." Julie said. How was she going to prevent this from continuing for the entire flight without being rude?

He babbled on and on. "I particularly like the China shop. That one about Greenhaven. I couldn't believe that."

"Are you going to Orlando on business?" she asked.

"No. Where are my manners? I'm Micheal."

"Nice to meet you, Micheal," she feigned interest.

"I'm going to the Bahamas on a chartered boat to hunt for the Treasure of Avalon..." He droned on and on. She thought it would never end. "I'm sorry. I've been rambling about a bunch of meaningless theories I know you couldn't care less about. I'm being rude. I ramble when I'm nervous. I'll leave you alone."

"It's no bother. It's an interesting theory," Julie said. On the other hand, she wasn't sure how much more she could take.

"Thank you for listening." He shut up after that. She breathed a sigh of relief when Micheal closed his eyes and fell asleep. She was able to relax for the rest of the flight.

Micheal woke up when they landed. Before they exited, he turned to her and said, "It was a pleasure to meet you."

"The pleasure was all mine," she said with a smile.

I: Best Laid Plans

MICHEAL'S original plans had to be thrown out the window. The arrangements he's made to be taken straight from the airport to the chartered boat in Port Canaveral couldn't be rescheduled. He'd taken a taxi to the accommodations suggested by the information desk. He'd have to figure out how to get to The Cape the next day.

After getting settled in his room, Micheal went to the lobby's front desk.

"How can I help you, Mr. Hall?" asked the young lady behind the counter.

"Where would you suggest for dinner?"

"Well, it's a bit pricy, but a block north is The Boheme, it's in the Grand Bohemian. If you want something else, there are more casual restaurants a few blocks farther north."

"The Boheme sounds perfect. Thank you very much."

The hostess at the Boheme lead him to his table, and said, "Your server will be Caitlin. She will be with you shortly."

The room had an elegant ambiance with beautiful wood finish, art on the walls, and mellow reddish lighting.

"Your tangerine juice." His server delivered the drink he'd ordered while waiting at the bar.

"Thank you."

"Would you like me to make any recommendations?" Caitlin inquired.

"Please."

"The escargot de Bourgogne is amazing, very tender in a garlic butter sauce and served with a baguette. They're one of my favorite appetizers, and the roast pheasant is very nice in a champagne green sauce with rainbow carrots."

"Well, that would be perfect," he said, taking her suggestions.

"I'll get that started and take that menu from you."

As she walked away, he thought she looked so familiar. He thought about where he might have seen her before.

All throughout dinner Micheal couldn't shake the feeling that he'd seen Caitlin somewhere before.

"What would you like for dessert?" she inquired with a smile as she cleared his empty plates.

"I think I'll have the pumpkin gelato," he replied, returning the smile.

"Very nice."

"Caitlin?"

"Yes?"

"Is your last name Anderson?"

"Yes? How did you know that?" Caitlin asked, a quiver in her voice.

"I saw a report about eight years ago on the *Esperanza*. You were the only survivor."

"How could you possibly recognize me? ... And they aren't dead!" She walked off with tears in her eyes. He realized how insensitive he'd been. Once again, his lack of social skills was rearing its ugly head.

The hostess came over. "Your gelato. I apologize for Caitlin," she said.

"Oh, no. It's my fault. I said something without thinking and opened some old wounds. Would you let her know I'd like to apologize?"

"Of course."

As he ate his gelato, he chided himself again for his social impropriety. A few minutes later, Caitlin returned.

"Would you sit for a minute?" he asked gently. "I'd like to apologize. I had no right to ask you such a personal question. My mouth moved faster than my mind. I'm sorry. And I'm sorry for your loss."

"They're not dead!" she protested again, tears coming to her eyes.

"I'm sorry," he said. She began to rise. "Please stay." She sat back down.

"I spent years dealing with it. You caught me off guard. No one ever recognizes me. No one here knows about it," she lowered her voice.

"You say they are not dead?"

"I don't think they are, but nobody believed me after I told the police what happened. Everyone said the trauma made me see things."

"I'd believe you. Do you want to tell me about it?"

"Why would you believe me? You don't even know me."

"I'm very open-minded, but you don't have to tell me if you don't want to. It's none of my business."

"Well..." She seemed hesitant, but then she began. "I was eleven at the time. We were out on my parents' friend's yacht celebrating something. I don't even remember what. I was on the bridge with the captain when the boat lost power, then we were surrounded by this cloud of green fog. A few times it was like the horizon changed from twilight to bright sun, and then back again." She paused for a second, staring at him, as though trying to decide if he believed her. She went on. "...everyone started panicking and running around the deck. Darren, my brother, ran past and accidentally sent me overboard. I drifted farther and farther away. There was a bright flash, and everything disappeared."

"I'm so sorry," he said.

"You believe me?"

"I believe you."

He rose to leave, and she stood with him. The tears welling in her eyes seemed about to burst. Micheal reached out and touched her shoulder. "I'm sorry about your family. Don't lose hope. Everything will be all right."

He was surprised when she threw her arms around him. He returned her embrace.

She looked up and said, "I guess I didn't realize how much I needed someone to believe me." She leaned her head back on his chest. For the first time, he felt he had made a true human connection.

As he lay in bed watching TV, he thought about what Caitlin had told him. It was a classic Bermuda Triangle story. He thought it was fitting that the show he was watching was trying to scientifically explain the Bermuda Triangle. Before he could finish it though, he fell asleep.

II: A Secret Matter

As JULIE was being driven to the hotel, she couldn't stop thinking of the man's theory about the Treasure of Avalon. Was it possible he was right? Of course she'd heard of the lost Treasure of Avalon. Who hadn't? It was usually believed to be a legend, like the Treasure of the Knights Templar or the lost city of El Dorado. He seemed so sure, and, while many treasure hunters usually do, he didn't strike her as the typical sort. This was more about his supposed family connection to the Lords of Avalon. At that moment, the car pulled up to the Grand Bohemian Hotel. She always stayed here when she was in Orlando.

After check-in, she headed to the rooftop pool. She brought her laptop so she could do some research of her own. She informed her production staff that something had come up, and she might be incommunicado for the rest of the day. Over the next few hours, she read everything she could find on the Lords of Avalon. They were the famous enigmatic noble family from England believed to be descended from King Arthur. They appeared on and off in England from the fourteenth to the eighteenth century, which was apparently when they all died off. There were others who thought some of them lived on in America. That must be where the man had gotten the idea he was related to them.

Avalon was a region north of Devonshire, bordering the Bristol Channel in Southwest England. The area was chosen by William Whitaker when Edward III made him a baron following his famous Black Death heroism, which saved the King at the Battle of Poitiers in 1356. Whitaker purchased the lands under special condition, granted by the King in the Contract of Avalon. He apparently chose the area because he said it was where King Arthur's Camelot had been located eight-hundred years earlier.

When Lord William's grandson performed a similar defense of the Duke of Bedford at the Battle of Verneuil in 1424, he was elevated to an earl. In honor of the event, he built the grand Palace of Avalon. The name was later changed to Camelot by King George II, under a stipulation of the Contract of Avalon, when the crown took possession of Avalon upon the death of the Seventh Duke of Avalon in 1745.

The Contract of Avalon was an interesting document. It established that the Avalon region was semi-autonomous. During the long absentees of the current lord, the family's taxes would be deferred. Upon return to England, they would immediately have to pay the back taxes. If the absentee was less than twenty years, they would owe three times the normal rate. If it was longer, they would owe four times the rate. Another interesting aspect was that the contract would only be in force when the lord was in England. That meant that the crown would not inquire about what House Avalon did outside the realm, including the source of their wealth.

Now, most historians believed the discovery of the Courtyard Vault at Camelot was the Treasure of Avalon. But skeptics pointed out that, while the find was valued at around fifty billion dollars, earlier estimates were far higher. But, if he had determined the treasure's location, it would be the greatest archeological find in history.

Julie called some charter companies near Cape Canaveral and inquired about chartering a boat. After consulting some maps, she was certain she had found the strange man's suspected treasure location.

She called Aiden to say goodnight, then relaxed in the jetted tub with a glass of wine. The stress and tension of the day evaporated.

Julie slid under the blankets, giving in to her exhaustion. Lost in the softness, she drifted off to sleep.

CHAPTER 4: THE FALL

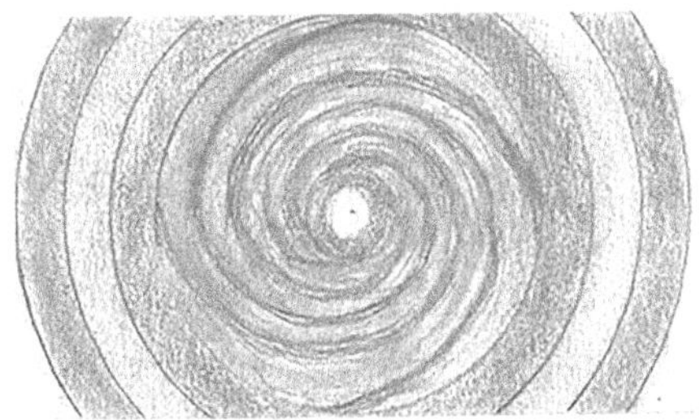

JULIE WOKE WITH A start. It was freezing. She surveilled her surroundings and was shocked to find herself in a snowy meadow somewhere in the woods. She only wore the slip she had worn to bed. How did she get here? The most obvious answer was that someone must have drugged her and abducted her.

She looked around the clearing. No one was around. Although, she feared they may be nearby. She felt her arm. Her skin was still warm. She couldn't have been out here that long, but she must have been unconscious for a while. She was in Florida and, while it was January, she didn't think it ever snowed here. Where was the nearest place that snowed?

Where Julie was or how she got there didn't matter. She knew she wouldn't last much more than an hour out here in the cold. She needed to find help. She rose and her head started spinning. She put her hands over her face to stop the world from turning. It had little effect. She lost her balance and fell.

MICHEAL opened his eyes and was blinded by the sun. He was outside. How was that possible? He'd gone to bed in his hotel room and now he was outside in daylight. He ran through all the possibilities he could think of. Maybe he'd been drugged?

He scanned the area and found himself alone in a forest with snow blanketing the ground. Deciding he was in no immediate danger; Micheal considered the possibilities. Maybe he'd blacked out and made his own way here? He ruled that out immediately because there were no tracks, not even his own. In Florida, the nearest possible snow was in The Panhandle, or maybe Georgia. That would be one hell of a blackout.

Micheal stood up, and the sun rose with him. It was obscenely bright. He shielded his eyes with a forearm and tried to get his eyes to adjust. As his vision came into focus, he noticed the ground where he'd been laying was devoid of snow. That, at least, could be a rudimentary sign supporting the theory of alien abduction. What other possibilities could there be?

His leading theory was abduction. But aliens? It didn't make sense that aliens would abduct him and leave him out in the snow. He doubted he had blacked out. The evidence didn't support him being drugged or kidnapped by some random person, so what else was there? The thought struck him. Maybe it's time travel?

JULIE had hit the ground hard. A bruise had formed on her right thigh. It hurt to put all her weight on it, and she feared it would slow her down. She was practically naked. No shoes. No coat. Completely exposed to the elements. She needed help, but where would help be?

Julie looked around, unsure which direction to go. She knew her life was on the line. If she made the wrong choice, she would freeze to death in the woods. She looked for any sign of civilization, but she saw none. She must be far from any cities, from anyone who could help her.

Cold and alone, she glanced around the clearing. She refused to give up on herself and headed in the direction of the sun. East was as good a direction as any. As she walked through the woods, the sun became eclipsed by a tree. A faint billow of smoke drifted above the treetops. It must be a cabin or something. She limped towards the smoke.

Her feet were numb. She wasn't sure how much farther it could be and stopped for a moment to warm her feet. Rubbing them didn't seem to have much of an effect, so she continued her journey. A few minutes later, she tripped on a stick and cut her left foot.

She sat on a rock, examining her foot. The cut didn't look too bad. She hoped it wouldn't slow her down further. She was getting colder by the minute. She got back up and pushed through the pain. She was getting closer. It was a cabin of some kind. A few minutes more and she would be there. The fact that smoke was rising from the chimney meant that somebody was home. At that moment, she thought of Aiden. She was supposed to call him this morning. He would be worried sick if she didn't.

The thought of Caitlin ran through MICHEAL with a shiver. He'd truly believed her story about the *Esperanza* and Orlando was on the edge of the Bermuda Triangle. It'd been theorized the Triangle was an energy vortex and a gateway through time, space, or dimensions. Perhaps he'd fallen through time, maybe even space, though he thought less likely, maybe a dimension? He scanned the sky again. Nothing. He hadn't seen or heard any airplanes, helicopters, or cars since he woke up. It was eerily silent. That was one piece of circumstantial evidence to support his new leading theory. A faint wisp of smoke over the tree line caught his attention.

He took a deeper look and confirmed that it was indeed smoke. He knew he'd have to investigate with caution. Micheal stopped for a moment to rest and care for his feet. He sat in the snow and pressed the soles of his feet against his thighs to warm them. As he sat and thought more about some of his ideas about what might have happened. Could it really be time travel? He thought of Caitlin.

Last night's talk with her might've swayed his thoughts. Just because he hadn't seen anything in the sky didn't necessarily mean there wasn't anything. If he was deep enough in the wilderness, there wouldn't be any roads around for cars, which could explain the silence. Micheal thought of Occam's razor. With all things being equal, the simplest explanation was usually the correct one. What was more likely? He was pulled through time and space by the Bermuda Triangle or he'd been drugged and left in the woods by people who didn't leave footprints?

He sighed. None of the options had enough evidence to convince him of one or the other, so he'd have to reserve judgment until he learned more. He wondered how much more trouble his bad luck would bring.

JULIE'S thoughts of Aiden brought warmth to her heart. It gave her the will to go on. Weak and out of breath, she urged herself forward with the only thought that helped. Aiden.

She came to a clearing. To her surprise, there were several cabins close together. A small village. She didn't see anyone as she neared the first house.

"Help me, please!" She cried.

A door swung open, and a man came out, wielding a gun. "Not one more step."

She stopped dead in her tracks. The prospect of Aiden seemed so real she began to yell even louder. "Please help me, I've been kidnapped. Call 911."

He stared at her with the gun aimed at her face. He appeared to be about 50 years old. His clothes were worn and old-fashioned. As she considered the man's British accent, more doors swung open, and more men came out, looking confused and angry. They wore the same style of clothing. All she felt, even above the cold, was fear. The commotion stirred the whole village and more people emerged from their cabins to gather nearby.

MICHEAL walked on, lost in thought. Suddenly, a cabin appeared in the distance, perhaps a hundred yards away. The sight snapped him out of his haze of ideas. He stepped behind a large tree for cover to reassess the situation.

There were other cabins in the clearing. He considered approaching the nearest one, but a man emerged from the front door and grabbed an armful of firewood from a pile near the door. He was oddly dressed in an early colonial, maybe seventeenth-century outfit. Was this a period film being shot? He didn't think so. There weren't any cameras or a production crew in the area. It could be an Amish village. If so, he was likely in Pennsylvania or upstate New York. He doubted the Amish brought him. If it was an Amish village, the question of how he got there remained. Another question came back to mind: was it time travel? The thought made him uncomfortable.

Micheal watched the cabins. People came and went about their business. All of them wore the same style of clothing. There were men, women, and children just going about their day. All the things they were doing fit the Amish narrative. There were no signs of electricity or any signs of modern life. He'd been scanning the sky, listening intently. Still, there was nothing. He was beginning to think the latter theory might be correct. He might have fallen through time. He'd investigate further with extreme caution.

***

A couple of dozen townsfolk surrounded JULIE. None of them had come to help.

"Help! Please? I've been kidnapped. Call 911. Call the police!"

They stared at her, whispering to each other. She couldn't believe it.

"Help me, please!" She turned toward the others.

"For Christ's sake, please help me?!" Tears ran down her cheeks, blurring her vision.

Some villagers crossed themselves while others pulled their children to their side and covered their ears.

Julie wiped her tears and focused on their faces. There was only shock and anger. None of them moved to help her.

One of the men stepped forward, pointing at her. "She blasphemes the Lord Almighty. She's of the devil. She's bewitched."

"What?! I'm freezing! Why won't anyone help me?" Her feelings changed from confusion to anger. How could they just stand there and do nothing?

A little girl stepped forward. Julie's spirit rose. The child stopped after a few steps, pointed at her and yelled, "It's the witch! The Witch of the Woods! She's the one that's been hurting me!"

Julie was stunned. She started to speak but broke off. What did the child call her?

With fists clenched, the townsfolk closed in on her. A murmur started. They were all chanting one word, "Witch!"

A woman stepped up behind the child. "Cover that witch before she bedevils us all!"

Another woman wrapped a blanket around Julie, and she was carried away by the mob.

PART TWO: THE PAST DIVIDED

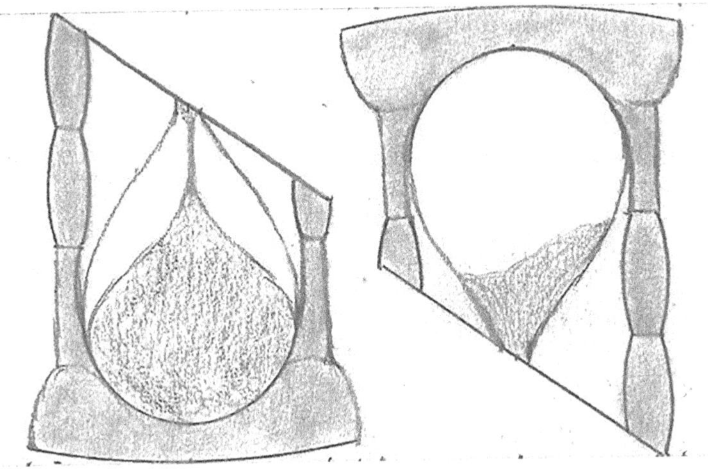

CHAPTER 5: A WITCH!

"LET ME GO! LET go!" JULIE yelled, to no avail.

She tried to free her arms from the men that rushed her. They held her tight. One was behind her, trying to pull her arms back as if to handcuff her. Another two were helping. Pulling, twisting, and kicking did nothing. She was too weak from the trek to break loose.

There were at least four individuals, all dragging her somewhere. They were filthy and smelled wretched. Julie begged them to let her go, but they wouldn't listen. As her strength gave way to compliance, she saw a tall building ahead, the largest in the village. The ground was frozen mud and the stink of manure filled the air.

The mob behind her continued accusing her of being the Witch of the Woods. They claimed she hurt little girls. The screams began to fade as the men led her to a small room. They slammed the door when they left. Clanks and creaks filled the space and were followed by fading footsteps leading away from her cell.

The only light came from a small window above the bed. The mattress was only about five feet in length. It was warmer in the room than it was outside, but not by much. At least they didn't take the blanket.

She yelled for a few minutes, but no one came. She sat wrapped in the blanket, overcome with emotion while trying to get warm. The pain from her wounded foot came back. Her body ached, but worst of all, she was alone. No one knew where she was. This had to be one of the worst days of her life.

As time passed, she settled down. Questions ran through her mind. Why were they all dressed like that? Why did they speak so strangely? Why did they say she was this Witch of the Woods? None of it made sense. Even if they were an Amish community or something like that, why did no one help her? Not only did they not help, but they also accused her of bringing... Devilry to their village?

She became angry at that thought. How dare they? She needed help. She wanted them to pay. To make them feel what she was feeling. The pain in her bloody foot was getting worse. She needed a hospital or at least a first aid kit so she could clean the wound. She was sure it was becoming infected.

She knew Aiden had already gone to the FBI. He had friends in the bureau and had connections in government. It was only a matter of time before they'd knock down the door to rescue her. She could see it now. When she didn't call, as she'd promised, he'd call the hotel to check on her. When she wasn't there, he'd immediately head to Florida to start looking for her. He'd call in a bunch of favors and, within a few hours, the best investigators the FBI had would be on the case. A slight smile came to her at the thought. Her horrible ordeal would soon be over.

More clanks and creaks filled the room. The door opening woke Julie to reality. Two men came in. She wanted to run, but there was nowhere to go. They grabbed her and dragged her into another room where a third man sat at a table.

The men pushed her forward. The one sitting at the table began to speak. "My name is SAMUEL PARRIS. I'm the minister of this town. What is thy name?" His breath was rank.

She hesitated for a second, pulling back to fresher air. "My name is Julie Buckingham. Why are you doing this to me? You should be helping me. I need help!"

She hadn't realized she was raising her voice. The man's expression tightened. He placed both hands on the table and slowly pushed his chair away.

"I will try to save thy soul if I can, but first I need to know why thou art bringing damnation upon our god-loving town?" Parris paced the room. The table was rough to the touch. And the floorboards creaked with each step.

Julie snapped back, not able to control her rage. "I'm doing no such thing! I'm warning you. The FBI is going to be here soon! You let me go and I won't press any charges—"

"Do not threaten this town with thy curses, demon woman!" Parris whipped his glare back at Julie. "After the hell thou hast put my own daughter through."

"This is ridiculous! I don't know anything about your daughter!"

"Thou hide out in the woods. Thou blaspheme the Lord our Savior. Thou speak curses with a strange tongue. Thou try to bedevil men in thy nakedness. And thou curse my girls with fits! Damn thee to hell, witch!" Julie heard genuine belief behind his words.

"I..." she began and then broke off. She wasn't sure which charge to argue first. She was at a loss. Before she could think of a response, Parris motioned to the men. They grabbed her and took her away.

They threw her back into her cell. She pulled the covers tight around her. After all the tears she'd cried, she found more to give. She kept thinking this was a horrible nightmare that she'd wake up from soon. How long would it be before Aiden and the FBI saved her from this... whatever this was? A cult maybe?

I: The Dungeon

JULIE had the blanket wrapped around her body, knees bent, feet bruised and hurting, but at least she was warmer than before. Her misery was interrupted by the door opening. Three men stood in the doorway. Two were short—shorter than most men she'd encountered, one with a mustache and brown hair, the other with blond hair and clean-shaven. He looked young and unsure of what to do. The one in the middle was tall and was dressed better than the others.

As she suspected, the one in the middle was in charge. He stepped forward, unrolled a piece of paper, and read: "Mistress Julie Buckingham. I, George Corwin, as sheriff of the County of Essex, do serve this warrant for the arrest of thy person on the charge of witchcraft."

She couldn't believe it. This was happening. Julie stood from her small bed but, before she could plant both feet on the floor, the two other men grabbed her and took her outside to a waiting cart. As she fought and screamed, the men overpowered her and proceeded to put shackles around her wrists and ankles.

"This is insane! You're all gonna pay for this! The FBI will be here soon and you're all gonna fucking pay!"

"She has the devil inside her, I tell thee," the older one said.

"This witch is trying to curse us," replied the boy.

"Dost thee really think this demon she keeps saying going a come will come?"

"May the Lord protect us," the older man replied, and both men crossed themselves.

Julie resigned herself to silence. There was no way these two were in any position to let her go.

"Fucking drones." She sat on the cart and pulled her blanket tighter around her.

The cart rolled down the road. Her silence wouldn't keep her from getting unwanted attention. Every person they passed stared at her in horror and whispered to each other. They were terrified of her. Once again, parents clutched their children tight and covered their eyes, so they wouldn't see the "witch".

The going was slow. Soon, the small village was left behind. The bumpy ride down a dirt road lasted for an hour through farmland and winter woods. They passed more people dressed in pilgrim attire.

The only thing that made sense was them being a cult. The leaders kept the townsfolk from knowing anything about the outside world. Made them live like pilgrims. She couldn't figure out why they picked her. Maybe the leader did it at random? Or maybe they had intentionally targeted her, but for what purpose? Whatever the reason, the village folk seemed to believe she really was a witch.

Anger boiling to the surface. How dare they?!

She thought of Aiden moving heaven and earth to find her. She knew her ordeal would be over soon. She closed her eyes, took a deep breath, and resolved to be strong until such a time came.

They passed over a small bridge into a modest town. It was a muddy mess. The smells were quite pronounced. The now familiar smell of manure mixed with wood-fire smoke and body odor from her captors. They came to a stop in front of a crudely built building in the center. They carried her inside and down a set of spiral stairs. At the bottom was a small, open door. She was forced inside. The room was tiny, with no windows. The door had a narrow opening, which was barred. She saw the look of fear on the boy's face as he slammed the door shut. She heard him uttering the Lord's Prayer as he walked away. The torch he carried went with him, leaving the room pitch black.

She curled up into a ball with the blanket wrapped around her and tried to get warm. The room was cold, damp, and smelled of shit and piss. Her stomach ached. She had had so little to eat since this all began. Images of food flashed through her mind. She thought of things like steak from one of her favorite restaurants, Bulls and Bears, cooked medium rare with a side of creamed spinach. Or a pizza from Gandolfo's! Sausage, tomato, with extra cheese...

Her breakfast with Aiden before she left for Orlando.

"Oh, Aiden. You must be such a wreck," she whispered. "I may have slept more since this happened than you have." Those words brought a sad grin to her face. She knew he would run himself ragged. Whenever he had a challenge in front of him, it was the only thing he could see. He'd push everything else to the side and attack it full bore. "If I could talk to you, I'd say, 'I need you to focus, my love. Just make sure to keep breathing.'"

Julie wondered why they'd move her here. She looked around the dim-lit room. In the murky shadows of the filtering light, she saw the chains, the tiny windowless room, the spiral stairs. A dungeon. She was in a dungeon.

A chill ran down her already frozen spine.

II: Inquisition

A few days went by. JULIE only saw light the few times they opened the door to give her food. She expected that eating stale bread and drinking their water would give her dysentery, but she was too hungry to care.

The door opened. Two men escorted her up the stairs and down a hall to what appeared to be a courtroom. A panel of men was seated to serve as the jury. The room was filled to the brim. The man seated on the pulpit must be the judge.

Master Parris seemed to be orchestrating this whole circus.

The judge pounded his gavel. The room fell silent. "Bring this court to order. On this day, 16 January, in the year of our Lord,

1692, we convene a grand jury to determine the charges against Mistress Julie Buckingham. Master Parris?"

Julie's mind paused for what seemed to be an eternity. 1692? What were they talking about? What was going on?

"Your honor, the town of Salem and the County of Essex, do accuse Mistress Buckingham of witchcraft," Parris said as he rose from the table.

The town of Salem... Those words echoed in her mind. A sense of despair came over her as she contemplated the word she'd kept hearing outside.

"What is thy evidence?" the judge inquired.

"Your Honor, Mistress Buckingham did emerge from the north woods. Mine own daughter and niece were thrown to madness and had uncontrolled fits. They said as they were bedeviled by a witch that did reside in said woods, wherein she did reside. Upon her arrival in our fair town, they did again go into fits of hysteria." Parris walked across the front of the room. He spat the word 'she' with venom on his tongue, shooting a blatant accusatory glare at Julie as he stepped between her and the judge. He then returned his gaze to the jury with emphasis, as if to gain favor. As he finished, he turned to the judge, his hands neatly crossed behind his back.

1692...Salem...Witch. It couldn't be. It was impossible. This must be a cult reenacting the Witch Trials. She was drawn out of speculation by the judge's question.

"Mistress Buckingham, what say thee?"

"I've done nothing to Mister Parris' daughters."

"Didst thou reside in the north woods?"

"No! I just woke up in the woods. I have no idea how I got there. I think one of you in this room is behind it. I must have been drugged and left in the woods. This trial is a sham. When the FBI gets here, you're all going away for a long time."

"This is even more evidence of her witchcraft. Mistress Buckingham has threatened the people in this town of punishment from a demon she keeps trying to summon, this 'Effbeye,'" Parris said.

"This is a fucking joke! This whole cult would be better off following the Jonestown example. All just drink the Kool-Aid and die! And good riddance!" she said, her anger boiling over.

There was a loud gasp from the panel room. She realized she might not have helped herself. The judge banged the gavel again.

"This is the exact devilry we've been talking about. Not only that, but she came out of the woods in nothing but a shift. Trying, I recon, to bedevil the good gentlemen of our fair village with her womanly charms," Parris explained.

"Is this true, Mistress Buckingham?" the judge inquired.

"I deny everything, and I refuse to participate in this sham any longer."

"Before I rule, is there anyone else that would like to be heard?"

A woman came to the front. Pointing at Julie, she yelled, "She used her siren's call to seduce my God-loving husband!"

Another woman stood up and said, "She visits my daughters in dreams."

Once again, Julie couldn't stop herself. "This is insane! You're all insane! They've got you brainwashed! Snap out of it!"

The judge banged his gavel. "This court will come to order. I hereby remand this to the grand jury. On the charges of malicious acts of witchcraft against Mistress Buckingham, shall we proceed?"

One by one, the members of the jury stood and said, "Aye."

The judge declared, "The aye's have it. I schedule a trial for three weeks hence on 6 February. This court is adjourned."

They threw her back into the dungeon where she la- crying in the dark. Why was it taking the FBI so long to find her? Was there any chance she could escape this psycho cult? How long until she would see Aiden again?

III: Enhanced Interrogation

JULIE spent the better part of a week in near-total darkness. She'd counted twelve meals of bread and water and was sure it was two a day. Outside of that, there was no reckoning of time. She'd been cold for so long she couldn't remember what warmth felt like.

Maybe their cult compound was so well hidden, no one even knew it was there, like that M. Night Shyamalan movie. Perhaps the leaders of this secret community keep the rest of the town in the dark, unaware of the outside world, like in the movie. They would try to force a confession for their sham trial and then burn her at the stake.

She decided that no matter what, she wouldn't confess.

The door opened. She was escorted into a different room. To

her surprise, her shackles were removed, and she was sat on a chair. The two men left. The door opened again, and two women came in carrying a large bucket full of water and what appeared to be rags and some clothing. They stood her up, took the blanket away, pulled the slip off over her head, and threw it into the fire. She might've been self-conscious, but she was too filthy to feel exposed.

She tried to appeal to them. "Please, help me."

"Quiet, devil woman," the one who seemed to be in charge said, glaring at her.

"I've been kidnapped—" The woman slapped her.

Julie would get nowhere with them. She kept quiet after that.

Two more women came in with two more buckets. They poured the first over Julie's head. With the second, they used a cloth and physically wiped her body down, pouring a third bucket over her head. The water was hot and, though they handled her roughly, she was at least warm and clean for the first time in weeks. She didn't think she'd ever been that dirty in her life. They dried her off and pulled a sheer, off-white dress over her head. They put her hair in an updo, placed a bonnet on her head, and left.

A few minutes later, the two men returned and took her to the courtroom. While she felt better being clean and warm, it brought some other pains into focus. The cut in her foot, which was obviously infected, sent shocks of pain up her leg with every step. She'd been trying to figure out why they'd made her more comfortable. They placed her in the same spot as the last time. One of the men, the boy, remained behind her.

The grand jury came in and stood in the panel. Master Samuel Parris entered. As he took his seat, the man acting as bailiff took a step forward to address the room. "Gentlemen. The Honorable John Hathorne, presiding Magistrate of the County of Essex. Gentlemen, be seated."

With that statement, Julie saw Hathorne take his seat at the pulpit.

Judge Hathorne spoke, "On this day, 23 January, year of our Lord,1692. We are here to examine Mistress Julie Buckingham. Master Parris, please proceed."

Julie looked over at Parris.

He placed his hands on the table in front of him and push off as he stood. With the backs of his knees, he slowly drove the chair back behind him. Parris circled around the front of the room.

Julie focused on the timing of his stride. The heels of his boot stomping on the hollow floor. The sound of coarse wool as he walked, like fine sandpaper on a wooden bench. His confidence. The tempo of his movement. All like an actor playing his role and moving to his mark.

Parris finished his parade to the left and was behind Julie. "We are here to physically inspect Mistress Buckingham for any marks of the devil. With your honor's allowance?"

"Proceed."

With that, he pulled the dress over Julie's head. It was clear why they had washed her. It was for her "inspection."

"What the FUCK are you doing!?!" she screamed and instinctively pulled her arms to her chest. Parris hadn't given in. He held tight to the hem of her dress while Julie tried to get away. She squirmed in motions she thought would yield freedom only to have her dress ripped off. She stood naked in the middle of the disgusting old men.

She looked up.

Parris' face tightened. The pronounced hook on his nose was reduced to a slim line as his glare met hers. She turned her glance to the boy next to him. He seemed more in shock than she was.

"The accused will remain quiet!" Hathorne stood up and towered over her.

Her feet wouldn't move. She wanted to run, although she couldn't compel her legs to abide by her will. Julie glanced back at Parris.

"The hell I will!" She flared in a panic. Her limbs finally took initiative and moved her toward the door on her left.

Before she could take two steps, a painful grip landed on her left arm. She swung around, lost her balance, and fell to the floor. Still, she made every effort to break free of her captor.

The guard to the right of Judge Hathorne rushed in. He grabbed her before she could make an escape. He picked her up and placed her on her feet. Hathorne nodded in the direction of Parris.

Parris punched her in the stomach, knocking the wind out of her.

Julie collapsed, clenching her middle in utter agony.

Parris ordered the guard to raise her up to resume the examination. He grabbed Julie by the jaw, moved her head to one side, and then the other. He pulled her head down and nearly tore the bonnet off her head as he inspected her back and shoulders.

"Raise her arms up!" The guard took the order and lifted her arms with a fast, jerking motion. Her breasts swayed and shook. For a moment, there was only sheer embarrassment until she caught Parris' eyes. There was concern, a deep loathing, and worst of all, conviction. Her heart dropped as his hate-filled eyes went back to his task.

He grabbed Julie by both shoulders and kicked the inside of her right ankle to spread her legs. She was helplessly exposed.

The scandalous gasps of the jury reminded Julie they were not alone. None of these men had any intention of helping her. They were all under the thrall of Samuel Parris.

His inspection continued. He bent his knee to survey further down. After a short examination, Parris' eyes widen with terror. He found the thing he'd been looking for. She couldn't imagine what he could have found.

Shame and indecency flooded her.

Parris directed everyone's attention to her inner left thigh where he singled out her birthmark. It was strawberry shaped, about the size of a quarter. Julie had forgotten all about it.

Parris said, "The mark of the devil!"

The jury's shock was even louder than before. They whispered and mumbled while some pointed. Others made endless crossing motions. They were convinced.

"We have found the devil's mark on thee. Does thou still deny being his servant?"

"Of course I deny it! It's a birthmark!" Julie tried to close her legs but Parris, now standing, grabbed her by the nape of the neck. He pulled her head back. With his left hand, he gripped Julie's left leg just above her knee.

"Thou is marked since birth? Of course!" Parris said with apparent glee. He let go of her leg and threw her head forward. The guard released his grasp, and she fell to her knees.

The boy who stood next to Parris lunged to Julie's aide but was immediately ceased by Parris. "Thou shall bide!"

For the first time, Julie remained silent. She looked at the young man, and he quickly dropped his gaze. She'd forgotten she was without clothes. Using one arm to hold her steady, Julie wrapped the other around her chest, collapsed to an almost fetal position, and tried to catch her breath. She couldn't risk inflaming such a volatile situation any further.

"For my next examination." Parris motioned to two other guards forward.

The two men grabbed Julie by her arms and forced her up. They didn't let her go.

Parris walked around to the front of Julie. He stood facing her. With a nod to each man holding her, they stepped away and pulled her limbs out wide. Parris made his way behind them to what she thought was his desk.

Julie, now in even more pain, broke out in a sweat from the rigorous maltreatment. She looked down. There was blood under one foot. She was overcome with perspiration.

Parris returned, holding out a pin. He moved a step towards Julie, the pin still held outward in his hand. When he noticed her heaving breasts, he took her entire person into view and stepped back.

"Witch! Said witch once more doth attempt to bedevil us all. In her nakedness, she doth attempt to appear clean, bare as a child. Vile temptress. Her unholy body doth take such cold. Do observe how it doth glisten!"

He shifted to the left to clear a view for the judge and jury.

"Even in her hour of judgment, she changes her body in an attempt to provoke our carnal weakness! I shall demonstrate her true nature if ye need more proof."

The sight of the pin being brought to bear sent a feeling of dread through her.

Parris stood. He looked into Julie's eyes as she tried backing away. The blood from her foot prevented any sort of traction. The two men held her still. He shifted his glare to the man on her right.

"Maintain firm constraint!" he demanded.

The man tightened his grip on her wrist and violently shoved the other under the pit of her arm, forcing Julie to apply more pressure on her injured foot and making her cry out in agony.

Her fears became a reality.

Parris brought the pin to bear on a discolored mark on her arm. With a slow and steady thrust, Julie's blood began to flow.

"What the FUCK are you doing!?" she yelled.

Parris then pierced another spot on her shoulder. The pain only increased.

"Let me go...Please...stop."

"Confess, and may you find solace in the grace of God," he whispered after pulling out the pin from a small mark under her collarbone. With his hands soaked in blood and his hair a mess, Parris took a few steps back. He picked up Julie's discarded dress and wiped his hands on it.

"Confess thy devilry!" Parris demanded again as he moved to insert the pin near her navel.

All her efforts to resist his torture were futile. The more she struggled, the tighter Parris ordered the men to hold her. Her writhing caused the pin to plunge deeper into her flesh.

The room remained quiet.

A steadily increasing sound began in the back of her mind and was getting louder by the second. It...it was a woman screaming. The sound became deafening. She needed to take in a breath before she passed out. She inhaled and resumed her shrieking in utter pain.

The probing progressed from her arms down to her feet. Parris paused on several occasions, supposedly finding a few witch's marks. Apparently, any mark that didn't bleed was the mark of a witch.

By the time the last pin was pricked, Julie was in pain from head to toe.

The two men by her side were struggling to stay standing. Suddenly Parris spoke again. "Set her down."

She hit the floor hard, knees first, with no help from her bruised and dead arms. Her face hit last. Julie's body was broken. She withdrew into herself, arms crossed over her chest. With She held her hand to her injured cheek.

The two guards moved away. Parris' boots were in her line of sight. They kept her stomach in knots.

Judge Hathorne took a deep breath and sighed. "Mistress Buckingham. Seeking truth be our purpose. The preponderance of evidence is most damning. Thou dost defy Their Majesty's noble justice at every turn and yet plead for mercy. Thou do cause such a spectacle, disrupt and befoul our fair town with devilry and threats... Mistress Buckingham. Confess thy witchcraft and thy soul may be saved!"

Julie's entire body shook. She couldn't feel the cold floor as she curled up in pain. Tears streamed down her face as she resolved not to break down further.

"Just breathe…" She used every bit of energy left to peel herself off the ground. She tried to cover herself with one arm while fighting to remain stable with the other.

Parris' boot steps slowly circling her beaten body. She had to answer or face more torture.

"I do," Julie finally let out. "I do confess. I confess to knowing you are all fucking insane! How can you do this to me? You evil, sadistic, perverted bastards! When the FBI gets here, you're all gonna fucking die—" There came a sudden and intense impact on the side of her face.

Julie went down. Her eyes failed to focus, although she could make out the rough outline of Samuel Parris' boots.

After being confronted with the new "evidence" and Julie's refusal to confess, the judge called the examination to a close.

The next day, Julie found herself back in the dungeon, dressed and in shackles. She'd been awakened by someone banging on the door. This went on for what felt like every half hour.

They would take her to a room where they'd try to force a confession again and again. This went on every couple of days for at least a week. On the last day of this torturous cycle, when she refused to give in to their insanity, they locked her back in the darkness. Deliriously tired and in constant pain, she passed out.

IV: A Dark Place

JULIE awoke to absolute darkness. She had no conception of time. It no longer seemed to matter. Every day passed like the one before.

She'd lost any hope of being rescued. It must have been weeks since this nightmare had begun. Yet she was still here. If Aiden and all his connections and resources were not able to find her by now, the likelihood of her ever getting rescued was pretty much zero. Time was running out.

The walls were closing in around her. There was no escape. She knew death would come soon. She had maybe a week to live, but it felt like an eternity. Sleep was her escape, but whenever she tried, she would have the most terrible nightmares….

Julie stared at the house. Aiden took her hand and asked if she was ready. Snowflakes fell on his face. She wiped one off his cheek and realized it was ash. The door opened. When she looked back, her mother took one step and collapsed to her knees, covered in ash. Then she was swallowed by the flames that were engulfing the house.

Julie tried to run to her mother but was stopped by Aiden's grip. She looked at Aiden, but it wasn't him, it was Parris. She ripped her hand away. The flames began running off the house, coming right for her. She turned and bolted, searching for safety, but there was nowhere to hide. No matter how fast she ran, Parris was right behind her, surrounded by flames, just plodding along.

She sought protection in the woods and tripped and fell. She knew he would catch her. She looked back, fearing the worst, but there was no one there. She stumbled to her feet and right into Parris' arms. They were surrounded by a mob. They tied her to a wooden post and fed her to the flames.

Her waking hours provided no consolation. She was losing her mind. She'd stare into the darkness and try to see something, anything at all.

Her eyes played tricks on her.

The door would swing open. A SWAT team would swarm through the cult village and rescue her from this hell. Aiden would run from the car, wrap her in his arms, and her nightmare would be over. Then everything faded back to horrible reality.

The effect of all of this brought Julie to a dark place. She knew she was going to die. She just wished it would come soon and put her out of her misery. That horrible thought produced at least one silver lining. She'd be with her sister again.

She closed her eyes and whispered, "Jess, I will see you soon."

CHAPTER 6:
HOMESTEAD

MICHEAL REALIZED THAT IF he had fallen through time, he'd be in a perilous situation. Time was a dangerous place. Particularly if you stood out in the wrong way. He'd need to avoid being seen until he'd confirmed things one way or the other.

How could he confirm it?

He'd have to get inside one of those cabins. After observing for a while, a family exited a cabin far from the main area of town. He watched the elder of the bunch help the smallest ones onto the bed of a cart before climbing onto the front. With a snap of the reins, they rode off down the dirt road.

He watched a little longer. When he was certain they'd gone around the bend and were out of sight, he crept through the clearing. Micheal stayed low and traced the fence on his way to the front of the cabin.

Just then, another person came walking up the road.

Micheal immediately doubled back until he was out of the stranger's sight. Much to his amusement, he made what he described as 'an awesome action movie jump over the fence whilst landing on his back-type move'. The reality, however, had him on the ground, leg split open from the fence, and what felt like a dislocated shoulder.

"I totally woulda made that if I had grown up in Sunnydale," he groaned. With a light chuckle, he proceeded to sneak behind this cottage. The cut on his leg soon stopped bleeding. His shoulder was more of a bruised ego than a bruised arm.

As soon as the road was clear, Micheal made his way across the small yard and tried to open the door. He recognized the type of door mechanism but needed a couple of pins to jimmy it open.

"How can I get in without a key?" he pondered. "Wait, I have an idea! Call the locksmith! Call the locksmith!" he quoted. "Maybe all of this would be easier if I had an English accent." he chuckled again. "Now, where can I get some tights?"

Suddenly, the distant stride of a horse filled the air. The family was coming back up the road. He made his way into a woodshed while the cart pulled up to the front of the house. The eldest climbed down, approached the door and, after what sounded like a latch coming loose, went inside the cabin.

After a minute, the man emerged from his home. Micheal heard footsteps coming closer and closer to the shed. He stood still, hoping he wouldn't be seen. To his relief, the man stopped short of the entrance. The next thing he knew, there were squealing sounds coming from outside. Micheal leaned forward to catch a glimpse. The man had grabbed a pig, loaded it onto the cart, climbed back in, and driven off.

Micheal breathed a sigh of relief and snuck out of his hiding spot. He examined the lock once more and concluded there were no suitable tools around that he could use to jimmy it open. Even looking at the fence for any loose nails was an effort in futility. Never before had he had the knowledge to do something but lacked the tools to do it. Micheal had no other choice but to try to break in using force.

He returned to the shed in a last-ditch effort to find some wire, a hammer—something to help him pick that damned lock.

He was out of luck. The only thing he could think to try was to use one of the split logs on the lock in hopes of breaking the latch. He picked up the first one he saw and made his way toward the door of the hut.

He cocked his arm back, cradled the log with the other, and took a step in as he swung the piece of timber as hard as he could up and under the pin of the locking mechanism.

The impact reverberated through the quiet yard. Micheal immediately looked around for any witnesses. When he turned back, he saw the door had come to a halt after having swung ajar. He took one more look around outside before stepping in.

He searched through the small two-room cabin. There was little of interest, mostly rudimentary items. He found a shirt and a pair of trousers and donned them over his pajamas. The clothes were a big sign of potential time travel. They seemed to be handmade and surprisingly fit. If he was in the seventeenth or eighteenth century, they usually made their clothes extra-large and would fit them with a belt. They were a little tight, but he could manage, and they'd help him blend in as he explored the rest of the town. He found a pair of shoes which were too small. His toes poked out through the split front, but they were better than nothing. He put them on and resumed his search.

He looked through everything but couldn't find anything that confirmed what year it was. No dated papers or correspondence. No newspapers of any kind. And, while he thought even modern Amish still would have newspapers or magazines, the lack thereof did not affirm his time travel theory. Even he had allowed for that conclusion. He still needed to know what year it was. Based on everything he'd seen so far, he thought he was in the late seventeenth or early eighteenth century. He needed more answers.

As he snuck out of the house, he had a sinking feeling in his gut. He didn't want to steal the clothes, but he needed them more in his situation. He'd be sure to compensate the family at his earliest ability. He slipped out of the house and back into the woods.

He circled the town, surveying the buildings, and kept an eye on its occupants until he noticed a larger house. He found a sense of comfort in imagining it belonging to somebody important to the community. Someone well off. Someone with means.

Micheal looked down at the trousers he now wore, and the sinking sensation came back. He really felt bad about taking things from a home that had so little.

A few hours passed. He took note of anything and everything he could hear. He could only make out a little from a distance, but it was important he was not seen. The first time he heard anyone speak in more detail was a shouting match between children.

His mind shot to holidays. Weekends spent with his siblings and their kids. This was not like that. Their words... "thee" and "thine."

His thoughts broke when a large man came outside and spoke to the children. "Hanna! Caroline! Clean thyselves. We depart presently."

Any other day, that would've been enough proof. Transitional modern English. Seventeenth to eighteenth century. But today, Micheal needed to see evidence.

The family left the house and walked down the road, but he wasn't sure if their home was entirely empty or not.

He snuck in through a back door and found himself in an unusual kitchen. The stove was heavy cast iron and copper pots and pans hung on the wall. The smell of coal fire emanated. The next room looked for dining with a rustic table and chairs. There was a large walk-in fireplace with the coals banked.

The next room was the front room, a door in the center. Basically a living room, but the furnishings were certainly period. A staircase led up to the second floor, but the room to the right was what looked like a library or study.

He darted to the shelves and began flipping through books. Most were definitely from an earlier time. But they were also well-worn, no guarantees there.

In a drawer in a small desk, he found something more convincing. Correspondence. The first sheet he read was on parchment and had been sealed with wax. It was a Christmas letter from Boston and asked about things in Waymouth, which was south of Beantown. It was dated 20 December 1691. His heart sank as he read it, and sank further when he read the next one, also on parchment. The wax was obviously fresh. He stared at the date. It was the final confirmation.

The letter was dated 10 January 1692. He held the parchment in hand and rubbed it between his thumb and forefinger. The texture drew him into his thoughts.

Micheal's heart fell when he heard his name. He'd lost track of time and had gotten lost in an old book about colonial times. It had a lot of pictures which were kind of useful, he thought, but he liked reading instead. Today, he'd snuck into his parents' study again and was catching up on his new favorite subject.

His mother walked into the room and let out a deep sigh. "Christopher! Come see what Micheal has done."

Micheal got up from the floor where he read all his books and watched his father's head shake slowly.

"Well, isn't this a sight..."

"Micheal," his mother added.

"Hi, Mom! Hi, Dad! Look! This says that our ancestors grew their own food and had farm animals they could care for! And this one says how a family worked back in 1692!" He could have gone on and on, but his father cut in.

"You read all of these?"

There were multiple volumes of an encyclopedia collection, splayed open and stacked one on top of one another, Micheal sprawled in the middle of them all.

"Yeah! And this one here shows you how they made baskets and clothes!"

Micheal saw his dad look at his mom and smile. "He's gonna be so bored in kindergarten." He placed his hand over Micheal's head with love and pride, then he walked out.

"Come here, honey. I wanna show you something special." His mom closed the door and walked Micheal over to the chair behind the desk. She went to the bookcase and pulled out a copy of Common Sense *by Thomas Paine. She opened the book, pulled out an old piece of paper, made her way back to Micheal, and placed him on her lap.*

"This is an old letter. I've only had it for a short time. It took me years to track it down." She handed Micheal the letter. He unfolded it and immediately started to read it out loud.

"Saratoga, 17 October 1777"

"My Dearest Elizabeth... Mom, is that you?"

She breathed in slowly and replied, "No, honey. I wanted to show you what they used back in those times. It's called—"

"Parchment!" Micheal interrupted.

Her smile grew wider. "Yes. That's right. You're so smart. Here, feel how strong and thick it is."

Micheal was still rubbing the letter, going over everything in his head: the strange dress, strange speech, the parchment. He couldn't believe it. Somehow, he'd fallen through time and worse; he was near Boston in 1692. The witch trials would start soon.

Micheal heard footsteps inside the house. He ducked down low and tried to make his way to the back door. It began to open. He turned to head back to the study, but realized he wouldn't make it in time. Micheal spotted the enormous table in the dining area, slid under it, and lay as quietly as possible. He was well hidden beneath it. He laid perfectly still while the family settled in, prepared and ate dinner, then sat around chatting.

As the hours passed, he considered everything he'd discovered. This wasn't how he expected to spend his birthday. A trip through time was something he'd have instantly signed up for, just not an accidental one. He placed his hands behind his head and wondered about the possibilities of this experience. Not to mention the dangers.

After what felt like an eternity, the family went to sleep. He slid out from under the table, slipped into the kitchen, picked up a knapsack, and filled it with food from the pantry. There were a few tools on the mudroom wall on his way out of the house. Believing they'd be valuable, he took them.

He crept to the door but, as he opened it, his sizable girth grazed a stack of pots that lay on the edge of a table. They fell to the ground with a sound like thunder.

The house filled with screams and panicked chatter. Someone hastily closed in on Micheal as he ran out of the house. The doorway was soon filled with the silhouette of a hunched individual holding a rifle. The shadow yelled obscenities but did not pursue Micheal as he ran as fast as he could into the woods.

I: Darkness

MICHEAL spent a few days living off the land. He slept during the day when the temperature was warmest and woke up before dusk to look for food. Every day, he moved a few more miles. First to the southwest, then eventually straight west. He was southeast of Boston and was planning to skirt around the city, foraging until he found a place to settle.

He started to make his way forward and thought about the cold. While it would be intolerable for most, he was more than glad to have such a high resistance to the winter seasons. The winter of '99 came to mind.

He and TC had gone to The Sundance Film Festival to try to get some day tickets to 'The Blair Witch Project'. They were standing in line outside the Tower Theater.

"We've been out here for three hours. How much longer is it going to be?" TC complained.

"Don't tell me you're cold. The sign says it's minus eight degrees." Micheal joked.

"Fahrenheit or Celsius? Cause to me, it feels like Kelvins."

"Kelvins don't go negative." The twenty-something man ahead of them chimed in.

"Hey Mike, did you know there's nothing colder than absolute zero? Me neither," TC deadpanned, then added. "It certainly feels colder than the vacuum of space out here."

The man looked embarrassed. The woman standing with him said to Micheal, "But seriously, we're from Northern Norway and this is cold to us. How are you out here in shorts and a t-shirt?"

"My Metallica shirt gives me great power...but no, I've acclimatized over the years to take colder and colder temperatures. Many people think I must be from Alaska or the North Pole or something." He could only laugh at the assertion.

Micheal came back to the present. If he could take minus eight degrees for three hours, no problems. He could certainly take the twenty degrees he'd estimated almost indefinitely.

But surviving off the land was not an indefinite option. He still had a few items left that he'd taken from the farm and had rationed most of it to supplement what he could forage. While food was rather scarce, he knew many useful tricks.

Micheal knew to dig. When the snow fell and the ground became a solid icy shell, he knew to dig deep. He was an eagle scout. Well, not officially. But he'd earned every scout merit badge by the time he was twelve. He dug under trees, dug beyond the top plates of frozen earth, and deep into the ground.

"Slimy yet satisfying," he sighed as he placed a worm in his mouth and swallowed, hoping for the best.

He picked up another bug. Suddenly, he heard footsteps behind him. They were headed his way.

Micheal dropped the beetle and moved forward to grab his bag of sundries. As he moved behind a tree, his foot caught on a root, and he came down on the dirt pile he made while foraging. His face was covered in icy mud, but he knew he needed to find cover.

He scrambled to his feet, jumped over a bush and ducked low, trying to determine the direction the sound was coming from. After a moment, a large black horse walked into the meadow. He looked around. There didn't appear to be anyone with it. It had likely escaped from a farm in the area. This was the perfect opportunity to better his situation. He'd have to win its trust. Some of the food he still had just might work.

He grabbed an apple and a carrot from the bag and slowly approached the clearing. The horse whinnied acknowledgment when he saw him approach. It looked like it was about to run away, but then it walked back to the middle of the clearing and circled the space, getting closer and closer to him with each pass, until finally stopping only a few feet away.

He made firm eye contact with the horse and held out an apple.

"Eeeeasy boy...I'm not gonna hurt you. I'm sure you're in need of a good meal just like me...Here, take it."

The horse, still a little uneasy, made as if it were going to take the fruit from his hand, only to pull back at the last moment and skitter back to the safety of his side of the clearing. Micheal tossed the apple toward the horse, making sure that it rolled more than flew. The apple landed only a few feet from the horse. It jumped back. After a moment, it slowly made its way to the apple.

Micheal took a couple of steps back to show this dark-as-night creature that it was in no danger. The horse sniffed at the apple a few times, then ate it.

Micheal held out the carrot next.

The horse looked at it and warily walked toward him. It paused a few feet away.

Micheal spoke calmly, raising his hand out in a fist toward it. "Don't be afraid...I won't hurt you..."

The horse sniffed his fist a few times, then walked close enough to eat the carrot out of his hand. It sniffed his fist again and ran off. Micheal was sure it would be back.

The dark stallion stayed close to the area over the next two days. On the third night, Micheal headed down on a hillside to the stream below. He'd been using it as a water source. Suddenly, he was met by an enormous wall of darkness, knocking him to the ground.

Micheal got to his feet slowly. The horse returned. It didn't seem too concerned with his presence. The animal gave a slight flinch at Micheal's initial touch but immediately regained its calm.

"Well, you came out of nowhere, didn't you? Appearing out of the dark."

Then it hit him. "Darkness."

The black stallion turned its head, blinked, then returned to its meal.

"Okay. Darkness it is."

With their relationship cemented, Micheal decided he'd try to mount him.

The next morning, after giving the horse his breakfast snack, it was time. He stroked his mane, then gave him a firm pat on its neck, maintaining eye contact.

"Good boy." He stepped to the horse's side.

He closed his eyes and remembered when he was ten. He repeated the steps in his head as he put them into action.

Grab the mane just before the withers, place your other hand on the back, then it's basically a hop, skip, and a jump.

He swung his leg up, but it did not go as high as he had hoped. Darkness was startled by his attempt and threw him off. He landed face down in the snow.

"Well, that almost worked," he said, laughing as he brushed himself off. He noticed Darkness hadn't gone far. That was a good sign. He knew he still had a good chance of taming the wild beast.

He tried and failed a few more times that day. The frustration of coming so close and failing made Micheal feel defeated. He decided to try again the next morning.

And the next morning: "Ready, Darkness?" Micheal slowly made his way to the horse.

It was a new day. He was determined to break him in. He kicked his right leg high, clearing the height of the horse, and pulled himself up to a sitting position. He held his mane tightly with both hands. Darkness shook his head a bit but seemed to calm down.

Micheal tightened his grip and gave Darkness a light kick with the heel of his foot, trying to urge his stallion forward. The giant beast took one step forward and Micheal perked up with satisfaction. He was immediately bucked off. Darkness circled around Micheal in a slow trot, snickering all the while.

"Laugh it up, fuzzball." Micheal sat up, watching his steed add insult to injury.

After taking some time to regroup, Micheal went to his supply cache and came back with a special treat for Darkness. His last apple.

Darkness perked up and quickened his trot. Micheal was delighted to see the trust this animal had given him.

Micheal took a step towards Darkness and held out a fist. The steed moved in and sniffed him. He opened his fist and placed his hand on the head of this mighty beast, then ran his hand up the top of this beautiful animal and took another step closer.

He took the apple and without warning nudged Micheal's cheek with its own in a sign of understanding. Darkness shook its head. Not in fear or dissatisfaction, but in preparation.

Micheal took a deep breath and slowly released it, preparing himself.

With a sigh, the black beast began to walk. Micheal followed its pace for a couple of steps, placing his right hand on the back of the steed. He clenched his left hand into a fist around the thick mane and kicked his leg over the mountain that was Darkness.

Micheal held tight to secure himself. He gave a slight cue and Darkness came to life.

While he experienced riding a horse bareback once, this was nothing like it. This was like flying.

Bushes, fallen trees, and boulders pass beneath them as Darkness cut through the fields in a thunderous roar. Rabbits and foxes scurried off in fright as he and his dark ally came riding in like the wind.

Darkness led them to higher and higher ground. Micheal was curious where his horse was taking him. It was a trust he didn't know he could give, especially to an animal. They rode into a clearing and Darkness slowed his pace to a light canter and down to a walk.

Darkness stopped as he came to a granite clearing. The silence of the land washed over him. He closed his eyes and thought back to all the maps he'd collected, all the research he had done in the name of his love of geography. He mentally traced his route along those maps.

If he was where he thought he was, there should be a lake

nearby. But he couldn't see one. His mind morphed the maps into one. Borders and names began to appear in his mind. His mental map expanded. There were only two possible points where he could see for such a distance. The first, the Blue Hills. The second was, "Moose Hill," he whispered.

This time, as he opened his eyes, the map in his mind began to spin and fall to face southeast, where the Providence River should be. His head panned from right to left, his eyes seeing shades of oranges, yellows, greens, and blues. He paused as the arm of the Providence River stretched out.

"Moose Hill. We're on Moose Hill," he said. Darkness nickered once more.

He reflected on the landscape and what it would eventually turn into in the year 2010. The soreness of his bruises started to ache. He'd lost count of how many times he'd fallen. The pain in his stomach reminded him his food cache was gone. It didn't matter. None of it mattered.

Darkness would make it easier to acquire the things he needed. They could go far together.

II: Homestead

MICHEAL had awakened just outside the town of Weymouth, near modern-day Quincy. He didn't want to establish his base of operations near that area since it was too heavily trafficked, so he rode northwest.

As the sun neared the horizon, they came to another river. Micheal believed the river they had forded earlier that day was the Charles, so this river had to be the Sudbury. He was probably just south of Concord, the center of the area due west of Boston. It would be the perfect base to gather needed supplies without going into Boston's hotbed. He'd be a day's ride from anywhere in the colony.

However, what he needed most was a permanent shelter. Micheal picked a spot by the river to camp for the night. He cleared a place for a fire and another for a place to sleep. He gathered several branches to weave together and stuffed them with all the leaves he could find.

Darkness circled around the clearing, stopping here and there to forage, seeming as if he approved of their resting spot.

The campfire had come to life, and Micheal was comfortable enough to be able to sleep.

A sense of urgency overtook him, but he didn't know where it came from. He spent half an hour digging for his breakfast before starting his day. When he finished munching down on a few insect treats, he motioned to Darkness and moved toward him.

"Hey, Darkness. Here, boy."

Micheal held his fist out, and Darkness trotted to it. As he opened his fist and moved to pet his equine friend, Darkness shook his head and circled back to his original spot.

"What's the matter?" he called out. "Are you okay? Darkness?" He gave himself a quick inspection and scanned his surroundings. He hoped to find a deer standing behind him or unwanted tree sap smeared on his hand, something that would tell him why his friend was acting strange, but nothing.

He took a few steps toward the horse and observed his actions. He was foraging.

Suddenly, a line from his youth came to mind. A quote from a never-ending tale.

"Oh, I know, it's time to eat!" Micheal walked more confidently and met his dark friend once more.

He referenced his scouting survivalist training files. "Those trees should be safe for you to eat," he announced. Darkness perked up and pawed the snow in approval.

Micheal swept the area in a systematic way to collect as many saplings and soft branches as he could find. That would probably serve Darkness for the time being.

He began tracing the river's edge to the south of the clearing and was happy to find the saplings in abundance. After about one hundred paces, he turned and swept back north and continued the harvest in this fashion for about an hour. He returned to the clearing where he could cut the arm full of branches down to more manageable sizes.

Darkness was drawn to the commotion. He dropped the segments on the ground and Darkness immediately began to eat them.

Micheal surveyed the clearing more closely. It was bigger than he had initially estimated—about half the size of a football field. This would be perfect.

He went to his experience from his youth when he had built a small ten-by-ten cabin in the mountains east of Park City. It was

October, and he was by himself. It had taken a week, but it was an interesting challenge of structural engineering and physics. All he was given in that case was a handsaw, an axe, and a hundred feet of rope. He would use that template for his new homestead.

—⋙—

The next day, he fixed Darkness with a harness to help with clearing the trimmed logs to be cleaned and then carved for stacking.

He used the stolen saw and ax to clear an area of trees near the river.

By the end of the day, he'd cut down nearly forty trees. Each time one came down, it was trimmed, cleaned, and moved. Branch after branch, he piled all the trimmings away for later use. Some were stored near what was to be the foundation of his cabin, and the rest were kept in a pile by the river.

As the days passed Micheal made steady progress on the homestead.

The first day Darkness nudged him awake, he got to work on the floor. He drove in four corner posts, marking the outline of the cabin. Then he laid down four notched logs as the floor's perimeter. It was about twenty by twenty feet. He split and notched the five longest logs to place in the center. They were about thirty feet long each. Placing them exactly in the middle would give him about five feet on the east and west sides as a porch. He loved the idea, but it was back-breaking work. Still, the relatively flat surface they'd created was worth the work.

The next day, he woke to a loud whinny. After a foraging sweep, it was time for the walls. He notched twenty more logs on both sides of each end, so they looked like giant Lincoln Logs. With Darkness' help, he used two smaller trees to create a fulcrum for leverage, allowing them to lift the heavy logs up to eight feet above the ground. He cut out doorways and windows as he went, bracing them with vertical logs. By day's end, he had three full walls and a fourth with a gap for a planned fireplace.

On the third day, he was wrenched from his slumber by sticks tossed into his face. He rubbed the sleep out of his eyes and grabbed a piece of what his friend had dropped. He used his thumb to scratch a bit of dirt off and saw orange begin to show. Micheal gave out a bit of a laugh and smiled.

"Thanks for the sassafras, Darkness." His steed had delivered breakfast in bed.

The morning sky was an ominous red. A storm was approaching. He needed a roof sooner rather than later. He cut five logs into thinner boards running lengthwise and used them to frame the roof, then laid more boards across the frame enclosing the cabin. He proceeded to shingle the roof with the trimmings he had set aside. As clouds darkened the western skies, he raced to dig out enough river mud to seal the roof. As the first flakes fluttered down, his one-room cabin was ready.

Luckily for him, the storm had passed by the next morning, leaving only a couple of inches in its wake. Days four, five, and six provided Micheal time to mortar the gaps in the walls, build a shelter for Darkness, and start an addition meant to be a bathroom to the south side and a chimney fireplace on the north side.

Nearly a week had passed, and foraging could only yield so much food. Micheal's stomach felt perpetually empty, but he'd tried to focus on the task at hand. While his regular hiking never helped him lose weight, it did give him stamina. But even with that, the days of constant chopping and stripping of trees were taking their toll. Every muscle ached and he had several bruises from log mishaps. And another problem had become apparent. The scratch on his leg from the fence had become infected. It was tender red and oozing puss. He thought this wound was shallow enough it would heal on its own. This wouldn't be the last cut he'd need to deal with, and the next time could be deadly. He needed penicillin. He'd synthesized it before in scouts, so he knew the process. He would need to initiate that quickly, as it would take some time. To him, antibiotics were history's single greatest discovery for extending human lifespans.

With so many things to deal with, he almost wanted to give up. Darkness had worked just as hard as he had and pushed on for both their sakes. Darkness deserved a reward, so he went to the morning's spoils in his knapsack, an item at a time.

"What food have we got? Let me see, oh yes...maple root...and look! More maple root!"

Darkness nudged at his hand holding the sapling. Micheal bit off a piece and gave the rest to Darkness.

"You know, I don't usually hold with foreign foods but this veiny stuff, it's not bad." Darkness began to sniff out the knapsack for more food. Micheal let out a laugh at his pet's eagerness.

"Nothing ever dampens your spirits, does it, Darkness?"

He looked at his friend and then back at what Darkness had helped him build.

"We need better food."

Micheal spent the evenings carving items such as spoons, plates, bowls, and spade shovels out of wood. He made a couple of jaunts into Concord, which was five miles north, to trade the items for food for both him and Darkness. As the days continued to pass, he saw a giant improvement in Darkness' overall demeanor. He figured the improved diet and regularity in feed may have something to do with it.

And there was one other project he'd been urgent to start, penicillin. He'd synthesized some in a personal experiment when he was in junior high. It had taken a month, and he'd gained access to the necessary acidic ingredient. He would need to make the acid this time, so this would be more difficult, but it was essential.

Micheal spent the days slowly adding more and more to his homestead. He thought Boston would give him his best chance to figure out his time dilemma, but only if he could move in the more sophisticated circles of society. If he couldn't acquire a fair amount of riches, he would just stay at his homestead. So, until he could come up with a strategy for wealth, he would focus on improving his homestead.

He insulated the cabin's ceiling with a few beams and what was left of the leaves and branches to prevent the heat from escaping.

He dug out a pit about five feet deep as a septic reservoir and, after putting up walls for the bathroom; he considered something. "A bed would be nice..."

And so, he put up another wall enclosing his new privy and left a hallway to his would-be bedroom. He cut holes in the floor of his bathroom where he intended to lay pipes. He would need to start metalworking to add any plumbing. To that end, he built a kiln outside the barn. Now he just needed some metal.

As Micheal fed Darkness some oats out of his hand, he took stock of what he had done. He had added another room on the other side of the bathroom and crafted a few furniture items. His mold cultures were growing, so penicillin was at hand. In about three weeks, he'd built a rather impressive little homestead.

He thought about all the unfortunate situations where his efforts were sabotaged. Of course, he'd been forced to test himself here. Normally, he avoided situations in which he might fail.

"So far, so good," he decided. The fact that he'd suffered no major setbacks since his arrival made him nervous that calamity was lurking around the corner. He likely wouldn't survive if it does come. He feared it was a matter of time.

Now he needed more tools and supplies. He had crafted a few things and traded them at nearby villages for some food. But he needed something more substantial to trade. But what was there?

III: Precious Metal

MICHEAL reached into the deep recesses of his mind until he stumbled into an interesting conversation.

March 1, 2009

TC arrived at the restaurant, late as usual, caught up in whatever he may have been up to since getting back from Boston. School, likely. Girls, more than likely. His friend had an addiction. TC loved women.

"Hey, Mike. Sorry, I got caught up with—"

"A girl?"

"You know, I don't need this type of negative thinking...."

They both laughed and ordered. Then TC exhaled and became serious. Micheal recognized that look. It was a girl, alright. No doubt about it.

"So I gotta tell you about this amazing woman I met in Cambridge. She's in the Exchange Clerkship Program from Stanford. We met after our orientation at Beth Israel Hospital. She's...wow. She's amazing."

'Head over heels', Micheal thought. TC had always worn his heart on his sleeve.

"I had to talk to her. I don't know what I was thinking or what I even said, but she agreed to meet up for a drink at her place. I

was so nervous when I got there that I don't think I said a word for the first ten minutes."

"That's a bit unusual, isn't it? I mean, you've never had a problem talking to women."

"That's just it. She's not just anyone. She's special. She had lights, like Christmas lights, running along the ceiling. She takes them wherever she goes so she can 'paint the sky with diamonds'."

"Diamonds?"

TC's smile grew wider as he continued to talk about this mystery woman.

"Anyway, she ran her own business to put herself through med school and does underwriting for Colonial General. She's..."

"Amazing?"

TC shot a glare at Micheal and they both laughed.

"I tried to impress her with random things I had read about New England. She topped all my facts by telling me she had seen a map saying there was gold next to the Merrimack River near the Massachusetts- New Hampshire border. Can you believe there was gold in New Hampshire?"

"That's... amazing."

"Shut up." They both laughed.

⁑

It wasn't much, but if the mystery girl was right, it might be just what he needed. He would need to go on a little expedition.

The next morning, he headed to a small town called Cambridge Farms, the future Lexington, and traded the carving kit for other tools. He needed a pick hammer, a pair of tongs, and the essential melting pot.

Micheal rode north most of the day until he reached the shore of the Merrimack River, a couple miles north of Chelmsford. He proceeded to follow the river upstream until he arrived at the New Hampshire border a little before dusk. He decided to establish a camp for the evening. He tied up Darkness and went to work on the fire.

He carved a groove in the edge of a four-foot-long branch to use as his ground stick. He sat with his right leg forward, bracing it to the ground, and began the Polynesian technique of fire starting. Using some forceful thrusts with his elbows out, as if he was preparing to make a chest pass on the basketball court, the friction stick began to smoke. He increased his pace, and he knew the spark was about to ignite.

"Easy as pie!" he exclaimed confidently to Darkness. But the expected ember failed to materialize. Darkness whinnied in what felt like a mocking tone. "You want to give it a try? I know I usually make it look easy, but few people or horses are as proficient as I am." He chuckled a little.

Still, as his efforts continued to fail him, he became frustrated and threw the stick. Darkness nickered in response, then retrieved it.

"I don't want your help!"

Darkness dropped the stick and stared at him.

Another half hour of failure had him on the edge. He tried to force it and the stick jerked. He burned his hand on the groove. "Damn it!" He tossed the stick into the river.

He cooled the burn in the cold flowing water and decided to give it one more try.

Micheal found another friction stick and refocused on his technique. He got a good rhythm going and a few minutes later, as the hint of twilight faded to black, a spark came to life. He quickly added kindling and slowly waved the ground stick through the air, feeding his ember some oxygen. The spark burst into a flame. He exclaimed, "I have made fire!" He turned to Darkness and added, "Wilson...sorry, I mean Darkness...I have made fire!"

Over the next few days, he searched high and low, from dusk till dawn. He wasn't sure how much longer he could go on searching. On the evening of the third day, when he was going to call off the search, the last rays of the setting sun glinted off something—something gold.

He investigated closer and thought it might be gold, but after digging most of the next day, he realized the ore was too hard, too brittle. His guess was pyrite.

Just when he thought his luck might be changing, it turned out the same old way. In failure. He'd even believed the way he'd discovered this, the fading sunlight catching something shiny right when he was about to give up, was a true sign his luck was changing. But things were never going to change. Being three hundred years in the past and two thousand miles from home still didn't change the fact he had the worst luck in the world. Maybe even of all time.

He knew if his friends and family were here, they would say the cabin he'd built proved he could do great things.

"Wow..." he said sarcastically as Darkness approached the pile of fool's gold. "I built a cabin." He stepped up to his friend and reached into his pocket for a treat. "Four rooms, though...." He held up a carrot to Darkness, which he happily ate. "Eh...it's just a cabin, and it took three weeks or so... Anyone could do the same."

Darkness nudged Micheal gently as if to agree. It was obvious his friend was of the same mind.

"The knowledge is there. Just gotta put in the effort. Now, rocket science, that would be impressive." He gave Darkness another treat.

Micheal would head back to his homestead in the morning. He gathered his things to get ready for the night and couldn't shake this feeling of failure as he did so.

So far, the only major accomplishment since this all started was losing a decent amount of weight. He estimated around thirty pounds or so. But it had nothing to do with him. He was starving. That, combined with nearly non-stop physical labor, was likely the cause. Nothing had ever worked before, so at least he had one positive.

With nothing but the build on the agenda, every day was sixteen hours testing his endurance. The faster he could cover the necessities, the sooner he could move on to the mechanics of time.

Some valuable resources could speed up the process, which was the whole point of this mission. Micheal was fighting his urge to quit. His stomach always ached and his whole body was a sore muscle. He hoped his body would adjust to the situation soon or might as well give up. Failures such as today only magnified the time travel mountain that still lay in front of him.

When he woke up, it was snowing. The terrain had lost most of its significance and no matter which way he looked, it all looked the same. He wasn't sure which direction was which. He would have to hunker down until the storm broke.

Snow covered most of the basic makeshift tent he'd erected for shelter out of a sheet of canvas he'd acquired on the way north. It had acted like an extra blanket during the night. It wasn't what you would call "warm", but it was noticeably warmer than it had been the night before. Upon extricating himself from the cozy little den, the sun had risen, and so he began making his way south. A few minutes into the leisurely ride with a clear blue sky, Micheal became lost in his own thoughts.

He snapped out of his daydream when a small strand of silvery metal gleamed in the rock face he'd been riding next to.

"Whoa, boy." He dismounted and took a closer look. He was nearly certain it was silver. A day of excavating later and his hopes were confirmed. This was soft. Much softer than the garbage he'd dug up before. The best part, it wasn't brittle. It wasn't just falling apart. It was definitely silver.

Micheal broke out his equipment and went to work on the vein with the hammer pick. Darkness didn't have much to do at this stage and Micheal was pleased to find his friend bringing the occasional sassafras treat. He was happy to have found a companion in this unbelievable mess.

Micheal went back to his experience when he was working toward his metalworking merit badge. A member of his church stake had their own blacksmithing forge. He'd spent a lot of time working with different metals. That would be helpful in this situation.

He spent the next few days extracting as much of the vein as he could. He hacked out multiple rock piles with silver ore for later processing. Dividing the silver from what he suspected was limestone would take some pretty intense heat. He made up his mind to build a makeshift kiln and smelt the raw ore in the location where he'd found the vein rather than haul hundreds of pounds of rock back to his homestead, only to have a fraction of that yield tradable silver.

First, Micheal took Darkness to the river's edge to find some rocks and gather mud to seal the base of his kiln. Leaving a vent on the side, stacking the stones, and filling in the gaps took less time than he'd expected.

Darkness approached as he worked on the roof of the kiln. Micheal noticed his friend's inquisitive expression. He said, "Think 'Pantheon', Darkness. I'm going for a ceiling with an opening just like the Pantheon." Darkness shook his head and made his way into the woods.

As he began hacking away at the stone wall, another mineral showed itself. It was silver-colored but was crystalline in nature. Definitely not silver. He grabbed a splinter from a chunk he'd been examining, threw it in the fire, and waited for a reaction.

To his surprise, the flame went from orange, to yellow, to white.

"Magnesium," he said out loud. This could prove quite useful later. He knew that other stronger metals would need higher temperatures for refining. Micheal took all the magnesium shards and stored them for later use.

Micheal spent the next day or so pounding the limestone and silver ore into a fine grade. After it was all ground up, Micheal stood and looked over his work. He was glad he'd strayed from his original plan. Taking all the ore to Homestead would have taken several trips, but the base of operation he'd built here was better than he'd hoped for.

At the same time, he considered his own thoughts: "Homestead."

"...has a nice ring to it," he murmured.

Darkness pawed at the ground. It caught Micheal's attention.

"Well, I was thinking, we call it homestead so much that it should be its official name, ya know?"

The vein proved to have a high concentration of pure silver. He knew he was rich. In two days or so, he and Darkness would arrive at Homestead. Their situation exponentially improved.

IV: Supply Run

MICHEAL knelt over the last bag, placing the remaining nuggets inside before tying it closed.

"All right. We processed the silver into nuggets. Each is about the size of a large grape. That means, on average, they weigh around one or two ounces each and they hold a value of about ten to thirty dollars apiece, in my time." He stood up, holding the bag in hand, and looked at Darkness again.

"This is our future, right here," he held up the bag of silver.

Darkness sniffed it.

"There's nineteen more where that came from." Darkness followed his gaze to the collection of burlap sacks. He nickered in approval.

"At twenty-five pounds each, that's five hundred pounds of silver." Darkness looked back and forth from the pile as if he was uncertain.

"If you're worried about the weight, I know what I'm talking about. My work at the post office gave me experience gauging weights. I know it's no more than five hundred pounds in total. Besides, you're a badass. You'll handle it without a problem." He pet Darkness on the nose.

"Do you know how much that is? In my time that much silver would be worth about"—he raised his pinky to his lips, turned his head slightly to the side, and with a raised brow said—"one million dollars!"

"Sorry, Darkness, I couldn't help myself. It's actually more like a hundred grand."

In 1692, that much silver was worth significantly more in a relative sense. If he went into some town and started flashing it around, it would draw far too much attention to him. He wanted to limit his interactions.

After returning from New Hampshire, he rode from town to town and made minor purchases. The first thing he needed was a horseman's set. He stopped off at Sudbury on the west side of the river and found a leather maker where he put in an order. He was originally told two days for a nineteen-hand horse, but he threw in a couple of extra nuggets to get it by the next day.

He made stops in two more villages—Maynard and Stowe—where he bought the last of the replacement items, the things he had borrowed on his first day in the seventeenth century.

He also acquired some parchment, an inkwell, and quills. He meant to write letters of apology and gratitude for his breaking in and for borrowing without permission.

That evening, Micheal sat by the fire and spent a couple of hours refining his contemporary penmanship. He knew it was important to continue a gentle stroke until the ink ran out. About every three to six words. He had learned to write cursive when he was young, but he knew writing in this century was an important social art form. Plus, he needed to be sure to write it in the local lexiconic style.

Along with the restitution for the borrowed items and letters of apology, he prepared some bags of silver. Despite the urgent need he'd had for the items and his plan to repay them, he still felt guilty for his misdeeds. He hoped his actions hadn't caused undue harm.

The next day, Micheal dressed in his newest set of clothes. After collecting the horseman's package from the leather maker, he rode to the place where he had first arrived. When he rode into the clearing, it looked almost the same as that first day. He could still clearly see the spot where he'd been laying, despite it being under a blanket of recently fallen snow.

For the first time in a while, he considered what that might indicate about temporal mechanics. He'd pondered his predicament here and there, wondering how the fall could have happened and if there was any hope of going back.

What was he thinking? Of course, there was hope. He was here!

Even so, could he figure it out? Was he smart enough?

He certainly hoped he was. He didn't want to spend the rest of his life in the seventeenth and eighteenth centuries.

He walked Darkness through the woods to the edge of town. Darkness looked around as if he didn't recognize their location.

"What boy? You don't think I know where I'm going? I promise you, I'm right. See? It's Weymouth. And that's the farm I first encountered." He pointed at the village.

Darkness nickered in response.

"Oh, what would you know?" They came to a halt in the identical location where he first saw the town.

The man and his family were doing chores outside the first home he broke into, rather than waiting to see if they would leave, he went to check out the other farm—the larger, richer one where he had confirmed the impossible fact of his current temporal location.

He left Darkness in the woods with the bag filled with silver, food, and clothes for the first household and quietly made his way across the farm and hid near the barn. He watched the house for a few minutes. When he was certain it was clear, he went and placed the bag of tools, food, and silver on the porch. They *clunked* against the wooden surface harder than he had intended, and he was once again running as fast as possible from this farm. He was able to get to the cover of the woods before anyone came out.

A man emerged from the house with a musket in his hands. He looked around, musket cocked, ready to shoot any trespassers. He looked at the package with a bit of surprise. Micheal saw the man step back a little, showing some reservations toward picking up the strange parcel. The man looked around again, this time musket down and less alarmed.

After investigating its contents, he read the letter. When he was finished, he looked through the package once more, this time dropping the musket to the deck of his porch. Six more people came outside as the man dropped to his knees with the letter in one hand. Seeing the reaction of the rest of the family made him feel like his restitution was accepted. He made his way back to Darkness and headed back to the first farm.

Micheal sat in observation for a moment, searching for any sign of the family's presence. The cart was gone. He was positive the family must have gone into town. He waited another minute to be sure the coast was clear and then snuck up to the door of the cabin.

Before he could put the package down, a voice behind him said, "That is far enough, friend." It was followed by the cocking of a pistol.

"Turn around slowly." As he turned around, his mind raced to come up with a believable backstory without implicating himself as the previous invader. Then the man went on, "What is thou doing on my farm?"

Then it came to him. "My name is Master Hill. I'm here on behalf of one Master Whitaker who had an unfortunate situation a few weeks ago and, in desperation, came to this farm for assistance. When no one answered, he regrettably made his way inside to find something to protect himself from the cold, so he borrowed some clothing from your house."

The man interjected. "And now you have come for more?"

"I've been sent on his behalf to make recompense," he replied quickly.

He held out the package. The man studied it skeptically. After looking thoughtfully between Micheal's face and the package, he seemed to relax. While he continued to hold the pistol on him, he said, "Open that package and show me my recompense." There was a hint of skepticism in his voice.

Micheal went to one knee and untied the package. He laid it open and explained the contents.

The man finally uncocked the pistol. He placed it in his belt and said, "That's quite a bit more than was taken."

"Master Whitaker felt the only way to make right the harm his sins had caused was to make restitution. That was severalfold what he took."

"And what are those?" the man asked, indicating the pouch and letter.

Micheal opened the pouch and revealed the silver and said, "For your trouble, and a letter of contrition."

He handed the letter and the pouch to the man. As the man read the letter, he could see tears in his eyes. The man looked up and said, "This is a godsend. Tell Master Whitaker I, Nathaniel Billington, forgive his trespass, and say God bless."

He held out his hand and Micheal shook it. Master Billington said, "My thanks, Master Hill. God bless thee—and Master Whitaker."

Micheal made his way back to Homestead feeling a great burden had been lifted. He'd felt guilty regardless of his moment of need and could tell that Master Billington must have been on hard times. His restitution may have greatly helped him and his family. So at least something good may have come from his unfortunate actions.

The whole situation brought one thing sharply into focus: he would need to develop a fully formed, believable identity. Darkness nudged him with his nose, as if asking a question.

"I'm trying to figure out who I'm going to be in this time." Darkness looked at him. His ears twitched.

"I don't appreciate your judgment. I can be whoever I want to be. Who are you going to be?" he challenged Darkness as he mounted up. The horse whinnied a snide reply.

"And don't say noble steed. I'm not sure you could pull it off." Darkness countered with a nicker.

"We'll see, we'll see." Micheal smiled and shook his head.

He thought it through as they rode, then it all became clear as the sun set on their arrival at Homestead.

CHAPTER 7: TRIAL AND EXECUTION

I: Escape

J ULIE AWOKE FROM HER nightmare of despair to the sounds of clanking keys turning in the lock on her cell door. Her back was turned as she slept. The dread of not knowing who or what was coming filled her.

She clenched her arms together under her covers, eyes shut tight. Suddenly, a warm hand was on her shoulder. A young man's voice intruded: "Mistress? I do beg pardon, are you awake?" It was gentle. There was concern in his tone. Her thoughts slipped to Aiden for the smallest of moments before the second guard's voice broke her fantasy.

"You shan't address the accused. Take her," He led by example and gripped her arm so tightly that the pain from her wounded foot faded away.

"Beg pardon, Master Putnam," the boy responded. He walked to her right side where he placed his right hand under her elbow and his left hand, gentle like before, around her arm.

Mister Putnam pulled sharply and walked at a pace that made her clench her teeth with every step. His body stench turned her stomach.

They arrived at her bathing room. The shackles were removed

by the young guard, which gave her a bit of comfort. He never made eye contact but was doing something he was made to do. It showed in the manner of his care for Julie.

The guards left and the same four women from before came in. She was stripped and a hot bucket of water was poured over her head. Unlike before, they didn't do much more. They just dried her off in a hurry and began dressing her in a fresh set of clothes. She was cleaner than before but by no means washed. Apparently, she wasn't required to be that clean this time. She guessed they wanted her to look dirty. Impure. Like a witch.

Julie had no more fight left in her. She set her mind to blank. She'd no longer participate in anything they did. She'd just sit there wherever she was going. Stoically.

After the women finished dressing her, they left. She was alone in the room for hours. At first, she just sat there, but after a while she wandered around the room trying to see if there was any chance to escape. Her arms and legs were light without the shackles.

Walking gave her some relief after all those days on end in the tiny dungeon. Even though her foot was festering, she had no way of keeping it clean, yet she suspected the infection was being slowed by the freezing temperatures of her dungeon.

There was only one door. It was guarded by one of the men, with only one window and it was barred. She eventually sat down again in exhaustion. A while later, she heard someone coming. The door opened, and it was the youngest of her usual escorts.

"Mistress, please follow me." He led her out the door.

Julie expected the other man to be waiting there, but it was just an empty hall.

"With haste, Mistress. We have not but a moment to spare." She almost paused, worried this was a trick, but she had to take the chance. Plus, what else was she going to do?

He led her down the hall and into another room. He guided her to the far corner and removed a board to reveal a small opening that led outside.

"Why are you helping me?"

"I do not believe you are a witch. Here. A blanket for your protection and some food for your journey. Now you must depart." He handed her the items. "Make your way north and you shalt come to a river. Follow the river northwest to the woods."

"Thank you." She crawled through the gap, then stopped. "Wait, what is your name?"

"Alan Reed, Mistress."

"Thank you, Alan." She slid out to tentative freedom.

Julie wasn't out of the woods yet. Or rather, she wouldn't be out of them until she was into them.

She soon found herself blinded by the day's light. She'd been kept in the dark for so long. Now there was too much light.

I have to keep moving. She extended her arms forward to feel her way around the back of the building where she'd been held. She moved slowly and painfully, her back glued to the north wall, her eyesight improving by the second. Her other senses were waking as well.

The buildings were made of crude wood. The roads were muddy and smelled like a farm. And sounds of horses amplified the effect.

The pain was dull now. She could manage at a faster pace. The snow on the ground and the cold chill in the air gave her new motivation to move out of sight, and fast.

She needed to move without anyone seeing her. She used the blanket Mister Reed had given her and shield herself from sight. Sure enough, as she reached the northwest corner of the jail, she heard voices in the distance.

She made out some conversation about today's events. They were talking about her. That brought an even colder feeling of dread. Everyone would be on the lookout once word got out that she'd escaped. Julie dragged one side of the blanket back to sneak a brief glance and survey her surroundings.

Two silhouettes stretch as their owners walked away. This was it. She had to move.

She reached for her bag of food but didn't account for her lost strength. The bag came up and back down, with some of its contents spilling onto the snow. Another chill washed over her. She stood frozen. She needed to escape, but she knew she needed food to survive. Another voice came. Julie moved into action with a two-step motion. She tossed the covering back over herself while grabbing the loose items and placing them in her burlap sack. She ducked down and hoped she wasn't seen.

Once again, the voice came and went. This time, as she moved the cover away to survey the situation, a wagon being loaded with boxes and sacks came into view. She made her way closer to see if she could use it as a means of escape.

There were two men, boys really, loading some final things before laying down a tarp over everything.

"Make haste! Not a moment to spare. If we're to make Fairmaid's Hill before midday, we must depart presently," said the younger of the two.

This was it. She spotted the river from the streets behind the jailhouse and made a play for it. She waited behind some barrels about fifteen feet from the wagon. The older of the two emerged from a barn-like structure and climbed in the front of the cart.

Bag of food held tight, blanket wrapped around her head and body, she crept up to the back and slowly placed her food in. As she started her effort to get herself on, the cart moved forward. Julie's heart dropped. She couldn't miss this chance.

She mustered enough strength to hop onto the moving transport and landed hard on her stomach. It brought about more aches and pains. As quickly and quietly as she could, she rolled to her left side. The uneven nature of the road bounced her up in the air. She came down on the arm that was wrenched by that horrible guard.

Julie placed her right hand over her mouth to muffle a cry. Her foot throbbed as she used it to steady herself as her right leg pushed her further under the cover of the tarp placed over the cart's items. Her eyes filled with tears of joy. She couldn't understand it. She wasn't out of danger yet. She could still be caught and end up right back where she started. Trapped.

But there was a certain happiness within this moment. Something positive had happened. At last, she had a chance to return to Aiden.

She carefully covered herself with her blanket to blend in with the items beside her. Her eyes focused on her bag. She pulled it closer and wept more intensely. This was it. This whole ordeal would be over soon.

The cart turned out of the alley behind the jailhouse and headed west. The cartwheels' steady noise was a pleasant hum. It shut out all the bad memories that inevitably popped into her head. The sound of the horses' steady beat upon the town's road took her away from the moment. She conjured up an image of Aiden beside her on horseback.

There were fields in the north. Endless fields. She could almost see herself riding when she noticed more and more people on the southern side of the road.

First, individuals walked hastily in the same direction she was going. Then, more people, in groups. Walking, and waiting, and gossiping. She couldn't make out any sounds or distinct conversations. Julie assumed everyone was talking about her, that everyone was talking about the witch's escape.

This brought a form of pride. Those fools would never again get the satisfaction of seeing her ridiculed over some piece of fiction. A witch? A witch?!

The cart slowed just outside of the town's courthouse. She was right. Everyone was there for her. Everyone was there to see the witch tried and burned.

Julie remained perfectly still as the cart came to a halt. The sinking sensation one feels after being caught out past curfew destroyed her hope. She was once again terrified. She still couldn't make out any details from the muttered sounds all around her. Just when she thought her nerves were going to cause her to explode in front of everyone, the wagon slowly rolled away from the crowds gathered outside the courthouse.

A wave of relief washed over her as the mob disappeared out of sight. She had a chance to catch her breath, but that only brought out her physical pain. This time, it wasn't as bad. The soreness and stinging and aching were just the same as before, but it all felt different. She could stand the pain. She could stand her foot's gangrenous condition. She could do it because she was going home.

The cart came to a sudden stop. Her breath quickened. Her heart raced. She was afraid they'd hear it pounding in her chest.

"I dare say, Master Edicott is coming up the road! Did you bring along such tools as we did borrow?" the younger of the two said.

"Indeed, for they be just there."

Julie's worst fears began to cloud her mind. She froze.

There were motions at the front of the wagon. One, if not both men, were coming down to check their stock.

Her courage was coming back. She wasn't going to be found. She wasn't going back to that hellhole. She was ready to run, regardless of how much it hurt. She was going to run back to Aiden.

To her surprise, a beam of light came through not six inches from her face. The men hadn't gotten out of the buggy. They were simply searching around behind them.

Still, she couldn't risk them getting a notion to look more thoroughly and find her. She was too weak to fight anyone off. She decided to exit as quietly and smoothly as she could. It meant walking and making things with her foot worse, but so be it.

"You are of a mind to return them upon this meeting of chance?"

"It will save us the road to the village. Restore the cover, and onward."

That was her cue. She rolled to the edge of the cart bed. She extended the arm holding her food out and lowered the bag as far as she could before dropping it. It made no noise. She was relieved.

Now, to wait until the cart began to move before she made one final roll to free herself from this possible capture.

As she expected, the wagon rolled forward slowly at first, but then the carthorse kicked into gear. With that, Julie rolled out and dropped to the ground. The pain was excruciating, but it didn't compare to the torture she'd face if she was thrown back into that cell.

She used all the strength she had to crawl out of the road and hide herself from sight.

Julie reached a point where the river branched south. She followed it to where the road bridged the river. As she was trying to cross, a horse-drawn cart came the other way. She ran as quickly as she could to the west end of the bridge and stumbled off into the woods to the south. She didn't know if they saw her or not.

She hid behind a tree and watched the travelers pass by. The cart stopped on the bridge. She crouched down, pulled the blanket over her head, and was paralyzed, not knowing if she should flee. The horses galloped to a halt.

"Ho there, have you seen a woman pass the road?" the man on the horse demanded.

"Not that we have. Beg pardon." It was a tense minute as the horseman scanned the woods in her direction. She was ready to spring into motion if he pursued her from the road, but he finally moved on.

Julie returned to her mission to put as much space between her and that cult village. She cut a path through the stark, cold trees. A sudden cracking sound, like a heavy foot coming down on a branch, made her run, fighting through the pain in her foot. She stumbled and tripped on a tree root, scrambled to her feet, and right into a tree.

She came to a road that opened to a large field and was fully exposed. They knew she'd escaped. This knowledge spurred her into action.

She dodged back and forth between the trees in the snowy woods. Julie almost lost her balance again, barely catching herself on a tree. She thought she heard footsteps behind her and spun around, ready to fight. As she slowly backed up, scanning for the threat, something touched her from behind. She turned to find a noose hanging from a tree branch. A sudden flood of terror made her lose her balance.

Julie was on her back, looking up at her implement of death, dangling like twisted dread. She rolled to her knees, collected the spilled contents of her carry sack, and plunged back into the paltry cover of the desolate forest.

She chased the sun to the west until its hopeful rays abandoned her to the night. She broke into a clearing and nearly ran straight into a river.

Julie didn't want to risk crossing in the haunting light of a quarter moon or in the middle of winter. Her westward progress halted until dawn. She was trapped by the walls of darkness surrounding her. She sank down next to a tree and pulled the blanket tight against the cold. Overwhelmed by the exhaustion of the day, she passed out.

She came to, once again lost in the woods, and remained alone with her thoughts. And the rumbling of her stomach.

Julie ate an apple, a roll of bread, and a wedge of cheese from the sack. It was the most substantial meal she'd eaten in weeks.

As she waited for the dawn to bring light to her dark world, she closed her eyes and thought of Aiden. Just one more day, she hoped, would bring her back to civilization and back to him. All she wanted was to hear his voice again.

Come dawn and the day was filled with dim sunlight. It was a murky gray day. The woods were misty and haunting. It would be impossible to navigate in these conditions, so she decided to follow the river.

The fog didn't let up all day. While she thought it'd hinder the hunt for her, it also slowed her down.

When darkness returned, all she could do was try to sleep and hope for better luck tomorrow.

Growling and barking dogs startled Julie awake. She sprung to her feet. It was still dark, and multiple torches approached from the east. She ran in a desperate attempt to elude the evil that pursued her.

She ran for what had to be at least an hour as the dreadful sound of hunters got closer and closer. And then—

"The witch! Right ahead!" Julie turned back. A man ran forward after her, a silhouette against the first rays of dawn.

The growling of the dogs nipping at her heels. She was surrounded, trapped against the river. She made one last desperate attempt to escape along the river's edge.

One of the dogs charged. She dodged it to the right and her foot slipped on the riverbank. She tumbled into the freezing water and flailed about before being grabbed by two men and dragged back onto the riverbank.

Julie had a horrible daylong ride back to the cult village tied to the back of a horse. By the time the sun was setting, she was dragged back to her dungeon cell.

As the door slammed shut, she curled into a ball and wept. Her short-lived freedom only amplified the hopelessness of her situation. How could she run for over two days and not find help? How much land did this cult own? There was no escape. And the likelihood of anyone finding her was probably zero.

Some time passed. Julie was relieved about one thing. It was certainly warmer in this prison than it had been outdoors.

Her eyes got heavy as her body settled in, warmth gathering under her covers. Her mind drifted as her breathing slowed. At least she could wait until morning to deal with the repercussions of her escape.

"Stand aside!"

Julie awoke to a voice she didn't want to hear. She closed her eyes, hoping it was just another nightmare.

"Beg pardon, Sheriff Corwin did decree no visitors," the guard replied.

"As God is my witness, I shall observe her myself. I shall not bide the will of weak men. Will you follow such a dark path, as did Master Reed?" Parris pressed his will.

There was a brief stint of silence. Keys rattled nervously in the lock.

"N...no, sir. I shall not fall prey, Reverend Parris" The lock turned. The door creaked open. Footsteps. Slow and calculated footsteps. They came closer.

"Rise..." Parris breathed. His voice was colder when he whispered. It frightened her even more.

"Witch, you shall rise. On my word, you shall receive the Lord's wrath."

Julie couldn't move. Her eyes were clenched shut. She heard one footstep come down hard and suddenly her covers were ripped off.

"Did you not hear me? Did you believe you could escape God's wrath? You shan't beguile more men toward your evil intention. True justice shall be served upon my word." His breath stank of rot. With that last statement, he turned and walked out. The door was shut and locked behind him.

This time, Julie knew no more help would be coming.

Julie didn't sleep that night. She didn't trust what would happen if her eyes closed. Her time was spent pushing aside thoughts of being burned alive. She found new tears to shed when she thought about Aiden and never seeing him again. If these people went through with killing her as a witch, Aiden would never know what happened to her.

She was holed up with her thoughts for what felt like three days. The door opened. She was dragged to the interrogation room where Parris stood menacingly over her.

"Pain, does it bring that the Lord's justice be delayed. Thy escape forestalled trial. Magister Hathorne, be absent on business. The Lord's punishment shall be greater for thy additional sin."

Julie cowered away from the repulsive monster and said nothing.

Sheriff Corwin stepped forward. "Mistress Buckingham, your

trial shall be Wednesday, 27 February."

"Lead not innocence into perdition! Confess your sins and your soul may be saved!" Parris slammed a bible down on the table, causing her to flinch. "Perhaps another week's confinement shall bring you to contrition." He stepped back and began to walk away.

"More like torture."

Parris turned his head slowly. "What did you say?"

Julie stood quietly.

Parris turned around and approached her, coming so close that a bystander would have thought they were slow dancing.

"You shall see justice and you shall feel God's wrath," he whispered and turned again to walk away.

"You mean your own desire to torture an innocent—" Julie shot an icy glare at her accuser.

"How dare you..." he turned once more to face her.

"God is not in this village. You are not serving him or justice. You're just as evil as the monster you claim me to be!" Julie replied through clenched teeth, fists tightly held beside her shaking body.

Parris lunged at her, both hands stretched out. She fell back with the weight of Parris as he knelt over her, hands around her throat.

She didn't know what to do. She was filled with both anger and fear. She grabbed his hands to try to pry them off, but she was too weak to give any opposition.

Suddenly, Parris was pulled from her. The voice of Sheriff Corwin yelled his commands of restraint. The guards burst into the room and helped the sheriff hold Parris back.

"I shall not bide your insinuation! Be assured, witch! You shall feel the hand of God!"

Sheriff Corwin ordered one of the guards to take Julie away. She was still shaking with terror.

All hope lost, Julie tried to sleep through the pain and emotional anguish until the day they would finally put her out of her misery.

II: Witch Trial

The morning of the trial came. JULIE was in disbelief. She was up before the sun, waiting to be retrieved, legs crossed, still favoring her left foot. It had grown considerably, and the pain became white noise. She was broken.

Two new men came in. The guards stood beside her. She half expected them to grip her tightly and force her to walk through the pain. Once her left foot had settled from pulsing with pain, her breathing followed suit.

"Mistress?" the man on her left said as he offered his hand behind her arm to show he was ready when she was.

Julie pushed off the platform she called a bed. The men took her by each arm and helped her to her feet. The man on the left led the way and Julie's body cringed as her injury sent a sharp stabbing pain up her entire body with each step she took with her left side.

They led her down the corridor and into the bathing room. The women followed. As the two men left, the last of the maidens entered, carrying the jug of water and towels for cleansing.

Julie stepped into the water basin. She stood in the middle, eagerly awaiting the warmth this bath would bring.

All at once, the pressure of the water hitting her head and cascading down hit her. Only this time, her muscles tightened, her eyes widened, and she drew in a breath that reminded her she was still alive.

The water was freezing. Even in her weak state, she flailed her hands and attempted to jump out. The women held her in place as they scrubbed away without concern. She suspected Parris was behind her cold bath.

The weight atop her head hit her again, and one more giant breath was drawn. She was made to keep her arms out for thorough cleaning or else Julie would have wrapped her arms around herself to find heat in this frozen room.

She shook uncontrollably. Julie had been breathing in so fast her hands began to go numb and her toes lost sensation, no matter how hard she tried to wiggle them. The women released her and, although she wanted to draw them close to her for comfort, her arms moved slowly as if her muscles were freezing from the inside out.

Julie was dried and dressed. The women left the room as soon as they were through with their duty.

She was led outside, where the roars of the crowds greeted her with anger and fear. A cage stood over the crowd. They walked her towards it and the crowd parted. She saw that it wasn't just a cage. They intended to ride her through the middle of town in this prison on wheels. She stepped into it and the opening was slammed shut and locked.

The people began to throw stones, mud, and even spoiled food, as the barred wagon moved forward. This was it. There was no turning back. This was really happening.

The ride proved short but dreadful. People didn't stop their name-calling and throwing. The carriage stopped in front of the courthouse, and the crowd grew in size and sound. They wanted her dead.

She was taken into the packed courtroom and led to the pedestal. The room was warm, with the musky smell of unwashed humanity. The jury was already empaneled. Master Parris sat at the table. After a few minutes, Judge Hathorne came and took his seat. The room was brought to order.

The judge was handed a paper and began, "This court is in session on this day, 27 February, the year of our Lord, 1692, to hear the charges of witchcraft against Mistress Julie Buckingham. Mistress Buckingham, to this, what say you?"

While she didn't want to participate in this sham, she knew if she refused to answer, the whole thing would drag on even longer. So she'd say the bare minimum.

"Not guilty."

"Master Parris, you may begin."

"Good people of Salem, I will expose the horrors that have been visited upon our fair town by the witchery of Mistress Buckingham," Parris said, walking up to her.

"Mistress Buckingham, will thou not spare thy victims the horrors of this trial? Will thou not confess thy sins?" He leaned forward to intimidate Julie.

"No."

"I appeal to thy decency. If thou have any left, confess!" He spat the words contemptuously.

"I have nothing to confess."

Parris turned back to the jury. "Mistress Buckingham be a stranger to our town. None saw her before, but spectrally. She come to my own home, my own daughter, my innocent niece, in her demon spirit, bringing about fits of hysteria." Parris motioned to the back of the room. "Bring them forward."

Two girls were brought to the front. Upon seeing her, they

began to cry, fell to the floor, and flailed around. Parris turned to her with fire in his eyes. "Why do you torment my innocent little girls so?"

"It's the witch of the woods!" one of the girls yelled.

"Make her stop!" the other screamed.

Julie didn't reply.

Parris stepped right up to her and said, "Have you no decency? Release my girls from your devil's spell!"

"They're faking it!"

Parris took a step back, surprised at her answer.

"You dare attempt to besmirch my righteous girls?"

Julie glared at Parris. "Oh right, because no child has ever lied before."

Parris took a step forward, cocked his hand, and swung. Julie clenched her eyes shut and waited for the impact. Nothing came.

He'd stopped inches from her face.

"Think not to provoke such a reaction with your evil tongue."

"They're clearly faking it! They are liars—just like their father and uncle!"

He didn't take the bait. He turned back towards the girls. "Remove them from the presence of this witch."

Parris turned to the jury and went on. "You have seen the effect this devil woman has had on our children. None saw her until she came out of the woods to the north, the same woods my daughter did swear their tormentor did reside. I tell you; she comes straight from hell! She come out of the woods wearing nothing but her shift, protected from the bitter cold by the flames of hell. She come in her nakedness to bedevil the gentleman of our good Christian town. A vile temptress, she did enrapture young Master Reed, whom we shall now hear testify."

Julie's would-be rescuer came to the front of the room. His ear was bloody. He'd clearly been punished for helping her. She couldn't help but feel some guilt.

"Master Reed, has it not been your assignment to escort Mistress Buckingham?"

"It has," Alan refused to look in Julie's direction.

"If it pleases the court," Parris presented the room to Alan, "would you testify of Mistress Buckingham's beguile?" Alan bowed his head and began to speak, all the while staring at the floor.

"To my shame, I did feel pity for Mistress Buckingham. She did exploit my good heart—" Alan was following the script Parris must have given him.

Parris cut in. "'Tis a weakness of men. Upon your vulnerability, did she pray."

"I was helpless, compelled to affect her release." Alan glanced in her direction, then quickly found his favorite spot on the floor.

"We understand your shame. You are excused, Master Reed." Parris moved toward the jury box. "Unfortunate as Master Reed's weakness may be, light does it bring to the next witness' testimony."

Parris walked over to his desk, looked at a letter, and said, "I call Mistress Martha Allerton."

A young woman about twenty-five came to the stand. Parris began. "Mistress Allerton, please tell us of the harm done unto you by the witch Mistress Buckingham."

"I did discover my husband in an adulterous act with Mistress Lynde. John has always been a good, God-fearing Christian. It was obvious he had been bedeviled by a witch's spell. That night I did see the witch in spectral form above my bed."

"Do you see said witch in this room?"

"It was her, Mistress Buckingham."

Julie clenched her fists to contain her urge to react.

Following the rest of Mistress Allerton's testimony, Parris called Mister Allerton.

"Master Allerton, do tell of the devilry brought about by Mistress Buckingham."

"I did lay in bed beside my loving wife, Martha, when a spectral form of a woman did come and despoil my mind with corrupt temptations of the flesh. My body was not my own. In my shame, I did betray my sacred vows with Mistress Lynde, whom was also under a witch's spell." Mister Allerton hung his head in shame.

"Master Allerton, do you see the spectral woman in this room?"

"It was that witch, Mistress Buckingham."

Julie closed her eyes and tried to tune out all the bullshit.

After Mister Allerton left the pulpit, Parris continued.

"During examination, we did ask Mistress Buckingham to recite our Lord and Savior's holy prayer. She could not proceed beyond the first line."

"I said it exactly!" Julie was still angry. They said she got the prayer wrong.

"You said, *who art in heaven*. All those faithful know our savior said, *which art in heaven.*" Parris turned back to the jury. "She completely omitted the final line as well."

The room was filled with murmuring. When it quieted down, Parris continued, "She does blaspheme with strange speech and unholy language. Upon our physical examination did we note the beastly size of Mistress Buckingham. The devil inside her did cause monstrous growth. She is taller than most men. Furthermore, we did find the kiss of the devil on her left thigh, as well as several other marks of the devil." Parris walked over to the table and picked up a stack of papers.

"These are sworn witness statements attesting to the same," he said, handing them to the judge. Parris went back to the table, turned, and said, "If it pleases the court, I have one more witness."

"If you please," Hathorne replied.

"I call Master Jonathan Corwin." The other man who had attended her examination came forward.

"Master Corwin, please explain to the court the threats given by Mistress Buckingham, not only against us, but our entire God-fearing community?"

"Mistress Buckingham, on numerous occasions, attempted to summon her master demon, the demon she calls 'Effbeeye'. She did threaten the wrath of this 'Effbeeye' would come and punish us for our attempt to protect this town from the witch."

Julie couldn't help herself. "It's the F.B.I. The Federal Bureau of Investigation, not some demon!" The room went silent at her outburst.

After a moment, Parris responded. "This devil woman curses in one instance and lies in the next. She attempts to confuse you good people with a false denial of her attempts to summon this demon, saying it is the what? The federal bureau of investigation?"

Parris looked legitimately confused, as if he had absolutely never heard of the FBI. Was it possible that the leader of the cult, who orchestrated the sacrificial abductions, had never heard of the FBI? She didn't think so.

The only possibilities that came to mind were: One, Parris wasn't the leader. She was sure he wasn't pretending not to know. Two, none of them actually knew about the FBI, which could mean one of two things—this was some kind of experiment to see how people who believed it was the seventeenth century would react to having someone like her dropped into their midst, or she had too quickly dismissed the possibility that she had actually fallen through time, that it truly was the seventeenth century, and she'd gotten mixed up in the Salem Witch Trials.

She looked over the courtroom. It certainly looked authentic. But it could still be the cult. Either way, she was likely headed for the stake.

Parris continued, "There is no such thing. Good people of Salem, in these troubled times, we cannot survive as a community if we do not purge this wretch of evil from our midst."

Judge Hathorne then instructed, "Master Parris, you may give your close."

Julie turned her head slightly to see Parris reach for his bible, stand up slowly, and push his chair with the back of his knees, like the time her accuser railed against her before.

"Gentlemen, the evidence has told the tale of the vile witchery rained down on our God-fearing town by this witch, Mistress Buckingham..."

Julie closed her eyes and tuned out the droning lies.

"...I, as well as Master Corwin, were witness to her numerous attempts to summon the demon, Efbeeye, to punish our holy attempt to protect our God-fearing community from her sorcery—"

At this point, there was a great commotion in the back of the courtroom.

She turned and saw a woman holding a baby with tears in her eyes. The woman pointed at Julie.

"She took my baby. She brought the plague of the devil to my baby boy. She come an suck the life from him in the night. He was perfectly healthy just the other day."

There was an uproar in the gallery.

Hathorne brought the room to order. "Master Parris, you may proceed."

Parris turned to the jury.

"As if all the horrible acts committed by Mistress Buckingham were not bad enough, she has now taken the life of a precious child. Worse still, she has apparently corrupted some amongst us. I beseech you, remove this scourge once and for all."

Judge Hathorne then said, "Gentlemen of the jury, I remand this case to thy judgment for holy justice." The jury filed out. Then she was taken to another room and locked inside.

As she lay there, her mind filled with confusion. She had been so certain of the cult theory, but doubt was beginning to creep in. She racked her brain for any tangible detail she could remember about the Salem Witch Trials.

She had never been interested in history; of all the subjects you have to learn, she had always found it the most boring.

She had been in the room for only a few minutes before the door opened. They brought her back to the courtroom. Apparently, the jury had finished "deliberating".

Judge Hathorne came in last, sat down, and began his address. "Gentlemen of the jury, in the matter of Mistress Buckingham being guilty of witchcraft, what say you?"

One by one, the members of the jury stood and said, aye.

"Gentlemen, our God and Their Majesties thank you for your service."

Hathorne then turned to her and said, "Mistress Julie Buckingham, having been found guilty of the horrific crime of witchcraft, I do on my authority as magistrate of the County of Essex of the Royal colony of Massachusetts Bay, condemn you to die. You will be hanged from the neck until dead. Sentence shall be carried out morning after next, 29 February, the year of our Lord, 1692 at nine o'clock in the morning. This court is adjourned."

III: Condemned

JULIE was taken back to the dungeon to await her execution. At least they hadn't put the shackles back on. Never in her life could she have imagined this is how she would die. At least she wouldn't be burned at the stake, although the thought of being hanged wasn't much better.

For a moment, she tried to figure out how she ended up here. She thought through the evidence and tried to decide which theory was more likely. She still thought the cult made the most logical sense. She thought nearly everything she had seen could be explained by that.

Time travel would also fit the evidence. Their manner of dress did certainly fit their stated time period. She thought their odd manner of speech was pretty convincing and had yet to see anything like electricity or any other modern items. Even how she'd die seemed to better fit the time travel theory. She'd been surprised to hear she'd be hanged. Everyone knows you burn witches. But could this time travel idea be correct?

She thought not. What difference did it make at this point? She'd still die in little more than a day. She couldn't stop the tears from coming and cried herself to sleep.

She woke up to the sound of the door opening.

An old woman entered with a small table and placed it at the side of the room with a stool. She placed an inkwell and feather with a stack of parchment paper, then placed Julie's standard breakfast of bread and water on the table.

The woman said, "If ya wanna write letters ta loved ones or a last testament."

The idea of letters to loved ones caused her to break down all over again. All night she had dreams and waking moments where she thought of friends and family. She knew how hard her parents, particularly her father, had taken Jessica's death. She wasn't sure he'd recover losing a second. They'd be devastated.

Then there was Aiden.

She didn't think they'd ever read these letters. She was glad she'd be able to write down some of the things that had been running around in her head. She spent the next few hours writing letters to everyone who truly mattered in her life. She was nearly finished with the next-to-last one, the one to her father.

I will always be with you. I know how hard it was for you after Jessica died. I don't want that for you again on my account. You have so many people who love you. They need you to be the best father, husband, and grandpa for them. I need you to be strong for me. You are the best dad a girl could ever have. I miss you and I love you, Daddy.

She broke down again. When she was able to gather herself. Her thoughts turned to her husband.

My beloved Aiden,

There are so many things I could say to you; if I wrote them all they would fill a library. So I will say what I think is most important: How generous you are, you give so much of yourself to everyone around you. The world is a better place because you are in it. You are the best husband—the way you swept me off my feet with your incredible charm, how you always know what to say to lift me up when I am down, how understanding you are when you listen to my problems. Your dynamic mind is always a pleasant challenge when we engage in intelligent discussions.

And how you love me so unconditionally. You accept all my many flaws. You make me feel like I'm the only woman in the world. You are my love; you are my life; you make me feel complete.

Now I need you to live a complete and fulfilling life. I know how driven and determined you are. I don't want you to spend the rest of your life looking for me and I don't want you spending the rest of your life mourning me. You deserve happiness. You can't sacrifice your chance to be a father or give up the business you love so much to put your life on pause on my account. So I need you to live life completely and you can't do that being haunted by the ghost of me. I need you to let me go.

I am so thankful to have had you in my life. There had always been a piece of me that was missing, then you came and filled that hole in the heart of me. You allowed me to live life completely. You are my love; you are my life; you are my whole world. You are my everything.

I love you. I'll miss you. I will be with you always.
Your loving jewel, Julie.

———※———

She'd been crying through most of the process, but the finality of completing her letter to Aiden felt like the end of her life, and she broke down completely.

In the midst of her total despair, her sister came to her mind. The closer the shadow of death had come, the more she felt Jessica was with her. And she suddenly felt a feeling of calm washed over her. She could hear Jessica say, "It's going to be all right, little sis. I can't wait to see you. I love you."

IV: Execution

JULIE lay awake; the candle had finally burned itself out, and she was surrounded by darkness. She could smell her uneaten last meal. While she felt terribly hungry, she had no appetite. Completely exhausted, both physically and emotionally, she still couldn't sleep.

There was a knot in her stomach that wouldn't go away. It was the dread of anticipation. She had no recognition of the passing of time and hoped it would be sooner rather than later. Just get it over with.

There were footsteps on the stairs. A moment later, the door opened and there were three men. The same two guards who always dealt with her, and a priest. Obviously here for last rites.

The priest stepped through the door. "Mistress Buckingham, I have come to save your soul."

Julie laid on her back, covers drawn. She laughed for a second. "Save my soul?"

"Aye, Mistress. Confess your sins to God, repent of your wickedness, and your soul may be redeemed. You can be buried in hallowed ground."

She laughed again. "You can't save my soul. You're evil." She sat up and turned to face the priest. "This whole damned place is evil. I've done nothing before God that a soulless bastard like you could save me from." She turned away, pulled her covers back over her shoulders, and laid back down.

"You truly have the devil inside you. Burn in hell, witch." He walked out in a huff.

The two guards returned and bound her hands behind her back, then lead her out of the dungeon. They escorted her to the other room, where she was washed and clothed. The women dressed her in one of those off-white dresses. They added a crushing gray corset and wrapped a gray skirt around her waist, followed by matching sleeves. They finished her pilgrim look by pulling her hair up and covering it with a bonnet. She was ready for her death walk.

Her escorts walked her through the main doors. As she stepped out, her eyes were blinded by the morning light. Aside from the two court visits and the candle she'd been lent for her letters, she'd been in near-total darkness for the last week or so.

She lost her footing on the stairs and fell to her knees. The men dragged her up and put her in the cage on wheels. By this time, her eyes had adjusted. For the first time in days, she saw a clear blue sky. The air was crisp and fresh, and a few late winter birds sung their morning songs. If she weren't about to die, she'd have said it was the most beautiful day she'd ever seen.

As the cart moved, the knot in her stomach came back. A few minutes later, they passed over the bridge from her escape. The cart took a left at the junction on the other side. People lined the road the whole way, but the crowd was growing exponentially. It was hard to see how a cult could grow so large.

As the road straightened out, she spotted a noose hanging from a tree. It was the one she ran into the day of her escape.

The crowd parted. They waded through and the people began shouting the most horrible, nasty things. Some threw things while others spit on her.

The cart stopped on the hilltop beneath the tree. They dragged her out and forced her to step onto a log. They slid the noose over her head and pulled it snug around her neck. The two men stepped away. She stood quivering, trying to keep her balance.

Sheriff Corwin stepped forward, pulled out a paper, and read, "On this day, 29 February, the year of our Lord, 1692, under my authority as Sheriff of Essex County, and authority vested in me by Their Majesties, I do condemn Mistress Julie Buckingham to die for crimes against the people of Salem and the County of Essex. Does the condemned have anything to say before thy sentence is carried out?"

She thought for a second, scanning the crowd of thousands. So many people. Originally, she was going to stay defiantly silent, but she didn't want to go out on that note. "I'd like to say how sorry I am that you abducted me. I'm sorry you tortured me. I'm sorry you falsely accused me and are going to murder me. And I'm especially sorry that I can't save any of your souls, for you are all pure evil. And finally, I'm happy that I will never have to see any of you evil bastards again because, while I will dwell in heaven with God and the people I love, you will all be burning in hell with Satan."

The crowd was silent for a moment. Then were outraged over her condemnation. Sheriff Corwin gave the signal. The log was kicked out from under her.

The pain in her neck was blinding. After a second, her toes

brushed the ground. The rope was too long. She'd thought it'd be over quickly. Now it seemed she might be conscious for the whole thing.

This can't be happening!

The rope was crushing, like her head might come off. Her face was tight and unbearably hot. The crowd was cheering while a look of evil satisfaction crossed Parris's face. The pressure built in her chest. She struggled to breathe. The rope started to feel like it was searing into her neck.

No! No! No! I don't want to die!

Her heart felt like it might explode. Out of all the horrible things she'd ever experienced, this was a thousand times worse.

Oh my God! The pain! Make it stop!

Her body screamed for air, but there was no relief. She went into a state of sheer panic and absolute terror. Every cell in her body was on fire. She was in unbelievably excruciating agony from which there was no escape.

I can't move! I can't stop this! I can't say goodbye.

It seemed to last an eternity. The constant ringing in her ears kept getting louder until all she could hear was white noise. Her body began to go numb. Her head felt like it was an over-inflated balloon that might pop at any moment.

I have nothing left. This is the end.

Her vision shrank to a pinpoint. In a flash, everything she'd ever done played before her like a movie. It went at the speed of light, but each individual detail came in slow motion. Then it was over. The last thing Julie saw was Aiden smiling at her.

A calm filled her. She felt completely at peace, like she was one with the universe. The last vestige of light disappeared, and everything faded to black.

CHAPTER 8: ENGINEERING RESOURCES

I: The Massachusett

MICHEAL HAD TWO CONCERNS now. And they kind of went hand-in-hand. Obviously, he wanted to get back to the future. But what was he going to do? Sit down, focus really hard, and boom, the schematics of a time machine were just going to come to him. He felt urgency to solve the problem but cracking the time code was going to take some time. He would need to engineer multiple tools to assist his investigation. This was an impossible task that he may never master. Before he could truly begin the monumental fight against the fourth dimension, he needed to ensure he would survive history.

Time was also an enemy. His prospects of a victory in this fight were so small he knew he needed to be realistic; he would likely spend the rest of his life in the past. That reality meant he needed to consider his life here in the seventeenth century. Eventually, he wanted to move to Boston or maybe London. There would be a much richer life in the city, but only if he was moving in the aristocracy. His discovery in New Hampshire was a start, but he had much more to do before he could move anywhere. In the meantime, Micheal would improve his comfort and safety at Homestead. Cause this might be his home for some time to come.

He spent several days gathering supplies from the surrounding towns. There was the acquisition of some weapons, namely a German musket rifle and a saber sword with a three-foot blade. He also built up a healthy surplus of metals, particularly copper, that he intended to use for plumbing. But the steel he acquired was used first. He crafted a condenser for making plastic.

And he took his other important project to the next stage. He had transferred the base penicillin into their second-stage cultures for fermentation. They might mature while he was gone. And he'd made some other ingredients in his homemade lab, including sulfuric acid that he could use to make hydrochloric acid, the final ingredient. Antibiotics would be at hand. Now he was making his most ambitious trek yet: traveling one hundred and fifty miles west to Albany to find a valuable resource. Shale rock.

Albany was the closest place where he could find it. While liquid crude would be easier to process, the nearest location he knew of was in Western Pennsylvania. Four hundred miles away. He could use oil to make plastics, which would be especially useful in medical implements. He knew how dangerous this time and place was, so preparing for potential medical situations was near the top of the list.

He'd traveled for nearly two days and had set up camp next to a river in the Berkshires, near where modern-day Pittsfield would be. He'd brought with him his new horse, Angel, a massive white mare he'd acquired during his trading runs. He left her and Darkness tied at camp.

Micheal went by foot to hunt for food. Horses were too loud. The wind direction was coming from the south. He worked his way around, a couple miles to the north.

Now that he was downwind from any potential game, he began moving south along the river. The flow of the water also hid the sound of his movement. He stopped as the river opened to a small meadow.

Micheal was pleased by the rifled musket he was able to pur-chase in Concord. It had been custom-made in Germany, specif-ically for hunting. It had a 40-inch barrel and used a relatively small 40-caliber ball. It was the closest thing to a modern weapon he would likely ever find in 1692 Massachusetts. The man who owned it had recently died and his widow sold it to him.

The accuracy was impressive for the seventeenth century. He'd tested it to a range of 100 yards. It had been a couple of years since he had gone to the gun range, but he quickly rediscovered his marksmanship form. It was more difficult with a musket, but he had used one. And aside from the loading process, it was just shooting a gun.

Micheal prepped his rifle. He measured and poured powder from a horn. He placed wadding on the end of the barrel and seated the ball with the ramrod. Opening the frizzen, he primed the pan with powder from a different horn. He cocked the flint hammer and closed the frizzed. Now he would wait.

Micheal had spotted a few deer and elk on his way into the river valley, so he knew they were in the area, and this would be a prime watering spot. After about an hour, a massive bull elk edged out of the woods to the riverbank. He took aim and waited until the elk finished his sip. The head came up, and he pulled the trigger. The bull jumped back and flailed its antlers, then stumbled into the woods.

Micheal climbed to his feet and ran in pursuit. He found it a hundred feet into the evergreens. The bull was on his knees laboring. He reloaded the rifle and aimed for the heart. While wounded, he didn't want to get on the business end of those antlers. His aim was true, and he put the animal out of its misery.

Micheal retrieved Darkness, then they slowly dragged the elk back to his camp. Shortly into the walk, he saw something glittering in a rockface. He left the elk with Angel. The light was fading, so he had little time. He rode Darkness back to investigate the potential thread of silver.

He and Darkness arrived at the location in good time. After a thorough inspection, he was disappointed to see it was another false positive. He was about to leave when he felt a hard whack to his head. Then it all went dark.

He regained consciousness and heard voices murmuring around him. His head was throbbing. He was having trouble focusing on what they were saying. He tried to open his eyes, but the flickering of the firelight hurt them and gave him a headache. His hands were tied behind him to some kind of post. He kept his eyes closed and tried to calm the storm in his head. After a few minutes, he was able to focus on what the people were saying.

Micheal went into his memory from a couple of weeks earlier.

He'd made a trading visit to Stow and decided to use the opportunity to hunt in a new area. He had no luck, but then ran across a small group of Native Americans.

Micheal had left Darkness at the bottom of the hills. As he blazed a trail near the stream, he was laser focused. He couldn't afford a careless injury. He heard a sound coming from the west and froze in his tracks.

He ducked down and assessed his surroundings. Peering through the forest in the direction of the noise, he saw them.

A small hunting party of about five.

Micheal knew he was taking a risk when he trekked alone, he was always hyper-vigilant and ready to flee if necessary.

Keeping a keen eye on the camp, he crept to a more secluded location from which to observe them. Before he began his study, he made a note of the time using the sun.

Micheal glanced to his left where an overgrown bush would offer him good cover. He'd see things coming downstream easily. On his right. A thorn-cluttered mess with a bend just beyond. Their horses would be watering down river.

He inhaled rather quickly but took his time. The hunting party he'd stumbled across was just over the ridge behind him. Both he and they were settling in after their day and he was lucky he was downwind, otherwise they would have detected him. But today Micheal found a rare opportunity. To learn a living Native American language.

But it was more than that. Since his arrival in colonial Massachusetts, he knew there was a good chance he would interact with the native people. And it would be quite beneficial to be able to communicate.

Micheal had always picked up languages easily. His perfect memory made it so that once he had heard the translation of a word, he could never forget it. But it was more than that. There were almost always patterns in the way people communicated and he'd been able to recognize the variables within context.

The first time he discovered his linguistic skill, he was two. The family had gone to the park for a picnic. He heard another family speaking in a way he had never heard before. When he asked his *mom why, she said they were speaking Spanish. The next time they went to the library, he studied an English- Spanish dictionary, and in just a few days, he could understand and speak Spanish.*

Over the years, he'd done similar exercises with other languages. It'd taken longer for him to attempt any Native American languages due to the general lack of the written word.

After seeing a documentary on the Navajo Code Talkers of WWII, he decided to take a road trip to the Navajo Nation in Southern Utah to learn from them directly. They had been generously welcoming, and he'd spent two weeks studying the amazing culture and becoming fluent in the language.

Following this experience, he'd sought out information on some of the other most prominent Native American tribes. Through this process, he became exposed to several other Native American language groups. The list included Sioux, Iroquoian, Algonquin, Athabaskan, and Uto-Aztecan, for which his home state was named.

"Knowledge. Knowledge is the key, Micheal. The more you learn, the more you can do. It's like knowing two languages rather than one..."

The voice of his mother echoed in his ear and pulled him into a memory within a memory. He smiled. He'd just turned three and his mom and dad took him into their study for the first time. The smell of maple was the same as the fragrance his senses picked up now. He was mesmerized by the wall of books as his mom carried him inside. The lights turned on and his mind filled with wonder.

The sound of the river at his feet was calming, and he let his memory take him in.

"Would you like to see one, Micheal?"

Micheal stretched his hand out and gripped the top of a spine. It wouldn't budge. He leaned forward with both arms stretched and slid out a massive book.

"Geh...neh...rah...tive. Mmmor...pah..."

"Fa. Morfa."

"Morfa... logy. Mor. Fa. logy. Morphology.

"Wow," his dad said as he entered the room. "Impressive, Micheal."

Micheal smiled but never broke eye contact with the pages of the book.

———⋈———

Finding the sounds from the stream before him relaxing, he secured his seat, placed his hands behind his head, and laid back and listened to the hunters' conversations, hoping to understand it.

He heard them say, "Winkan nupes waapiti," many times.

That word. "Waapiti." Where had he heard that before? In his current location, they could be speaking in a language from either the Algonquian language family or the Iroquoian language family.

Micheal visualized the letters he thought were in the spelling. He then bounced from left, to right, to middle, to left again, like a piece of a jigsaw puzzle his mind was trying to place. Only the puzzle was comprised of millions of images of memories. He recalled his study of these languages, magazine articles, and television documentaries. Then it hit him.

Moose! The memory was located. It unfolded like an old map that had been doubled over and pressed many times. Kindergarten. Miss Martin's class. That day, she taught them about the first Thanksgiving. He recalled his hunger for more information and his sneaking into his parents' study to use their reference books, which he adored.

Waapiti meant white tail in Algonquin. He learned that this Anglophonic term for elk was originally confused by the British settlers. In England, they said what we call a moose is an elk. When they saw the giant size of what in modern times we label an elk, they believed the animals must be related, and so called them by the same name.

This meant that the hunting party must be speaking one of the languages in the Algonquin language family. If they were from either the Massachusetts Tribe or the Wampanoag Tribe, they would be speaking Wopanaak, which was a member of the Algonquin language family. His listening session had greatly improved his understanding of the Wompanaak language, but he knew he would need more to approach fluency.

Micheal came back to the present and began to formulate a construct of the Algonquian vocabulary in his mind. He first laid a template of a polysynthetic morphology system, one which is also primarily verb-based, and incorporated base-line prefixes to develop a growing library of what he understood. In his mind, it looked like metal. Liquid metal. Weightless, waiting to take form.

Images of planes, examples of Native American tools and daily activities, the flora and fauna of the region. Words appeared on top.

Next, he analyzed the Algonquian vocabulary he had, took the new elements he derived from his earlier observation, and filed them into their proper locations in the template.

While he thought running an algorithmic analysis might account for much of the missing data, he wanted to gather more information. He kept his eyes closed and listened.

He focused through the pain and began to understand what they were discussing. They were trying to decide whether to kill him or not.

When he felt confident, he could maintain his focus enough to have a conversation, and was mostly sure he could communicate with them, he'd try to reason with them.

He had spent the last week or so organizing Algonquian linguistics in his head and trying to expand his potential vocabulary. The chances of an encounter had already been high, but when he decided to go to Albany, they went up dramatically because the colonial settlers had forced the native people west into the Appalachians.

He'd wanted to be prepared for just this type of situation. This would test his preparation in a trial by fire, perhaps literally. He opened his eyes and alerted his captors that he was awake.

Everyone went silent. It appeared to be a small village. There were perhaps one hundred or one hundred and fifty people. They were all staring at him.

One of the elders, perhaps the chief, spoke. "Ki-wencitaw-we-kw?" What is your purpose? The elder looked toward another man to his left. The man was about to speak, to translate, Micheal thought.

Micheal replied first in Algonquian.

"Ni-lawa-kepehkawe-wa-ki-skakana-me-wa." I pass through.

"Ne-lawa-anwe-nemahwe." I am not a threat.

There was a small gasp and murmuring spread through the crowd.

The chief said, "Ki-kexke-lentamwa-o-atot?" You know our words?

Micheal responded, once more in Algonquian. "I know some."

Another man stood and said, "We should kill him. He knows our location. He will bring warriors of the English to enslave or massacre us." His tone was filled with hatred. He stood as the tallest of the men with blue feathers in his hair and war paint on the right side of his face. The left was plain, exposing the scar that ran down the middle of his left eyebrow and down the left cheek.

This sparked a wave of popular support for his death. The chief sat silent for a few minutes, listening to multiple arguments for or against his death, then he raised his hand and the whole crowd went silent. The chief rose and walked closer to Micheal and looked at him, searching his face. After a moment he stepped back from Micheal and asked, "What is your name?"

Micheal thought for a second then said the name he had been using, his mother's maiden name. He had chosen it because it was one of the oldest English names.

"Micheal Whitaker."

A smile came to the chief's face, and he gave the order to cut him loose. "My greatest apologies, brother Whitaker."

At that moment, the man who stood to call for his death, the man who appeared to be one of the great warriors of the tribe, perhaps the war chief, stood again and protested outrage at Micheal's release.

"Pisintam!" They called for silence.

"Many of you are too young or were still with your mother Earth to recognize a true friend to the people. But in my youth, I remember a visit by a Whitaker. Brother Whitaker is a true friend."

The chief raised his arms to preempt any potential retort, then went on.

"For generations, when our people have been on hard times, our adopted brothers and sisters of Whitaker have brought great assistance. In our time of need, Brother Whitaker has come." The chief then called for a feast.

Micheal was struck by something from the chief's story. He had stated that Whitakers had been visiting them for generations. He had also indicated that he had met one of them as a boy, which would mean over fifty years ago.

Micheal then considered the other odd element. Why would the chief recognize him?

He figured it had something to do with the Lords of Avalon. The lords, he knew, were "enigmatic." Perhaps they spent some of their time away from England visiting America. He wasn't sure whether it was the name or his face that convinced the chief. He would have to ponder it further.

In the meantime, Micheal couldn't help but see the people didn't have much and were using a great deal of their resources to celebrate him.

"What do I call you?"

The chief replied, "Mahinkana Nyipawi."

Micheal translated that to "wolf of the night." Nightwolf. Micheal smiled.

"Chief Nightwolf, I have a great blessing from the sacrifice of our elk brother, as well as other supplies. I will share with the people."

A big smile came to Nightwolf's face. He called some men of the tribe and instructed them to accompany Micheal to his camp and retrieve his supplies.

The two men that Nightwolf assigned to accompany Micheal were an odd pair. First, he introduced Peaceful River, a broad and semi-heavyset man with a big smile. The second, Eye of Eagle, was tall, thin, and with a permanent scowl on his face certainly made him seem like the perfect sentry. He was aptly named.

They brought forward three horses. As Micheal gripped the borrowed horse by the mane, he wondered where Darkness might be.

Just then, a thunder of hooves rumbled through the trees and Darkness burst into the clearing and sidled up to him.

"Hey there, boy! Where have you been?"

Chief Nightwolf approached Micheal with a laugh then turned and said, "Your beast has a mind of its own. Peaceful River and Eye of Eagle were unequal to the task." He joined the chief in a brief laugh, and they were off.

After a short ride, perhaps ten minutes, they were back at the place he had gone to inspect the wall. From there, he led them to his camp, which was another twenty minutes away.

He was glad to see Angel. Everything looked to be in order, and so he directed the broader of the two, Peaceful River, to the elk. His new smiling friend motioned to Eye of Eagle to follow while Micheal broke down his camp.

———⊠———

They then returned to the village and feasted late into the night.

When the village quieted down, Micheal found himself alone with Nightwolf.

"I'm glad you've come back." The Chief said.

"You said *we* came in your youth."

"It was you and a female Whitaker."

"What is our relationship?"

Nightwolf examined him closely. "I understand how complex the agents of the Great Spirit might be. You may not follow the progress of the seasons."

"What does that mean?"

"After your last visit, I asked my father about you. He said the guardians of the Spirit have come and gone throughout the history of our people. They don't live by the seasons or the moons. He told tales of the ancestors in the time of giants. And in the many seasons, the guardians come and go. Whitaker has gone by many names but are always friends of the people."

Micheal didn't know what Nightwolf was talking about. It sounded like he viewed Micheal as some kind of mystical protector. "What if we are not able to protect the people from what is to come?"

"It has been trying times since the coming of the white man. But that is not the purpose of your guardianship. I know you live beyond the limits of what the British call time. And you know what is to come. The Great Spirit has told me that our existence lives on in the great beyond where my fathers now sit by the eternal fire. Whatever happens to our people in this world will be accounted by the Spirit. Our lives are about harmony with him, and we must live them. As the guardians, you serve the betterment of all peoples, not just our people. I am grateful for your friendship." Nightwolf rose from his seat. "I have something for you. This came from trading with the nations to the west." Nightwolf presented him with a large stone embossed with cubic crystals. He would need to study the crystals to see what elements they were. "I sensed the spirit wanted you to have this. Now, harmony requires an old man to get rest."

The departure of Nightwolf left Micheal as the lone holdout. He was tired after the eventful day. Micheal navigated the sleeping people to exit the longhouse. He was greeted by a half-moon kissing the western horizon. His thoughts went to what Nightwolf said. How were the Lords of Avalon related to these guardians that he spoke of? Why did he think Micheal was one of them? He talked about living outside of time. How would he know about that, anyway? A time of giants? It was all too much to contemplate. He found the small house they'd arranged and slid under the skins. In a matter of minutes, he was out.

The next morning, he continued on to Albany with Angel and Darkness. He didn't go alone. Nightwolf sent Peaceful River and Eye of Eagle to assist in his mission. He left all that could be spared and promised to make a return visit, along with more periodic visits, so long as he was in Massachusetts. He was, of course, an honorary member of the tribe.

The shale deposits were located quite easily in the mountains near Albany. After a couple of days of work, they began the four-day trek back to Homestead with a metric ton of shale rock. He had engineered a plastic-making machine. He had enough hydrocarbon to produce perhaps four hundred pounds of plastic, and he could make many useful things with that.

Micheal's friends accompanied him to the Ware River where he set up camp. They unloaded their shale burdens and said their farewells. He would need to return here to retrieve the extra load, but his friends didn't want to venture too far into the settled areas. He was only a half day's ride from home.

Now that he was alone, he went to collect water from the river. The sun had already sunk into the trees. He would lose the light soon. With his waterskins full, he was about to head back to his camp when he heard the snap of a twig. There was a flash of tan and he reflexively ducked. A sharp pain scratched his back.

Micheal turned to the attacker; it was a mountain lion. The big cat lunged, and he blocked its jaws with his left arm. The teeth sank in, and its claws hugged his shoulders as they fell to the ground. Adrenaline numbed the pain, and he drew his knife. He punched the cougar's underbelly repeatedly. The cat screamed, releasing his arm. The animal retreated, and the tan turned to red.

Micheal struggled to his feet and approached the mountain lion, knife at the ready. It panted a few more times, then went silent. With the threat neutralized, he assessed the damage. There were scratches on his back and shoulders, but they didn't compare to the bite on his arm. It was oozing blood and hurt to flex his hand.

Making a painful fist, he plunged it into the ice-cold river. He wrapped fabric around his arm and secured it with a strap of leather.

A restless night was followed by a painful daylong trek to Homestead. By the time he unloaded the shale and put the horses in the stable, he could feel the infection taking root in his arm. He cleaned the wounds as best he could, but the canine punctures went deep. He feared he couldn't stave off the infection but hoped it would pass without severe complications like the scratch on his leg had. He'd rarely had issues with infection in the 21st century. But the 17th century was a different story. Could his body weather this storm?

II: Biological Warfare

MICHEAL woke in a hot sweat. He felt his forehead; he felt on the warm side. He removed the wrap around his arm and found the wounds inflamed and tender-red. He pressed on the scabs and a thick white pus bled from the punctures. This was not good. If the infection deteriorated, he could face mortal danger.

His best hope was the penicillin he'd been working on. His cultures might be close to ready, and he had no more time to wait. He still had to extract the penicillin to make it useful. He hoped his mind would hold up long enough for him to do that. Now it would be a race against time.

Micheal went to his storage and collected the ingredients. The cultures were light brown. That made him confident that there was enough penicillin in the growth containers. Before he could extract the penicillin, he needed to make hydrochloric acid.

He placed the container with water in the snow to keep it chilled. Using a leather funnel with a leather tube, he prepared the apparatus to feed the gas into the water. Then he put a dish of salt in the snow and covered it with the funnel.

Now would come the most dangerous part. He took the container of the sulfuric acid and slowly poured it in through a crack beneath the funnel. Pressing the funnel as airtight against the salt dish as possible, he could feel the heat of the reaction. By the time the chemical process was finished, the snow beneath the dish had melted.

The rancid odor wafting off the water dish signaled his success in the formation of hydrochloric acid. One step down, much still to do.

Micheal bowed his head into his hands to support his weariness. Then rubbed his eyes to clear his mind. The warmth of the oncoming fever reminded him he needed to press on.

He placed a cheesecloth over one of several large jars to strain the mature cultures. He'd worked in volume, knowing that he'd need a lot to treat any major infection.

Starting with about two gallons of solution might yield enough for two major infections. Hydrochloric acid was added to the strained penicillin to adjust the ph. He didn't have a way to test the PH, so he would have to estimate how much acid to add.

After mixing the hydrochloric acid into the penicillin, he dipped his pinky into the liquid for a few seconds. The burning on his skin told him the PH probably was around 2.

Micheal felt drained. He closed his eyes and sucked in air to try to bring him enough energy to finish this medicine. The final ingredients were buried in the snow outside. He mixed the ethyl acetate with the penicillin solution and separated the final strain from the mixture. Now the final step was to add the potassium acetate, then it would be a waiting game.

With the penicillin just about ready, he needed to find a way to inject it.

The barn shop was the next stop. He was in a fight against lethargy to complete his task. His forearm was swelling, which made his grip weak. Carrying the shale would be a challenge. He picked up a large slab from the stash in the barn and walked it into the shop. A shock of pain shot through his arm and the rock slipped from his hand. The stone came down on his toe.

"Mother fucker!"

His toe was throbbing, and he dropped to his knees, then spun to his butt. The throb was pulsing through his temples. He collapsed to his back.

Laying on his back, Micheal wondered what he was fighting for. He'd been a failure in the 21st century. And despite his early successes in the 17th, he was starting to realize he'd fail here as well. So why fight? He wasn't going to solve time. All he had to look forward to was a miserable, lonely life in the past. His body relaxed as he accepted his fate.

"Why are you here?" A shot of recognition came in the face of a woman who spoke.

"Amanda?" She looked much older.

"Am I that different?"

Micheal approached his sister. They were on a familiar mountaintop. Her strawberry hair was back, beautiful, and flowing. But those emerald eyes were the same.

"You're all grown up. And you look beautiful."

"You told me I was even more beautiful without hair."

"You always look beautiful." He embraced her.

A long moment passed, and she pulled back. "What are you doing here?"

"Is this the afterlife?"

"No. Do you remember Mount Olympus?"

"You know I can't forget." She just stared at him. "I kept my promise. This was just nature."

"I also made a promise that day. That I would look out for you in death, the way you did for me in life. That's why I'm here. You can still live, but you must fight for yourself, the way you fought for me. Will you do the hard thing? For me?" She searched his face.

"If I couldn't save you, how can I solve time? My life will amount to nothing in the past."

"There are no guarantees in life. The point is to live it. I wish my time was longer. Will you live life for me?"

How could he say no? "I don't know how."

"You do. You will." Amanda touched his cheek.

Micheal woke to the morning sun shining into the barn. His face felt hot. The fever was starting to win. He needed to fight, and his window was closing, but he had promises to keep. Removing the cloth from his arm, he found the wounds festering and swollen.

Pressing his fingertips into the infection produced a bursting response, and the puss bled to the ground. He forced himself to his feet and stumbled across the yard to the cabin. The smell of ethyl greeted his entry. He waited for it to air out, then found the basin, and removed the cloth cover. Plunging his arm into the cold water felt good and helped wake him up. He scrubbed the wounds with soap and felt the burn. Then wrapped his arm with a clean cloth.

Micheal was alert but also knew this wouldn't last. The fever was persistent. He needed to work fast. His toe hurt with each step to the shop. And he decided to take out his frustration on the offending stone. Using the smithing hammer, he pulverized the shale. Now it was time to bring the heat.

With the shale in the condenser, he fired up the kiln. As the flames grew hotter, he fed them with a billow. At the smith in Concord, he bought a raw stone that he'd identified as containing zinc. That element's melting point matched the temperature he needed to make plastic.

He placed a piece of zinc and a piece of lead on a conductor plate on the kiln. When the lead melted, he knew the temperature was getting close. He slowed the amount of oxygen gain to the flames until the zinc began to melt, then the task was to maintain the temperature.

While he monitored the heat, he prepped the syringe mold he'd crafted. His mind began to cloud as the intensity of the heat in the shop magnified his fever. He guzzled a full pitcher of water to satiate his thirst. Then he added a catalyst to the polymer to form the final version of polyethylene.

Micheal dispensed some liquid plastic into his molds and set them aside to cool. He mediated the dispensation of the remaining plastic into small chips, then removed the catch from the hot zone. His vision blurred with a flush of heat to his head. Falling to his knees, he crawled over to the molds.

He fumbled the die in his swollen hand. He finally slipped the form out of one cast, then the plunger out of the other. Testing found they fit. He was a needle away from salvation. His eyes kept shifting their focus.

It was a herculean effort to locate his pre-forged injection needle and fix it to the new syringe. Fighting the broiler in his brain, he slogged through the smoke and fire, and crossed the yard. Reaching the porch, his bruised toe cursed him again and tripped him into the snow.

Lying there, his tank was empty. His whole body hurt. He could barely think. All he wanted was to give in to his fatigue. But the cold shocks of the falling snow foretold doom if he took the slumber.

Micheal summoned Amanda's strength to force his legs to the task. He trudged through the dim light of the cabin to his penicillin jar. His eyes failed him, so the dosage was more of a guess. Half went into the bottom wound; the other half went to the top of his arm. The heat took him, and the lights went out.

III: Miner Engineering

MICHEAL spent an indeterminant amount of time in an opaque haze of fever dreams, temporary lucidity to inject more penicillin, and foggy actions to tend to bodily needs. Now he awoke to a chilled forehead. The fever had passed.

Normally, the internal clock of his flawless memory would tell him the day. But the fever clouded everything. Now that the light of day had chased the fog away, he needed to recalculate the date.

Meditation allowed him to sift through the chaos of his fevered mind and determine that the date was Thursday, February 21.

It had been nearly six weeks since his temporal fall. And now that he was on the mend, it was time to get back to the task. He did a mental rundown of his time in the seventeenth century.

Micheal had confirmed that he had awakened in the field on the morning of his birthday, January 12. He built Homestead, and he was finally working on some more modest engineering projects, namely a wind-powered generator, which cost him five days and a big chunk of his resources. But he'd had no ability to harness the generator until he could insulate the wiring. Now, with plastic at his disposal, the electricity to power Homestead was nearly available.

He'd made the generator a secondary priority because he knew one of the most ever-present dangers of the past was fire. When you are lighting the night with candle flame, there's always the threat of conflagration.

Micheal had already pulled the requisite amount of wire from some copper rods. Now he needed to produce the plastic insulation tubes. He distilled another batch of plastic. And using a funnel die dispenser he pressed out dozens of feet of clear plastic tubing. He used a different catalyst to produce a softer, flexible plastic.

As he soldered the insulator around the copper wire, he realized the insulator by itself would work as an I/V tube. And after how close he'd come to death, by way of dehydration, an I/V drip would have removed that threat. So once the wire was housed, he used some of the extra to craft the medical tubes. Then improvised another mold to fashion a few I/V pouches. With the synthesis of some pure saline, he'd have some I/V hydration at the ready if another medical emergency befell him.

The plastic would also allow him to fabricate other medical instruments. His extensive medical knowledge and experimentation wouldn't amount to much without certain tools of the trade.

With the wire at the ready, he needed to fashion a few light bulbs. And he had an unusual concept for illuminating Homestead. The crystal-embedded stone that Nightwolf had gifted him proved quite interesting. He determined the crystals to be perovskite. Before insulating the wire, he'd placed some of the crystals in a solvent solution to enhance the luminescence properties of the crystals. He could use those to produce LED bulbs. The production process would be simpler than trying to manufacture incandescent light bulbs. Then the threat of an inferno could be laid to rest and the lighting would be more proficient for working after dark.

Micheal worked all day and as the sunlight began to fade, Homestead was electrically wired. It was time to test his LEDs. The windmill was rotating slowly so the generator should produce enough energy.

He stepped into the main room of the cabin and reached for the switch. "And let there be light."

The LEDs worked. They were generally white, but there was a bluish tint. But that didn't affect the overall effect. He blew out the candles but would keep them close as the wind was an unreliable energy source. He would need to build a water wheel to supplement, as a power generator.

Even though some of his latest accomplishments had come through good fortune, Micheal was pleased that his LEDs had worked. Juxtaposed against his near-death experience, that gave him unusual confidence.

It was time to reward himself for his hard work. He'd laid pipe in the bathroom, and the tub he'd constructed was ready for testing. Maintaining hygiene with an ewer and basin was less than ideal. He hadn't had a bath since high school. Showers were more practical. But he was looking forward to this.

Micheal tested the water temperature, it was hot. As he sank in, the scratches on his back reminded him they hadn't quite healed. Eventually, the heat soothed the itch away and he tried to relax. But the pain in his forearm pulled him out of his luxury.

The infective swelling was gone, but the magnified sensation of the cougar's jaws penetrated the wounds. A muted ache throbbed in his arm. Despite how this bath had emphasized every cut and bruise, he let the heat seep deep into his core, bringing total relaxation. He closed his eyes and let his mind be drawn from the challenges of the past.

Micheal's mind never stopped. Relaxation was always a challenge. The best method he'd found was to recompile the databases in his head. Taking the memory files from the past two months, he organized them from least to most important. By the end, the front of the drawers were of family.

He'd used the distraction of survival to obscure what he was feeling about his friends and family. When Amanda died, a sickening twist racked his insides. It was like a part of him died with her. And now he was marooned in the past with little chance of return. The separation from his family felt permanent. As if they were all now dead. He tried to mitigate the effect by reminding himself that they still lived in the 21st century.

Micheal went to the last experience before he left. His mom gave him a ride to the airport.

⎯⎯⎯⎯◄►⎯⎯⎯⎯

"I've been meaning to talk to you about this trip. I know you've been particularly interested in my family lineage recently. Does that have anything to do with this?"

"Why would this have anything to do with that?"

"I worry you are looking for something you'll never find. No lost treasure is going to change what's important in life."

"I'm not treasure hunting."

"Don't feel like you must keep secrets. I know more than you think about my family's secrets."

"It's been ten years. All I do is study. Learn this, learn that. I just feel like I'm spinning my wheels. My thirst for knowledge never stops, but it's losing its meaning. And if I must abide this world, something needs to change."

"I know I failed you when you were struggling in school. I should've recognized that the system was failing you. I should've fought harder."

"It wouldn't have made a difference. No one would've supported me. I have to do it myself."

"You don't need the Treasure of Avalon to do that. The fact that you've found the drive to take this trip tells me all I need to know. I fear you might get lost in this quest." They pulled up to the drop-off.

"I don't do this frivolously." Micheal climbed out of the car.

His mom joined him on the curb as he grabbed his bags.

"I hope you find what you're looking for. You do have amazing potential. No matter what happens, just remember how much we all love you. I am going to miss you." His mom gave him a bear hug. In this rewind, it felt like a true goodbye.

"I love you too, mom." She didn't seem to want to let go. After a long while, he broke the embrace.

"I will be here for you, no matter how long you're gone." She was in full tears.

"Okay Mom. See you in a week?" She was being so dramatic.

She sniffled and wiped her eyes. She forced a smile. "Time is relative, as you know. Whether it's a week or a year, or something else, I will truly miss you. But I know you're ready. And I love you." She hugged him again, then stepped back.

"I love you, Mom." As the sliding doors made way, a chill went down his spine.

He reached the check-in kiosk and, after a final glance, saw his mother crying in her hands.

Micheal's eyes opened to the 17th-century reality and her words seemed prophetic. Much of the aches had relaxed away, and then it took him.

He woke, and the water had chilled. Refreshed anew, it was time to get back to work. With his most pressing concerns about health and safety being addressed, it was time to attempt his most ambitious engineering project yet.

Any two-bit high school science teacher could probably do most of what he'd done so far. Perhaps even the generator. For the first time, he was going to try to engineer an idea he'd first conceived of when he was twelve. A mining bore. Over the years, he'd worked to build a prototype in his head. One of his biggest challenges in this century was where to get the rarer and useful elements. A mining bore would solve that problem.

He'd been looking from town to town for certain high-class engineering metals before he found a smith in Providence, who had a piece of metal, obviously a meteorite, that he couldn't forget. That told Micheal it might contain metals such as tungsten or titanium, metals he might be able to use for this project. Because of the apparent special nature of the meteorite, it took much bartering and more silver to acquire.

All his running around the past couple of weeks had given him plenty of practice with his accent. He felt he was close enough not to be singled out because of his speech, but it could still use some work. He was running low on silver, which put even more pressure on him not to fail. He had decided he would move to Boston when he felt he could develop a believable backstory. But only if he was at least able to portray upper-class. If he couldn't get to that level, he might as well stay at Homestead.

If he was able to move into Boston high society, he might be able to gain access to more resources—resources that could help him figure out how he fell into the seventeenth century. And perhaps even help him find a way home. He knew the odds were long, but what else was he going to do in this century?

The idea he had envisioned for his mining bore included a drill head, which he had already fabricated out of the alloys he had produced using the meteoritic metals. It would bore through the ground and process the material through a smelter filter, expelling the unwanted minerals and filling the hold stocks with only the more valuable metals, which could then be extracted for further processing. He would then combine that with extreme heat to allow it to cut through the ground with relative ease.

He had built the superstructure of the bore. It was about five feet long and a foot in diameter. He had been making a tether cable, and it was currently about half a mile in length. His next challenge was to find a power source. The engine was an electric engine but to get electricity; he needed to turn to another idea he had. This one was inspired by one of the greatest geniuses of the twentieth century, Nikola Tesla. His ideas of electricity being pulled straight out of the buildup of kinetic energy in the atmosphere and channeling it without wires from one point to the other had made so much sense to Micheal. If you could pull energy straight from the atmosphere, then the energy available would, for all intents and purposes, be limitless. And it would always be there. You would never run out of gas.

By the time he had envisioned this concept, the family emergency had stolen away his attention and so he'd put the idea on the shelf. His primary focus became curing cancer. But after that abject failure, he didn't dare test the limits of his intellect. After she died, he had promised her he wouldn't kill himself. And he knew if he failed again, he might not be able to stop himself. Better not to tempt fate. The last thing he wanted to do was break his promise.

Now under extreme circumstances, Micheal had dusted off his *Da Vinci level* inspiration. He spent several days of effort, to no avail. Obviously, he'd bitten off more than he could chew. Once again, he was a failure.

"You were actually starting to believe you could invent something new? Did you believe you could match Tesla or any other genius from history?" He laughed at the ridiculousness of him remotely imagining he was that intelligent.

He walked over, saddled up Darkness, and said, "I guess we're stuck together. If I can't make a kinetic energy extractor, what possible chance do I have to make a time machine?" Darkness whinnied in reply. If he couldn't finish his mining bore, he would go for a supply run. For speed's sake, he took only Darkness. He brought his mining equipment, including a new piece of his arsenal. Dynamite. He'd made a few sticks which would speed up the job.

Micheal and Darkness rode all day north to New Hampshire, back to the location of the silver thread. He wondered if he would fail again. He had only performed one test of his dynamite so the rest could easily be a dud. If it worked, his haul would be far higher.

It was time to put his dynamite to the test. He lit the fuse and sprinted for cover. A few seconds later, the detonations went off in sequence.

"Well, at least I wasn't a total failure. With my luck, I probably excavated almost all the silver on my previous—" His train of thought was interrupted by the sight of the shelf he had collapsed. The entire shelf he'd dislodged was sparkling in the sunlight—and not just from silver.

"There's gold in them thar hills." A smile came to his face.

Over the next couple of days, he smelted as much ore as he could. The vein was far richer than he could have imagined. After two days, he'd processed around half a ton of silver and more than a ton of gold. He estimated the value of the gold at around fifty million dollars in 2010 and the silver at perhaps a quarter of a million. He wondered why this find wasn't in the history books. This amount of gold would have sparked a flood of people from Europe seeking fortune.

It made him consider how time operated. There was a chance that it was never found because he found it. If that was true, he'd already been in the history books, but just didn't know it. If he was, obviously, he hadn't done anything significant enough to notice. He decided that it didn't matter at this moment. He needed to find a hiding place for most of the gold and silver; there was no way he would be able to carry it all back, even if he had brought Angel with him.

After burying nearly all of it, he determined he would head east to Portsmouth, then run the coast southwest back to Homestead. He loaded up a large pouch of silver, perhaps fifty pounds, for trading along the way. He spent two days trading down the New Hampshire and Massachusetts coastline and was about to cut inward toward Homestead, keeping north of Boston. There was one last stop on the coast. Salem.

The streets were like a ghost town. Usually by this time, maybe nine in the morning, there'd be people everywhere, going about their daily routine. But it was eerily silent. He rode to the town square. Surely there would be people...but nothing. Something wasn't right.

Micheal brushed off the uneasy feeling and reassured himself with the prospect of trading for goods in other towns along the way.

He exited the Salem Peninsula the same way he came in. His thoughts were interrupted by a quiet murmuring to the southwest. As he crossed the bridge out of town and approached the junction, he heard the rumblings of a mob. Traveling in the opposite direction, the different angle allowed him to see down the road. South of the intersection was a large crowd.

He approached them slowly, periodically tugging on Darkness' reigns to slow his stride.

"Easy boy," he whispered. "We're in Salem. In 1692. We can't be too careful."

The trees parted, and the full crowd came into view. It had to be a couple thousand strong. That kind of crowd would only come to one place for a single purpose. An execution.

In these times executions were public spectacles. He knew to expect whole families in attendance. Nearly everyone in the general area was probably here, vendors and all. They treated it like a sport.

He wondered who was being executed and why?

His thoughts cut off as he reached the edge of the clearing. Something felt wrong about the entire scene, like it shouldn't be happening. Darkness came to a stop as if reacting to the surprise before Micheal's eyes. It was a woman.

Women were rarely executed, and if they were, the most likely reason would be witchcraft. But it was only February. It was too early to be the witch trials. He knew the first accusations didn't come in until mid to late February, and the first execution wasn't until June 1692. Whoever was being killed was doing it four months ahead of schedule.

As he focused on the woman's face, he was shocked to realize he recognized her. It was Julie Buckingham!

CHAPTER 9: NEAR DEATH

JULIE BECAME CONSCIOUS AGAIN and was relieved to discover the pain was gone. She was standing in front of the crowd. Why was she no longer bound? She reached for the rope around her throat but found it, too, was gone.

The people in the front row were still shouting the most terrible things about her. She turned instinctively to run away and found herself staring into the lifeless eyes of a woman. They were bulging wide open. Her large, dilated pupils were like a deep abyss in the center of bloodshot eyes that stared into nothingness. It looked like her.

It couldn't be. She didn't want to believe it, but the horrible truth was hanging right in front of her. It was so surreal that she almost didn't recognize herself. The face of the woman was swollen and purplish-blue. Even though it felt like it was someone else, she knew she was staring at her own reflection.

Julie collapsed to the floor. Hands and knees pressed against the snow, yet no feelings or sensation to speak of. She should have felt the cold of the icy ground, but all she felt was despair for what she'd lost. She tried to cry but found no tears. What would she do now? After a long moment, she pulled herself up. Was this what death was?

She floated up and looked down on the entire situation. The crowd looked like a festival. People were talking and laughing near food stands. She couldn't understand how people could so casually come and celebrate the death of someone they didn't even know, someone who had done them no harm.

As she watched the crowd, a glow began to emanate from the people. It was like a cornucopia of color. She wasn't sure what it was. Maybe it was the people's auras? The two most predominant colors were orange and pink. She floated back to her body and a stream of orange light seemed to aim right for her.

An odd vibration flowed through her. She was overcome with a strong feeling of hate for this crowd of wretchedness.

She stepped aside to avoid the next stream of orange and stepped straight into a blue streak that was coming from a woman in the third row. This reverberation brought on strong feelings of sadness.

Julie couldn't understand what was happening to her. What were these streaks of color, and why did they seem to be targeting her?

Before she had time to think, a pink stream shot through her. This time, she felt terror.

Julie felt her entire body quivering. It was like these colors came with emotions attached. Her connection seemed to be expanding. She could sense the animals recoiling from this field of negative emotions. She could even feel the imprint of history in the memory of trees.

The chaos within intensified and her reach expanded beyond the earth. She was flying through space. She flew past our yellow sun, then accelerated out into the vast emptiness. A brilliant white sun raced by, followed by a giant red one. She continued picking up speed, soaring past a stunning blue sun until she saw something truly terrifying: a black hole!

A dark orb spinning incredibly fast was drawing matter from a companion blue star that was whipping around it. She focused on the event horizon. The awesome gravity seemed to bend the universe to its will. The background stars were all distorted like looking through a fish lens. As she neared the horizon, the stars behind her seemed to speed up. She turned back to the termination point and could see the battle between the speed of light and the force of darkness. Then she was back at her death scene.

The whole experience left Julie out of sorts. She was distracted and lost in thought when a red stream rushed toward her. Fists clenched and eyes firmly shut, she braced herself for the sensation of anger but, to her surprise, the feeling didn't follow.

The expected rush of rage was not there. Last time it overtook her senses, but now she could see them coming and withstand their force.

She tested it. A rose-colored stream took off from another member of the crowd. Her fists clenched again, but this time with determination. She stood her ground while the pink streak met her full-on. Her thoughts concentrated on what she had felt before. Fear. Once again, the emotion was not there.

Julie couldn't make sense of the changes happening all around her. Perhaps she was now immune to the effects of the auras.

That thought led to others. Where were the pearly gates? And the harp playing angels? Where was her spirit guide explaining how death works? Was she a ghost, condemned to haunt this wretched town for all eternity? What was she supposed to do now?

As her eyes adjusted from the barrage of colors, her sight narrowed. A familiar face stood out amongst the crowd. Samuel Parris. At once, she saw the distance between herself and Parris close in until she was face to face with her accuser. He was glowing bright with orange and yellow, a look of satisfaction on his face.

She thought of Parris holding her against her will, ripping her clothes off, beating her and throwing her to the floor. Her hands flew up and shot at Parris' face. A feeling of static traveled down her hands and through her arms. It didn't hurt. There was no pain, just a sensation like when an arm falls asleep. She tried again, but her swings went straight through him, leaving only the feeling of numbness in her limbs.

She tried to focus, tried to clench her fists tightly enough to strike this evil thing, but it was no use. Every swing, every attempt, resulted in failure, and the man just kept standing and smiling.

Is this all death was? You become a ghost?

The faith she was raised in taught that if you were a good person, you would be with your loved ones in heaven. That had given her the hope she would see Jessica again. But now she felt like she lost her sister once more.

Maybe this was hell? Or at least purgatory? Perhaps she was not as good as she thought, and she wasn't going to heaven, at least not for a while. She crossed back to her dangling body; she tried to touch her face, but her hand went right through it. She slid back inside her body, but nothing happened. She came back out and looked into her lifeless eyes.

"I wish I was back in New York with Aiden." If she'd had tears to cry, they would've been streaming down her face, but she couldn't feel a thing. "He'll never know what happened to me! I'll be buried in some unmarked grave. No one will ever find me!" She sunk into the depths of despair.

As she leaned against her body, a most peculiar thing snapped her out of her malaise. Her body and spirit began generating a dark element, like a black light.

The once beautiful sky turned a murky gray, then a ray of light pierced through and brightened. She floated above the trees. It looked like an explosion of light. She was drawn to it, like it was calling to her. She looked back down for a moment; the crowd was fading into the distance.

Julie advanced through the beam of light and found herself back at the event horizon of the black hole. She felt torn between two options before her. The first was drawing her toward the center of the hole and what might be on the other side. The other was driven by her fear of the unknown, pushing her to flee this location and return to the world she knew. If she went toward the center, would she be erased from existence or be sucked into hell? If she went back, at least she was the ghost of herself. But then, how far could she go as a ghost? Could she leave that cult behind? If she went back, would she ever get this chance again?

She closed her eyes and moved past the horizon. It was like she had passed through a doorway. Everything became much darker. After a few moments, her eyes adjusted to the mellow scene. He was there.

It was Aiden. He was standing on a beach looking at the sunset. He bent down and grabbed a handful of white sand. He observed how the fading twilight sparkled off the grains.

"Julie, where are ya, luv?" Tears streamed down his cheeks.

Julie moved so they were face to face. He was generating waves of purple and blue. She knew blue meant sadness, but what did purple indicate?

She reached into the lavender glow that lit his face and felt the strength of his love for her.

"I'm right here!" She tried to make him hear her.

He almost seemed to reply. "Were ya but a grain, I might hold ya once more."

He let the sand slip between his fingers, but one glowing speck seemed to hover in mid-air, like a tiny star. It was captivating.

She became so entranced with it that everything else disappeared. She took it between her fingers and placed it in her palm. As she focused on the glow, it sucked her in.

I: The Other Side

The grain became a brilliant light at the end of a circular tunnel. Light was radiating down the sides and was rapidly getting brighter. When the tunnel came to an end, she was in the midst of pure light. Maybe she was going to heaven after all.

The light was blinding. It took a few minutes for JULIE'S eyes to adjust. Even as the world began to come into focus, she still felt wrapped in a blanket of light.

She was on what looked like an outcrop overlooking a beach. The water was a deep royal purple with lavender caps. As the waves washed over the white sand, the beach looked like a crescent of fine-grained table salt curving into the distance. The sky was an aquamarine with various tints of blues and greens interspersed. The sun was a silvery blue, floating low near the horizon.

A warm breeze tickled her face. She noticed the deep red wheat blowing in the wind and ran her fingers through the heads. They felt like silk.

On her right there was a whole array of the most stark and dynamic colored flora she'd ever seen. The vibrant colors made her feel like she had walked into the most beautiful painting imaginable. It reminded her of a Leonid Afremov palette knife she had once seen at a gallery in New York.

Julie went to one knee in a patch of sand and grabbed a handful. Each grain sparkled like a million diamonds in her hand. As they slipped between her fingers, the wind caught them, and a grand spectrum illuminated their wake.

Her thoughts went to Aiden on that beach. The tears breached her closing lids, and she wished she was that sand, so he might hold her once more.

It was at this moment of grief that a sensation of all-encompassing, unconditional love washed over her, like every cell of her body was filled with it. She'd wondered where she was, now she thought out loud, "Is this heaven?"

Then she heard a voice call her name, an unmistakable voice. She turned and Jessica was standing in front of her. She emanated light and wore a flowing, white dress. She was so beautiful, the image of an angel.

Julie was overwhelmed with emotion. She gave her sister a passionate embrace, a release of everything she'd suffered alone. Jessica held her with tender love in her arms.

Following this catharsis, her thoughts turned to Jessica and their family. She was excited and she pulled back, speaking a mile a minute.

Jessica smiled and touched Julie's shoulder to make her pause. "Slow down there, little sis."

Julie still had trouble containing herself. "I've missed you so much. There's just so much I want to tell you."

"I missed you, too." Jessica gently touched her cheek. Julie tensed slightly, taking a small step back as she felt the storm rise behind her eyes. Jess stepped up and blanketed her with loving arms.

The hug lasted a long while. Jess pulled back and looked into her eyes. It felt like their souls were connected. Julie's feeling of guilt made her want to look away. Jessica's fingers on her chin stopped her.

"It wasn't your fault." Those words brought the rain.

"I know I could have done something more." Julie's tears blurred her sister's image, and she turned away to the edge of the precipice.

"No Julie, I know you always thought you should be able to do anything you put your mind to, but you were only fifteen and human. You need to allow yourself to be human." Jess joined her on the edge.

Julie shook her head in argument. "It was my fault. The lake was my idea. If only we—"

"Shh." Jess took her hand, stopping her. "I need you to forgive yourself."

"How can you still—"

"I could never not love you."

Julie turned to face her sister. "Can you ever forgive me?"

Jess pulled her into her arms. "There's nothing to forgive." Julie tried to pull back to reply, but Jess squeezed her tighter and instructed, "Say: 'It wasn't my fault.'"

"But—"

Jess stopped her. "No, I want you to say, 'It wasn't my fault.'"

Julie had been wracked with such guilt for the last fifteen years.

She shifted uncomfortably, then surrendered and finally said, "It wasn't my fault."

"Say it again."

Julie hesitated, then repeated, "It wasn't my fault." Julie broke down and cried on Jess's shoulder for a while. It felt like a massive burden had been lifted off her shoulders.

After a long embrace, Jess finally pulled back and asked, "Now, little sis, how is everyone?"

Julie explained everything that was going on with their family and friends as they walked down to the shoreline. They ambled through the warm surf until they came to a small estuary where they sat on an ivory sandbar.

"And what's going on with you?"

Julie sat with her feet in the lavender river and began telling her everything, "My TV show is a huge success—"

"You have a TV show?"

"For five years. It's called Bull Markets."

"Of course. I know how much you love business."

"I try to improve myself every day. I'm at Columbia so much taking one class after the next that people say I should move in."

"Gotta keep that mind sharp." Her sister tapped her on the temple. "Have you earned your place on Mount Genius yet? Up there with Da Vinci, Newton, and Einstein. Have you solved one of the greatest mysteries of science? Like how life began? Or what came first, the chicken or the egg?"

"Not yet." Jess could always make her laugh.

"What's the last thing you studied?"

"Software design and programming languages. I was learning how to become a hacker."

"You were always a natural with algorithms. Your handle could be Gravity Vixen." They laughed together. "You know, Newton's muse."

"So you're living in New York?"

"For over twelve years now. Aiden and I live in a penthouse near Columbus Circle, overlooking the park. I love to go for runs." Julie felt a pang at the thought of him.

"Aiden? How did you not start with that one?"

Julie stood up and walked a few steps into the violet surf. "We were so happy..."

"What happened?"

"We were planning on having a child, but...It doesn't matter."

Jess stepped right up next to her. "Tell me about Aiden."

Julie wiped the tear from her eye and mirrored her sister's half-smile. "He is the sweetest Irishman you ever met."

She went on for what seemed like an eternity; It felt just like old times. She and Jess would go off for hours just talking. They were like twins born three years apart.

She could've gone on for days, but Jess finally said, "We need to talk about why I'm here."

"Isn't it about why I'm here?"

"It's the same thing."

Julie opened her arms, indicating her incredible surroundings. "Is this heaven?"

"No, it's more like a stopping point." Jessica went and sat down on the riverbank.

"Then where is heaven?"

"All I can tell you is that it's not here."

Julie turned and kicked the waves in frustration at Jess' answer. "Aren't you supposed to be my guide or something? To explain how all this works?"

"I don't have all the answers. I'm here to assist you in whatever you decide."

"Decide? What possible decision could I have to make?"

"Come here!" Her sister patted the bank.

Julie walked to her sister. Jess took her hand and sat her down. "This doesn't have to be the end for you. You can still go back."

"Back? Back to what?"

Jess stroked her hand lovingly with her thumb. "To your mortal life."

"How? I was hanged as a witch." Julie was still confused. She concentrated on the satin silt between her toes.

"All I know is you get to choose. If you choose to stay, I will guide you through what comes next. If you choose to go, you can live again."

"How can I choose? What's the right choice?"

"There is no wrong answer. The choice is entirely up to you. But time is short."

Julie was flooded with images of her family and friends, and especially Aiden. Then she looked at where she was—beautiful beyond description, no pain. She felt loved completely, unconditionally. And if she stayed, she would go to heaven. Which she imagined had to be even better. How could she possibly choose?

Aiden's face came to her mind again. She closed her eyes and imagined her life with him once more. The decision was clear. She had to take the chance of seeing him again. "I have to go back." She stood, determined.

Jess gave a half smile and a nod. "I told them you'd choose to go back." Her sister threw her arms around her. "It was so good to see you, little sis." After a minute, she pulled back. "You have to go now."

"Jess...." Julie traced the curve of her sister's face, trying to memorize every detail. "I love you."

Jess' eyes began to water as she brushed the hair out of Julie's face. "I love you so much."

"I don't want to say goodbye." Julie let the tears flow.

"Then don't. I will see you again."

Julie saw the light radiate through the tears on her sister's face. She felt a pull from behind. It was like an irresistible magnet. Her fingers lost contact with Jess's outstretched hand. Then there was a falling sensation.

She was back in the tunnel. She saw it go from bright to dim. It all faded to a point of light, then she felt a sudden impact. She was back in her body, then everything went dark.

II: Stranger Dreams

...JULIE moved through barren trees, light filtering through the branches. It was haunting. The mists of night trying to silence the last rays of life cutting between the bones of the forest. She couldn't remember how she got here. A chilling wind bit her naked skin, and she heard a branch snap. Was that a footstep? She heard a rustling sound. It had to be. They were getting closer. A sense of dread washed over her, and she started running. She looked back and there was a shadow darkening the carpet of leaves beneath her feet. No matter how fast she ran, it kept getting closer. She was gripped by fear. She tried to look back and tripped. When she turned and looked up, he was right on top of her. It was the man from the plane...

⟶⟨※⟩⟵

...Julie's limo pulled up in front of The Met. Her door was opened, and she stepped out onto the red carpet. This was her first premiere event, and though no one knew who she was, all the cameras were flashing. Everyone was yelling for her to pose. She was making her way around the party when a friend grabbed her and said there was someone she should meet. A charming Irishman, six feet tall, reddish-blond hair, and green eyes. As they approached the bar, the crowd parted. "Aiden O'Leary," he said, as he kissed her hand and led her to the floor. They danced the night away. They kissed by the fountain in the park. When she drew back, it was the man from the plane...

⟶⟨※⟩⟵

...She was at the rooftop bar of the Grand Bohemian and two men were chatting her up. As she laughed at one of their jokes, the bartender served her another drink, one she hadn't ordered. The bartender motioned to a man at the end of the bar. His shaded face made her feel uneasy. She turned away and found herself sitting next to the pool and was confused about her feelings of unease. She relaxed into the chair. As she stroked the water with her toes, she noticed the same man staring at her. Her head began to spin as he approached her. Before she passed out, she realized it was the man from the plane...

⟶⟨※⟩⟵

...Julie woke up, tied to a chair. She had no knowledge of how she'd gotten there. A camera was on, with a teleprompter rolling. She instinctively began to read. A man came and said her husband had failed to pay the ransom, and it was time to die. Suddenly, the FBI broke through the door. The man knocked her out. She woke up next to Aiden in the penthouse. Her reflection in the vanity was older. She and Aiden had a daughter and a newborn son. They were playing in the park now. The first spring flowers laid across

the memorial at Strawberry Fields. She was perfectly happy. The leaves turned autumn colors, winter snow began to fall, whipping to a whiteout. When the air cleared, she was back in the chair. Her captor pulled out a piano wire and began strangling her. She could see their reflection in a mirror. His mask fell off. It was the man from the plane...

...She accidentally walked into what had to be the set of a movie. The people were dressed as pilgrims. When everyone saw her, the director came and said, "You are perfect for this picture! The starring role, the Witch of the Woods!" He elaborately framed the air with his hands. "Hold out your hands." When she did, they slapped the shackles on. "I want this to be as authentic as possible. And action!" He clapped the slate. They started pricking every inch of her. She struggled against her binds. The director acted impressed. No matter what she did or said, the director would just say, "That was perfect." During the scenes of the trial, they continued to verbally abuse her. "What an Oscar-worthy performance!" He gave two thumbs up. She fought as the noose was slipped over her head. "This scene will make you a legend. You'll thank me later." He smiled and kicked the stool out from under her. Before everything went black, she recognized the face of the producer in the shadows. It was the man from the plane...

...Julie was walking on a beach. A figure appeared ahead. It was Jessica. They chatted about school and boys as they both strolled down the beach. "Wanna go for a swim?" Julie asked. With a smile as her response, they were soon jumping with the waves. Julie was suddenly caught in a rip current that rapidly took her away from shore. Her head went under regardless of how hard she fought to stay afloat. Jessica dove toward her, but as her hand brushed Julie's, something grabbed her leg and pulled her even deeper. She immediately placed her hands on her mouth to keep from drowning as long as possible. In a moment of panic, she looked to see what had dragged her down. It was a man. He ripped

her hands away from her face. She couldn't hold her breath any longer and took in a full breath of water. Before it all went dark, a face come out of the murky depths. It was the man from the plane...

...Julie was flying over a small town, but without assistance. She circled around, then flew up to the clouds. A lightning storm formed overhead, blocking her ascent. Whichever direction she tried, it spread. As she tried to round the edge, she was struck and began to fall. The ground was coming up quickly, and she landed hard. She was in a bathtub, naked, and she couldn't move. A man, a faceless man, came to her side and began running his hands all over her body. She was terrified and even though his every touch disgusted her, she couldn't move to avoid him. The man reached between her legs. Julie's breath was staggered from his intrusion. He began sucking on her nipples when she heard a knock on the door. He stood up and turned to leave the bathroom when she realized it was the man from the plane...

...She was in a bed. She was finally able to move. She thought it was still a nightmare, then she woke up...

CHAPTER 10: EMERGENCY MEASURES

I: The Horseman

MICHEAL'S FIRST THOUGHT WAS that this was impossible. But of course it was possible. He was here. He didn't think it was a coincidence that someone who sat next to him on the plane would randomly fall to the same time and place he did.

He focused on her face. He was probably too late. He noticed her feet were touching the ground. Perhaps there was still a chance. He felt he had to try to save her. If nothing else, he could give her a proper burial, as opposed to some unmarked grave.

He needed to act quickly if he was going to have any chance of resuscitating her. The crowd was still fully engaged in the spectacle; he didn't think anyone had noticed him yet. But how *was* he going to get through that massive crowd? He thought they might scatter if he could instill panic. They are superstitious. He could use that to his advantage.

Darkness turned his head to the side and let out a blow from his nostrils in the frigid air. It looked like dragon's breath. The image reminded him of the four horsemen.

How could he bring the horsemen to life? "I need dark. I need fire...." He walked Darkness back about a hundred yards into the shadow of the forest.

"It's time for battle," he told Darkness as he pulled his bandanna up below his eyes. "A demon rider for a demon horse," he declared as he pulled the cape over his head.

"One more thing to complete the effect." Darkness made calm eye contact as Micheal drew his sword down a palm of grease and prepared to set it on fire.

"Let's do this." He sparked the blade on flint and, with a roar, his sword flared with flame.

He tightened his grip on the sword and wound the reins with his left hand. He looked up in time to see two people on the outskirts of the mob turn to look at him. He raised his fiery blade above his head. He could see more people begin to turn their gaze.

Micheal pulled on the reins and reared Darkness fully back. The demon horse let out a loud cry and came down with a clap of thunder and launched into a full gallop. He could see men pointing in his direction, screaming alarm. Women were pulling their children close, rushing out of the path of this monstrous beast. The crowd went into a panic, tripping over each other in their attempts to flee.

A priest was pushing his way through the scattering masses. He stopped in between Micheal and the gallows. Micheal could see a bible in his left hand. The priest stretched out his right in a halting motion while screaming inaudibly.

"Not today." The crowd parted like the Red Sea.

Darkness was weaving through the melee with expert precision, dodging left then right, then hurtling over someone who was falling to the ground. Micheal whipped his sword like a madman and for a brief moment he wondered if he became the inspiration for the legend of the Headless Horseman. To the casual observer, Micheal would appear to have no head. His horse moves with absolute grace despite his size, and he was wielding a fiery sword.

As quickly as the thought came, it left with the shock of something striking the blade of his weapon. They were near the top of the hill, with bullets flying all around them.

He turned Darkness into the line of fire and pushed forward. The searing pain in his side indicated a bullet hit home. He felt another as he charged. He tried to ignore the burn. The thunder of his horse's stride immediately broke several of the men, making them drop their muskets before running away. Two men were ready to draw, so Micheal swung his sword right at their heads. They dove out of the way, dropping their arms in the process.

Micheal coaxed Darkness to kneel, pulled Julie's left leg over the saddle, and wrapped his left arm around her waist. As Darkness rose to his feet Micheal, cut the rope with his sword. Making sure she was fully secured in front of him, he turned to the west. His heart was beating loudly. He couldn't believe he'd done it. The clearing was empty. The whole crowd had dissipated. His thoughts quickly turned to Julie.

"We need to get out of here as soon as possible."

And with that statement, Darkness kicked to a full gallop straight out of town.

II: Emergency Measures

MICHEAL rode hard for a few minutes until he was sure no one was in pursuit. Darkness came to a halt in a small grove. He dismounted and pulled Julie to the ground. Her lifeless eyes were staring straight ahead. She was cold to the touch, and he could feel no pulse. He wasn't sure if her swollen neck was hindering his efforts. The noose was still incredibly tight and cutting into her neck. With much effort, he forced the knot loose and pulled it over her head. He cut the binds holding her hands behind her back, laid her down, and immediately began mouth-to-mouth.

After the first round, he drew a knife from his belt and, with one stroke, sliced the threads of her corset, then tore her shift open. Micheal placed his right palm over his left hand which rested above her heart and intertwined his fingers.

"One-one-thousand. Two-one-thousand. Three-one-thousand." As he counted the compressions, Darkness paced in circles, keeping a constant perimeter of security around Julie while Micheal counted and continued mouth-to-mouth. Just as he was about to give up, she began to cough. Her eyes blinked a few times, and she started breathing regularly. After a moment, her eyes fluttered closed again, and she seemed to go unconscious.

He was genuinely surprised and relieved. But how much permanent damage had she sustained? He had noticed her toes touching the ground. But who knew how long it had been since she had taken a breath?

Micheal listened to her breathing. While labored, it was better than he expected. Her swollen neck and wrists made it difficult to feel her pulse. He pressed two fingers to the center of her chest and found a stable rhythm.

He inspected her bluish-purple hue. He could only imagine the hell she must have experienced.

She was still in danger; he needed his medical equipment at the Homestead. Over the next few minutes, he could see her breath and felt her pulse, her vitals remained stable. So he wrapped her in his cloak, mounted up, and headed for home.

The afternoon sun beaming through the windmill signaled their arrival at Homestead. As he was about to enter the house, a ray lit up her face. Filth covered every inch of her, but her color was much improved.

Upon laying her down in the bathroom, she was cold to the touch. He didn't want to raise her core temperature too quickly. He turned on the cold-water faucet, then added some hot water. As the tub filled with lukewarm water, he slowly removed what was left of her corset, as well as her skirt. Now that his adrenaline was back to normal, embarrassment washed over him as he let the tattered remains of her shift drop to the floor.

He averted his eyes. He had never seen a woman naked in person before, let alone touched one.

Micheal retrieved the bar of soap from his sink, along with a few clean pieces of cloth.

His first concern was any injuries that might need urgent care. He bathed her gently, making sure to inspect her for any maladies. The bruise around her neck was the most obvious, but she was covered in scabs and lacerations, and there were deep bruises around her wrists and ankles.

"What the hell happened to you? These look like marks made by crude shackles..." Micheal carefully turned Julie's wrists to wash the dried blood off.

"It looks like they had you in those for some time." He saw similar injuries on her ankles. A quick rush of anger came at the thought of anyone doing this to Julie. He let out another deep sigh and focused on the sore on her stomach.

"What is this? This has festered. It's small but..." He looked at her face. Her eyes were closed, as if she was sleeping. "Who the hell could have done this to you?"

Micheal finished by cleaning the infection on the sole of her foot. He began to wonder how she had survived these injuries for so long. She was obviously malnourished and dehydrated.

Micheal gently patted her body dry then carried her into the bedroom.

"I cleaned it up all nice just for you." He laid her on the bed and pulled the blanket up to her chest.

He wrapped rags packed with snow around her neck, wrists, and ankles.

The infection in her left foot still looked bad.

Before placing the cold cloth over her eyes, he opened them. Her pupil response was encouraging. While she appeared to be in a light coma, there were clear signs of brain function. She was breathing on her own, so chances for recovery were good.

Micheal looked down at this sleeping beauty. "If you don't wake up soon, you probably never will." *And there's absolutely no way a kiss from me would do the trick.*

III: Intensive Care

MICHEAL realized Julie likely wouldn't survive even a short coma due to dehydration. He needed some way to get her moisture. He went to work crafting his solution out of some of his raw plastic. First, he made two thin sheets that he worked into soft bowls. Soldering them together to create a pouch.

Next, he fashioned a piece of metal to have a hole approximately one-half inch in diameter, in the center. But he left a smaller round piece in the middle of the opening, about a quarter of an inch wide.

When he forced liquid plastic through the opening, what came out was a tube that was split open on one side. After soldering the gap closed, he had himself a decent I/V pouch and tube. He completed the essential equipment with one of a couple of needles he had crafted to administer the Penicillin he had finally finished synthesizing.

Micheal's new antibiotics had proved their muster against infection. And after inspecting Julie's foot, it might be the only way to save it from becoming gangrenous.

He then processed a saline solution to help with the threat of dehydration. All these tasks took many hours, but it was necessary.

Was his new I/V going to work? He took a moment to reflect on how beneficial all those years of medical research were to his current situation. And while he had failed his family, maybe Julie could benefit from his efforts.

The days passed, and Micheal spent them caring for Julie. He kept the I/V pouch full and rinsed and re-bandaged her wounds until he saw the signs of infection clear up. The only wound that still required more time was the one on her foot.

Micheal sat by her bed and took her hand in his, observing how much the bruises had faded from her wrist. He checked her vitals, all normal. The more time passed, the more normal and beautiful she became.

Rising to leave, he reached out and traced the deep purple ring around her neck. "I had hoped you would have awakened by now." And with that, he left her to her slumber.

There was a loud scrape. Micheal let out a light grunt, cleared his throat a bit, and resumed singing his favorite song by another artist, Wind of Change by Scorpions.

While making his way to a small wheelbarrow, he saw the white mare jump slightly and come down with a steady beat. Her hooves making a thudded drum. And he resumed the tune.

Angel's step came in again, two steady thumps, as he dumped the last of the manure. He leaned the shovel just inside the supply room and grabbed a pitchfork, then he continued singing.

Without fail, her legs came down on beat, her white main flowing and whipping down. This time with a series of stomps. This was one of Micheal's favorite times. Singing, with his friend providing well-needed backup. He stepped to her, ran his hand down her face, and scratched under her chin. Not to be outdone in the affection department, Angel nickered and began to nuzzle him.

Darkness was not going to let Micheal forget the task at hand. Suddenly, and quite silently, Micheal felt Darkness push on his back.

"Hey, boy..."

Resting the handle of the barn tool on his chest, he reached for Darkness' chin. He saw the horse take a step back, pull away from Micheal's reach, and shake his head, his mane tossing about wildly.

"I know..." Micheal grabbed the pitchfork and headed to the feed stall. He took a good chunk of hay out of a pile in the back. He had regularly purchased bundles of hay from the market in Concord. "Okay. Here's what I'm thinking." With a quick and short swing, he tossed the hay into Angel's stall and began to spread it about.

"First, I'm going to take my mother's maiden name."

Darkness watched as Micheal walked back and forth with a fork full of hay. Micheal thought he saw a bit of confusion in his eyes.

"It's well-known and respected. It's English as opposed to Norse, and it'll go with the persona I've come up with. I could easily portray myself as a math or science professor."

While the surname Hall did exist in England, it was obscure, as most of the English Halls had moved to Scotland shortly after the establishment of the house, just after the Norman Conquest. Hall was a highly prominent surname in Micheal's Father's ancestral place of origin in Norway. But Whitaker was one of the oldest and most respected surnames in England.

His voice faded and came back as he walked more hay to Angel's stall.

"It would be extremely beneficial to have an identity with some authority. I mean, a position as a professor somewhere would help boost my social standing. So," he hurled the last of the hay intended for Angel's quarters, walked over to Darkness, stuck the pitchfork in the ground, leaned on the handle, and continued, "I'm thinking. Harvard. What do you think, Angel?" he asked as he spun around to meet her gaze. "Professor Micheal W. Whitaker."

She was always Micheal's biggest fan, so it was not surprising to him that she approved of his new identity. She gave a blow and nosed his outstretched hand.

"She's on board! Wadda ya say, Darkness?"

Darkness was still for a moment, tilting his head slightly. Micheal knew that look and let out a deep sigh.

"I know..." He took the pitchfork back to the supply closet and walked out with a bag of oats for Angel as the last part of his routine. As he made his way to her stall, he turned to Darkness with a bit of a tilt in his head, as well.

"Yeah, I'm working on it. I have the certificate complete, for the most part. I just need to perfect the signatures," he explained, referring to the mathematics and science degree from Cambridge Trinity he needed to forge.

Micheal had seen an image of Isaac Newton's degree from Trinity in 1665, during his study of another of history's greatest minds. And through that, he had happened to come across a list of the Masters of Trinity. So he knew the current Master was John Montagu.

He poured the feed into Angel's trough and resumed his explanation. "And the seal should be ready tonight." He gave Angel another scratch, this time behind her ear. "The stagecoach is nearly complete. Another week and it'll be ready. But we'll need a lot more funds once we arrive in Boston." His thoughts turned to worry. He walked over to Darkness and pet him.

"I'll have to make another run or two for more gold and the rest of the silver." Micheal then took the empty bag, wrapped it around his hand, folded it, and placed it in a bucket hanging on the wall near his stall.

"Julie's been in a coma for nearly a week." Micheal stared at the ground. His horses listened as they had learned to do.

"If she doesn't come out of it soon, she may be in a coma indefinitely. I don't know the extent of the damage done." He looked up to see Angel slowly stride to Darkness' side.

"I could never leave her—and I don't think I can just let her die." The thought of having to pull the plug made Micheal feel very sad. He hoped he wouldn't have to make that choice.

Darkness let out a huff that broke the thoughts Micheal had been slipping into. His loyal friend could always be counted on to stay on task. He smiled at his horses, brushed off bits of hay from his pants, and gave them one last loving scratch behind their ears before heading inside.

The Massachusett were in need of supplies, and Micheal's word was his bond. It would, however, be a five-day round trip and the thought of leaving Julie unattended shook him to the core.

Micheal wasn't sure what to do. He dithered between the horses, Julie, and back again. He shook out and refolded the sets of women's clothing he'd made a day's journey to Concord for.

He finished saddling Darkness, then a muffled noise came from the house. He looked up, and the door opened.

PART THREE: COLONIAL LORDS

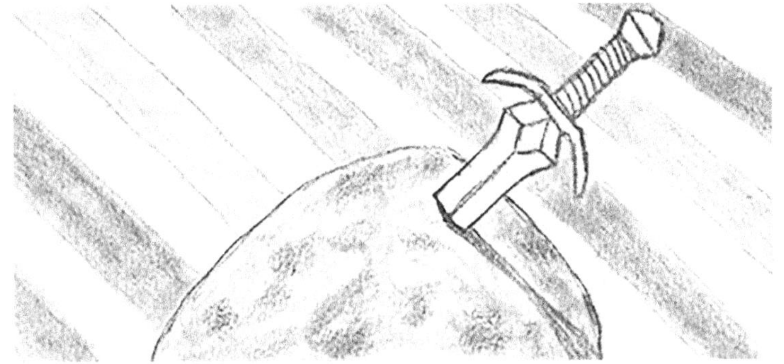

CHAPTER 11: AWKWARD INTRODUCTION

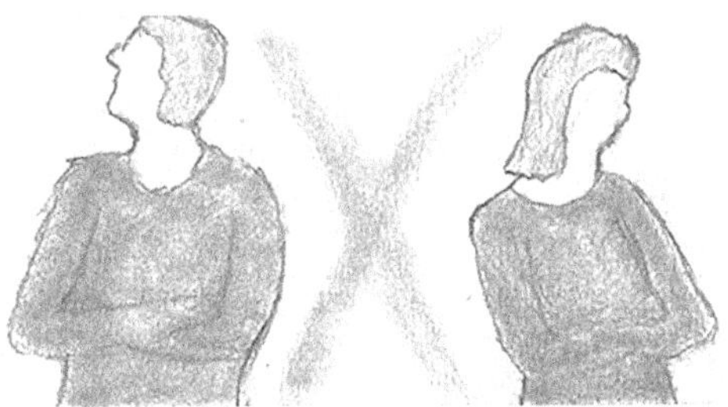

JULIE BECAME AWARE OF her surroundings. Her back was sore, and it was quiet save for a lone bird she could hear chirping. The smell of lavender filled the room as she slowly opened her eyes. The light was blinding; she had to close them again. As she blinked them open, the room began to come into focus. It had to be a cabin. Her bare skin against the blanket evoked questions about how she got here. Wherever here was. She looked to her right and a shock of pain ran up her neck. She felt a bruise that went all the way around.

There was a plate of food that made her stomach growl. She felt so hungry she could die. As she began to move, she realized there was something in the back of her left hand. It was an I/V tube. Removing the needle, she attempted to sit up; her head began to spin, so she laid back down. Focusing on her breath, eyes closed, she worked to steady herself, then tried again. She sat up and squeezed her eyes to tamp down another dizzy spell. Then opened them all the way, sat up, and felt her toes touch the floor.

The food consisted of what looked like oatmeal and scrambled eggs. There were two cups of liquid. One smelled like some kind of soup, the other was water. Before she could stop to think about any possible malfeasance, she devoured everything.

Feeling better, her surroundings came more into focus. The room was modest, perhaps ten by fifteen feet, with a large closet at the end. Aside from the bed, two nightstands made a vain effort to fill the empty space. On top of a dresser was a stack of clothes. The sight reminded her of her lack thereof.

Julie began to put weight on her right foot; it wanted to betray her. Stretching her tired limb brought a question. How long had she been out? She was about to go gingerly on her left foot and was surprised to find it felt normal, even if every muscle in her body was aching.

Her calf began to cramp, making her stumble over to the dresser. The clothes appeared to be from the Middle Ages. There was what she supposed was the undergarment, sleeker but similar to the one they had dressed her in. That sparked all sorts of terrible memories.

She felt the bite of the shackles on her wrists and the chill of her dungeon cell washed down her spine. A thousand needle pricks took their turn. Then she felt the noose tighten.

Julie looked around defensively. They could come back at any time. Standing there, naked and vulnerable, she searched the dresser. It was empty. Finding no other choice, she slipped on the underwear from the stack of folded clothing. The next piece appeared to be a skirt. It looked as if the clothes were laid out for her in sequence. The flowing black skirt was a challenge, but she was able to wrap it, then tie it off. The next piece looked like a corseted bodice with sleeves. It was dark purple with black ties. It took a bit of effort, but she was able to thread the ties.

While weak from the coma and still shaken from the shock of a strange place, her goal was to leave. And as soon as possible. After securing the corset, she walked to the door. She reached for the knob but was frozen in place. She didn't know what would be on the other side. She hoped it was freedom. However, her last experience taught her to throw away any scrap of hope.

Guided by desperation, with one motion, she turned the handle and pulled the door open. If there was going to be a person on the other side, she wanted to have the upper hand.

There was no one. Julie stood in place for a moment, trying to hear footsteps, people talking, something to give her a clue as to where her captor might be. But she saw no one.

Her first step led her to a better view of the room just outside her door. A sudden urgency caused her to quickly step into the bathroom she saw to her left. As she cleaned herself up, she saw a pale reflection in the mirror above the sink. She tried to find recognition there but failed.

Julie moved back to the matter at hand. Where was she? The cabin was tidy and spartan and a confusing mix of details—some very old, some completely implausible. Like her memories... There were some things that she was sure of, but others that were muddled. Much of it felt like it had been inside her dreams or, more accurately, inside her nightmares. By the end of the trial, she had begun to entertain the idea that she had somehow fallen through time. Now she wasn't so sure.

Wasn't this cabin proof of that? The I/V in her room...even this bathroom was a piece of the future. Her future. The thought frightened her, and she immediately pushed it to the side. This wasn't the past. This was the present and her only goal was to get the hell out of here and return to Aiden.

She reached for the handle and again stood frozen. What if they can see me?

How much more of this could she take? Would this continue forever? It couldn't. It mustn't. She pulled the door open and made her way into a large room where she saw what appeared to be a kitchen beyond the fireplace at the far end of the room. A table and chairs were strewn about, some near the fireplace, and to her right was a bed in the corner. There was a door that looked to lead outside. Julie's heart beat faster.

She was afraid that the cult leader would jump out of nowhere at any instant and this would all turn out to be just part of the nightmare she'd lived through. She crossed the room with caution and opened the door slowly. The light was blinding at first, but soon things began to move into focus. She was able to make out a figure. It was him. It was the cult leader. It was the man from the plane.

Terror and rage filled Julie. She considered fleeing but didn't think she could escape from him. She'd confront him. She noticed the rifle next to the door. Perhaps she would kill him after she got some answers.

The man came around a large horse. "I'm so glad—" He stopped in his tracks.

"You evil bastard. You deserve to die for what you've done to me!"

"Huh?" He was playing stupid.

"You drugged me! You kidnapped me and probably raped me! You threw me to your cult, who tortured me and hung me as a witch. Then you bring me back from the brink of death to do it all over again. Do you want me for your bride? Was this some kind of initiation ritual? Well, it's not going to work." Her finger urged to squeeze the trigger.

"Well, if I did all of that to you, then you really should kill me."

"What do you mean, if?"

"Well, I didn't do any of that. And whoever did is likely responsible for both of us."

Julie became angry again. "I'm not going to believe your lies. Why did you try to make me think it was the Salem Witch trials? And why 1692?"

He chuckled. "Wait, after everything you've seen, you still don't know it really is 1692?"

"That's what you want me to believe."

"Why do you think I'm the one who did this to you? The only time I was ever around you or said anything to you was on the plane."

"Exactly! I'm supposed to believe you 'accidentally' sat next to me and then I coincidentally disappeared from my hotel room and ended up in a random field on my own?"

Julie had an odd memory flash. "I saw you at the bar... You were the one molesting me in the bath..." It felt like memories and dreams were blurring together. She inhaled to steady herself. "I was completely naked in your bed! Did my clothes just fall off?"

"Uh..." His face flushed and his eyes fluttered. "I'm sorry, you were filthy, I had to clean you up."

"You *had* to?"

He stammered for a second. "Yeh...Yes! You were covered in dirt. I needed to know if there were any cuts that needed tending. And to prevent infection."

She'd noted that her two worst sores were basically healed, the one on her foot and the one on her stomach.

"This is not how I saw this conversation going," he shook his head. "But I'm running late. I have to go."

She wasn't sure what was real, some of the things she thought were real now felt more like dreams. "What do you mean, 'How you thought this would go'?"

He shrugged, snorted, and rolled his eyes. "Now thinking about it, I guess I should have expected this. Of course, if *I* try to do something to help someone, it all blows up in my face."

She couldn't figure out if it was all an act. For the first time, she was beginning to doubt he was the one responsible.

Then, he looked at her and said, "Oh, I stupidly thought I might get thanked for saving you, for caring for you. But it doesn't matter. I'm glad you're feeling better. I have to go." He turned to the horse.

Her pulse was pounding. "Don't move! Where do you think you're going?" her voice trembled.

"Look, there are people who are depending on me. If you're going to shoot me then shoot me. I have to go."

Julie wasn't sure what to do. She now had so much doubt. Could she really shoot someone? Especially someone she now thought more likely innocent than not. As she started to lower the weapon, her finger clipped the trigger. She was stunned by the loud pop. She looked up, and he had blood streaming down the side of his face.

In a calm voice, he said, "You missed. Do you want me to reload so you can try again?"

She looked at the gun and dropped it.

MICHEAL touched the side of his face; the bullet had grazed his temple, starting at the corner of his eye. He looked back at her as she dropped the gun and was beginning to cry.

"Don't worry about it. It's nothing. You just grazed me," he reassured her.

He could tell she had likely never fired a gun before. She was in shock. He wanted to try to make her feel better, but he checked the sky and saw that he was already late.

"Look, I'll be gone for four or five days. I'll understand if you're not here when I get back."

"You're leaving me here alone?"

He rubbed a hand over his face. "First, I'm some kind of cult leader who did unspeakable things to you. Then, I molested you in the tub. And now, you don't want me to go?" He threw up his hands and gave an exasperated laugh.

"Well, I don't want to be left here by myself."

"I'm not keeping you here."

"Where would I go? I don't even know where *here* is."

He sighed. "Okay, so the closest decent-sized settlement is Concord. It's about five miles up the river to the north. Boston is about fifteen miles that way," he said, pointing to the east.

"When you've gathered your strength, you can take Angel and any supplies you need along with the rest of the silver—"

"Silver?"

"There's about thirty pounds of silver from my last haul. It will help you get established in Boston."

"Where did you get thirty pounds of silver?"

"It doesn't matter. Just take what you need and good luck to you."

Micheal prepared to mount up. "I'll come with you." Julie surprised him.

He knew literally nothing about women, but her see-sawing attitude toward him was giving him whiplash.

"You don't want to do that."

"Why not?"

"You're in no condition to ride on your own. You'd have to ride with me, and I wouldn't want to subject you to that."

"Subject me to what?"

How could she not realize? "You'd have to ride with me, you'd have to sit in front of me, and you would be in close contact with me."

She tilted her head to the side and said, "So?"

He felt he should better explain. "While I'm not the monster you believed me to be, I am repulsive. I'm sure you don't want to be in such close contact with me."

"You're not repulsive. And I don't want to stay here alone. So I'm coming with you."

He folded his arms. "Okay then. Don't say I didn't warn you. Now, let's get you ready to ride. We really do have to hurry."

Once inside, JULIE could see he still had blood down the side of his face. "Oof. I am so sorry for shooting you... There's something I never thought I'd say."

"Oh, I'm sure it looks worse than it is. Don't even worry about it."

She was incredulous. "Here, sit down." He obeyed. She cleaned the blood off his face.

After she was dressed for riding. She caught a glimpse of herself in the bathroom mirror. She looked closer and almost didn't recognize herself. She came into the main room as he was finishing packing for the road.

"I think I'm ready."

"Not quite. You need to cover that," he said, pointing at her neck. "Use one of the scarves I got for you."

As they walked out the front door, he turned to her. "You probably don't remember my name. I'm Micheal."

"It's nice to meet you, Micheal. My name is Julie."

I: Keeping Promises

JULIE watched Micheal walk over to the big black horse and give it an apple. "Hey Darkness, I'm going to need some extra effort today." He patted him on the neck and said, "Now boy, this is Julie. She's a friend." The horse seemed to look at her for a moment.

"His name is what?"

"Darkness." He clicked his tongue and pointed to the ground. Darkness knelt, then Micheal said, "Climb on, my lady."

Once in the saddle, he gave the order and Darkness rose. As he mounted behind her, she felt a bit anxious and tensed with surprise at the assertiveness with which he wrapped his left arm around her waist. He clicked his tongue and yelled, "Yah!" And Darkness began to trot.

Julie's thoughts were scattered. So many things had happened. As Darkness slowed his pace, she felt she needed more answers. She just didn't know what questions to ask. She was skeptical about this entire situation.

"So...the year is 1692?" She didn't know what else to say. She guessed that she just needed someone to talk to—about everything. "We...time traveled?"

"Yes, and yes."

"How do you know what year it is for sure?"

"After I woke up in that field, I went to a nearby village, where, in one of the houses I found correspondence dated between late 1691 and early 1692."

"You really believe time travel is possible?" She was still trying to convince herself.

"I always knew it was possible. I just never expected it would actually happen to me."

"But that cabin had plumbing. The I/V? The windmill?"

"I made it all."

"You made it all?... How long have you been here?"

"About two months. And yes, all of it. Now, we need to get our seventeenth-century faces on. Try not to speak unless spoken to, and if you must speak, try to fake the accent."

"Yes, sir!" she saluted sarcastically.

They stopped at a crossroads. A man rode up to greet them.

"Good morrow, Master Gardiner, how does all at home?" Micheal said in greeting.

She was surprised how naturally authentic he seemed.

Gardiner tipped his cap and replied, "What cheer Master Whitaker, Mistress Whitaker." Julie felt odd being addressed in such a fashion. She hadn't even taken Aiden's name when they were married.

"All be well, this be my son John." John tipped his cap as well.

"Good morrow, friend John."

The Gardiners guided them to a caravan of six horses packed with supplies.

"How fare the road of Boston?" Micheal inquired.

"We made good speed."

As Micheal inspected the caravan, Julie decided to walk around a little bit. She saw people coming and going about their business. Many smiled at her and said "good morrow" or tipped their caps. She didn't think it was possible that a secret cult could control so much area.

It is, it's 1692. Her heart sank at the firm realization. All of her hopes of getting back to her family, to Aiden, were dashed. What was she going to do now?

As she returned to the crossroads, she heard Micheal say, "I thank thee most kindly." He handed Gardiner a bag of silver.

"Your servant, sir."

"Sir, I am yours." Micheal finished.

As they headed out of Concord, Julie wondered how Micheal was able to sound so spot-on. If she hadn't heard his normal manner of speech, she would never suspect he wasn't from the seventeenth century.

It was now sundown and Micheal had barely spoken to her since leaving the cabin. After they set up camp, he went to tend the horses. A silent dinner followed, then Micheal immediately went to sleep. She was so exhausted from the long day she did as well.

They rode most of the next day in silence. She had been so caught up processing the idea of time travel she never thought to ask before. "Where are we going?"

"To visit the Massachusett."

"*The* Massachusett? I don't understand."

"A local tribe of Native Americans. They have a village in the hills near the New York border."

He was full of surprises. "Friends of yours?"

"Yes. A couple of weeks ago, I was headed to Albany when I happened to meet them. Following an initial misunderstanding, I saw they were in dire straits, and I promised to return with enough supplies to get them through the rest of the winter."

"Now you are going to all this trouble on their behalf?"

"Yeah, so?"

"Just out of curiosity, how much did all this cost you?"

"I don't know, two hundred pounds of silver."

She just about said, "Holy shit!" but was able to hold it in. She calculated the value at maybe north of fifty thousand dollars in 2010.

Before she could say anything else, two men stepped out from the trees. She was surprised again when Michael began conversing with them in their language. He said something, and they all laughed. They each greeted her, grabbed something off one of the horses, took the reins, and began guiding them into the village.

"You never told me you could speak their language."

"How did you think I communicated with them?"

"I don't know. They had someone who could translate."

"They do, but—"

"How could you possibly speak their language?"

He seemed to get irritable. "I read something a while back about how to translate Algonquian into English. Their language is in the Algonquian family. I was able to utilize that to build a framework and the more I heard of it, the more I could begin to fill in the gaps."

At that point, the entire village had come out to greet them, and they were ushered into a longhouse. All she could do was sit and watch. He translated for her whenever someone addressed her directly, but most of the time, she sat quietly.

There was a feast and storytelling around the fire. Micheal took a turn, to the great amusement of everyone. After that, he left with a couple of men.

Julie felt abandoned. The people were all engaged in jovial discourse, and she felt invisible. She stepped out for fresh air. She wrapped her blanket tight and looked to the stars.

"My fathers watch over us from above." Chief Nightwolf joined her.

"You speak English?"

"When I was young, I learned the language of the guardians."

"Who are the guardians?"

"I could see you were new to the family. Your husband speaks our words, but you do not."

Julie didn't know what to say. "He has not spoken of this role."

"I can see why you were chosen. It takes a special person to accept this role. The gift of intelligence was bestowed upon you by the great spirit. I am pleased by your protection. You will find your place amongst them. I hope you are comfortable here. Now I should get back." Nightwolf entered the longhouse, she followed.

The night became late, and they were shown to their private sleeping quarters.

She saw the single cot in the tiny hut, looked at Micheal, and asked, "I thought everyone slept together in longhouses? I thought I saw that somewhere."

"They wanted to accommodate our cultural differences, to give us 'privacy.'"

A pit formed in Julie's stomach and feelings of unease came over her as the walls seemed to begin to shrink. "I don't think—"

"Of course I know you would never do anything like that with me. But they think you're my wife. You don't have to worry; I'll take the ground. But we do need to pretend we're, yah know." He raised and lowered his eyebrows quickly. She started to get angry, then he broke out in a laugh. "I'm kidding, relax. I promise nothing will happen in the night." He laid down and fell asleep.

The entire village became silent. But Julie was still awake with her thoughts. She still knew nearly nothing about Micheal; he'd barely spoken to her during their two-day ride, and usually only when she spoke to him. Despite her initial thoughts about him, which were clouded by what she realized must have been coma dreams, she was impressed by his seemingly unconscious generosity and ability to forgive things others did to him.

She knew some of it was based on his obvious depression, but she thought it went deeper than that. It seemed to be his true baseline nature.

He also seemed to be intentionally keeping her at a distance. She wasn't sure why, but it was beginning to make her feel all alone again. Here in 1692.

II: The Choice

MICHEAL did feel bad for how he was keeping Julie at arm's length, but it was for the best. When they got back to Homestead, he would help her get established somewhere. Then he would be back on track. He knew she would feel out of place for a while, but once she accepted her new reality, he felt she would be able to make a good life for herself here in the seventeenth century.

He helped Julie down from Darkness and said, "Go get cleaned up. You can have whatever food is inside. Angel and Darkness need tending. This might take a while. You don't have to wait for me."

As Micheal tended the horses, he thought about what he would have to do about Julie. He had originally thought that when she woke up, he would give her whatever she needed, and she would go on her way. He knew how intelligent she was. Despite how difficult this century was for single women; she would be just fine. Certainly better than if she was with him.

At that moment, Julie walked into the barn. Her aspect nearly took his breath away. Her giant turquoise eyes in the mellow light almost seemed to glow. Her shoulder-length, dark-brown hair was loose about her face, contrasted with the red bodice and yellow skirt. He took a deep breath to steady himself.

"I thought you would've been asleep by now," Micheal would have preferred that.

"You must be hungry. I made dinner."

"Really? You didn't have to do that." It would be rude to refuse.

"It was my pleasure. See you inside?"

JULIE set the table while Micheal cleaned himself up. She had found some meat and vegetables and made a stew, used some apples to make a strudel, and she found something that looked like some kind of apple-flavored beverage.

He came into the main room wearing fresh clothes. "Wow. This looks amazing. Allow me," he said, grabbing her chair.

"Thank you." She sat down.

As he took a seat, it occurred to her this was the most normal thing she had done since this whole crazy situation began. It felt good, at least for the moment.

Wanting to keep that feeling as long as possible, she steered the conversation to trivial subjects like music and movies. They had a particularly deep breakdown of the last movie they had both seen, James Cameron's *Avatar*. By the time they moved on to dessert, the conversation had sort of died.

After not saying anything for a few minutes, he cleared his throat and said, "There's something I need to talk to you about."

She knew those were usually not words you want to hear. "Okay, what's that?"

"We need to discuss your future, what you plan to do now that you're back on your feet."

She had been contemplating this since Concord, where she had confirmed in her own mind that it really was 1692. "I don't know. I don't know the history very well. What are you going to do? Live here?"

"No... But it doesn't matter. We're talking about you."

She could tell he had something in mind for himself, so she continued to pursue it. "It does matter. I need to know what you're planning, so I know what my options are. You're not staying here. Where else would you go?"

He seemed to consider whether to tell her or not. "Okay... I've been planning to move to Boston. I just needed to create a believable backstory."

She considered that for a second. "So you move to Boston and just live the rest of your life there? In the seventeenth century?"

He seemed about to say something, then stopped.

Ever the reporter, she kept prodding. "No. There's something you're not telling me. What are you planning?"

"This is about your future, not mine."

"No. This is about both of our futures. What don't you want to tell me?"

He seemed unused to being pushed so hard. "I didn't want to influence your decision with false hope but if you want to know my plan, it's this: I will move to Boston—or even London if I must—to gain access to whatever I think will help me figure out how this happened to me, to us, and how I can get home."

"Is it really possible?" her heart began to rise.

"Anything's *possible*. But *probable*? No. I don't have anything else to do while I'm here. But you could have a real life. I know it's hard, but once you realize you're not going to be able to get back, you can find someone here who you can love, maybe have children—"

"You're telling me to move on, to forget about Aiden and my family?"

He rubbed his hand across his face. "No, I didn't mean it like that. I just—"

"Maybe you can move on from the people you care about that easily, but I can't!" Tears came to her eyes. "You say you have nothing else to do? Well, I have something else you can do. You can go to hell!"

He looked away, like he was gathering his thoughts. "I'm sorry. I know I'm a terrible person." She was about to cut in, but he raised his hand to stop her.

"No, it's true. Which was the point I was trying to make earlier." She considered interjecting again, but he gave her a look to stem any further discussion on *that* matter. "I was just trying to explain that you need to make a decision about who you are. I don't know if you understand the intricacies of seventeenth-century society. Once we affirm who you are, it's difficult to change."

"Why can't I just be me?"

"Do you know much about history?"

She had lived in the present her whole life. History had always bored her.

"Well, not a lot."

"The culture here is quite different from ours, particularly for women, which is why I have to help you get established."

She rolled her eyes in annoyance. She remembered, "Of course I need a man to take care of me!" He just stared at her until she said, "I'm sorry, please continue."

"I didn't want you to cling to a pipe dream of getting home. I was worried it would cloud your judgment—"

She raised her hand to stop him. "I'm curious to hear what you think the odds are against it."

"I'm not going to call myself an expert but, I've studied temporal mechanics since I was young and let's pretend I'm really as smart as I always claimed to be—"

"Wait, I'm just curious. How smart did you always claim to be?" Julie had to force back a grin.

"Well..." Micheal stammered. "...I always said I was a modern-day Leonardo da Vinci." He rubbed his face. Then continued. "But I digress... I would say maybe one in a million? And even then, it would probably take most of the rest of my life."

She believed he was truly saying what he thought the odds were.

"You think it's really that slim?"

"Yes. I'm sorry. I will simplify the choice you have to make. Option one: we make you a backstory, you take most of the gold and whatever other supplies you need, and you go on your way. I know how intelligent and resourceful you are. With that kind of money, you would be fine. Or two: you pose as my sister, come to Boston with me, and when you are ready, in a year or so, you marry some upper-class gentlemen and have a real life."

"You want me to forget about Aiden and marry someone else?"

"I never said forget about Aiden. He will always be a part of you. I know it's a difficult situation, but you will have to marry someone."

"The hell I will!"

"You will if you want any kind of social life. I'm not going to make you do anything you don't want to do. If you want to be a celibate spinster for the rest of your life, I won't stop you. I will even help you if that's what you want!"

"You forgot option number three."

"Option number three?"

"I go with you and we try to figure this out together."

He shook his head. "That's the last thing you want to do."

"I know the odds but—"

He held up his hand again. "No, you're better off without me."

She was getting annoyed. "Why do you—"

"It's the truth. If we do what you suggest, you'd have to pretend to be my wife. And we both know that's the last thing you'd want to do."

She decided not to argue with his negative comments. "Why would I have to be your wife?"

He came out of his malaise. "The only single women of age, not including girls, are usually prostitutes. Unmarried girls usually live with their father. Unmarried men and women don't live together."

"I could be your sister."

"You could, but then you would be pursued by every eligible man in the colonies. And if you rejected them all, people would think something was wrong with you. You would be a social pariah. You might think you won't care, but I know what it's like to be a loner. I'm used to it, but most people want a social life."

She was already tired, and his constant self-denigration was exhausting.

"So, I'm your sister if I want to move on. I'm your wife if I hope to get home? What about you?"

"What about me?"

"If I pretend to be your wife, won't that prevent you from having any intimate relationships? Maybe you would want to marry at some point."

He laughed out loud. "That's funny."

"What's funny?"

He laughed again.

"Married? The only way a woman would marry me was if I were rich. And while I suppose that's more possible here than in our own time, I don't think I would ever do that. And the only way a woman might share a bed is if I paid them, so don't worry about my nonexistent sex life. If it hasn't happened by now, it probably never will."

She was stunned and felt terrible. She could tell he was beyond embarrassed but couldn't help herself. "You're a—"

"A virgin," he finished her sentence. "I'm sure you already guessed by looking at me." He rose from the table, grabbed the blanket off the bed, and said, "Good night, my lady." And walked out the door. Through the window, she saw him going into the barn.

As she made her way to her bed, Julie tried to organize all the information. At the heart of it was the choice he presented to her. Could she accept that she'd lost Aiden and everything she loved to have a "real life" as he had put it? Or could she accept being in a state of suspended animation on a fool's hope to get home, and risk never truly living again? She was too tired to even think about it. She would need more time and consideration to make 'the choice'.

CHAPTER 12: PREPARATIONS

MICHEAL HAD NEVER BEEN so embarrassed in his entire life. The discussion had turned into a total debacle. As he lay in his makeshift bed, he wondered if she was still laughing at him.

He did his best to put those thoughts aside by distracting himself with his latest project. The kinetic energy extractor. He got up and went to work.

During the night, he'd dreamt about energy. From the type one uses to raise an apple and take a bite to the type that is in the air all around us. He saw currents of particles as they wove around and through one another. They all coalesced into what he could only describe as a plus and minus sign on its ends. A magnet. He needed a magnetic component for his channeler. Over the next hour or so, he worked the meteorite he had acquired and refined the mineral he needed: Magnetite. Unlike the lodestone variation, this would have a softer magnetism.

He spent countless hours on efforts to realize his midnight inspiration. He hardly slept or ate. He didn't want any distraction to derail the momentum of his progress.

Micheal installed his latest version, which was about the size of a toothpick, perpendicular above the test plate, a quarter-size copper disc.

As he pulled the lever, he said, "And then there was light."

And with that, a spark lit up the needle.

JULIE spent the next two days exploring the house. Micheal seemed to be avoiding her since the argument on the night they got back. The modern comforts he had engineered into the house gave her a feeling of normality. Simple things like cooking or sitting by the fire with a hot cup of tea made a world of difference.

As Julie lay in a hot bath, eyes closed with a warm folded cloth over her face, she imagined she was back in New York, and this was all some horrible nightmare. She thought of seeing Aiden when she opened her eyes. Thought of him joining her in this soothing bath. He'd be there, and he'd take her in his arms.

Suddenly she slipped, caught herself by gripping the rim, swiping the towel off her face in panic, her eyes finally opening, and all she saw was her seventeenth-century reality. The thought of Aiden only solidified the decision she had already made. She would hold on to hope no matter the odds, come what may.

But what about Micheal? She had so many questions, and he was the only one that had any answers. She wasn't sure if she wanted to intrude on his solitude, so she decided to let him come around on his own time.

She dressed and made dinner. When Micheal still hadn't come back from the barn, she went to find him. After checking the stables with no luck, she tried the door at the end. She came through the door to what appeared to be some kind of lab. She saw him experimenting on something.

"What are you doing?"

He seemed surprised. "Oh! Uh, Julie. It's just something I've been working on. What's up?"

"I was worried about you. Have you been eating?"

"I don't know? A little something here and there," he shrugged.

She touched his shoulder. "Come to dinner."

MICHEAL got cleaned up and nervously approached the table. He stood as Julie entered with some kind of casserole.

"Wow, that looks amazing."

"It's oyster fricassee, my mom's recipe," she said with a smile. "It almost makes it feel like home," she added as she sat down. "I want to apologize, I—"

"You have nothing to apologize for."

"Then how come I haven't seen you in two days?"

"I've been working on a problem. I had an...inspiration about how to solve it. I've been pushing nonstop since to see if it worked."

"And did it?"

"It doesn't matter. How have you been?"

She looked as if she might pursue an answer to her inquiry, then she said, "I have come to a decision. I don't care what the odds are, I won't give up on the ones I love." She hesitated for a second, then continued. "Despite how certain you are that you will never get married. I don't want to—"

"Don't even worry about it. So you want to pose as my wife?"

She took a deep breath, then said, "Yes." She seemed a little unsure.

"Well, if you ever decide you do want to marry, I will help you, no matter what it takes."

"And I will—" He tried to cut her off, but she said, "No! I promise the same." She gave him a look to stem any further argument.

"Okay then, we need to get you ready."

"Hold that thought." She rose and disappeared into the kitchen and returned with a pie. "My grandma's famous peanut pie." She served him a piece, then said, "What do I need to do?"

I: Seventeenth Century Lady

Over the next week or so, JULIE was put through a crash course in colonial etiquette. She worked on her accent, learned proper greeting, and common speech patterns. Micheal taught her the history of the times, explained the political dynamics of the region, and warned her of the potential dangers. If only he had been there to warn her at the beginning, she wouldn't have had to go through all that hell.

He even taught her some of the more common dances of society, including: the Minuet, the Allemande, the Contredanse, and the Assemble. He was a very good dancer.

He guided her steps across the ground. "And present and curtsy, face me and curtsy, come together, forward and curtsy."

He went and grabbed a cup of water. "I think you've just about got it. A little more practice and you'll be ready for a ball."

Julie had routinely been surprised by Micheal's breadth of knowledge, but she felt compelled to ask: "Where did you learn Baroque dance?"

"My mother taught me when I was young. She had learned it when she was young. She also taught me many other dance styles, but...." He shifted nervously.

She decided to take the pressure off. "Time for dinner?"

During a visit to Concord, Julie was able to practice her speech when they stopped at a seamstress to commission full wardrobes. She tested her etiquette as they shopped for other needed supplies. This entire process also allowed her to get to know her horse, Angel, much better. By the time the week was over, she was beginning to feel like a real seventeenth-century lady.

II: Major Engineering

MICHEAL had a breakthrough. And, unlike Edison's ten thousand tries, it only took one hundred and twelve attempts to finish the prototype for his mining bore. He had spent every spare moment he had working on this project, and it was time for a test. They took the bore about a mile south for its trial run.

"So this is supposed to mine or something? Mine what exactly?" Julie inquired skeptically.

"Well, just about anything. I did design it for heavier metals, but I ought to be able to rework it to gather whatever elements we might need."

"I have a dumb question. If this works, why didn't anyone from our time, make something like this? It seems so much easier and more efficient than normal mining."

"I honestly don't know why no one tried, but if I had to guess, it would be how to power it. Most conventional methods of power would make this explode like a bomb."

She seemed to want to flee, but instead asked, "What does power this thing?"

"Kinetic energy."

"What? You mean like friction or something?"

"Yes, that's precisely it." He held up one of his extractors and said, "This is a kinetic energy extractor, or KEE for short. It can pull nearly an unlimited amount of energy straight out of the air."

"But isn't it underground? How does it access the air underground?"

"It creates nearly all the energy it needs from the friction of cutting through, and it has a small battery to make up the difference."

JULIE grabbed the KEE Micheal had set down. It was a silvery-gold three-inch long pin with rounded gray tips. "So, this is what you were experimenting with that day? It supplies the power?"

"Precisely."

"That's incredible."

"Another stupid question. Why hasn't anybody done something like this KEE before?"

Micheal laughed.

"No, seriously, it doesn't seem like anything someone else couldn't have done a long time ago. No offense."

"None taken. I had that same thought. It's likely a combination of greed and unimaginative myopia. It's a lot easier to make money by selling the same thing over and over, rather than to increase the overall amount of resources in the most efficient way. Now, I think we're just about ready. Let's see if this thing works."

"Why didn't you make this sooner?"

Micheal became quiet and looked away. "It would have been a life and death proposition."

"What do you mean by that?"

"Nothing. Let's run the test."

Julie realized there was something dark behind his statement, but he didn't seem about to reveal it.

She watched the bore as the drill heads began to rotate and quickly cut through the surface. It disappeared from sight with a ground-shaking vibration, like when a large truck passes by. Small bits of earth flew through the air. The whole effect was of a prairie dog burrowing into the ground.

As they sat there waiting, she couldn't help but consider what the implications would be if someone had invented this in the twenty-first century. The friction he was talking about was mostly air molecules crashing into each other. Tapping into that would likely solve all the world's energy needs in a completely green way.

She looked at Micheal and thought how much different or better the world would be if he had applied himself in their own time. The thought angered her. She wanted to give him a piece of her mind, but decided she didn't want to hurt his obviously fragile confidence. After all, she was beginning to believe he may actually be another Leonardo da Vinci, and she needed him at his best to give her the greatest chance to get home. She had never met someone who might be smarter than her before. She would encourage him going forward, and she was even more confident she had made the right decision.

After they ate their picnic lunch, the bore finally returned. The collection pods were full of what looked like metallic gravel.

"Is this what you were hoping for?" she asked.

"Absolutely." There was a big smile on his face. He looked at her and said, "We're going to need to make a bigger bore."

III: Final Preparations

A month passed, and they had spent it preparing everything for their move to Boston. Micheal had said he originally planned for some time in March, it was now the middle of April. Outside of JULIE'S courtesy training, they had used the time to engineer an even bigger and better mining bore. The amount of precious and rare earth elements they had acquired would easily make them the richest people in the colonies.

"Julie, here are your wedding rings. It's official, we're married," Micheal said with a sarcastic smirk.

Ambivalence filled Julie. She looked at the rings. She was still having trouble with the idea of wearing them. It kind of felt like she was cheating on Aiden. She finally accepted them.

"Don't worry, it's just for show. I promise I'll never try anything, not that I would ever have a chance. I'm just saying I know how much Aiden means to you, and I promise nothing will ever happen between us."

She felt like she wanted to be alone.

"I'm going for a ride," she said as she walked out the door. She saddled up Angel and headed north up the river.

MICHEAL focused on the image of the signatures on a certificate from Cambridge University he had seen during a scouting mission to Harvard. After weeks of practice, he was able to faithfully recreate them, completing his degree in mathematics and science.

He now had a plan for what his position in society would be once they got to Boston. Setting up a Department of Mathematics and Science at Harvard College could prove to be a challenge but, if successful, becoming a professor there would be easy. He knew Harvard wouldn't have a science department for over a hundred years and, while he wasn't sure about the effect that would have temporally, he felt it would be small.

Micheal was making his final preparations. With their documents and identities firmly established, they had gone over their story and backgrounds several times to make sure Julie's role was flawless.

Micheal briefly thought about a moment he had with Julie during preparations.

"So, tell me again. Your background is..." Micheal was running Julie through her drills.

"We've been going over my background numerous times. Don't you need to go through all of these same memory drills? I mean, some of this stuff we just made up on the spot."

"No. I won't forget anything."

"I don't know if I want to trust our success on your new-found confidence."

"It's not about that. I literally can't forget anything. Now, can we get back to it?"

"Whoa, wait. You mean you have an eidetic memory?" She seemed to be studying him. He felt under a microscope.

"Eidetic, photographic, photo-autobiographical.... I just combine it all and call it total recall." She was still staring at him, so he felt compelled to explain further. "I think Leonardo da Vinci claimed to have it, too. Which is partially why I identified with

him."

"You haven't mentioned this until now?"

"It's not a big deal."

"Do you know how rare that is? You might be the only person in the world who has all three."

"Can we just get back to the task at hand?" Micheal always felt weird discussing his "ability."

"Okay, but this might change some things between us." He didn't know what she meant but resumed the exercise.

⁂

Micheal came back to his present.

One relief was that they had everything they needed financially. The gold and silver alone was worth millions, and the minerals the bores harvested would give them plenty of resource materials for anything they needed to build. The question was, would it be enough? Would high society question their legitimacy? He was unsure of his success. His lack of social skills might prove to be their demise, inevitably leading them to become social pariahs. The only thing in their favor was the fact he'd worn a mask of courtesy since he'd withdrawn inside himself. He'd become a competent actor, portraying an air of normality in public. This would be just another role.

His thoughts turned to Julie. Obviously, she was unbelievably beautiful—the most beautiful woman he'd ever seen. But, at first, she was an inconvenience who delayed his move to Boston. He had tried to pretend she was just a pretty face, but it was her mind that he found most appealing. He had never met anyone who seem to pick up things so quickly. She was like Einstein in a supermodel's body.

He was beginning to fall for her. Not that he would ever have a chance. And even if he did, he had made a promise. His word was pretty much the most important thing to him.

⁂

JULIE rode a couple of miles up the river and stopped next to the large outcrop about halfway to Concord. She had come here once before when she wanted to think.

"Good girl." She patted Angel on the neck, then went and sat on a rock next to the river. There were blossoms on the banks, their coloring hinting at new beginnings.

She closed her eyes and listened to the water flowing over the rocks. It was so peaceful. A slight breeze blew through her hair. She heard the chirping of the first birds of spring signaling the change of the seasons, signaling the impending change for her.

Her anxiety had been building as the move to Boston got closer. It was April 15, the last day at Homestead. Julie was about to jump into the great unknown with a man she barely knew, and she was going to have to do it as his wife. She felt trapped, like she had no way out. Was she ready for this? Could she successfully portray the aristocratic image? She wasn't sure of what she was about to walk into. She wasn't an aristocrat. She was a nobody from Richmond, Virginia. She felt like a fraud. They would see right through her.

Julie looked at her actual wedding ring and, for the first time in weeks, she wondered if she would ever see Aiden again. She had been so caught up in their frenetic efforts that she hadn't thought of much else. Doubt was creeping back in. Even if she was able to get home, how long would it take? If it took too long, would Aiden wait for her?

"Aiden, please don't give up on me." Tears ran down her cheeks. In her own mind, she could almost hear Aiden say. "My precious jewel. I could never give up on you. I will never stop loving you. Be strong for me." She closed her eyes and gathered herself, then headed back.

As she came through the door, the table was set and there was a wonderful smell.

"Just about ready," Micheal said from the kitchen.

"So, what do we have here?"

"It's my mother's tater-tot casserole, one of my favorites. A little home cooking for our last night here."

She raised her glass and said, "For luck in our endeavor."

He raised his. "For luck."

CHAPTER 13: BOSTONIAN

I: Boston 1692

JULIE had taken an extra-long bath this morning, as she wasn't sure how long it would be until she could have another. She dressed in her finest dress. The skirt was sky-blue, and the bodice was off-white with green interlays. The satin felt opulent. The shoes were navy blue heels, and she was wearing an emerald and gold necklace and earring set Micheal had made for her. They were elegant and would be worth several hundred thousand dollars in 2010.

The carriage and trailer had been loaded up the night before. Micheal had prepared his bath before removing the generator. It was the last thing loaded.

Julie stood waiting for Micheal. She was still in awe of the job he had done on the stagecoach. The door opened behind her, and she heard Micheal step out onto the front porch. She turned to greet him and was stunned by what she saw. He had lost a significant amount of weight. She hadn't really noticed with all of the preparations. He still had a few extra pounds, but he was looking quite strapping.

"Wow!" Julie said. She could feel her eyes widen with admiration. When she took account of that and the fact that she hadn't taken a breath in a few seconds, embarrassment washed over her.

"That new suit looks sharp," she finished, hoping Micheal didn't notice her reaction to how good he looked.

"I don't know. I kind of feel like I'm going to the prom or something. I'm still not sure about these colors, purple and turquoise." He opened his jacket.

"You look fine." Julie was so frustrated by his negativity.

"I guess.... and you, look every bit the lady." He appeared embarrassed by his compliment, then he said. "Can we start over?"

"Okay."

As he returned to the porch, she focused on his newly chiseled face. He was a handsome man.

That made her feel guilty. She considered his commitment to her and how that would prevent him from taking advantage of the opportunities she knew would come.

He walked over, removed his tri-corn hat, and gave her a proper bow.

"My lady," he said in his aristocratic British accent.

He stood, held out his hand, and said, "Please?"

She took his hand, and he helped her into the carriage. After one final look at her first real home in this miserable century, and they headed down the path.

A few hours later, they intersected the main road between Boston and Providence. They had been quiet most of the way.

Her thoughts were filled with what she could only classify as "stage fright." Things had gone well in Concord. She had even impressed herself at times, but this was different. She felt like she had been nearing the point of no return, but now she was here. Waiting behind the wings of a stage for her cue to play the part of a stranger and make it her own.

That's what really scared her. The commitment of being someone else. Her stomach sank at the thought of how few interactions with others she'd had. Now she had to convince the entire city of Boston.

Micheal looked over at Julie and said, "Is everything all right?"

She took a deep breath. "Just a little nervous."

"You'll do just fine."

"Really? Because I'm not so sure."

"Of course... Do you think we would have left if I wasn't sure? I would have thought you'd be excited. Didn't you say you did your grad studies at Harvard?"

"Yes, but I was only fourteen when I moved here and spent most of my time near campus to focus on my studies. It's not like I could have ever fit in cause of the age disparity."

"I thought you said your family always lived in Richmond?"

"I was emancipated at fourteen so I could move to Boston on my own."

"Impressive! So it was fourteen and out the door, huh?"

"It wasn't a big deal. I'd already felt like an adult for years. I knew how to take care of myself." She clenched her teeth and looked away.

"Sorry, I wasn't trying to upset you. I actually felt the same way."

"Really?"

"Now I wasn't running off to grad school, but I never fit in with people my own age. When my mom went back to work, we were sort of left to our own devices. And I didn't have much of a childhood. Children did, well, childish things and I didn't have time for that."

"I know what you mean about childhood... I'm curious to see what it looks like in this time era."

"Well, you're about to get your chance," Micheal said as they crossed a bridge.

There appeared to be tidal plains on either side. "Are you sure this is Boston?"

"Yes. Boston was, or should I say is, practically an island."

Entering the city was surreal. As the land widened, the building numbers increased, and the muddy track became paved in cobbled stones. The clopping of hooves echoed. The standard manure smell was dampened by the previous night's rain. And the people walking on the road were stopping to stare at them. The sight of the period dress turned her stomach.

A church greeted their arrival at the main square. The most prominent building in town was to the right. It had an overhanging upper floor, and two pinnacled turrets crowned the roof. It had to be an important building.

They came to a stop and a man in a waistcoat and tricorn approached.

"Good morrow, good sir, my lady. How may I serve you?" he asked, tipping his hat to Julie with a smile.

"Good morrow, sir. Where might we find lodging?" Micheal asked, returning the smile.

The man considered for a second, then said, "Upshall Red Lyon Inn. Take the road past the docks, follow Ann Street to the right, and it will be on your left. If you see the meetinghouse, you have gone too far."

Micheal tipped his hat and said, "Your humble servant, sir."

A moment later, the harbor opened to the right. It was a forest of masts and rope, and a fresh breeze carried the call of seabirds. Most of the wooden buildings on the waterfront showed their years of salt air and freeze cycles.

A couple of minutes later, they arrived at the inn. It resembled a large wooden, gabled house. The upper floor overhung the street by a few feet. The stable hands took charge of their little caravan, and they went inside to inquire about a room. Entering the building was surreal. It was like a standard tavern out of a period movie. Except the movies never included the smell. A horrid concoction of body odor, bad breath, ale, and piss, mixed with food.

The entire room eyed them with interest. She felt overdressed. Like leaving the opera and grabbing a quick bite at the local diner.

A middle-aged woman stepped from behind the bar. "Might I be of service, Master? ..."

"...Whitaker. And my wife, Mistress Whitaker." Micheal briefly removed his tricorn, then replaced it. "Might we trouble you for your finest accommodation?" A man with a scar on his face stared at her.

"Whitaker?!" Her eyes lit up. "We have the best in the colonies."

A few minutes later, Julie surveyed their "fine" accommodations. It was two rooms. One room had a bed and a dresser with an ewer and a basin. The other room was a sitting room with a fireplace. Some of their luggage had been brought up, and the innkeeper had promised to send up dinner.

"Not exactly the Ritz Carlton," Julie said dryly.

"I'm sure this is high-class for the time... I mean, it does have a fireplace."

"Well then, I must say, this is the lap of luxury."

There was a knock on the door.

"Oh, and don't forget about room service," Micheal said.

He went to the door and turned the handle. He was immediately ambushed. A man rushed forward and hit Micheal with the butt of his rifle, then turned his deep-eyed gaze on Julie. Micheal caught his balance after the hit. His face was bleeding. The scarred man from before joined the first, and they went after Julie. She couldn't take her eyes off Micheal as he reached for a candlestick on top of the fireplace and threw it at the gunman with immense force. The gunman was out cold.

The man with the scar had reached her and taken hold. He positioned Julie in front of him like a shield and drew a knife and put it to her throat.

She saw Micheal, again, being ambushed by two new thugs. She saw that even with the two of them it took some effort to take Micheal down to the ground.

They began to kick him fiercely, then, out of nowhere, he caught the bald man's foot, rolled with it still gripped, and took him down hard. His head hit the wall. Julie felt the floor shake with the force, and she felt the man behind her begin to quiver with fear. Micheal was on his back staring at the last man. The long-haired coward took out a pistol in a panic and fumbled around like he had never held one before. Micheal took the opportunity and kicked it to the side as it went off. To her surprise, the man that Micheal had just taken down screamed in pain. The misfire had hit him in the leg.

Once again, Julie was impressed with Micheal's stature. He rose from the ground, fists clenched, and towered a full head above the thief who was trying to reload.

The man dropped the pistol and pulled out a knife. Micheal grabbed a cloth, and they started circling. The man lunged swinging the knife, Micheal caught it in the cloth and tackled the man to the ground. He pulled back and punched the man hard in the face. Micheal rose again with the knife.

The man holding her pressed the blade into her neck. His rotting breath tickled her throat. Micheal's eyes were fixed on him with a look that would intimidate anyone.

"I kill er! I swear!" the man warned. "Drop—"

Sudden footsteps at the door distracted him for a split-second and in that instant Micheal threw the knife and it stuck in the man's forearm.

She realized he was stunned and pried the hand holding the knife away from her neck. As she stepped away from his reach, he fell back through the bedroom door.

The deep-eyed bandit was getting up. Micheal took a step and punched him in the nose, and he went back down.

Several men stood in the doorway, armed with pistols. The black-clad leader stepped forward and pointed a gun past her.

"That will be enough!"

Scar-face had risen; he dropped the blade.

"Take them away," he ordered. Six more men came and collected the bandits.

The man in black said, "My apologies for our late arrival. It does appear you handled it."

"My lady," he said, tipping his cap. And he followed the others out the door.

A moment later, another man in fine accoutrement came through the door.

"Lord Whitaker, Lady Whitaker, my most humble apologies for this unfortunate assault upon your persons. My name is Thomas Fisher. I am here on behalf of Lord Governor Bradstreet. He requests your presence and humbly offers accommodation."

II: Lord Governor

They got cleaned up while the governor's men prepared their wagons. Mr. Fisher had addressed them as lord and lady. MICHEAL wondered if Bradstreet thought they were the Lords of Avalon. Using his mother's maiden name was yielding unexpected benefits. Julie approached the coach, and he helped her in, then climbed in after her.

"Julie, are you all right?"

"I've been better. Why do you think those men attacked us?" she asked, rubbing her neck.

"Probably to rob us. It's always a risk. Our manner of dress says money. That could be a motive."

"Maybe we shouldn't have—"

"No, it's a risk in any time, and now we have an invitation to see the Lord Governor."

"And how does that help us?"

"He can help us get into society. Introduce us to people of importance. And help us purchase some land."

"Why do you think the governor sent for us? How did he even know we were here?"

"I'm not sure, but this still is a small town. Word travels fast. He's likely curious about some new upper-class people moving in?"

Just a short carriage ride later and Master Fisher had them rolling up to a modest mansion house. The governor came out to greet them. He was an old man in his eighties.

Master Fisher stepped forward, opened the coach door, held out a gloved hand for Julie, and gave an elegant bow as she stepped down. He held his bow stance as Micheal made his way down. Micheal gave him a polite nod and with that, he made his way to the bottom of the steps to announce their arrival.

"Lord Governor Bradstreet, Lord and Lady Whitaker." Master Fisher gave another bow and stepped back.

They bowed and curtsied.

The governor took Julie's hand and kissed it. "A divine pleasure, Lady Whitaker," he said flamboyantly. "With great honor do I receive you." He extended his arm to show them inside.

As a dinner of fish, cheese, and vegetables was served, Governor Bradstreet exchanged basic pleasantries, then casually asked, "What brings you to Boston?"

"There was a tragedy in the family, we desired a new beginning," Micheal feigned regret, attempting to sell their story.

"My sympathies. Are you looking to settle down?"

"We were to inquire after some land," Micheal informed him.

The governor's eyes lit up. "My lord is in luck. An old friend of mine, Sir Richard Pemberton, must return to London. He owns a large estate across the Charles on the peninsula north of Charlestown. Five hundred acres and the largest estate in the area. He must sell to finance his business interests. Shall I make an introduction?"

Micheal looked to Julie for a moment then said, "Very intriguing proposition."

"Splendid! I shall make all arrangements. Until such a time, my lord and lady are most welcome guests."

After the meal, they retired to their room.

"This is so strange," Julie was staring at nothing.

"In what way?"

"Why the overwhelming interest in us? And why does he keep calling us my lord and my lady? Aren't those noble titles?"

"I think he might think we are related to the Lords of Avalon. They don't disappear for another fifty years or so, and we are using their name. I can see how he might make that assumption."

"What if they find out we aren't the 'Lords of Avalon'? Will we be arrested? Run out of town?"

"I think as long as we play the part and keep the power brokers happy, we won't have any problems," he said confidently to reassure her. "And I doubt he believes we are the actual Lord and Lady of Avalon. He probably assumes we are related and addresses us in such a style out of respect for the family."

"He sure seemed excited about assisting in the sale of his friend's estate," she said suspiciously. "The real estate market never changes. I guess we need to see this 'estate'."

"Indeed, we do."

III: Bostonian

They spent a few days making casual introductions with the governor's inner circle, allowing them to make many useful connections. To MICHEAL, the time passed quickly, and now they rode with the governor's grandson to the Boston-Charleston ferry.

"If we buy this place, it won't really be Boston," Julie said. "So what would be the point? Should we buy land in Hoboken, too?"

"Good one..." he chuckled. "...then we will have to do something about that."

"Like what?"

He shrugged. "Build a bridge?"

"We can't do that!"

"Of course we can. We'll have to discreetly modernize any place we buy. Why not a bridge?"

The ferry was arriving, so they mounted up. They soon reached a fence.

"This is the property line. There are two hills within the property boundaries. The one on the right is Breed's Hill. The one in the distance is Bunker Hill," Master Bradstreet explained.

Julie looked at Micheal and asked, "*The* Bunker Hill?"

"I assume so."

As they rode, Master Bradstreet pointed out different features and details. Micheal surveyed the lands. He already thought it was perfect. It was about the same distance to both Boston and Cambridge time-wise, which might change if they built the bridges.

They spent a few minutes passing through fields of crops until they reached the north end of the property and came to the main house.

It was a large mansion built in the colonial style. It had at least four floors and there were multiple chimneys. He estimated it was over thirty thousand square feet.

He turned to Julie as they dismounted. "The finest estate in the colonies indeed."

A couple they took to be the current owners of the estate approached them. "Lord Whitaker, Lady Whitaker. I am Sir Richard Pemberton." He bowed in greeting. "My wife, Lady Ellen Pemberton."

They exchanged courtesies.

Lady Pemberton smiled. "It is our great honor to receive people of such esteem."

"The honor is all ours," Julie said.

⸻ ⬗ ⸻

The Pembertons were giddy as they gave a rundown of the property. JULIE couldn't figure out why they were so excited about meeting them, even if they thought they were the Lords of Avalon. The Pembertons were acting like star-struck fans. She had experienced it a few times because of her show, but not quite like this. She almost expected them to ask for an autograph or a picture. The thought brought a smile to her face.

After the sales pitch was over, Sir Richard called another man over. "This is Master Smith, the overseer."

"My lord, my lady," Master Smith said. He whistled and within a few minutes, all the workers formed up in two lines.

"These the indentures," Smith said of the first line. "These the slaves," he said of the second line. Some of them were in shackles.

Julie clenched her fists, then instinctively rubbed her wrist as the heat was building inside her. She was about to give them a piece of her mind when she noticed Micheal staring at her. She took this look to mean, "compose yourself."

She was stunned. She couldn't believe Micheal was going to let this happen. Julie shot a glare back at Micheal.

The next thing was unexpected. Micheal gave another look, but this one said he understood. It gave her a sense that the situation would be dealt with.

The sight of the shackles had brought a flood of horrible memories. She felt queasy and lightheaded.

"Dear me, are you all right, my lady?" Lady Pemberton sounded concerned.

"Will you excuse me," Julie said and then walked off quickly. She sat down by a tree, trying to quell her outrage. A moment later, she heard footsteps approaching.

"Are you all right?" Micheal asked.

"Hell no, I'm not all right! Are you actually planning on buying slaves? I didn't even know they had slaves in Massachusetts."

"I can't free them if we don't buy this place. I'm sorry I didn't warn you."

"How can you be so calm?"

"I need you to look at the big picture here. First, we can't solve every problem or right every historical wrong. And we still don't know how the temporal mechanics work. We need to tread carefully until we know more about how our actions affect history or we may never be able to return to our loved ones because they wouldn't even exist."

She thought about Aiden and her family and, for the first time, considered whether any of her actions to this point could have changed her future.

She gathered herself and they returned to the manor house.

A few days later, they purchased the property and drove their belongings to their new home. All the staff was waiting for them as they pulled up. They stepped down from the carriage and everyone bowed.

"Master Smith."

"Yes, my lord." Master Smith stepped up dutifully.

"Would you be so kind as to remove the shackles from these good people."

"My lord?"

"Please. Now," Micheal said with emphasis. Smith obeyed and a few minutes later, the shackles were gone.

"Master Smith, you and your men may take the rest of the day off."

The caretaker and his men walked off toward the stables.

All the servants looked at each other and then snapped to attention when Micheal stepped up to address them.

Micheal raised his head and spoke loudly enough for everyone to hear him. "I own this land, but I can never own you. It is against God and decency to own another person. You are all free. If you wish to leave, no one will stop you. I know many of you were taken from your homes, that you are far from home. If it is your wish to return home, we will assist in your passage. You may remain in our service if you wish. You will be compensated, and you shall have the freedom to come and go as you wish. If you would like to leave our service but remain in the colony, we will assist you in whatever way you require. You are all free. I will shortly have documents attesting to that fact and you may come and claim yours. The choice is yours. And to all of you under indentured contract, I am forgiving all debts. And all the same offers of assistance are available to you as well. That is all."

That night Julie and Micheal discussed the property over dinner. At the end, she asked, "So, what are we going to call this place?"

He thought for a second. "I don't know...It's a little unimaginative, but how about 'Bostonian'?"

"I suppose that works...for now."

IV: Harvard College

MICHEAL decided they should hold meetings with all the service staff. All but one of the indentured couples decided to stay, so twenty-four out of twenty-six. Six of the former slaves decided to stay, one requested assistance to be set up as a smith, and the other seventeen wished to return home, two to the Caribbean and the other fifteen back to different parts of Africa. Master Smith wasn't pleased with the changes and opted to leave. Most of his men took work on Micheal and Julie's forthcoming construction projects.

With the estate business tended to, Micheal rode to Cambridge to meet with the Harvard College Fellows. It had been arranged with the assistance of Governor Bradstreet.

"Lord Whitaker, Governor Bradstreet informed us of some interest you may have in our college," Master Brattle, the head of the council, said.

"I have interest in serving as instructor of mathematics and the scientific arts."

"My lord, President Mather is in London and no date of return is known at this time. Aside that, this institution is more clerical in nature," Brattle explained.

"Does not this board envision a future where Harvard is on terms with my alma mater, Cambridge University, a haven of knowledge and learning?"

"Despite our lofty aspirations, we are but a small institution. We do not even possess a department of the sciences." Cotton Mather said.

"Perhaps a benefactor might invest in building this college into a university on par with my alma mater?"

The members of the court whispered to each other, then Brattle inquired, "What is my Lord Whitaker proposing?"

"I am prepared to invest in the building of a campus that would surpass Oxford and Cambridge."

Brattle then said, "Would my lord leave us a moment to discuss your proposal?"

"Gentlemen." Micheal bowed and saw himself out.

A few minutes later, he was summoned back.

"Lord Whitaker, might we see your certificate?" Brattle asked.

"Indeed," he replied and presented his BA in mathematics from Trinity College, Cambridge University.

After they all had inspected his carefully crafted document, Brattle said, "Under normal circumstances, we would require input from the president. However, since there is no date forthcoming for President Mather's return, we have decided to accept my lord's patronage, and we look forward to my lord's more detailed proposal."

As Brattle led Micheal on a tour of the grounds, he explained the history, gave a detailed profile of John Harvard, and presented him with a map of Cambridge.

"So how did it go?" Julie asked as Micheal walked through the door later that afternoon.

"They like the proposal. They want a detailed version of my plans for the university."

"Didn't you say we should tread lightly? Aren't you worried you will change the future?"

"Yeah, I've been thinking about that. I think we're ok. If time travel is possible, and we obviously know it is, then it doesn't make sense that the butterfly effect would be in play. If it was, the moment you traveled, you would be thrown into a new universe and we probably wouldn't have ended up in the same one, since we didn't start in the same place. Well, we were in the same time and the same city, but we didn't leave there or arrive here together."

Two days later, Julie and Micheal rode to Cambridge to discuss the plans with Master Brattle and the rest of the college council.

"Gentlemen, this is Lady Whitaker," Micheal said.

After some pleasantries, they sat to discuss business over tea. The council seemed uncomfortable with Julie's presence.

"Is something amiss, good sirs?" Micheal asked.

Master Brattle, the chairman, addressed the council. "You all understand about the ladies of my lord's house?" They all murmured agreement, and the discussion went forward.

"So," Micheal detailed the campus, "the Department of Math and Sciences will be down by the Charles, Academic Row will be along Cambridge Street, with Harvard Yard to the north flanked by boarding houses. As part of the project, all roads will be paved, and Cambridge Street will extend east to the Charles and a bridge will be built to connect to Boston." They all seemed impressed. Plans were made to begin construction immediately.

———⋈———

Several days later, as the spring planting deadline approached, JULIE was working to organize the management of the property. She had taken charge because of her business acumen.

Her first item on the agenda was to appoint a new management team. After conducting interviews with all the staff, she decided on two women and one man to lead.

For the head management position, Julie had really liked Rose. She was a middle-aged African American woman who clearly knew the property well. She had a quiet intelligence and was respected by the rest of the staff.

"Rose, please sit." Julie offered a chair in her study.

"My lady?"

"My lord and I would like to ask if you would be willing to take a greater role in the operations of the estate."

"A bigger job?"

"Yes, you will oversee the property and all the operations. We will increase your compensation and I will personally teach you all you shall need to know."

"My thanks, my lady."

Rose departed and Julie called in her other choices. They were a young French couple, Yvette and Filipe. They were both in their early twenties. Filipe was nearly as tall as Julie, with brown hair and eyes.

They both bowed.

"That is not necessary. You may sit...I was keen on your quality. The both of you. Filipe, I would have you as overseer of the stables and fields. Yvette, I would place you in charge of the entire staff. You shall manage compensation and petition for all who work for us. Should you accept position, you will answer to Rose, and shall acquire a great deal more compensation. Do you accept these positions?"

"My lady, I do not feel equal to the task." Yvette averted her eyes.

"I shall enlighten you to whatever you lack."

Yvette looked at Filipe, then back at her. "We will, my lady."

"Very well, that is all." Julie excused them.

———⋈———

Micheal had been overseeing the planting of the crops and she went out to inform him of her decision. As she rounded the side of the barn, she saw him take his muddy shirt off and begin to wash himself. She had to fight back some lustful thoughts as the water streamed down his rippled chest.

She suddenly felt guilty, as if her thoughts betrayed Aiden. She was about to turn and go.

"Julie? Did you want to talk to me?"

"Oh, um..." She stammered in embarrassment. "Uh, well, I came to tell you I'm putting Rose in charge as property manager."

"Good choice.... Are you okay?"

"Of course... Looks like you lost some weight."

Her words had betrayed her.

"Yeah, it's called the time travel diet. It'll be the next big fad when we get back," he laughed. "Did you need something else?"

"Oh...no," she said, then left.

Once back at the house, she sat down and took a deep breath to try to settle herself. This was not supposed to happen. Micheal was never ugly, but she certainly never viewed him in such a fashion before. She almost wished he had stayed chubby. Now she had made a total fool of herself, and he would know she was becoming attracted to him. She would have to stay strong for Aiden.

Julie sat looking in her vanity mirror.

"It's only physical," she told herself.

Later that evening Micheal came to their rooms. She was worried he would be awkward.

"So the training with Okafore is going well. By the time I'm done, he'll be the best blacksmith in the colony," he said casually.

"That's great," she said. He didn't seem any different. "How did the planting go?"

"Everyone did well. They picked up the use of my planting machines perfectly. And we followed the Massachusett method of complementary farming to maximize yield. How's everything on your end?"

"I think my plan for the property is just about set. Pretty soon it will be running like a well-oiled machine. At least once the new mansion is finished. How long do you expect it to take?"

"I hope it will be done by the end of the year." Micheal fidgeted.

"You think that monstrosity you designed can be built that quickly?" she teased.

"I wouldn't say it's a *monstrosity*. It might be a little big."

"A *little* big? It's practically a palace!"

"I suppose I may have gotten carried away when I designed it."

She felt aggravated. "Why are we spending so much time and resources on this property? Shouldn't we be focusing on time travel?"

"There's nothing stopping you from making that your focus, but this is a challenge on par with interstellar travel. I feel we need to establish ourselves first. And this estate must reflect the perception of us."

"Fine, you don't have to justify it to me. I'm just tagging along on your plan."

"You know that's not how I feel."

"Do we really have to be in the same suite together?" she lost herself and felt her eyes go wide.

"Of course not. I have some things I need to attend to anyway. Good night." He quickly exited.

Julie didn't understand her reaction.

MICHEAL thought of the limited interactions he had with women. His time with Julie was easily the longest he had ever spent with a woman—longer than with every other woman combined.

"How pathetic am I?"

He didn't know what he could have done to upset her, but it was obviously something bad. He felt bad that she had to deal with all of his flaws. He decided that the best thing he could do was give her space.

Micheal spent the next few hours reconfiguring several of the mining bores into machines to help lay the foundation for the bridges.

Later that night, he climbed up to the loft to lay in his sleeping bag and watch the stars. Even stranded across the centuries, he could at least depend on the familiarity of the night sky. The moon had already set, and the Milky Way blazed across the sky. He could see the reddish glow of Mars as well as Jupiter.

His favorite constellation, Orion, was low toward the horizon. Alnitak, Alnilam, and Mintaka traced the unmistakable belt. The mellow red of Betelgeuse above was contrasted by Rigel's brilliance, not yet sunk below the horizon. In his mind, he could see the misty nebula.

As he stared at the sky, he thought about his family and friends. For the first time since he got here, he realized just how much he missed them and wondered how they were dealing with him being gone. He had always told himself no one would care if he were gone. He knew that wasn't true.

Micheal wondered if any of his family were looking across the centuries at the same night sky. He hoped they were, but that was likely as close as they would ever get to each other again.

He was sure he would ultimately fail. He could never bridge the distance of time.

V: The Governor's Ball

JULIE checked Micheal's room. It was apparent that he hadn't slept there again. Anytime they had an argument, he'd disappear for a couple of days. Normally she'd give him space, and he'd eventually come around, but two days ago an invitation came from Governor Bradstreet; he was hosting a ball in their honor.

She checked his makeshift lab, but he wasn't there, then checked the stables. Darkness was still there, Micheal had to be around somewhere.

She started to walk out of the barn when she heard a noise above her. She climbed the ladder to the loft.

He was in his sleeping bag near the sky door.

"Is this where you've been sleeping?"

"I *am* sleeping," he said and rolled over.

She climbed into the loft and stood over him.

"Well, normally I would let you sleep, but we have a ball to get ready for."

"What ball?" he asked, still turned away from her.

"The Governor's Ball. The invitation arrived two days ago. Why are you sleeping up here?"

"I watch the stars at night."

"I'm sorry."

He turned toward her. "Sorry? For what?"

"I was in a bad mood the other day, and I took it out on you."

"You have nothing to be sorry for. I know how hard it is to have to put up with me on such a regular basis. I—"

"No! That's—"

"No. I've lived on my own for the past ten years and I got used to it being just me. I don't know how to live with anyone else. I'll try to give you more space, to make things easier on you. And I will scrap the current designs of my"—he paused for a second—"monstrosity."

"No! You aren't changing the house plans over some stupid argument. Now get up and get dressed. We need to leave soon if we're going to get to Boston in time."

"Yes, ma'am."

Julie appreciated the sarcasm.

MICHEAL was ready before Julie and dressed to impress in his new satin blue dress suit. As she began to descend, the sight of her was heart-stopping. Her hair was up, and her long delicate neck was accented by a laced choker that flowed perfectly into her chest. Her body was framed by her lavender corseted dress.

He took a breath to steady himself. She always had this effect on him. He had practiced his poker face when she decided she would be living with him. He didn't want to cause the situation to become awkward, so he didn't want her to know how he saw her.

He stepped forward, took her hand, and said, "My dear, you are a vision." And he kissed her hand.

"And you look dashing as well."

The carriage ride around the Charles was mostly quiet. It was their first time in Boston since they bought the estate.

"I was becoming worried about you," she said finally.

"Worried? You were worried about me?"

"I didn't see you for two days."

"I was busy working on some things."

"And sleeping in the loft?"

"I was giving you space. We are around each other an awful lot.... I don't want you to feel smothered. And I need some alone time as well."

"Still, you don't have to sleep in the loft."

"Don't worry about that. It was like camping. I was stargazing. I miss doing that."

"Did you do that often?"

"Oh, all the time. I even had a twelve-inch telescope. That was my first portal through time. When I stare at the night sky, it makes me think that perhaps someone who cares about me might be looking back across the centuries. I feel closer to them in a way."

Julie turned to look out the window. He thought he saw a tear on her cheek.

A herald announced their presence as they entered the governor's mansion.

All eyes were on them. They had been acquainted with some, but there were many strange faces. This was Boston society.

JULIE felt like she was in a movie. She thought she did as well as could be expected under the circumstances. By the end, she was rather enjoying herself and Micheal was so debonair she could almost believe he was from this time.

Julie went looking for refreshments when a very theatrical woman popped up excitedly. "Lady Whitaker, 'tis such an honor. I am Mistress Cecily Penn."

Julie opened her mouth to answer, but at that moment there was a commotion. She turned toward Micheal and saw he was embroiled in a debate.

"Do you believe that because of who your family is, you can come here and make everyone bow down to you?" a man said angrily as she walked up. "You can go back to whatever hole you crawled out of and take your whore with you." He shot a glance at Julie.

Before she could think of a response, Micheal stepped forward and punched the man in the stomach.

"Sir, you will apologize to my wife." The man seemed about to resist but one look at Micheal and the gathering spectators seemed to change his mind.

"My apologies, my lady," the man said. Then, gathering his courage, "You will pay for this." He stormed out.

Julie was immediately joined by her new acquaintances.

"Are you all right, my lady?" Mistress Penn asked with dramatic abundance as Micheal turned to address the guests and the governor.

"My most sincere apologies for this unfortunate disruption," Micheal said to the room. "And my personal apology to the governor," he said with a bow.

Later that night Julie asked Micheal, "Did you really have to hit him?"

"I cannot allow such an insult to you to go unanswered."

"It's not like I'm your actual wife. Plus, he's hardly the first creep I've had to defend myself against."

"To them you are, and it cannot be known that I don't defend your virtue."

Later that night, after Micheal was asleep, she stared out the window at the night sky and thought of Aiden.

She felt closer to him already.

CHAPTER 14: THEORIES ON TIME

OVER THE NEXT COUPLE of months, things settled down, and they fell into a normal routine. MICHEAL started considering what the science behind their predicament might be. He'd spent years researching temporal mechanics. He ran down the list of theories of how it might work.

Einstein's theory of relativity says the flow of time is relative. Gravity and velocity both affect the relative speed of the temporal flow. But Micheal didn't see how either of those aspects applied to their situation. Not that he could say for sure, as he was asleep when it happened.

Could there have been a gravitational flux near their hotels?

"Julie!" He saw her passing by his office door. "I'm working on...how we got here. Care to discuss the possibilities?"

"You really want me to try to figure it out with you? Physics is not my area...."

"You don't give yourself enough credit. Now please sit so we can discuss this."

She sat, then said, "So, are we going to talk about all the ideas from pop culture?"

"Do you want to?"

"I would be interested to hear your thoughts on them."

"Well okay...First, we don't have a DeLorean and there's little useful details about the flux capacitor, so we don't have anything there we can use."

"You mean Doc Brown and Marty aren't going to be showing up anytime soon?"

"You never know. But I don't think we can expect them or Sarah Connor to come to the rescue. And don't plan on stumbling across a TARDIS, either—it rarely crosses the pond."

"There's a book series I've been reading since grad school. The heroine travels through stone circles which are energy portals or something."

"Hmm…. The concept of energy vortices is likely more pertinent."

"What do you think actually happened?"

"Tell me your experience again?"

"I went to sleep in my hotel bed—"

"And this was the Grand Bohemian in Orlando?" he interjected.

"Yes. I went to bed in my room and when I woke up, I was in a field of snow."

"Which is precisely what happened to me. My hotel was only a block from yours in downtown Orlando. And we both ended up in 1692 Massachusetts."

"But what could've possibly caused us to fall through time?"

He pondered for a minute. "The night we fell when I ate dinner at the Boheme, my waitress, Caitlin, was the only survivor from the *Esperanza*. Have you heard of it?"

"No. What is it?"

"It was a luxury yacht that disappeared off the coast of Cape Canaveral in the summer of '02. No trace of it—or anyone on board—was ever found again. Except for Caitlin, of course. She told me what really happened. The *Esperanza* lost power and then was surrounded by a cloud of green mist. She said she saw the surrounding horizon flicker between what I believe was either an alternate dimension or another time and place. She was knocked overboard in the commotion and then the yacht disappeared in a flash."

"How does that relate to our situation?"

"Both events took place in close proximity to the Bermuda Triangle, which is supposed to be an energy vortex. I'm sure you've heard the stories about all the weird things and disappearances."

"Have any of the missing ever returned?"

"Not that I know of, but I doubt there has ever been anyone more capable of figuring it out than us," he said as confidently as he could. But her look of doubt reflected his own.

"You don't really believe that, do you?"

"Are you trying to kill any confidence I can muster?" Micheal rubbed his hand over his face. "Of course I don't believe that because it includes me. You made a mistake putting your hopes in me." he quickly left the room. He felt like a failure already.

JULIE was confused and annoyed. She knew Micheal was depressed and what she was considering was risky, but she couldn't handle this anymore. She followed him out to his lab in the barn. She didn't recognize the device Micheal was working on, but he looked surprised when he saw her there.

"I've tolerated this long enough," she stared him down.

"Tolerated what?"

"You run off to your pity party anytime we have a disagreement."

"Pity party?"

"Yes! Exactly what you're doing right now."

"No one is forcing you to be here. If it's so bad, I can help set you up somewhere else."

"Oh! So now you want me to leave?" She gripped her skirt.

"I told you; you were better off on your own."

She rolled her eyes.

"You are the dumbest smart person I know!" He was about to respond, but she cut him off. "No. Shut up. Don't say anything. Just listen." When she was sure he wasn't going to try to interject, she said, "I know you're struggling to find confidence, so I've been trying to play it soft on you. But that ends now. You always say how intelligent you think I am. So with that in mind. I want you to believe me when I tell you that the things you've been able to do here are impressive by any standard, and I know how intelligent you are. I need you to help me out of this situation. I need your best effort. I trust you. I need you to trust me. Do you trust me?"

He had been averting his gaze while she was speaking, but at that, he finally looked her in the eyes. "Yes," he said simply.

"I realize how fragile your confidence is, so I want you to lean on me. Anytime your confidence is slipping, put your trust in my belief in you."

He seemed to soften, then said, "Okay."

"I know it won't always work, but I want you to give me your word you will try."

He looked at her for a moment, then finally said, "I promise."

I: The Order of Harvard

They rode to Cambridge to inspect how the construction was coming along. Most of the roads had been laid down in just two months. MICHEAL had several of the bores working covertly on the underground elements of the bridge-university project.

"Lord Whitaker! Come to inspect your 'monstrosity' of a campus? It will never be done in time for fall instruction. I would never have approved this ridiculous plan of yours. You may have a degree from Cambridge, but only your family would be so arrogant to believe they could outdo such an institution." President Mather glared at Micheal and Julie.

"President Mather, we would never deign to compare to such grandiosity," Micheal said flippantly. "I do, however, believe that President's Row on Cambridge Street and the mathematics buildings shall be completed in time for instruction."

"For your sake, my lord, they better be. For you are not your noble cousins, and regardless of support from the fellows, I shall expel you from these halls."

"That is entirely your prerogative. However, should you decide on such an outcome, I suspect you won't be long for your office, 'Mr. President.'"

Mather scowled at him, then, sneering at Julie, he said, "My dear Lady Whitaker, I would have thought you might spend a little more time at home where you belong."

Julie cocked her head to the side and said, "President Mather, I might have thought you would spend a little more time at Harvard, though I am not quite sure you belong there."

He seemed about to respond, then stormed off, mumbling to himself.

"Your servant, Sir," Micheal said in a mocking tone.

They'd had a few exchanges of "pleasantries" since Increase Mather, the college president, had returned from London along with the new governor, Lord Governor William Phipps, of the newly established Province of Massachusetts Bay. The president's views about tradition had caused friction from the beginning—and he especially didn't like Julie showing up as often as she did. After all, a woman's place was in the home.

"Is it going to be ready for the fall?" Julie asked Micheal once Mather had left.

"Not all of it, but the math and science buildings should be, along with University Row and a few dormitories."

"Is that the science building?" Julie was squinting with her head cocked.

"Yes. Why?"

"It's exactly like I remember it from my time there. Did you do that on purpose?"

"No. I was given a map by the council and designed the campus and individual building how I thought worked best."

"You didn't copy this from some picture you've seen of Harvard?"

"No. I've never seen a picture of Harvard."

"That's hard to believe."

"I only ever read about the university. I swear I have no idea what it looks like. Why?"

Julie looked away for a moment then said, "up until this point, none of the things we had done had clearly shown our impact on the timeline. But this…" she indicated the science labs, "…means we must be having some kind of effect on history."

They sat down on a bench overlooking the Charles River on a newly finished section of the Riverwalk. JULIE returned to their favorite topic.

"If our actions are already baked into history, does that mean we never got home?"

"Actually, it might be a good thing."

"You mean if we had been here all along but didn't know it, at least we are in the correct timeline?"

"Yes. That was definitely a concern."

"If it's not the multiple timelines in effect, then what do you think it is?"

"It could be the preventative."

"What's that?"

"It's like in the 2002 movie version of H.G. Wells, *The Time Machine,* where time prevents Alexander from saving Emma."

"Why would it prevent him from saving her?"

"In the movie, Hardigan builds the time machine because of Emma's death. So he can't use the machine to save her, otherwise he would never build it. If he somehow did, it would create a paradox, and while that can happen in the movies, it could never happen in the real world."

"So you think this demonstrates the preventative effect?"

"Maybe, or it could be a third option."

"What else is there?"

"When I was five, I saw *Back to the Future* for the first time and it sparked my interest in how time works. Over the next few years, I researched everything I could about temporal mechanics. And after a lot of contemplation on the matter, there was a moment of inspiration. My family had gone camping in the Uinta Mountains, east of Salt Lake. My sister Vanessa and I were sitting, throwing rocks into the Weber River. I watched the ripples from each splash. Upstream there was a boulder, and the water was breaking around it. I thought about the timestream. What if it was like the river? What if the stones we were throwing were like small changes by a time traveler? And the boulder was like a major change? Where it actually diverts the flow of time."

"Why would it work like that?"

"It never made sense to me that if you could travel through time, you couldn't actually do anything because you would automatically be sent into an alternate timeline."

"Because of the butterfly effect?"

"Yes. It made more sense that you could make small changes and the force of the timestream would smooth them out. Like the ripples from the stones. And no one would ever know it happened."

"But if you did something major like kill Hitler. That would divert you into an alternate timeline, like the boulder."

"Exactly."

"So time is like a river constantly flowing. We can throw a few pebbles, but we need to be careful of the boulders."

They looked at the river, then back at the rising Harvard campus, then to the river again. As she stared at the slow-moving currents, Julie wondered if she could ride them back to Aiden, or if she would be drowned by the temporal undertow.

II: Martial Arts

JULIE had a restless night. She'd had nightmares on and off since waking up at Homestead. But these were particularly bad. She wanted someone to talk to. She slowly opened Micheal's door, but he was gone. Ever since they had moved into the new partly finished house, he had been gone nearly every morning before sunup. She usually just went back to bed, but today she decided to go find him. She checked all the usual places. The last one was the labs. On her way, she heard muffled sounds coming from the Tier Gardens.

She reached the garden's edge and saw him doing something like Tai Chi in the first light of dawn. She made her way down the steps and could see he was punching and kicking a padded board. When she reached the bottom tier, he did some kind of roundhouse kick but stopped in the middle of it.

"Julie!" he said breathlessly, with a surprised look on his face. "What are you doing up?" He was shirtless, which was distracting.

"I came to find you." She broke off. "Could you put a shirt on or something?"

Micheal put a shirt on then said, "You wanted to talk to me?"

"Yes... What are you doing out here?"

He was still breathing heavily and sweating. "I had always intended to do this, and now that things are situated, I'm teaching myself martial arts."

"You're teaching yourself martial arts?"

"Yeah. Well, when I was young, I studied the forms and philosophies of every martial art I could find. I never really trained in any of them, but I do need to be a better fighter if we're going to survive this century."

"How long have you been doing this?"

"Oh, nearly every morning since we bought this place. So far, I've been focusing on Kung Fu."

Julie threw up her hands in annoyance. "When were you going to tell me about this?"

He shrugged.

"And were you planning on teaching me?"

"I don't know. You want to learn how to fight?" He raised a brow.

"Of course! The creeps and the witch hunters are after me, not you. You want me vulnerable to any two-bit thug? Stuck, a damsel in distress, needing you as my knight in shining armor to protect me?"

He leaned back, averting his eyes. "Of course not... knight in shining armor?" He shook his head, laughing to himself. "I train nearly every morning a little bit before sunup. If you're serious, meet me here tomorrow morning and we'll train together."

Over the next few weeks, they trained faithfully every morning. After a while Julie started to get the hang of it but she wasn't improving as quickly as she would've liked, so she started riding with Angel to a secluded grove at the top of Breed's Hill to practice on her own.

Julie had spent a few days practicing solo. While she was repeating her daily lesson, she heard a small cough behind her. It was Master Liu. He was a bit of an enigma. He'd shown up at the house a few weeks after Micheal and Julie had freed all the slaves. Word had obviously gotten out about the curious habits of the new estate owners, and he'd come around offering his services as a tailor. Julie certainly wasn't planning on taking up sewing and she eagerly snatched him up.

"Master Liu, you startled me."

"My lady practices the arts?" he asked, a delighted look on his face.

"Oh, well, yes. I'm not very good yet."

"I studied under Master Wong. I train with my lady?"

For the next week or so, Julie trained every day with Master Liu in the grove on Breed's Hill. She liked having her own little secret from Micheal.

One morning Julie did a few moves MICHEAL hadn't taught her.

"Wow! Where did you learn how to do that?"

"I've just been practicing on my own."

He raised an eyebrow, then said, "Well, keep it up, you're doing great. I think that's enough for the day."

Micheal watched Julie leave; he felt like she wasn't telling him something. Later that day, after his smithing training session with Okafore, he saw Julie riding Angel south toward Breed's Hill and followed on Darkness. As he got closer, he saw Master Liu heading up, also.

Micheal dismounted and slowly approached the hill. He heard what sounded like fighting. So that was it. Master Liu knew Kung Fu and was teaching Julie. He left quietly so they wouldn't see him.

Later that evening, he sent for Master Liu, then asked Julie to join him in his study.

After they'd both arrived, Micheal said, "Please sit, there is something I would like to discuss with both of you."

They passed odd glances back and forth, then Master Liu sat down.

"It has come to my attention that the both of you have been meeting up on Breed's Hill." Micheal began.

"My lord, it is not—" Master Liu started to explain.

Micheal raised his hand to stop him. "I know what you've been doing, and I was wondering...when are you going to include me?" he said, looking back and forth between them.

Julie grinned at him and tossed his own words back at him. "I don't know. You want to learn how to fight?"

He rolled his eyes at her joke and turned to Master Liu. "Master Liu, you are skilled in Kung Fu?"

Master Liu looked at Julie, then turned to him and said, "I study under Master Wong."

Micheal thought for a second, then said, "I would like you to become our Kung Fu master. You will no longer attend to any other duties. You will train individually on your own. And you will instruct us in the arts on a regular basis. Are these terms agreeable, Master Liu?"

Master Liu's face lit up. "My lord wants me to be his master of the arts?"

"We would be honored," Micheal said, bowing respectfully.

Master Liu bowed back and said, "Thank you, my lord, my lady." Then he left.

III: Summer Festival

Much of the primary structure of the new mansion was now erected. The Charlestown Bridge connected Boston to the peninsula, opening earlier in the week to great fanfare by the new Lord Governor, Sir William Phipps.

JULIE felt things had become boring and routine. Since Micheal was *too busy* to work on temporal mechanics and she didn't know where to start. She decided to distract herself with a summer festival, planned for the first Friday and Saturday in July. Invitations for the formal events were sent to all of Boston society and tents were set up across the property so commoners could attend the general festival.

Musicians, games, and other entertainers from around the colonies were brought in. And they also brought in many extra cooks and temporary staff to prepare the food for everybody.

Julie was at the west entrance of Bostonian, overseeing the arrivals. "Rose, how is everything going?"

"My lady, there are far more people than expected. Word has spread from New York to Maine," Rose's eyes went wide.

"Do your best to accommodate everyone. I have the utmost confidence."

"My lady. There are more people wanting to set up stalls," Yvette said. She was one of the former indentured servants. Julie had seen that she was a hard worker and quite savvy. She was her second in command after Rose. Yvette had come from France and, not a surprise, she was quintessentially French. She had slightly squinty green eyes and a petite nose. All framed by canary blond locks.

"Find a spot on the north side. Thank you, Yvette."

Micheal came up to her. "It looks like a smashing success."

"Maybe a little too smashing."

Micheal laughed. "I was told there are people from all over New England and many of our Massachusett friends have come."

As if on cue, Chief Nightwolf approached.

Julie greeted him in Algonquian. She was trying to learn as much as possible.

"Lady Whitaker," he replied in Algonquian.

More than half the tribe had shown up, as well as thousands of people from around New England. Many were gawking, and they were all excited to meet her.

Even incomplete, Bostonian was impressive, with multiple towers rising toward the sky. It reminded her of some of the European palaces she had visited. She couldn't remember if it was there in modern Boston. She'd been so busy with school that she never really saw any of the sights.

Julie took a break from hosting duties and got her hands dirty. She'd been helping Micheal engineer an assembly line in a secret underground factory beneath the palace. Her time there was always a respite from the seventeenth-century lady.

A couple of hours later, it was time to get dressed for the ball. Her dress had a pastel peach skirt and a bright yellow bodice. She was wearing a simple pendant with matching earrings she designed herself.

There was a knock on Julie's chamber door.

"Just a minute," she said.

Julie emerged.

Michael was dressed in a dark red suit with silver adornments and blue trim. "My dear, you positively look of summer."

"That is the very idea, my darling. And you look very flashy this evening. I wouldn't have expected so daring a color."

"Well...having lost some weight, I felt I might be able to pull it off... Let's go." She took his arm, and they descended to the ballroom.

"Lord Governor Phipps, Lady Phipps, welcome to our humble abode," Micheal said in greeting and Julie gave a curtsy.

"Lord and Lady Whitaker, quite a wonderful festival," Lady Phipps marveled.

"And marvelous for the economy. Boston is positively filled to the brim with visitors," the governor added.

Micheal deflected the praise to Julie. "It is to my lady's credit."

They were making the rounds when Julie heard a name that stopped her in her tracks.

"The Honorable John Hathorne and Mistress Hathorne."

Julie had a sudden urge to flee. She began to take a step and stumbled.

Micheal caught her, then asked, "Are you all right?"

Julie looked at Hathorne, and Micheal followed her gaze.

"He was the magistrate who oversaw my witch trial," she said, taking deep breaths and trying to steady herself.

The Hathornes were making a beeline toward them.

"Everything will be okay. Try to compose yourself."

"Lord and Lady Whitaker, John Hathorne, at thy service, and this is my wife, Ruth."

"Quite a beautiful place you have here," Ruth said.

"It does keep the rain off our heads," Micheal joked. Everyone laughed.

"Lady Whitaker, the governor tells us this festival was your idea." Ruth looked only slightly older than Julie and perhaps half of Hathorne's age.

Hathorne looked at Julie in confusion.

"Have we met somewhere before, my lady? You seem familiar for some reason."

The butterflies in Julie's stomach felt like they were going to burst right out of her.

Before she could respond Micheal cut in, "Master Hathorne, that is impossible—unless you visited here in the last few months. We have only just arrived in Boston and we have spent most of our time attending the property. Was there a visit I am unaware of?"

Hathorne looked at Micheal, then back at Julie.

"My apologies, Lady Whitaker. I meant no trespass." He still seemed unconvinced.

"No offense taken, Master Hathorne. Enjoy the ball."

Hathorne gave her one more long look, then he and Ruth left.

"Let's get some air," Micheal led Julie out to the waterfront.

The herald announced the fireworks and people started to head out in the opposite direction.

Once they were outside Micheal started, "Are you—"

But she threw her arms around him, and tears started down her cheeks.

She felt like she was back in the courtroom, standing naked for everyone to see. He wrapped her in a comforting embrace, whispering soothing nothings in her ear.

Micheal's protective embrace was a shelter from the storm of emotions that had been stirred up by the encounter. His lightest touch began to pull the tension out of her.

The grip of the noose she had felt tightening around her throat began to loosen. For the first time since she fell through time, she felt completely safe.

IV: Liberty

A week after the Summer Festival, MICHEAL was doing his final inspection. Everything looked in order. It was time for the big reveal. "Ladies and gentlemen: the *Liberty*." Everyone cheered as the *Liberty* drifted out of the water-filled dry dock and into the Mystic River.

"I don't think it's big enough," Julie said facetiously.

He decided against going along with it.

"It's only one hundred and twenty feet. It does need to be ocean-worthy."

After the christening, they went for a cruise around Massachusetts Bay.

Afterward, as they docked at Bostonian, Micheal said, "I think it will do. We will leave in the morning."

They held a going away party that evening. It had taken three months to build, but those who wanted to go back to Africa and the West Indies would finally be able to get underway.

The ship had KEE powered engines and water jet propulsion. Defensive systems to fend off potential attacks. A desalinization system. Proximity detectors. Sonar and radar systems. And a stellar/solar orientation system he had designed for open-water navigation. It was three decks above and one below. The interior had numerous cabins and lounges and a full kitchen. The top deck was the bridge.

The next morning, they were out to sea by sunup.

"So we are still going to practice, right?" Julie asked.

"Well, I had something else in mind. Since we are fairly proficient in Kung Ku and our Master is absent, I decided we would begin a new form. One that is useful for someone like you—"

"Someone like me?!"

"Someone of limited strength. It's Aikido. It's primarily about energy misdirection and redirection."

"Using your opponent's strength against them," she said in understanding. "Which martial arts forms have you studied?"

"After relentless bullying at school, I decided I needed to be able to defend myself. I knew my parents could never afford to put me in formal martial arts, so I began researching every form that I thought might help. For the core, I focused on the most balanced forms of Kung-Fu, Karate, and Tae Kwon Do. I added some grappling with Jujitsu and Judo. For power, I included Muay Thai Kickboxing. And for a little evasion and flair, I added Aikido and Capoeira, respectively. I had decided that those eight forms would pretty much make me as well-rounded a fighter as possible. But then I thought there were a few other things that might be advantageous to include, so I studied weapons forms like Kendo, Fencing, and Longsword, for swords. Bojutsu for staff fighting. And finally, I watched a lot of demonstrations of Parkour that would help enhance agility."

"So that seems like a lot to learn. How proficient did you become in all of that?"

"I spent some time practicing a variety of things from all the different forms, but some other things became more of a priority. Once I was confident I could defend myself against the bullies, I decided to focus my time on other things."

Micheal felt like Julie was studying him. As if she might want to explore something from his past. To quell his discomfort, he said. "Should we get started?"

After a short hesitation, she agreed.

The next evening, they arrived in Port-au-Prince. With all of Micheal's modifications, the *Liberty* was suspiciously fast, but JULIE still wondered if they were in the right place as there was barely a port.

"Have you ever been to Haiti before?" Micheal asked Julie as they sailed through the harbor.

"I did a couple of shows out of here a few years ago. You don't remember?"

"I said I watched your show most of the time, not all the time."

"How could you possibly miss my show?"

"I..." His face flushed.

She laughed. "I was joking. If you had seen every one of my shows, *then* I'd be worried."

Julie gathered all the passengers at the gangplank to address them. "Everyone stay close to the ship. We will depart tomorrow evening."

Port-au-Prince, known as Hôpital, was a notoriously dangerous pirate port, so they assigned someone to tend the ship at all times. The next day, they used their financial influence to help set up the two former slaves in Haiti.

Upon departure, two ships seemed to try to pursue them, but they pushed the liberty up to fifty knots, leaving them in their wake.

Four days' sail later, they docked in Lagos in the early evening. "How dangerous is Lagos in this century?" Julie asked Micheal.

"I don't know that much about Africa in these times. Best be on your guard."

Even dressed down, they got all kinds of odd looks. Their towering height alone made them stand out. Julie was taller than nearly everyone else in town and Micheal looked like a giant. At six foot four, he was at least a foot taller than most of the people there.

They spent four days making arrangements and even put in some shipping orders with some merchants. They said their final farewells to the dozen former slaves.

Julie reflected on the past few months and the friendships she had made. She would miss her language lessons. She had been teaching the servants the basics of reading, writing, and arithmetic. She thought she could greatly improve all of their lives through education. In return, many of them had offered to teach her and Micheal their languages.

This exchange had been rich linguistically. She and Micheal had learned four different languages from Africa, along with many languages from all corners of Europe. And their Kung Fu Sensei Master Liu had been teaching Micheal Mandarin Chinese.

They returned to the *Liberty* to depart, only to see that the ship was being ransacked by at least ten men. MICHEAL saw four near the bow, two across the ship, and four to the left. Two of which were on the bridge.

"Hey! Get the hell off!"

Without a word, the men to his right began a blitz attack.

He used a sidekick to send the first man off the boat. A second man had nearly reached him, with a third one closing in. He rotated, using the second man's forward momentum to toss him in the water, then met the third man with an elbow. He spun and landed an uppercut, sending him backward over the rail.

Micheal turned in time to see Julie demolish one of the men with a spinning sidekick that sent him flying off the ship. The second man was stunned. He seemed frozen with fear. Julie took a step forward, grabbed the man by his left arm, and with it held tight, tucked herself under, and threw him over her shoulder and off the ship.

He turned to see a man with a patch draw a sword, while another man rushed him from the other side. Micheal kicked the blade hand as the other man plowed into him. He began to fall. He allowed himself to go to the ground just in time to see the sword slash past his face. As they came down, the Patch stumbled over the other man's leg, and he began to fall on top of them. Micheal used his feet to propel the Patch into the harbor. Bringing an elbow down on the other man's face.

He was getting up when Julie yelled. "Micheal!"

He turned. Two men were holding her and the third had wrapped a rope around her neck. He ran full speed into a sliding sweep and all four went down. He grabbed the man with the rope as if to body slam him, then tossed him off the ship.

Julie freed her arms and landed a vicious right cross on one man's chin, knocking him out. The other man attempted to rise, so Julie kicked the side of his knee. He fell, hit his head, and was out cold. The last three ran away. They threw the incapacitated men onto the docks and got underway as quickly as possible.

"Are you all right?" Micheal asked.

She rubbed her neck, breathing deeply.

"Let's get you cleaned up."

Micheal guided JULIE into the bathroom.

"You fought well," he said.

"Not well enough."

"We were outnumbered thirteen to two, and you took out four all by yourself. I'd say you fought well—and no arguments."

Julie gave a little smile. "When you put it that way...."

He was wrapping a cold towel around her neck.

"Why do they always go for the throat?"

Julie had to fight back thoughts of her execution. Over the last few months, her mind had cleared everything up, and she had come to recognize she had actually died. Her conversation with Jessica on the other side was seared vividly in her mind. She realized she had never told Micheal anything about that experience or of Jessica. She had been hesitant to open up to him fully. She knew he was holding back from her as well.

At that moment, she also realized she had never thanked him for bringing her back from the dead. She was flooded with guilt. What kind of person was she? Even though she had originally thought he was responsible for her predicament, once she knew he wasn't, one would've thought she might have expressed a bit of gratitude for having her life back.

He hadn't said a word or even alluded to it. She knew he wasn't opening up to her. There was an emotional wall that she couldn't penetrate. What if that was the reason?

As the *Liberty* lost sight of land, Julie sat on the bow, enjoying the sea air.

"Beautiful sunset, huh?" Micheal handed her a drink.

"Incredible. At this moment, I can almost imagine I'm in the twenty-first century."

"Doesn't that cloud look like a seahorse?"

"Oh yeah. And the one over there looks like a giraffe."

Micheal sat on the portside bench near the front. "I used to spend hours watching the sky and searching for shapes amongst the clouds."

Julie sat on the starboard bench. "In the summer, I would climb on the roof of our house and the clouds became my fantasia. Those days of innocence seem so long ago."

"The past is certainly relative. We would visit my grandparents in Manti, Utah. My favorite thing to do was lay at the top of the temple hill, with my head at the edge. I'd look backward and the sky would appear upside-down. It made you feel like you were floating above a sea of clouds."

Micheal leaned on his elbows and looked backward. Julie copied him and the colorful twilight took on a new image. Then she sat up. "What do you think you would be doing if we never fell through time?"

Micheal came upright. "If I was able to find my family's treasure, I'd be trying to see if I could invent some of my crazy ideas. But with that being unlikely, I'd probably still be searching for the truth of my family legacy. How about you?"

"I'd be six-month pregnant shopping for the baby and preparing to take a hiatus from my show. I would also be scouting nannies because I couldn't quit the show. Now, in regard to you, you would've found the Treasure of Avalon."

Micheal gave a slight smile, then stepped to the bow and gazed at the twilight. "I've always had terrible luck. That was the only reason I sat next to you that day–"

"You think sitting next to me was bad luck?" She tried not to laugh.

"Do you want me to answer that?"

"Wow!"

He laughed. "That was the only good thing that happened on my flight debacle. I mean, when do you get to meet a celebrity?"

"I was almost famous. I'm not exactly Scarlett Johansson."

"You're more of a young Jennifer Connelly."

"You know what I mean." She shook her head.

Micheal sighed. "Our first meeting wasn't the only unusual encounter I had that week." He became reflective.

Julie joined him at the bow. "An odd encounter?"

"I was on break from my deliveries when a strange woman interrupted. She spoke in Latin." He paused.

"What did she say?"

"Our family motto. The words of Avalon. 'A Deo, et in Terra, Rex in Caelis'."

"A God on Earth. A King in Heaven. That's quite a statement. Did she say anything else?"

"No. She just vanished into the snow. And her accent was quite unique. Usually, I can parse out the regional inflections when someone speaks. But hers gave me nothing."

"I also had a strange encounter. On Christmas Eve an old man in a robe briefly spoke to me. At the time, I brushed it off. But maybe there was more to it."

He shrugged. "I don't think it matters now. And look, the night sky has replaced the day." Micheal laid on the deck looking skyward. "Come on. It's like the clouds, only with stars."

"I don't know." He looked silly on his back.

"And I thought you longed for those old days."

She huffed. "Fine."

Julie tried to sit on her ass, but fell on it instead, when her foot slipped. As she came down, Micheal showed his reflexes, catching her fall. She felt a tickle at the close contact.

"Very graceful." He chuckled.

She laughed off her embarrassment.

"Are you okay, then?" He still held her.

"Yes, thank you." She drew up on her hands and briefly made eye contact, then rolled onto her back. "So, I forgot what we were doing down here."

He turned his head to face her. "Trying to revisit those days of innocence through the stars. Now tell me what you see."

The faint distant suns began to illuminate new features in the ancient heavens. She began to see her childhood in the patterns.

V: Research Triangle

They spent the three-day voyage from Lagos testing the equipment they had engineered for studying the energy flows in the Triangle. Despite the fact it may be responsible for their current dilemma, MICHEAL was curious to research the Triangle. One of the greatest paranormal mysteries.

The *Liberty* came to a stop. "We are on the edge of the Bermuda Triangle. Puerto Rico is about fifty miles to the south," Micheal said, pointing at a spot on a map.

"What are we supposed to be looking for?"

"Spikes in EMF energy."

Julie was scanning the west horizon with a spectrometer. The morning sun was shining red behind a blanket of clouds. They ran scans all day, with the strongest readings coming from the northwest.

"Another false positive," she said with disappointment.

"I don't think so. I think they are like whack-a-mole. They come and go. This data is pretty interesting. These variations are far more prevalent here than they were on the way to and from Lagos."

"Look at this pattern. Doesn't that look like it's radiating out from an apex somewhere to the north?"

"You're right. I think we will head toward Bermuda tomorrow and spend a few days running scans. If they correspond with the last few days' results, we may be able to triangulate a center of energy,"

Julie joined him at the back of the top deck. "This last week at sea has me feeling like myself again."

"How so?"

"I haven't had to pretend to be something I'm not. I can just relax."

The next few days were spent tracing the data until they had isolated a potential vortex. Micheal was a bit apprehensive as they were approaching the triangulated location.

"It's about one more mile. Just kill it and we will drift in," Micheal said.

"These readings are off the charts."

Micheal performed a preliminary sweep of the area, pointed, and said, "The apex is probably about one to two hundred feet off the starboard bow."

As they were drifting toward the energy source, Julie was focusing the spectrometer on the area in question. There was a buzzing sound like cicadas.

"It's fluctuating, it's moving in a circle... Wait, it's... I think it's stabilizing," she sounded confident.

The area began to glow with some kind of light below the surface. The ship's KEE lights began to flicker. The buzzing sound became like a loud Harley.

"Are you seeing this? And what's that noise?!" she yelled.

Micheal stepped up next to her.

"Yes, I don't think we should remain here." He hurried to the bridge. He couldn't get the engines to respond. The noise sounded like a freight train.

Julie ran up from the back deck.

"Why aren't we moving?!" she yelled.

"The engines won't respond!"

The glowing light from underneath the surface of the ocean burst through and became a green mist. Micheal could see it slowly start to spiral. It was all around. It kept rising until it was above their ship. He looked up to see the vortex of the mist begin to widen, as if its goal was to swallow their ship whole.

"What are we going to do?" Julie was beginning to panic.

Micheal felt helpless. He tried to think of what he could use that didn't require the engines. Then an idea came to him: the defensive systems.

"I'm targeting the port side."

"What? What are you targeting?"

"If I use the explosive rounds, it might create a wave to jar us loose."

"Jar us loose? From what?"

"From the vortex!"

The horizon shifted. There was a mountain right in front of them, underneath a glowing violet sky. It faded away and the green glow returned.

Micheal targeted the port guns as far down as possible, firing all simultaneously. There was a loud concussion, and a massive twenty-foot wave slammed the port side. The impact knocked them off their feet as the ship rolled thirty degrees. Micheal regained his footing as the *Liberty* righted itself. Two of the engine indicators lit up. He fired the engines, and the ship began to push through the fog.

As they cleared the edge of the mist, the winds picked up rapidly. The anemometer read eighty miles per hour through sustained winds. The waves grew to more than thirty feet in height. He ran to the Doppler; Julie was right behind him.

"What's going on?" The roaring wind and rain nearly obscured her words.

"It's a hurricane!"

"Where did it come from?"

"I don't know, but we are about to enter the eyewall!"

Over the next ten minutes, the wind speed increased to over one hundred and fifty miles per hour. Wave heights reached upward of one hundred feet. The *Liberty* was violently rocking and twisting like it was in a spin cycle. It was a battle with the elements to secure the boat and take shelter. As they reached the back deck, the ship took a one-hundred-foot wave broadside, and Micheal was washed overboard.

He was pulled under the roiling waves. There was no light. He lost any sense of orientation. Up could be down, right might be left. He fought to find the surface. It felt like his chest was going to burst. He couldn't hold out any longer and took a deep breath.

JULIE realized Micheal had gone over. The waves looked like mountains. The terrible storm was a real-life monster. It was thirsty, attempting to suck her up like through a straw. She latched onto the rail, holding on as tight as possible so as not to be blown away. The *Liberty* was spinning and with every rotation her cabin shield would fail her, exposing her to the mercy of elemental horror. The storm would try to suffocate her with the full force of its winds. She tried to think of what she could do. She grabbed a weight belt she saw on the wall and wrapped it around her waist. What else was there? Then she remembered the emergency surface inflator. She quickly retrieved it, then attached a retractable anchor line to her ankle, took a deep breath, and dove in after him.

Panic set in as the water entered MICHEAL'S airways; the anoxic reflex paralyzed him.

Micheal slipped into the protection of his mind.

He was seventeen, sitting in his first apartment just after he moved out, and reading a book about what it's like to die.

Drowning:

- The victim typically holds their breath for sixty to ninety seconds, then reflexively takes a breath. Panic rises during this period.

- As they start to take in water, the anoxic reflex usually closes the throat, so very little water gets into the lungs.

- The water that does get in the lungs sears like fire.

- The reflex generally causes a state of shock.

- If this happens, the victim usually blacks out shortly after.

The door opened, interrupting his reading.

"Hey man, you doing all right?" TC shut the door behind him.

"I'm fine." Micheal closed the book.

"I can see that. Doing some light reading?" TC grabbed the book and looked at it for a moment. "Why don't we go get something to eat? There's this new place over near campus."

Micheal left with TC, leaving the book behind him.

He returned to the quiet world where he felt just as numb as he had that day. Then everything went black.

JULIE was searching frantically, but it was so dark she couldn't see anything. She dove several times, trying for deeper depths each time. As the minutes passed, she feared she would never find him. Images of her sister's arms sinking into the water came flooding in. When she came up for air, her whole body was shaking. She felt herself begin to cry. She couldn't let this happen again. She wouldn't let Micheal leave her. She focused on Micheal's face, took one last deep breath, said "Jessica, help me," and dove under.

MICHEAL saw a glimmer of light in the darkness. It increased in intensity. The light was blinding, then his eyes seemed to adjust, the light focused into...a woman. She was ethereal, a soft luminous glow emanating from her entire being. She looked like a beautiful angel. Her blond hair flowing in the current, her piercing sky-blue eyes shining like brilliant stars. She looked about twenty years old, her white dress whipping all around her. She looked familiar to him; he wasn't sure why, and she seemed surprised he could see her.

You can see me? But it wasn't him. Those words hadn't come from his thoughts. He just heard them as he could hear himself think.

Yes, he thought in response. *Am I dead? Are you an angel?*

You are going to be all right. She communicated.

A calm came over him and he felt completely at peace. He thought she must be his guardian angel.

Just know you are loved, she communicated.

As she turned to go, he realized why he recognized her.

You look like Julie!

Before he could ask her name, she disappeared in a brilliant flash of light.

JULIE'S body was exhausted from treading the waters, and her mind was full of regrets. She couldn't save her sister, and now, she couldn't save Micheal. She was about to give up when her eye was caught by a glimmer below the surface. She took a deep breath to give it one final try. She dove, fighting toward the light.

As she drew near, the light disappeared in a flash. Julie desperately kicked deeper. Her hand grazed something that had to be an elbow. Micheal! She dropped the weights, wrapped her arms around him, opened the surface inflator, and they were pulled quickly toward the surface.

The waves were becoming much calmer as they broke the water and she could see the Milky Way shining brightly in the sky. She scrambled back on board, lugging Micheal behind her.

She began CPR.

"Come on Micheal...." She counted in her head.

"Don't do this to me...."

"What was that light for if I wasn't meant to save you?" All that effort just to fail in the end.

She gave a couple more breaths.

"Come on!"

At that moment, he started coughing up water and opened his eyes.

"Oh my God!" She hugged him.

After a minute, he said, "Help me to the safety pod. We're in the eye of the hurricane. Once we're inside, we should be safe."

Julie helped Micheal in, and she sealed the pod door after her. She immediately placed the safety harness around him, then secured herself. A few minutes after it was sealed, everything started shaking and swaying. They rode out the storm in silence.

"Why did you do that?" Micheal finally asked. He had been quiet for a while.

"Why did I do what? Save your life?"

"You could have died."

"And? I'm not supposed to risk my life for you, but you can risk yours for me?"

"Thank you for saving me, but I'm not worth your life."

"You don't get to tell me what my life is worth."

"You have people who care about you—"

"I don't want to argue."

He was being stubborn, so she decided to drop it. She was just happy he was all right.

He stared off blankly for a moment.

"Death, honestly, didn't seem so bad," he said softly.

She felt the anger rising again. She took a few deep breaths to suppress it, then said. "What do you mean? You didn't die."

He seemed to be considering something, then he said, "I think I did for a little bit. I went under and it was totally black. I was disoriented and couldn't find the surface. When I started taking in water, I knew it was the end. After what seemed like a lifetime, everything became peaceful. I felt a warmth wrap around me like a comforting blanket and then I met an angel."

"An angel? Not the horse Angel?"

He looked longingly.

"There was a light. It got brighter and then," he paused for a second, "she was so beautiful. She was floating in the water. The light was emanating from her. She was dressed in white, her dress and her blond hair floating about her. Her soft blue eyes seemed to pierce right through me...She seemed surprised I could see her. I asked her if I was dead. But in my head. She said I would be all right, and that I was loved. She said she wasn't an angel, but what else could she be? At that moment, when it seemed all was lost, she showed up to comfort me." He seemed to finish, then added, "It was probably all in my head, now that I think about it."

"What do you mean?"

"Well...because of how she looked.... She looked like you." He considered things for a moment. "I must have just confused it all in my mind," he said, shaking his head.

She couldn't stop the tears from flowing.

"Are you all right?"

"Jessica," she said.

"What?"

"My sister... that was my sister, Jessica."

"Your older sister?"

She told him all about Jessica and what had happened to her—about going to the other side, about asking Jessica for help, and how an unusual glint of light had helped her find him.

When they came out of the pod, the sun was shining; the sails were all gone, and all but one of the KEE engines were broken. They limped into Bermuda for repairs. The silver reserves stashed in the security vault made everything go smoothly, and a week later, they sailed for home.

CHAPTER 15: SUMMER OF FEAR

WHEN THEY RETURNED IN early August, "witch fever" had spread throughout the colony and Boston was in chaos.

"That certainly went south while we were gone," JULIE said as they walked after dropping off Angel and Darkness. They had just gone for a reunion ride into town.

"We are approaching the climax of the trials. They called it 'the summer of fear.' Anyone could be accused."

"Don't I know it," she said rubbing her neck.

"Micheal?"

"Yes, Julie."

"There's something I have to tell you." She had been putting this off for too long.

"Okay."

"I think..." She hesitated. "I think I'm pregnant."

"Why do you think you're pregnant?"

"Well... I'm not sure I'm comfortable talking about this, but I..." She took a deep breath. "I haven't had a period since we fell. And Aiden and I... Well, we..." She broke off.

"That was seven months ago. You'd be showing by now."

"Haven't you ever heard of those stories in the news about how some women found out they were pregnant only when they went into labor?"

"They were usually overweight and typically had five or ten kids already."

"So you don't think I'm pregnant?"

"You haven't..." He hesitated.

"No! There isn't anyone here I would ever do that with!"

Only she wasn't being completely truthful. She looked sidelong at him. Still, every time she had lurid thoughts about him, the guilt over Aiden pulled her back to reality.

Micheal touched his chin and squinted at her.

"What are you thinking?" she averted her eyes.

"It could have something to do with the temporal mechanics."

Julie looked back. "How so?"

He thought a bit longer, then said, "There is a concept in temporal mechanics that something outside time is unaffected by time. If we were outside time in some way, we wouldn't age."

They reached their riverfront deck overlooking the Mystic River and stopped at the center.

"Really? ... You don't seem convinced."

"In those theoretical scenarios, to be outside of time meant literally being outside of normal time. But we are obviously living through the days."

They both stood lost in thought, watching the river.

Then: "Fire!" The screams came from behind them, inside Bostonian.

As they ran in the direction of the screams, Julie saw that the north wing was on fire. The sprinkler system was already dousing the flames.

They heard someone yell "Fire!" again, this from the direction of the barn.

Julie saw a hooded rider about to throw a Molotov cocktail into the servants' quarters. Micheal pulled out his pistol and shot the bottle out of his hand. The man turned and rode off to the west at full gallop.

"Angel!" she yelled as she ran toward the barn.

Micheal was right behind her. They freed Darkness and Angel along with the rest of the horses and made for the exit. They were near the door when the front half of the roof collapsed. It was about to come down on Julie, but Micheal tackled her, and they rolled away, just clearing the flaming mass.

Some staff, under Rose's direction, were already coming over with water and wet blankets to help put out the barn. Stable hands calmed the horses while inspecting them for any injuries.

Micheal helped her to her feet and, after all the fires were put out, assessed the damage. The north wing of Bostonian had some minor damage. One of the fields had been set alight but was doused in moments. The barn was a total loss.

"Who do you think would do this?" Julie asked Micheal.

"There are some that may not be too happy with our taking the limelight in the society circles and many more who are envious of my family." He thought for a moment. "I have a few people in mind, but no one is the clear culprit. Many are using this summer of fear and suspicion to settle scores."

Tensions ran high over the next couple of weeks while everyone tried to recover from the attack on the palace. This distraction had delayed MICHEAL'S routine maintenance on the mining fleet. Then, while he was running diagnostic tests, he cursed, "Dammit!"

"What?" Julie looked up from the robot she was finalizing for the second assembly line.

"One of the bores is not responding. I'm going to have to go up to Portsmouth to deal with it."

"New Hampshire?"

"Yes, it will take a few days. I will be back as soon as possible."

The next morning, everything was packed. Micheal stood next to Darkness preparing to mount.

"Be vigilant my dear, I will return to you promptly," he said dramatically. He had come to look forward to this small, yet charming, tradition.

She responded in kind. "I shall count the days until you return."

In public, they played the loving partners. He would give her tokens of affection and make elaborate proclamations, and she would respond by fawning over his gifts and showing devotion, all to give the perception of a happily married couple. But it was all a charade. He knew she would never have feelings for him.

He had, for the first time, been able to lose weight, so he was in good shape, but that couldn't make up for all his other shortcomings. And of course, there was Aiden. He could see how much the separation was hurting her. He was determined to do whatever it took to get her back to him. All he cared about was her happiness. That thought led to a sudden epiphany: *Am I...in love with her?*

Micheal had never been in love before so maybe he was wrong about it, but she consumed most of his thoughts. He knew she could never know. He would do what he always did in these kinds of situations, although this would be harder than ever before. He would have to build a wall around his heart.

His thoughts came to a halt when he reached the location of the bore. Once he found the bore's precise depth, he was able to coax it to the surface. One of the gaskets in the drill motor had broken down, allowing some of the molten ore to leak inside. This was going to take longer than he had expected.

It took three days of work to overhaul the engine system but, with the bore back in commission, Micheal finally started home. It was an irritating delay, what with everything going on. He needed to get back to Julie.

He had strong feelings of déjà vu as he rode into Salem. There were at least a thousand people crowded around the gallows. Eight people, six women and two men, were standing on the gallows with nooses around their necks. Then he remembered it was September 22; these were the final executions of the witch trials.

"Lord Whitaker, come to see justice carried out against the devil's children?" John Hathorne said jovially.

"Justice? Yes, Master Hathorne, I've heard much about the 'justice' taking place up here," he said as he rode up to the front of the crowd.

Hathorne detected the cynical tone.

"My lord, if the sight of justice being served disturbs you, you may be on your way."

"Oh no, Master Hathorne, it's quite the spectacle, something to be proud of I'm sure."

Hathorne shifted in his seat.

When the execution was declared over, Micheal rose and turned to the dignitaries in the front row.

"A great act of justice, gentlemen," he declared, dripping with sarcasm.

Hathorne and the Corwins looked incensed. Parris was clenching a bible; he seemed to be the most furious, but they all seemed intimidated by him.

He mounted Darkness and said loudly to the crowd, "Ladies and gentlemen, a proud act of justice, to be sure. Don't hang your heads in shame, look! Look at the great justice before you."

The crowd grew quiet, most averting their eyes with their heads bowed. "Hold your heads high, proudly before God."

He eyed the crowd for a moment, then rode off towards Boston.

⸺⋈⸺

JULIE had been fluent in several languages before the fall. She had learned Latin at the university, and for the sake of business, she had learned Mandarin, Japanese, Arabic, Hindi, and Russian. Now, she had begun to get the hang of many others while working with her staff, adding nearly all the other main European languages.

"Bonjour!" Yvette said as Julie arrived for her French lesson.

"Bonjour, Belle matinee, s'il vous plaît," she said, gesturing for Yvette to sit.

After her lessons, Julie was overseeing preparations for dinner.

"Rose, inform everyone supper will be served at sundown."

"Yes, my lady," Rose said.

"My lady!" Yvette said urgently as she ran to Julie. "There are men here for you!"

"Men?" she replied in confusion, opening the doors to the mansion.

"Lady Whitaker?" one of the men said.

"Yes?"

"Sheriff Samuel Gookin. I arrest you on charges of witchcraft and high treason." His announcement was followed by two men grasping her by the arms and escorting her to a coach.

As they drove toward whatever horrible dungeon she was sure she was to be thrown into, she wondered how much longer it would be before Micheal returned.

⸺⋈⸺

Julie woke to the sound of the lock on the door rattling. She rolled over as the door opened and when she saw Micheal she instinctively ran into his arms and started crying.

"Sh… You're safe. Everything's going to be all right. Let's get you home," he touched her cheek with tenderness. She looked up at him. He wiped the tears from her eyes, then escorted her out of the room.

"You think yourself so special, don't you, 'my lord'!" She turned, and it was the man from the Governor's Ball.

"You and your Devil's whore."

"That will be all, Master Nash." The sheriff restrained the man.

Micheal gave him a stare that could stop a heart and said, "This will all be settled. Soon."

"I am so sorry I wasn't here. How are you feeling?" Micheal asked as they rode away.

"Much better, but I still face charges?"

"Yes, but the governor is about to put a stay on all prosecutions. It will never go to trial," he said, his knowledge of history lending certainty to his words.

"That's good. How was Portsmouth?"

"Well, the stupid bore took forever to fix, but it's back in commission and I ran into your three favorite people in Salem."

She felt the hate begin to build, but she suppressed it. "Which three?"

"I encountered Hathorne on the way to the executions, Sheriff Corwin, and Parris were already there."

"What executions?"

"The last eight of the witch trials."

"Did you try to stop it?"

"No, I didn't want to alter such a major piece of history. I did dress down the entire town after it was over."

"Well, no one deserves it more."

I: The Professor

With Julie safely at home, it was time for MICHEAL to prepare for the start of his classes. In a few weeks after the harvest, he'd begin as Professor of Mathematics and Science Arts at Harvard.

He had a meeting with the board and, as he rode toward the university on the River Road, he saw the Harvard Bridge. It was nearly complete and scheduled to open next week. As he continued on, he saw the science labs. The fully completed building was just as impressive as he had envisioned it in his own mind. The large circular building stood out with all the windows and almost looked like a UFO had landed. He continued up to University Row on Cambridge Street.

"Professor Whitaker! I must say impressive the developments at the University." Master Brattle said jovially. "A world-class institution!"

"Yes! It has been a proud effort by the masons and craftsmen."

"And it has been a pleasure to see a taste of Avalon in these parts, my lord."

Micheal hoped Brattle wouldn't probe too deeply into his relationship to the Lords of Avalon.

"We just wanted to contribute to this great community."

"Now, my lord, the fellows are eager to hear your curriculum," Brattle said as they entered the President's Hall.

"That is a rather ambitious proposal, my lord," Master Elliot seemed concerned.

"I have laid out my process with thorough reason, I assure you." Micheal spoke with confidence.

"I have reservations about your proficiency." Cotton Mather questioned.

"Master Mather, you may inquire on any subject you wish."

"My lord, I would have a demonstration of aptitude." Mather challenged.

Micheal looked at the windows and got an idea. "Allow me a moment."

He excused himself, then returned with two prisms and a lens.

"I shall demonstrate Master Newton's discovery that white light contains a spectrum of color within it."

Micheal arranged the prisms to the precise specifications, then placed a paper to catch the end result.

"Using this optical lens..." He held it up for all to see. "...I shall focus light through the prisms and onto the parchment. Through this process you shall see white light enter one prism, it shall separate into the color spectrum, then reconstitute itself back to white light."

He went and pulled the curtains closed until there was only a small gap for light to pass through. Then he placed the lens in just the right spot so that it concentrated the beam on the first prism. The rainbow spectrum connected the prisms, then a circle of white lit up the parchment.

"Impressive demonstration, Lord Whitaker, a Professor of

Mathematics and Science Arts, indeed." Master Brattle said with approval.

II: The Harvest

Two weeks after her arrest, JULIE was in much-improved spirits. A message had come from the governor.

...Therefore, with most humble sincerity, and with a most gracious heart, express our deepest apologies for thy plight. It is my honor to inform the most noble Lady of Avalon that these grievous charges have, by my order, have been categorically expunged.

—Sir William Phipps, Lord Governor of the Province of Massachusetts Bay

The letter had brought relief, and now she could focus on the harvest.

Bostonian felt like a madhouse with everyone coming and going. It had become a bit hectic, and Julie decided she needed a break.

She took a carriage down to Boston to visit her friend, Cecily Penn, and take some time to relax.

"Julie!" Cecily was already down the steps before Julie could respond.

They had become fast friends at the Governor's Ball and had visited each other on and off since.

"Cecily! All is well with Master Penn?"

"Matthew is quite well. We do spend a bit of time trying for a child, if you catch my meaning." Cecily's smile grew wider as she led Julie inside. She continued, "And when he is not tending to business." She gave a light cough, poised herself, then asked, "My lord is well?"

"Micheal has been busy at university preparing instruction."

"With that and the harvest, how much time do you spend,"—Cecily drew closer as they walked—"trying?" And they both laughed.

"Unfortunately, not much," Julie said in a disappointed tone as both ladies composed themselves.

"Julie! You are not letting that handsome man go to waste, are you?"

From the first time they met, Cecily gushed over the idealized relationship she imagined Julie and Micheal shared. She did feel some pangs of guilt for deceiving her friend, and for preventing any possible prospects for Micheal. She was sure many other ladies in the colony viewed him the same way Cecily did.

On the other hand, she wasn't sure she would like to see Micheal with any other woman. Julie wasn't sure what she wanted, and that vague conclusion made her feel guilty all over again, like she was cheating on Aiden.

They were joined by several other ladies for tea, and the conversation turned to the gossip of the day.

"How terrible are these scurrilous accusations against you, Julie," Cecily said in disgust.

"All charges have been dismissed," Julie sighed and smiled.

"Lord be praised," Alice Windsor rejoined, and all the ladies echoed their agreement.

"Let us leave this unhappy discussion. I just visited the children at Carehouse." Carehouse was an orphanage Julie had opened in Boston.

"I love those children." Mary Rainsford regularly visited the orphanage.

Following tea, Julie and Cecily made their farewells to the other ladies, then they headed off to go shopping.

When the spree was finished, she left Cecily at her estate and returned to Bostonian.

"How are the ladies?" Micheal asked as she was passing him in the hallway.

"Very well. It was nice to have a frivolous day of shopping and gossip with the ladies. How was work?"

"A lot of effort to ensure the Harvard Bridge opens in time for classes. But I think it will be done in just a couple of days. On a different note, I thought we could take a day away to celebrate the Governor's letter."

"What did you have in mind?"

"A surprise."

"Sounds fun."

"Nice hat. I'm sure it will look good on you." He gestured at her new purchase.

"Thank you!" she smiled."Tomorrow then. Good night, Jules." Micheal disappeared into his suite.

<hr>

The next day they left on the Liberty, after breakfast. Micheal had been coy about their destination. JULIE knew they'd headed south after passing Cape Cod. By midday, the sandy cape of an island drew near. She thought about where it could be.

"Nantucket?"

"I tried to think of a beach that would be empty. This was what I came up with."

Micheal brought the Liberty into the shelter of the west side of the peninsula. She had been here in the 21st century, but she flew in and never visited Coatue Beach.

"So it's a beach day?"

"That's part of it."

He opened the lower access, and she saw that Angel and Darkness had come along for the day.

"Hi sweety!" Julie stepped down and greeted her friend.

Micheal met Darkness. "Ready to ride?"

They were met by a big blue sky. It was perfect for mid-October. They ran the horses in and out of the surf. This was another transportive experience that made her feel timeless. The wind in her hair was therapeutic. Micheal was majestic with Darkness beneath him. He was dressed down in just a simple shirt and trousers, but the shirt was well-tailored in purple with fancy buttons enclosing the front. He'd let his hair down. To match the aristocracy, he'd grown his hair since the fall, and now it was just above the shoulder. Normally, he wore it back in a ponytail. But here it flowed like Fabio.

"Race to the end?" She prompted Angel and left Micheal behind.

They weaved in and out of each other. The race was an exhilarating five minutes until the horses tired and slowed to the end of the peninsula.

"Looks like I won!"

"Darkness had more to carry."

"Excuses, excuses."

"You're right, Congratulations. I do have some other things. Let's go back a little way."

They rode back a few minutes to the beach next to the second point of the peninsula.

Micheal laid a large blanket at the top of the sand, then set out a picnic lunch.

"You can eat whenever you want. But I'm going to get in the water."

He removed his shirt, then slid his trousers down, revealing his custom swim trunks.

"Your swimsuit is packed in your saddlebag with a towel. If you did want to use it. And I promise I won't look."

Micheal waded into the waves. What was the big deal? It's not like he hadn't seen her before. And it was a bikini. She'd wear it at the beach or the pool in the 21st century.

Using Angel for a shield, she stripped down and slipped into her bikini, then joined him in the water. He dove under, then emerged with streams rippling over his abs.

"The water feels nice, doesn't it?"

"It's calm, like a swimming pool."

"I haven't been in a pool since high school. And this is the first beach I've swum at. Not counting the Great Salt Lake."

"Isn't that pretty big? I think that would count."

"It's nothing like this. It smells terrible. The primary reason to go is that you can float on it due to the salt content. It's five times saltier than the ocean. But mostly it's used for boating."

He went quiet and leaned to float on his back. It looked relaxing, so she joined him.

"This reminds me of the lake. Whenever we went to Saltair, I would float with my eyes closed and pretend I was suspended in space. For a moment all my troubles drifted to the background, and I could pretend I was someone important."

Julie would've argued his statement but didn't want to rob him of his solace. Instead, she drifted into her own tranquility. Following a good few minutes, she turned upright. Micheal remained calm. As the minutes passed, she thought he looked dead. That's when she got an idea.

She crossed her thumbs, then pushed through the surface of the water, spraying him. He sank under, then popped back up, wiping his face.

"Was that necessary?"

"I worried you were dead." She muffled a laugh.

"Is that right?" He sprayed her in the face. And the water fight was on.

Julie dove under and pulled his legs out from under him.

Micheal got back up. "I see how it is."

He pursued her through her spray attacks until he caught her under the arms and dumped her in the surf. She found the surface, then made her way toward the blanket, kicking water at him the whole way.

Julie toweled off, and he joined her for the picnic.

"What was your favorite thing about growing up in Virginia?"

"The diversity of the options being in the center of the east coast. One weekend we might go to Shenandoah or the outer banks. The next might be DC or Atlantic City. What about you? I hear Utah is beautiful."

"The natural beauty is amazing. We mostly went camping in the Wasatch Mountains. But a few times we did go a little further. Southern Utah is all like a national park. We'd work our way from St. George to Moab, stopping at each national park. My favorite is Bryce Canyon. The furthest we ever went was Vegas and the Grand Canyon."

Julie opened the basket and found sushi rolls.

"Interesting choice for lunch."

"You said sushi was one of your favorites."

"Where did you get the seaweed?"

Micheal plated one of the rolls.

"Last week I went to the shallows and collected kelp. After we acquired the rice on our trip to Africa, I wanted to make sushi, so seaweed was necessary."

Julie was touched by the consideration. She enjoyed the Japanese treat. There was more sun and fun, then they returned to the Liberty by sundown.

Micheal's distraction felt like a date. She'd become comfortable in their *marriage,* and Aiden crossed her mind for the first time all day. How did that happen? She felt terrible.

They reached Bostonian late, so Julie woke late the next day. She stopped by Micheal's suite. "I really enjoyed Nantucket."

"It was good to get away."

"Indeed, I'm going to oversee how the harvest is coming along."

Julie made the rounds, then needed a break. She was leaning over the main fountain in front of the palace when she felt something hit her hard on the back of her head and everything faded black.

As she started to come around, she got a slap to her face.

"Wake up, 'my lady,'" a man said with a scratch in his voice.

She thought she recognized the voice. As she opened her eyes, three faces began to come into focus and in the center was Master Nash.

"Now, whore of Avalon, I will see justice served," he said coldly. Her hands were bound behind her back, and she realized there was a rope around her neck.

"Justice? Have I done you wrong?"

He had a knife in his hand. "That special family a yours wronged me twice over. And that lying whore, so-called Duchess, in particular..." He paused and slid the blade into a shoulder sheath. "Whores a Avalon know not their place. Ladies' place cooking and cleaning, not making promises unkept," his teeth clenched, his eye quivering.

"What promises unkept give allowance for murder?"

"In his mercy, God Almighty has provided for my suffering. My Lord in Heaven will forgive me," he said self-righteously as he slid the loop tight against her throat.

"If you believe in God's forgiveness, do you not believe in your own? I have done no offense to you."

"You are just like 'Her Grace,' the whore promised to save my daughter and my wife," he said with tears in his eyes. "Whore let them die, now you will serve recompense," he gave a signal and the two men threw the rope over a tree branch and began pulling her up.

"Please! No..." Her feet rose from the ground.

MICHEAL was working on his latest project in the labs when Yvette burst through the door.

"My lord! My lord!" she said breathlessly. "They have taken my lady!"

"Who?!"

"Two men...on horses."

"Yvette, send word to the sheriff. Which direction did they head?"

"Northwest! The road to Cambridge."

He sprinted past the Tier Gardens to the stables, mounted Darkness, and rode full gallop toward the isthmus. Once across, he searched for any signs they might have left on the main road. As he discovered a trail of fresh damage leading north into the woods, the Sheriff of Suffolk came riding up from the west with two deputies in tow.

"Lord Whitaker!" the sheriff called.

"Sheriff Gookin. Two men abducted my wife. Their trail leads this way into the forest."

A hasty ten-minute ride up the trail, and they spotted three horses tied to a tree. As they slowed to assess the scene, they could hear some rustling in the leaves through the thicket.

The rope was thinner than the previous time and it bit more deeply into JULIE'S neck. The pain was agonizing and, as the dreadful minutes dragged on, they felt like hours. She knew she didn't have much time. A state of terror and disbelief threatened to send her into a panic.

Julie doubted Micheal would arrive and save her this time. She would have to do it herself. She had to fight through the excruciating pain to focus on the task at hand. The walls were closing in again. Everything started to sound distant. She had tunnel vision, and her body began to go numb.

She had been fighting the binds that held her hands the entire time. They finally came loose. She reached up and grabbed the rope above her head and was about to try to pull herself up when she saw Master Nash charging at her.

She swung her legs forward, then back. As Master Nash got in range, she swung her legs up and wrapped them around his neck. He grabbed her thighs in shocked response. She flexed her neck against the rope and let go. She ran her hand down Nash's arm to his shoulder and found the knife. She pulled it out, reached up, and cut the rope. It gave way and, as she fell, she used her momentum to flip Nash.

She pulled the rope loose around her neck. The sudden pressure change caused her to get lightheaded. She nearly passed out. At that moment, she realized Nash's henchmen were closing in from both sides. She took a deep breath to steady herself. The first man reached her; his arm was stretched out holding a gun. She deflected the pistol as he fired, spun around, and used his momentum to send him headlong into a tree.

The second man hit her from the side, tackling her to the ground. He straddled her and pulled the noose tight behind her back, attempting to strangle her as he reached for the knife. She was starting to feel helpless. To calm herself, she focused on her training. Jujitsu bridge roll...and she was on top of him, then a Muay Thai elbow brought down hard...and he was out for the count.

Before she had a chance to rise, she felt a punch to her chest. Julie saw the handle of a knife sticking out. He was trying to pull it out again. She grabbed his thumb and twisted his arm back. She pulled the knife out and jabbed it into his inner elbow, splitting his lower arm open to the wrist.

She loosened the noose around her neck. She turned to the second man and saw him writhing on the ground with blood pouring out of his arm. Her adrenaline dropped, and she remembered she'd been stabbed. In the chest. She lay on her back and put pressure on the wound. She fought to stay awake. She knew that if she fell asleep, she might never wake up again. As she had that thought, everything went dark.

MICHEAL and the men by his side pushed into the clearing to see a bloody mess.

"Julie!" he screamed as he ran over to her.

Her whole chest was wet with blood. There was a noose around her neck, and she wasn't moving. He checked her pulse; it was faint but there, and her breathing was shallow. She had lost too much blood.

CHAPTER 16: CELEBRATIONS

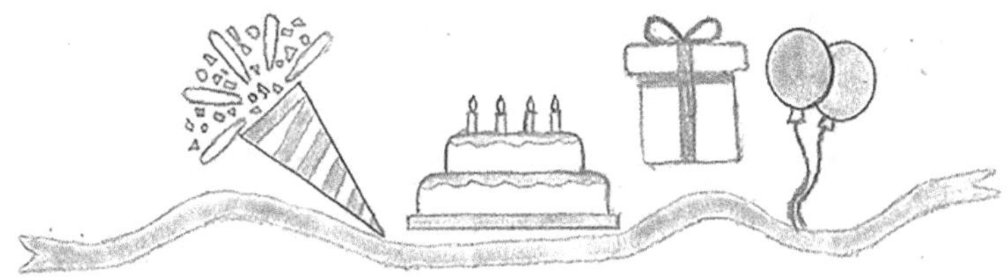

J ULIE SLOWLY OPENED HER eyes. Micheal was holding her hand; Rose and Yvette hovered nearby.

"My lady!" Yvette said excitedly.

"My lady, we are so pleased." Rose was smiling.

The two rushed to Julie's side. Rose reached out and took her other hand, tears flowing down her face. Yvette touched her shoulder.

"Ladies, might we have privacy?" Micheal asked.

"Yes, my lord," Rose said as they exited.

"Here drink this," Micheal said offering a cup of water. It went down hard at first, then it got easier.

"How long have I been out?"

"Two days. I almost lost you there a couple of times." He paused for a second. He seemed like he was holding back tears, then he steadied himself. "You were fortunate. The knife missed your heart by less than an inch. It nicked your right lung and your right pulmonary vein. A few millimeters to the left and you would've been dead. Are you in much pain?"

"A little. But surprisingly, not much."

"I synthesized some morphine."

Julie couldn't help but smile. "How did you find me?"

"Yvette saw them take you. She told me what happened, and I tracked them. Do—" He broke off and took a deep breath. "I'm so

sorry. I should have been there sooner. The hell they put you..."
His eyes were watering.

"It's not your fault. I know you feel like you're supposed to be
Superman, but there's only so much you can do. That's why I'm
learning to protect myself."

He was averting his eyes, obviously feeling guilty. She gently
pressed her other hand over his. He looked up and met her gaze.

"I don't blame you for anything that's happened to me. You've
been protecting me with no thought to the danger to yourself since
we first met." Julie looked into his eyes. She needed to know he
was truly listening. "I want you to say, 'it's not my fault.'"

He seemed truly concerned about her. They had become good
friends in the past eight months, but a part of her wondered if he
cared for her as more than that. He was normally so composed that
he was difficult to read. His emotions were a complete mystery.

"I want you to say it."

He shifted his eyes, then said, "It's not my fault."

She recognized how hard that was for him to say, so she didn't
push further.

"What happened to the men who attacked me?"

He looked away for a second, then looked back. "They're all
dead."

Julie felt tension fill her stomach. "Dead? Did I kill them?" She
didn't want to be a killer.

"It was self-defense."

Her heart sank. Despite how bad they were, she didn't want to
personally kill them.

"How did they die?"

"Master Nash had a broken neck. The other two, Talmage
and Gibbs, one had a cranial hematoma that likely caused an
aneurysm, and the other bled out from the gash in his arm. The
sheriff and his deputies had met me on the road. They dealt with
the bodies. The sheriff won't be pressing any charges. Now, take it
easy, get some rest. Yvette will look after you while I'm gone." He
stood up and rubbed her hand with his thumb.

"Feel better." He kissed her on the forehead, then walked out
of the room.

She was a little surprised that his intimate gesture didn't feel
uncomfortable or wrong. It felt nice to have that caring touch.

I: First Class

"Salve, nomen mihi est Dominus Micheal Whitaker. Hic est provectus studiis in Arithmetica et Acientia Artibus," MICHEAL said in greeting. He had to brush up on Latin in preparation for acting as a professor, as it was an academic requirement in the seventeenth century.

"Who can translate that into English?" he asked. "Master Rainsford?"

"Welcome, my name is Lord Micheal Whitaker, Professor. This is advanced studies in Mathematics and Science Arts."

"A credit, Master Rainsford. Aptitude in Latin is a requisite for this course. These books shall be referenced throughout," he said as he passed out copies of textbooks he had prepared for his courses.

As he began his lecture on the course overview, several of the fellows and President Mather himself came and sat in the upper rows. They appeared to want to hear his first lecture.

"These courses will cover many aspects of scientific arts, aiding in the exploration of the Lord's creation. Friday courses will be in the laboratories on south end. Do not be tardy. That will be all gentlemen," he said, dismissing them.

"Quite the claim, Professor," President Mather said snidely. "A poor attempt to interject the Almighty into a blasphemous search for knowledge."

"Blasphemy you say Mr. President? Do you not see the Lord's hand in all creation?"

"How dare you! Your arrogant quest to elevate man to the level of God."

"It is blasphemy to muse that men might even aspire to such heights? Was it blasphemy when man discovered fire? Or when man created the wheel? These are simple concepts in this day. Our knowledge is but a single candle flame in God's noonday sun. What is God's greatest limit of ignorance, Master Mather?"

Mather was speechless.

"Your servant, Master Brattle," Micheal said and walked out the door.

He was in a hurry to return home. He felt terrible having to leave Julie in such a condition. The thought of how they parted made him a little nervous. The hand holding and the kiss. Had he revealed too much?

He had built a wall around his heart, but the horrible situation made it difficult to maintain. All he wanted at this moment was to hold her and soothe her, but he knew that level of intimacy would never be wanted. He would need to do better to hide his feelings for her.

When she nearly died, he realized just how much she meant to him and, in spite of everything, he couldn't wait to see her again.

II: Happy Birthday

It had been over a month since the incident in the woods. JULIE had nearly recovered from her wounds. She would train in martial arts in the morning, teach her class for the staff in mid-day, and spend time with her friends in the evening. She was also finally able to go see the children at Carehouse.

The estate was operating smoothly under Rose's management and Micheal spent most of his time at the university. He had withdrawn a bit since the day she woke up. At first, she thought he was just focusing on his classes, but aside from that, it seemed he was putting up more walls between them. She felt he believed he'd gone beyond what a friend would do and was trying to respect her boundaries.

The thought was a little upsetting. While she fully intended to stay faithful to Aiden, she couldn't deny the affection she had developed for Micheal.

She was also longing for intimate contact.

It had been ten months since the fall, and aside from a few moments with Micheal, she had had no meaningful human contact.

Not only was he being emotionally distant, but he'd also been disappearing for hours at a time and had been vague about the reason why. They had agreed to live separate lives with no obligation to keep each other apprised of what the other was doing. She typically let Micheal do his own thing, but her boredom and curiosity finally got the better of her.

She slipped off her shoes and discreetly followed him into the lower basement of Bostonian. As she came to the end of the hall, she was surprised to find another new hallway to her left; a temporary wall had been removed, and the hall was dark. She followed Micheal's trail through the curtain at the end where she found a set of stairs leading to a door. She approached it slowly; there was a black glass circle in the center. As she reached for the handle, she heard some kind of mechanism engage.

Julie took a deep breath and opened the door. She was stunned to find herself in a glass-walled hallway. To the right was what looked like a modern lounge complete with a television, couches, and even a refrigerator. She went through the door and down the stairs. She started walking around the room, exploring. There was a workstation next to the stairs.

At least something interesting happened on my birthday...

Of course, no one knew it was her birthday. There would be no party and no birthday cake or gifts. She had considered telling Rose, Yvette, or even Cecily, but with all that had happened in the past year, she wasn't sure she felt like celebrating anyway. But where was Micheal?

She suddenly heard what sounded like music coming from the hall.

Julie stepped into the hall and in the final room she found...

"Micheal? You can play? And you can sing?"

In her amazement, she stumbled back and sat on a bench she didn't notice was there while keeping her gaze on him the whole time. She didn't recognize the song. It was a slow rock melody about living in dreams.

Over the next hour, he played and sang about a dozen songs, all unrecognizable. She thought he must have written them. This was just what she needed, a true birthday gift. She considered going in when he finished, but then she liked the idea of watching him unaware.

"Time for one more. Recent events have brought this back to the forefront. From August 2000, this is *Failure.*" Micheal began playing.

It was a song full of melancholy. She wondered at what was behind it.

Micheal finished and put the guitar away. She was considering whether to wait for him to exit the studio to talk, then heard him speak to himself.

"Should I tell Julie? No. Not yet. She'd just think it's an amateur hour performance." He laughed and shook his head.

Hearing all of that, she decided to leave the studio before he knew she had been there.

After dinner, she lay on her lounger, thinking about what she had discovered. Why hadn't he told her he could sing? He sounded smooth, but sad.

There was a knock on the door. She gathered herself, then opened it. Micheal was standing there with a birthday cake with one candle on it.

He serenaded her with the birthday song. She was stunned; she didn't know how to react.

"Make a wish," he said with a smile on his face.

She blew out the candle and took the cake.

"Please, come in." She couldn't stop the tears from streaming. "How did you know?"

"I watched your show. What's wrong?"

"I don't know that I want to celebrate the last year," she said, sniffling.

He stepped over to her. As he wiped the tears from her cheeks, he said. "Every year of Julie Buckingham needs to be celebrated. The world is a much better place with you in it."

The tears came again, and she threw her arms around him. He wrapped her in his warm embrace. He was so tender and caring; she could feel her resolve weakening. As they parted slightly, she was sure he was going to kiss her, and if he tried, she wouldn't be able to resist.

He paused like he was considering it, then said, "I have something for you."

He broke their embrace, stepped out of her chambers for a moment, and returned with two wrapped gifts.

She opened the first. It was a leather-bound journal, and her name was engraved in gold on the cover. It was beautiful. The second was a box. Inside was an inkwell and a quill tip matching set with a set of writing quills.

"It's cut diamond," Micheal said of them.

He had clearly planned this for a while. The amount of thought he had paid to her birthday brought the tears back to her eyes.

"Micheal.... Thank you so much." She hugged him again.

After a little while, he pulled back a little, looked down at her, and said, "Happy birthday, Jules. Want some cake?"

III: Holidays

Bostonian had been completed the week before, and they were preparing for an official opening gala that would also serve as a Christmas party. MICHEAL had built an apartment above the labs. He occasionally spent the night there whenever things were more intensive at Harvard.

As he returned home and headed for the stables with Darkness, he saw Julie approach.

"Micheal?" Julie said.

"Yes?"

"I have an idea that I want to run by you." She was fidgeting.

"Okay...?"

"What do you think of a Christmas concert?"

"You mean bringing in a local minstrel or something?"

"No, I thought we might sing." Her big eyes looked hopeful.

He looked away for a second, then looked back.

"I don't know? I'm not sure anyone would want to hear me sing," he said with a laugh.

"I highly doubt that." There was an odd amount of confidence in her statement.

"How do you know? I might sound like a billy goat," he said, trying to convince her to drop this idea.

"I know you are vocally gifted. How many languages do you speak?"

"Only a few, fluently."

"How about in part? And don't forget your perfect aristocratic accent."

"Perhaps a dozen." She was too smart to fool.

"So anyone who is that gifted linguistically can likely sing, at least passably. Please? It's a tradition in my family and it would mean so much to me." Julie gave him the puppy-dog eyes and touched him on the shoulder.

How could he possibly say no to her? He put his hand on his face, then said. "Okay."

He smiled, and she hugged him.

"Thank you so much!"

"Well, I don't see a way out of this one," he said to Darkness. Micheal took the saddle off and was putting it away. A part of him wished he was stronger, more able to resist her. He would do anything for her.

JULIE was having tea with her friends in Boston.

"So, are you doing a concert?" Cecily asked hopefully.

"I always heard the Duke and Duchess perform a concert for Christmas," Alice added.

"As a matter of fact, we are. . ." Julie raised her chin with a proud smile. All the ladies gushed with delight. ". . .and we hired the finest minstrels from all the colonies."

"What to wear to the palace?" Cecily cocked her head, looking up.

"I have a new one in from Paris, already, Cecily." Alice straightened up.

Julie couldn't help but smile. "Not quite a palace, Micheal argues."

"Quite impressive, only half finished. I am certain tis positively captivating now." Cecily began to rave about the castle.

Julie had been amazed at the speed in which Bostonian had been built. Its towers reaching heights of more than two hundred feet with ramparts and majestic spires, ornate interiors, and ceilings twenty feet high, complete with a grand ballroom that was straight out of a Disney princess movie. It was a true fairy tale palace.

Her private chambers were fit for a queen. It had taken a little getting used to. On the adjacent side of the ballroom were Micheal's chambers, a mirror of her own. If Micheal's idea of grandeur was a family trait, it was little wonder everyone viewed them as Lord and Lady.

It was the night of the Christmas Ball, and it was about to begin.

"You look positively festive my dear," Micheal said as she emerged from her chambers.

She was wearing a holiday green skirt and red bodice with a modest décolletage, which made her feel like a posh Mrs. Claus.

Micheal was wearing a suit to match hers. He looked like Christmas itself.

She took his elbow, and they descended to greet their guests.

"Master and Mistress Penn."

"My lord," Master Penn said, bowing.

"My lady, you are a vision of grace and beauty." Master Penn kissed Julie's hand.

"Master Penn, your servant Sir. Mistress Penn, welcome to our humble home", Micheal said.

After a second, Cecily laughed. "Humble indeed, my lord," she said, with a smile on her face. "I am in great anticipation to hear you sing, my lord. To believe the stories, you must possess the voice of an angel," Cecily said, fawning over him.

Julie hadn't realized there was such a reputation.

"Julie, your tiara is positively royal!" Alice complimented Julie's platinum headpiece.

"Emeralds and rubies, Julie?" Cecily ventured of the earrings and pendant that matched the headpiece.

"Indeed!" Julie confirmed. "Quite the French fashion. Both of you are positively divine."

———⟡———

About an hour later, it was time to take the stage.

"Ladies and gentlemen," the herald began, "in the great tradition of House Avalon, my lord and lady are pleased to present, Christmas in Avalon."

As Julie waited in the wings, she thought about her last six weeks of observations of Micheal's music sessions in the secret rooms. He had covered all kinds of genres and topics. But more than learning about his singing voice, she had found out a lot more about him.

There was a family tragedy, sometime around the year 2000. One of the stranger things he commented on, on a few occasions relating to his fight against depression. He used it as lyrics in one of his songs. He said, "Everybody's always telling me my perfect memory and so-called genius must be such a blessing. But if they took a moment to think about it, they would know it's a curse. Do you really want to remember all the terrible things in your life? In my case, time heals no wounds. And there's no escaping all the bad things I've done in my life. My *perfect* brain dooms me to the reality of my terrible nature. How can I ever be a good person?"

Julie was struggling to fully grasp Micheal's rationale. But at least she was confident his voice wouldn't be bad. Now it was time to start.

They had selected their favorite songs and included some traditional ones as well to satisfy religious expectations.

They opened together with "Have Yourself a Merry Little Christmas." Micheal took the lead, much to the surprise and satisfaction of the females in attendance, and Julie had to hold back a chuckle. Then, she stepped up to her cue as Micheal sang "...miles away".

She walked out of the right wing of the stage. A soft light traced her steps until met she Micheal in the spotlight and began to sing.

The audience was captivated. They alternated singing songs with the occasional duet. The lights of the ballroom and the charisma they shared seemed to enchant everyone in the room.

As their concert was coming to a close, Julie sang a rendition of her favorite song, "Somewhere in My Memory."

They closed with a duet of "O Holy Night." As they finished, the audience rose in ovation, and they went and bowed to the applause.

MICHEAL, despite his original reservations, felt privileged to discover just how talented Julie was. But more importantly, she appeared to be having a tremendous time. He was glad he could give that to her.

Master Robert Rainsford approached with his wife, Mary.

"My lord, my lady, compliments on a fine performance." Master Robert gave a leg.

"Our most humble gratitude for your gift." Mistress Mary dipped in deference.

"We're so pleased you enjoyed yourselves." Julie was beaming with pride.

"'Tis but a small token of our appreciation." Micheal nodded to Mary.

"Professor, might I inquire after this commemorative coin?" Robert held up the personalized disc.

"My apologies, my lady. I did wonder after these sweet items?" Mary inspected one of the pieces of candy from the gift basket.

"Julie, simply marvelous!" Cecily heaped praise on their singing. She was echoed by Alice and the two began to draw her away.

Julie paused, then said, "Mary, join us and I'll explain everything."

Mary complied and the four of them headed off, boisterously chatting.

"Come, Robert, I shall explain everything, as well."

Micheal and Robert made the rounds with the aristocracy and discussed many things besides the coin.

The party ran late into the night, and he escorted Julie to her suite.

"Micheal?"

"Yes?"

"I wanted to thank you again for singing with me. And you definitely didn't sound like a billy goat." She couldn't hold back a giggle.

"It was my pleasure. Good night, Jules."

"Good night, Micheal."

Micheal went out on his balcony to reflect on the night's events. He could honestly say it was one of his best nights. There was, however, something he couldn't shake. A thought that emerged during the party.

He had knowledge of the Queen's Concerts. He knew that the Lords of Avalon performed them periodically, as well as their annual Christmas concerts. If the family stories were true, the Lords of Avalon were his distant ancestors. He was convinced more than ever that the stories were true. Chief Nightwolf had recognized him as one of the lords. More than a few of society's elite who had met the Duke and Duchess of Avalon in England had commented on the family resemblance. He didn't believe in coincidences, so they were almost certainly his ancestors. It was known from contemporary sources that the Lords had claimed definitive proof of Arthurian descent. Which would mean he really was a descendant of King Arthur.

Two days passed, and it was Christmas. JULIE awoke to falling snow. She wrapped herself in her robe and went out onto her private rooftop terrace. She closed her eyes and felt a snowflake land on her nose. The quiet peace of a snowy day embraced her, and it felt like Christmas magic.

"Julie?"

"Micheal! You scared me to death."

"My apologies. You didn't answer the door. I got worried." He explained his intrusion.

"I was enjoying the snow." She suddenly remembered something. "I have something for you!" She made her way inside.

"Merry Christmas, Micheal," she said, handing him a wrapped box.

He opened it and stared for a moment. "These are incredible!"

She had been at the market, trying to find a Christmas gift, but what do you get someone who can make whatever they want? Julie had settled on a set of clay tablets.

"I saw them at an antiquarian's storefront," she said as he took one in his hand. "The dealer didn't know much about them except that they were very old. He had bought them from a merchant many years earlier, and they had just sat there ever since. They were extraordinary and old, so I thought you might like them."

"Do you know what these are?"

"No, what?"

"They are ancient tablets of record. They were used for trading purposes between cultures that had different languages. The writing on the left is cuneiform, the writing on the right... I've never seen anything like it before." He seemed transfixed. "This is the most amazing gift I've ever received. Thank you so much."

He spent another minute studying the tablets, then told her to hold for a second and pulled himself away.

He returned a moment later with a smile. "I have something for you." He let a scarf drop down from his hand.

"I think that's mine already." She laughed.

"It's a blindfold. Do you trust me?"

"Must be some gift."

"I hope so."

Julie turned to surrender sight.

Micheal took her hand and guided her across the chamber, and she heard the elevator open. The ride came to a halt and the scent of paint greeted their exit. Her heart was beating out of her chest with anticipation.

His fingers traced her arm up to her shoulders, then paused on the scarf shielding her vision.

"You ready?"

"I can't wait."

The scarf fell away, and light filled her vision. Then things came into focus slowly. It was a large, circular room. There were canvases on easels everywhere. She saw paints, palettes, and many other instruments of art all over the place. On one side was a pottery wheel, along with any and every other art supply imaginable.

"An art studio?!" She couldn't believe her eyes.

"You've told me on numerous occasions how much you loved to paint. Now you can, whenever you want.... Merry Christmas, Jules."

She hugged him and kissed him on the cheek. He was starting to get inside her head. He was starting to get inside her heart. If only she weren't married.

IV: Anniversary

"So classification of elements." MICHEAL quizzed. "First? Master Rainsford?"

"Gases."

"Second? Master Smith?"

"Non-metals." Smith had an abundance of confidence.

"Third? Master Arkinson?"

"Metals." Arkinson seemed unsure.

"Which kind, Master Arkinson?"

There was a lingering silence.

"Master Rainsford?" He pivoted.

"Trans-metals."

"Quite right. Master Arkinson, would that you were more attentive? Four? Master Bradford?"

"Weak metals."

"Five? Master Scott?"

"Heavy metals."

"Six? Master Baxter?"

"Chalks?"

"Master Smith?" He had raised his hand.

"Soft metals?" A hint of uncertainty in his voice, Rainsford raised his hand.

"Master Rainsford, please enlighten these gentlemen."

"Alkalines," Rainsford said with confidence.

"Indeed. If only you were all like Master Rainsford, we would be a great deal farther along. Observe his example. That is all, gentlemen." He dismissed class for the day.

Julie had come in during his lecture and sat in the back. They all bowed as they passed her on their way out.

"I don't believe that's the usual periodic table of elements," she nudged.

"No, I made an adapted version. The one we are familiar with is not to be for nearly two hundred years. What brings you here?"

"Nothing really, just interested to hear one of your lectures."

"And?" He was curious about her thoughts.

"You certainly have a professorial air about you," she said with a grin.

"I guess I'm doing a good job of faking it." While he could fool the seventeenth century, he was sure he wouldn't pass muster in Julie's modern classes.

She rolled her eyes, shaking her head.

"Care for a walk?" he asked, leading her outside.

"I realize a lot has happened since Bermuda, but we are approaching a year since we fell. When are we going to focus more on the temporal mechanics?" Julie seemed impatient.

"I have been. The biggest challenge is how do you study time? The only thing I could envision was subatomic particles. I've been trying to engineer such a scanner."

"Why is this the first I've heard of this?"

"Your impatience made me not want to get your hopes up."

"Aren't we supposed to be working on this together?"

"I understand your urgency. But you need to be more realistic. I will try to work closer with you on this, but it takes time to invent new tools to study time."

"I just want to get home." Her teary eyes tugged at him.

Micheal put his arm around her. "So do I. Now, after what happened out in the triangle, I tried to assess what it all meant, along with your...situation."

"My situation?"

"The nonoccurrence of your...cycle."

"Oh, well, we know I'm not pregnant. But what do you think it means?"

"Perhaps some form of suspended temporal animation," he said as they reached the Charles.

"You mean like the theory you mentioned the day I first thought I might be pregnant? The one where someone 'out of time' is unaffected by time. How would that work, exactly?"

"In theory, the fourth dimension would require some kind of energy to exist. So, if temporal energy flowed through the three spatial dimensions and you were sort of above the four-dimensional plane, you would be unaffected by the temporal energy and wouldn't age."

"And you think that's what's happening to me, or perhaps both of us?" She concentrated on the river.

"The problem with that idea is we are obviously in the four-dimensional plane." He considered for a moment. "Conceptually speaking, you could make something phase or go invisible by changing its frequency, like tuning in and out of radio stations."

She seemed to consider things, then looked up and met Micheal's eyes. "When we were in the vortex, things seemed to be fluctuating between solid and transparent. Is that what you're talking about?"

"Precisely. Only, in my theory, everything had a temporal vibrational frequency caused by the temporal energy flowing through it. In theory, it's possible that when something or someone is out of place temporally, that they might be out of sync temporally. So they would be 'out of time' and wouldn't age. Your situation might be an indicator of that effect. We will have to discuss this further."

It had been two weeks since Micheal gifted Julie an art studio. He was curious about how she was using it. He took the elevator up the Lady's Tower. Stepping into the studio, he found her stroking a canvas.

"That's beautiful. What is it?"

"Remember what I told you about my near-death experience?"

"Oh. That is how you described it."

Micheal examined the scene. A mystical beach of surreal color.

Julie set down her brush. "I wanted to put it to canvas. Just in case the memory fades."

"The empty spot is for Jessica?"

"I saved her for last. When I picture her in my mind, it always hits me emotionally." Her eyes became watery.

Micheal considered sharing his own loss, but it was too difficult. That thought alone encouraged tears. He fought them back.

"Are you okay?"

"I got something in my eye." He rubbed his eyes.

Guilt replaced sorrow. The first time they ate dinner together, after returning from the Massachusett, they discussed their families. He left out one important person. That memory belonged to him. What did it matter, anyway? They weren't going to remain together. But then she stayed. And after she pulled him from death in the hurricane, the dilemma reemerged. He went back to that moment.

"Jessica's dead? You spoke of her like she was alive."

"It's not something I like to talk about." Her tears hit close to home.

In that moment Micheal thought about sharing his own loss, but he didn't want to cause another fight. How could he explain such an important discrepancy in his family history?

"You don't have to say anything."

"No, it's okay." She wiped her face. "Now I may not fully understand what it's like to remember everything, but the day she died is permanently etched in my mind…"

Julie recounted the memory. As she spoke, the feeling of intimacy was potent. He felt like an intruder. Like it would be selfish to seek empathy for his own loss. So he buried his urge to share.

Julie finished, and he touched the top of her hand. "I'm so sorry."

Back in the present past, Micheal suppressed the moment of weakness. If he was falling in love with Julie, carrying the guilt of such a secret would stay any thoughts of acting on those feelings. He didn't want to dwell in this headspace.

"So, what else are you doing in the studio?"

"Come on. You might want to put on some coveralls."

He donned a set and joined her on the large tarp. She placed two large canvases on the ground.

"Are we going to get messy?"

"There's always a chance it could splatter on your clothes. And we wouldn't want that." She handed him a bucket with painting tools.

Micheal drew a brush. "Are we going to make some happy accidents and friendly trees?"

"I don't know if Bob would approve of this method. But then he did say to find freedom on the canvas."

"I always like to beat the brush."

They both laughed.

"Okay, dip a knife or brush in one of the colors and spray it on the canvas."

Julie swung a knife and pink streaked her canvas. He sprayed his with a cluster of purple. Another knife of orange Xed her pink. He slowly circled his cluster with drips of black.

"If you want to make a circle, you do this." She whipped a brush around, and a curved green spray arced her X and continued on to his shins.

"Sorry." She suppressed a smile.

He dipped a brush in turquoise. "So like this?" His paint showered her legs. "I don't know what happened. But I like your technique." He laughed into his hand.

"I have other techniques." Julie grabbed a can and threw red on his chest. "You were supposed to move. I was trying to improve your painting." She laughed.

He retrieved a can. She was already moving, but he caught her side with blue. Then it was a paint battle. She was winning, so he tackled Julie to her canvas.

"Is this technique improving your painting?"

She rolled them over until she was on top of him on his canvas. "I think it does. But there's one more thing." She streaked his cheeks with her fingers. "That's better." They both laughed.

When the levity subsided, Julie rose to her feet. "I think it's a masterpiece."

Micheal stood up. "What about mine?"

"Well, I am an amazing teacher, so it's almost as good as mine."

"I want to try your last lesson." He smeared paint below her eyes with his thumbs.

"Want another lesson." She attacked, and they went for another battle.

Having lost the war, Micheal lay in his secondary bath, washing the colors from his body. He closed his eyes and enjoyed the memory of Julie's playful smile. Love would never fall between them, but she did feel like his first friend in more than twenty years. At least he no longer felt awkward in their fake marriage. They were just friends hanging out.

⎯⎯⎯⎯▷◁⎯⎯⎯⎯

Three days later.

"Hap—I mean, *un*happy anniversary," Micheal said in greeting.

JULIE wasn't feeling celebratory.

"Definitely unhappy."

"I know. It's been particularly rough for you, and I'm sorry for everything you have had to go through, especially at the start. There's something I want to show you," he said with an air of mystery.

"What?"

"Come with me. It's a surprise."

As they walked through the second basement, she saw the corridor she had passed so many times on her way to catch Micheal's show and realized he was about to lead her to the secret rooms.

"Here we are," he said as he opened the door.

"To the right is a complete twenty-first-century lounge and to the left is a music studio. Only the two of us can access these rooms." She saw a look of pride as he turned to face her.

"Wow! This is amazing," she said, attempting to feign surprise.

"Is there something wrong?" He raised an eyebrow. "Not quite the reaction I had expected." His head lowered and his eyes averted. It was ever so slight, but she had come to know his intricate movements enough to tell when he was working things through.

She paused for a moment.

He let out a sigh and was about to speak when she took a quick step to confess. "I already discovered them. I'm sorry. I followed you down here on my birthday and heard you play. Please don't be angry?" Her heart was going crazy. She wasn't sure what was going through his mind.

He stood in thought for a second, then put his hand to his face.

"This whole time?" He said, not looking at her.

"Don't worry, you were great." She sensed he was about to say something self-denigrating.

"You mean if I were in the shower?" He shook his head, hiding his face.

"You are so annoying sometimes! I swear, sometimes I just want to slap some sense into you." She couldn't believe he was doing this again. Not after what the whole of Boston had seen.

"Well..." He began to turn away.

"Don't you dare." She warned, and he stopped.

"I can't understand how, after everything you've accomplished; you can still think like that. You promised me... Remember? Now, I'll make you a promise. I will only ever tell you what I truly think. Obviously, I won't always tell you everything, but if I say it, I mean it."

His rejection of her praise was painful. And, as a flood of other similar moments came to mind, she wondered if it could have something to do with her.

"The next time I give you a complement just accept it. You may not realize it because of your shortcomings in personal interactions, but when you throw my compliments back in my face, it hurts me. . ." Julie's voice broke as she held back tears.

"Julie... I'm sorry. For so long, I never received a compliment that I believed. ... I guess it's just reflex. This whole year has been confusing..." he paused and looked into her eyes. "...emotionally. Sometimes the old me just comes out. Can you forgive me?"

She knew he meant what he said. His word was his bond. Julie looked at him and remembered the other acts of selflessness she had seen. Now, his reveal of their own private retreat. She took a deep breath, wiped the tears from her eyes, then smiled.

"Okay." She said simply. "Will you show me the music studio?"

CHAPTER 17: TEMPORAL WALL

I: Nightmares

*J*ULIE WOKE UP TO *the buzz of her alarm. She reached through pitch black to silence it when she saw a faint green light begin to glow in the corner. The buzzing turned to a vibration as a vortex burst to life. She tried to run, but the floor kept sliding beneath her feet, defying her will, and drawing her towards doom. She reached out, digging her fingers into the side of her mattress. This only supplied temporary solace as she and the entire bed were dragged into the portal.*

What followed was an abyss of nothingness. She felt like she was falling forever, surrounded by darkness and a complete feeling of emptiness. Then there was a murky light below.

The ground began to take shape. It moved like grass on a windy day. As she fell, shapes became apparent. There were people everywhere. The crowd grew in size. The faces looked like melted wax, with black holes for mouths and eyes.

An unknown force seemed to bind her arms behind her, and a noose slipped around her neck. The rope cut into her neck, and she stopped inches from the ground. She strangled in agony for an eternity. The crowd was cheering her pain, and it appeared death would never come...

Julie woke up in a sweat. Her hands reached for her neck as if to find the noose still there. She could feel it around her neck. She was having trouble breathing and even now; the nightmare felt real.

After an hour or so, she fell asleep, only to fall back into another lucid nightmare. She cried in anguish. She knew she couldn't handle this for much longer. She didn't think her heart could take it. She had never felt so lonely.

She didn't want to be alone tonight. She made her way to Micheal's quarters. She started seeing glowing green eyes in the shadows coming after her. She ran as fast as she could. The empty ballroom seemed like a black void filled with terrifying creatures. She reached the doors to his chambers, and she fumbled with the knob; they were closing in on her. She came inside and slammed the door shut.

She stood with her hands placed firmly against it, as if to barricade herself from any intruders. She caught her breath and slowly backed away. She turned and ran into a dark figure. At first, she hadn't known who or what it was, and her panic made her arms flail around her as retreated back towards the door.

"Julie. Shh...shh...it's okay, you're okay. You're safe." The sound of his voice was calming, and she surrendered into his arms.

Her emotions overwhelmed her. She drew her arms to her chest and her face to her hands. Micheal held her close while she cried. She was finally beginning to feel safe.

Her cries calmed to a light sob as her head rested on his chest. The rhythm of his breathing helped to calm her down.

MICHEAL could still feel the tension in Julie's body, but at least she was no longer hysterical. He relaxed his embrace slowly, then asked, "What's wrong?"

She locked eyes and opened her mouth to speak, but tears flooded back, and she covered her face. He held her tight once more.

"I can't do this anymore!"

"Do what?"

"It feels like ages since I've slept." Julie paused and her head dropped.

"Come here, let's just sit and you can tell me all about it." Micheal led her to his dining table, poured her a cup of fruit tea, then sat beside her.

"Now, why can't you sleep?"

Julie took a sip, sniffled, and her body relaxed slightly. "I have these nightmares. They've come nearly every night since my execution and tonight was worse than ever because of the anniversary...and...." Her tears came rushing back.

"Why didn't you tell me this sooner?"

"I thought I could be strong. I thought I could handle it on my own. But I'm not strong. I don't want to do this on my own."

Micheal could see she was shaking. This wasn't just some nightmare. This was destroying her. It broke Micheal's heart to see her in such terrible despair.

"You are not alone. I will help you in any way you need." He would go to the ends of the earth to keep her from feeling this way again.

"Can I stay with you tonight?" she asked. His eyes met hers; the loneliness in her eyes said this was a desperate plea.

"Of course."

He led her to the spare bed in his sleeping chamber, pulled the covers over her, and ran his hand down her face. He climbed into his bed, and they fell asleep.

Micheal woke to Julie's cries. She was tossing about on her bed. He grabbed his covers, about to throw them off to rush to her side, when she sat up in a panic.

"Julie? Are you—"

She said nothing and climbed into his bed with tears in her eyes. He wrapped himself around her and held her throughout the night. As the hours wore on, Micheal could see that her battles seemed to subside. She finally relaxed comfortably in his arms, and then he fell asleep.

———⋈———

When JULIE woke up, she felt more rested than she had in a

long time. Micheal's protective embrace had comforted her fears and for the first time since she died, she didn't remember any nightmares.

She turned over in his arms. For a moment she thought he was still asleep, but then he opened his eyes, brushed the hair from her face, smiled, and spoke, "Good evening, Jules. How did you sleep?" His voice was soft. It made her feel safe.

She drew closer to him and nuzzled up against his chest.

"I think that's the best sleep I've had in a year. And what do you mean evening?" she asked, suspecting humor.

"We slept all through the day. It's about seven p.m."

"Why didn't you wake me?" Her thoughts jumped to Rose and the day's report, to Yvette and the orders that she was managing.

Micheal, as if knowing her mind was spiraling out of control, cut in. "I thought you needed the sleep," he explained. She appreciated that more than he could know. But now, other thoughts came to mind. Her feelings for him rose to the exterior, and she felt guilty.

"I'm sorry I imposed, I..." She realized how this might confuse their normal arrangement. She didn't want him to know what she was beginning to feel for him.

"It's no imposition. I will help however you need me to." His reassuring words meant the world to her.

Her head felt clear. Her thoughts were beginning to settle. Julie shifted against him, then noticed her legs were straddling his thigh. She also realized the slip she had worn to bed had ridden up around her hips.

She had been so comfortable in his embrace she hadn't really thought about it. She pressed her chest into Micheal's stomach, trying to hide her body's natural arousal.

He seemed to notice her discomfort. "Do you want to get up?"

"I'm okay," she decided and laid her head on his chest.

Despite her stated ambivalence, she relaxed back into his arms. He slowly ran his fingers through her hair. It was very soothing; she soon fell back asleep.

MICHEAL woke up sometime in the night. She shifted in his arms and as her firm chest pressed into his side; he knew that if she did attempt something, he would be powerless against it. Eventually—finally—he fell back asleep.

The next time he woke up, Julie wasn't in the bed. He sighed deeply, the scent of her lingered in the air. It had been one of the most unusual days he had ever experienced. He didn't know what to think.

How did she actually feel about him? Not that it mattered. She already belonged to Aiden. And, with everything she had said about him, Micheal knew he could never compete.

"Good morning, Micheal," she said, bringing in some breakfast.

"Good morning, Jules."

"I made breakfast. You must be famished. I could literally eat a horse." Her eyes widened as she gasped. Then, with shifty eyes, said, "I'm sorry, Angel. Sorry, Darkness." Her smile widened.

They laughed as he sat at the table.

"How do you feel?" she asked.

"Rested. You seem chipper this morning."

"I finally got some quality sleep, thanks to you..." She broke off. He sensed a bit of shyness in her voice.

"This isn't going to change things between us, is it? I know what you said last night, but I'm worried that I crossed a line. I—" Her shoulders slouched, and she averted her eyes.

"There's not really a line," he cut in. He didn't know how to express what he was thinking; he'd never had to do this before. He looked her in the eyes and said, "If you're comfortable with it, so am I. If you ever want to sleep in my chambers, or have me sleep in yours, to help you deal with this, I am here for you." Then he changed the subject: "These omelets look amazing!" He poured some apple juice. "Care for a glass?"

"Coffee, please," she said smiling. She paused for a moment. "I thought about something this morning."

"Yes?"

"We've been here for a year, and we never celebrated your birthday. So it would have to be before we got together." He saw she was trying to work it out.

"It's January 12th." He averted his eyes, knowing how she would react.

"What?!" She leaned forward, eyes wide. She took a deep breath, then relaxed. "How come you didn't tell me?!"

"I didn't think it was a day worth celebrating."

"Micheal, we talked about this!"

"It's not about that." His muscles tightened. "It's the day we fell... into this hell of yours. I didn't think you would care to celebrate. I thought that if you knew, you'd feel obligated, whether you really wanted to or not. That is why I didn't tell you."

"What was it you said to me? 'Every year of Julie Buckingham needs to be celebrated. The world is a much better place with you in it.' Well, I'm here to tell you that every year of Micheal Hall needs to be celebrated. The world is a much better place with you in it," she said with a smile. "So, we are celebrating it today."

Micheal found her determination rather charming. "I do have a lecture in a couple of hours."

"Tonight, then—and happy late birthday, Micheal." She rose from her seat and leaned in to kiss his cheek.

JULIE baked a cake then joined Micheal in the secret lounge. "Want some cake?"

"I would love some."

She serenaded him. He took the dessert, and they sat on the couch.

"Did you have a good day?"

"Indeed. Knowing I had a party waiting for me helped." They sampled her baking skills. "That's so good."

"I found some passion fruit pulp in the freezer. I know it's one of your favorites."

"Thank you for the special treat."

"I didn't have time to get you something else."

"This is perfect." He took the last bite.

"Is there anything you'd like me to do for you?"

He locked eyes with a slight grin. "Want to join me in the music studio?"

"What are we going to do?"

"One of my favorite things to do for my birthday is improvise music."

They entered the studio, and Micheal took a seat at the piano. Julie selected a guitar off the wall.

"When I first showed you this studio, you said you could play multiple instruments. Which ones can you play?"

She sat in a chair. "I learned piano as a child. Saxophone in high school. Violin in college. Then I learned guitar while I worked on Wall Street. And learned drums after starting my show. The one I was studying when we fell was the harp."

"I'm impressed. You talked about the Christmas concert tradition, but I didn't realize you were so musically gifted."

"Well, I was equally impressed when I spied on you. That was partially why I knew about your voice. I'm not on your level, but I've always loved music. My mom got me the piano lessons and once I'd mastered that, it just made sense to learn a new one."

"My love of music has always been there, and I knew if I didn't play the instruments myself. The melodies in my head would remain there. And finally, on my twelfth birthday, I wrote and played my first song. And I did that every year until the fall. Here's this year's it's called 'Across the Stars'."

Micheal played a tender song about longing and loss. Julie clapped at the end. "That's beautiful."

"Thank you. It is a bit melancholy, so we should lighten the mood. Let's see what you've got."

She tried to think of something to play. Then her pick began strumming the melody of 'Waking up in Vegas', and she began improvising the lyrics. She struggled to keep the giggles out of her voice but brought it to a conclusion.

Micheal gave her an ovation. "I would've pictured you a Katy Perry fan."

"What can I say? I like the classics." They laughed together.

"A worthy gift. My turn. In that same spirit, do you know 'The Climb' by Miley Cyrus?"

He played a parody in one of his female vocal impressions.

The rest of the night was spent playing music.

Micheal set down the guitar. "This is probably the best gift anyone's ever given me. I've always kept my music to myself. But I felt comfortable with you. Thank you. Good night, Jules."

Julie was tired but took a moment of reflection. This jam session proved her friendship with Micheal was real. She didn't want to contemplate anything beyond that. She decided to distract herself with another song, and her fingers worked the keys.

II: The River of Time

JULIE was in much-improved spirits these past two months since she could lean on Micheal when things got rough. She did worry about getting too comfortable in the situation. It could increase the odds of her slipping up.

"Are you sure about this?" The motion reminded her of break-dancing, and she felt like a preppy cheerleader trying to be cool.

"I know it feels a little silly at first but when you get the rhythm down, it will allow you to flow into the cartwheel combinations," he said, demonstrating the back-and-forth dance motions involved in Capoeira, the latest martial art form she was learning. "The key to Capoeira is all about keeping the momentum going through the attack." He immediately did a front kick-flip.

"Once you become proficient, it will be effective against multiple foes, allowing you to be evasive and on the attack at the same time." Micheal demonstrated this principle by alternatively kicking one dummy then avoiding the next through the continuous attack. "Ready?" He was in the stance, prepared to go through the motions together.

"Let's go." She was determined to get this right. She practiced the motion for a while, then attempted to rotate into a cartwheel. Once she felt she could duplicate the motions successfully, he called an end to the session.

"We need to take a voyage." His statement came out of nowhere.

"A voyage? To where?"

"Back to the Triangle."

"Do you really want to? After what happened last time?"

"We'll keep our distance from any vortex we detect, and hurricane season is three months away." While she remained skeptical, his air of confidence and reason convinced her. Then she thought of something.

"What about your lectures?"

"After this week, it's spring break."

"Spring break? Florida and whoo hoo?"

He smiled at her joke. "A little less of that. In this time normally you have two spring breaks: the first in March for the spring planting, and the second for Easter week. But this year Easter falls on March 22, so both weeks fall together. So, I thought we might put my neutrino wave detector to the test." He was excited about their research projects.

"You got it to work?!"

He had been working on it for months and if it did what he thought it would, it might be the next breakthrough in their study of temporal mechanics.

"There have been some detections in my tests, but I'm hoping for more useful data in the Triangle."

MICHEAL continued testing the Subatomic Particle Apparatus, or SPA, during the day-long voyage to the Triangle. The neutrino density increased the closer they got.

"Every time we come out here on the *Liberty,* I wonder if it wouldn't be better to just live on it full time. It would probably be safer." Julie seemed only half joking as she approached the bridge from the back of the sun deck.

"It might be a good idea."

"We can't leave like that, especially now that we have our own Kensington palace. What would our subjects say?" she said with a grin. She always liked to tease him about Bostonian.

"Why would my lady ever want to leave her fairytale palace?" he said in an elegant aristocratic accent.

"Shut up."

"Okay, we are approaching an energy vortex."

She picked up the SPA. "How does this work again?"

"I used a torqued KEE channeler to affix a static EM field which is able to return a trace signature of any neutrinos passing through the field. So, we should be able to detect the flow pattern of all the neutrinos passing through this area. Neutrinos are one of the least understood subatomic particles. Some theoretical physicists believe they might be a portion of what they label dark matter. I theorize that is where temporal mechanics live in the structure of the universe."

"So, it's just a guess?" She raised her eyebrows.

"An educated guess."

"Technically, you don't even have a high school education," she said with a devious grin.

"Observe my young padawan."

"I'm older than you... I really just admitted that."

"Your secret is safe with me."

She hit him on the shoulder with the back of her hand.

"Shut up."

"Sorry." He tried not to laugh.

They tracked the neutrino flow from energy apex to energy apex throughout the day. To JULIE'S surprise, the SPA seemed to be working much better now that they were in the Triangle. Their cursory scans had been tepid at best during the cruise. There was a higher concentration of neutrinos the closer they came to a vortex.

Julie saw what looked like water circling the drain. It appeared as a whirlpool with various turbulent currents twisting in toward the center. There also seemed to be some kind of anti-cyclone spinning in the center.

"What do you think these distortions are in the vortices?" she asked as Micheal studied the data patterns on the screen.

"When we were stuck inside the vortex last year, do you re-member how the whole ship seemed to be in flux and how the horizon was changing?"

"How could I forget?"

"If the vortices are a nexus point between two different points in space and time, then these distortions might be showing the inverse reflection of the temporal flow."

"You mean these gaps might literally show the movement of time? Maybe the gaps show temporal inflow from the other side of the space-time nexus." She thought it was the logical next step.

She saw him shake his head and her confidence wavered. "What? You don't think so?"

"No, that's an amazing insight. This is why I wanted your help with this."

A wave of relief came over her.

"I think we got some good work done here. Are you hungry?"

Julie had had something on her mind for some time now. She didn't know how to bring up the subject and as she gathered some ingredients suddenly heard herself ask, "Micheal?"

"Yes?"

"Never mind." She turned her gaze away, but through, the cor-ner of her eye she saw an air of suspicion on his face.

"No. What did you want to ask me?"

"We're friends, right?"

"Of course. Do you consider us friends?" His head dipped a little and his brow furrowed as he raised an eyebrow.

"Of course!" she answered quickly. "I'm screwing this up. I just...okay. I...I wasn't sure how to bring this up..." She stalled, then: "Do you remember last year before we went to Boston? You were so sure you had zero prospects romantically?"

"Yes."

"Do you still think you would have zero prospects?" Her heart was beginning to beat faster.

He didn't immediately answer and rubbed his chin thoughtfully; she began to worry.

"No," he shrugged.

"You sound pretty certain about that." She felt her eyes widen; feelings of jealousy were beginning to build.

"Well..." She couldn't believe he was pausing again.

"I have been propositioned on numerous occasions."

Micheal's blunt statement felt like a gut punch. "What do you mean you've been propositioned?"

"It means on many occasions some of the society ladies have offered to be my mistress."

"Who?" she asked sharply. She couldn't understand why he didn't tell her about this before.

"It doesn't matter. It's not like I would ever do anything."

"Tell me!" Her jealousy overcame her reason.

His eyes went wide with surprise, then shifted, and he leaned back slightly, answering through his teeth. "Are you sure you want to know?"

The curiosity was too great, so she took a deep breath and clenched her fists to rein in her emotions, then calmly said, "yes, I do."

Julie knew that he would be desired, but she was not prepared for the possibility that other women might pursue him. She couldn't believe Micheal had gotten her so worked up.

"Well..." She felt anger and jealousy rise again as he listed them off, one by one, in a casual manner. At least a quarter of the ladies she knew had apparently come on to her "husband".

"...and, particularly, Mistress Alice Windsor. She's been pretty persistent."

When he finished with the last name on his list, her head began to spin. *That bitch!*

Alice was one of her regular teatime acquaintances. She was pretty, with strawberry blond hair and green eyes. Julie had been starting to think of her as a friend.

"I thought you said pretending to be married would prevent that kind of thing from happening?" Micheal's apparent lack of concern for the matter was getting on her nerves.

"I said for you. But it's common for high-class men to have dalliances. And usually, the wives just tolerate it." He was just going about preparing the food like this was a normal conversation.

"You never told me that." Julie started going over the list in her head again.

"That's because originally, I thought there might only be a few. And it's not like it matters anyways. They're only interested in the money."

"Why do they believe they had a chance with you? And why Alice? She's supposed to be my friend!"

"First, I can't really blame Alice. With two daughters, and since Arthur's death, she is in a tough situation. If she doesn't remarry someone of stature, her daughters won't receive their inheritance. Secondly, there are rumors that we are having trouble. A lot of these women are most likely angling for an affair with me to get pregnant, which would set them up for life, in their minds anyways."

"Well! Don't let me stand in the way of your prospects." She began to walk away but stopped when he answered with a large amount of certainty.

"I would never do that."

She turned and faced Micheal. She had her arms crossed and was beginning to form tears behind her eyes.

"Why not? What's stopping you?" Her thoughts filled with ridiculous answers like 'because I'm fat' and 'because I don't deserve it', but nothing could have prepared her for the answer he gave.

"You." She was stunned. Her feelings of anger and jealousy all faded away after this confession.

"I would never dishonor you like that. You and I aren't actually married, but everyone thinks we are, and many would blame you if I gave into temptation." She couldn't think straight. His confession had certainly helped settle down her thoughts. Then she thought of the last word he said: Temptation.

"Temptation? Then you are tempted to?" she asked, the jealousy rising again.

He laughed in exasperation, rubbing his hands over his face.

"Of course I'm tempted. I'm a twenty-eight-year-old virgin if you haven't forgotten. And how could you possibly? I have never had even a single woman show interest in me before in my whole life. Now there are dozens offering themselves up on a silver platter. Any man would be tempted, but I doubt almost any other man would have resisted as I have. I don't know why you're jealous. It's not like we're actually married. You still have Aiden waiting for you, so why would you care?"

And there it was. The question she had been trying to avoid this whole time.

"I'm going to the top deck," he said, and she saw him exit the cabin, leaving her with more thoughts than she could handle.

She stood in stunned silence. Her unusually strong feelings of jealousy started to morph into guilt. She had no idea how much he was giving up for her sake. Then she quietly reflected on what had just happened.

Why would she care if he was spending time with other women? The only answer she could think of was she was starting to fall in love with him, and she didn't want to see him with anyone else. She felt guilty all over again. If not for her, he would've been able to experience the intimacy that everyone deserves.

She loved Aiden, now she thought she might love Micheal. It was a confusing mix of guilt and jealousy. She wanted Micheal to be happy and live fully, but she also couldn't stand the thought of him with someone else.

Micheal went to bed, but she didn't think she could sleep, so she decided to take a page out of his book. She just started focusing on the work.

She re-analyzed the flow data, still uncertain about how to test her hypothesis. She took out the neutrino scanner and ran a full 360° sweep. There was a new anomaly. She retested the sweep, and it was still there. She realized the anomaly was...Micheal.

After multiple checks to be sure, she ran a scan with her in it. Just as she expected, she, too, was an anomaly. She closed her eyes and thought of the ramifications. In her mind's eye, she saw a river with the water flowing around two stones. They were the two stones. They were temporal anomalies and perhaps that's why the neutrino flow passed them by. If that were true, the reverse echo of the neutrino flow might be the literal river of time. How could she prove it?

She noticed that they were a few hours from the nearest land-mass and made for it. They arrived a little after midnight. She decided to test the butterfly effect. There was a town of some kind on the other side of the island.

"A couple of tests on the unpopulated side and then a couple in the port should suffice," she said out loud, working out the location of the next tests.

She fired a gun at the empty beach while scanning it and just as she thought; it created a temporal anomaly which, after a few seconds, dissipated.

Micheal came running down at the sound. She filled him in on her hypothesis and repeated the tests, recreating the same result.

They sailed into the small port and ran scans as they interacted with the harbormaster, as well as some seamen in a pub. The scans proved that most of their interactions left different-sized anomalies that dissipated over corresponding lengths of time.

They made their way back to the *Liberty* and left the harbor.

"This definitely looks like your corrective time theory," she said confidently. "We change something, and the flow smooths it out. The temporal anomalies are the pebbles thrown in the river of time," she concluded. Julie had almost forgotten about their fight. Now, feelings of shame came rushing in.

"Great work!" She knew that to him the issue was already for-gotten, but she needed to say something to him.

"Can you forgive me?"

"You were already forgiven."

III: Project Certification

They made some steady progress in their understanding of time, while MICHEAL'S students made steady progress in their under-standing of basic sciences.

"Scoring shall be made both individually and as a group. I shall divide you into groups of six." He broke the class into two teams of six, calling one Group A and the other Group B. "Group A, your task shall be the making of a one-meter reflective telescope. Group B, your task shall be the making of a one-meter refractive telescope. Everything you need is in the laboratory. Please choose one project manager, you have two weeks to complete this project, and I shan't help. Good luck, gentlemen." Micheal finished the instructions for his class certification project.

"Professor Whitaker, of what plans do you have for these telescopes should your students prove successful?" Master Brattle asked with great interest.

"Donated to the Astronomy Department." He had already prepared an observatory on top of the Astronomy Building.

His days grew long, and he began sleeping at his apartment on campus. As the days became weeks, he worried about Julie. She had been doing better, but there had been a little more distance between them since their voyage.

"Lady Whitaker is here, my lord." Apparently, she was coming for a visit.

"My dear, so unexpected." Micheal kissed her hand in greeting.

"Dear husband, I have not seen you these weeks past." Julie seemed to be acting for the university audience.

"I would be home so late," he replied in kind. He guided her to a bench, then sat with her. She took his elbow and leaned on him. He met her eyes, and he thought she wanted to talk to him, so he called a halt to the work for the evening.

"Shall we walk, my dear?" he said, and they exited through the south labs and strolled along the Riverwalk. "Is there something wrong, Jules?" They took a right and followed the Charles up campus.

"I've barely seen you in the past two weeks and...well, the nightmares have been bad the last few nights." He could hear the fear in her voice.

"But I thought you—"

"I was, but I'm dreading the night alone."

Micheal pulled her into him then said, "let's go home,"

While JULIE did dread the night, if she was being honest, she had missed him over the past two weeks. And it felt longer than that ever since their argument on the *Liberty*. He had seemed more distant.

"So, how's the project coming along?" she broke the silence.

"Oh, they're just about finished, probably tomorrow or the next day."

"Have you run scans on these telescopes to see how much wake they are going to leave?"

"Yes, it's actually less than I expected. And have you been able to come up with a way to calculate how long we have until our temporal frequency will sync up?"

"Nothing one hundred percent yet, but I found an anomaly in the vibrational differential. If it is what I think it is, then it's probably at least five years and maybe closer to ten."

"Damn. That's longer than I'd hoped for. Well, let me know when you have a more accurate number," he finished as they rode into the barn.

After dinner, they went to their own chambers to prepare for bed.

Julie knew he had some level of affection for her, but he hid his emotions well and she wasn't sure if they went so far as love. She was in love with Micheal, and she felt guilty that her presence was interfering with him living fully, so she decided that she would let him experience that with her. She had always intended to remain faithful to Aiden, but she never thought she would fall in love with someone else.

She also thought Aiden would understand on her account. They would make love once, sometimes twice, a day. When they saw each other. Now, to have her Aiden drought precede these many months of forced abstinence was torture. She'd only had sex a couple of times in nearly two years.

She took a deep breath and headed for Micheal's chambers.

He was already in bed when Julie came inside. The heat of the day had almost dissipated, and Micheal was lying without covers.

"Jules," he said as he rose slightly to meet her gaze.

"Hi," she said. She was trying to keep calm.

Julie made her way to the other side of the bed. Micheal rolled to his side to receive her, and she slid under the covers, so he was spooning her.

A few minutes later, his breathing became slow and deep. If she was going to show Micheal what lovemaking was, it had to be now. Her whole body swelled with anticipation. She took his hand and slowly brought it up to her breast.

He didn't pull his hands away, so she squeezed it to give him the true feel of a woman. She moved closer, grinding her butt against his penis. He had tensed a little with surprise, and she could tell he was responding to her movement. She felt him grow between her thighs. He was much better endowed than she had expected. He started breathing heavily against her neck, sending chills down her body and making her quiver.

She turned to face Micheal, her body twisting to meet his. Her leg slid up, pulling her slip to her waist. She ran her hands up Micheal's chest and slowly laid him on his back. She sat up, hugging his body with her thighs, aching to have him inside her.

Her gown had slipped off one shoulder, she caught Micheal's eyes on her, so she reached across to slide her slip off completely. She took his hands and slowly traced the curves of her waist and up to her chest. She shook at his touch as she felt his hands enjoy her body. She was out of her mind at the thought of his throbbing dick rubbing against her pussy.

Julie dove at Micheal, opened his shirt, and ran her hands down his muscular body. His broad shoulders looked so strong, and his stomach appeared chiseled from granite. Her nipples became hard again, so she pulled Micheal's hands back to her breasts. She couldn't take it. She arched her back, rose slightly, then ran her hand down his enormous cock. Julie reached down his pants when she felt his hand stop hers.

"Jules?"

"What's the matter?" She was trying to figure out what was happening.

"We can't do this."

"Why not?"

His breath was labored. He took his hands off her and sat up, leaning on his elbows.

"I know you will regret it later."

"I want this." Julie tried to kiss him, but he turned his head to avoid it, dropping from his elbows.

"It may feel that way now, but it will be different in the morning."

She couldn't believe he stopped her. She could see in his eyes he had come to his senses. She felt immense disappointment about how the night unfolded. She collapsed on his chest, and she felt his arms wrap around her.

"I'm sorry, Jules," he whispered.

Julie knew he meant it. He would never take advantage of her, and this was proof. Even after going as far as he had let it get, he was still a gentleman. He was still her knight in shining armor.

She slid off Micheal and grabbed his arm once more but this time to pull him over. He rolled to his side and held her tight.

Emotionally exhausted, she fell asleep.

She woke up to Micheal caressing her hair. The embarrassment of the previous night rushed back.

"Are you all right?" She looked up and met his eyes.

"I don't know what I was thinking." She turned away.

He turned her back to look at him. With a gentle gesture, he then caressed her lips and said, "I've never been so tempted."

He let out a slight laugh, and she joined him.

"It's probably good you stopped me." She would have felt guilty. She didn't know what to do in this unique situation.

She excused herself to take a bath.

Julie's thoughts returned to the memory of the night as the heat embraced her. Micheal had rejected her. The initial thought angered her. She was only trying to do him a favor. She was setting aside her feelings for Aiden, not to mention her marriage, so that Micheal could have the chance to experience something. She stewed in anger for a moment, but thoughts of the other parts of her night with Micheal crept in.

She was extremely attracted to Micheal. She thought of the way his hands felt on her body. The way he let her take control. And his dick. It was amazing...

As more thoughts of Micheal filled her head, her need for satisfaction got the better of her and so she traced the curves of her body and touched herself the way she had wanted Micheal to touch her.

MICHEAL was saddling Darkness for the road, but he couldn't shake last night. His mind pulled him in.

Michael had nearly drifted off to sleep. He was stunned back to consciousness when Julie placed his hand on her breast. Her nipple pressed into his palm, her breast was soft and firm... Is this really happening?... He didn't know how to react... Maybe she's just cold?... She overwhelmed his senses. He felt his hand about to move, but stopped it. His thoughts were turning to lust.

Now he couldn't prevent another reaction. He thought "down boy" to no avail. She was slowly pressing her ass into him, grinding against his groin. Her slip had ridden up. He could see the curve of her hip in the light of the moon and feel the heat between her legs. He didn't want her to stop.

Julie pressed him on his back and straddled him. She slid the strap from her shoulders. Her perfect breasts looked irresistible. All he wanted was to feel her large erect nipples between his lips. His head was swimming. He didn't know what to think. He knew what his body wanted.

She guided his hands back to her amazing breasts, then she grabbed him down there. That reality shocked his brain back into control and he stopped them from making a mistake.

Micheal came back to the moment wondering if their occasional sleeping arrangement had confused their friendship. There was no other way this goddess of beauty would try something like that with him. He was average at best. His mind drifted back.

Micheal woke to her sleeping beauty. He worried about her. "I wish I could tell you how much I love you," he whispered. But that was a selfish thought. What if the facade he put on in this contrived marriage even fooled her into seeing him as better than he was?

If they went through with such a mistake, he'd make Julie violate her vows, and he'd break his promise to her, ruining one of his few good qualities.

He tried to soothe his emotional turmoil by running his fingers through her silky tresses. This caused her to stir. They had a brief exchange, then as Julie rose from the bed, her slip fell away and he could see every inch of her. He was tempted to pull her back to the bed and finish what they started last night. But he was able to control himself, barely. He sighed deeply, watching her walk away, then released the tension by growling into a pillow.

Guilt pulled Micheal out of the memory as Julie was approaching. He quickly restored his facade.

"Will you ride with me?"

She went and prepared herself and Angel for the ride.

As they headed for Cambridge, she began, "I don't know what came over me last night. It's been difficult this past year and a half."

"I'm not sure I can understand your situation. I've been abstinent my entire life, so I don't truly know what I'm missing. I get the feeling you're not used to being...alone this much. I understand why you might try to do something you would never normally do."

"No! It's—"

"It's okay." He didn't understand why she would try to argue this. "I know that's what happened last night and if we had...gotten together, you would have hated yourself for it. And probably resent me as well."

She continued, trying to argue. But she didn't need to spare his feelings.

Micheal spent the last part of the ride just going over everything between him and Julie. He worried about what state she would have to be in to have attempted such a thing with him. He would need to be more careful to maintain their arrangement.

But now he had to play the role of the professor. The students were waiting as they arrived at the labs.

"Master Rainsford, Master Oliver, you may commence," Micheal instructed.

Over the next few hours, he supervised while both teams made final adjustments to the telescopes. They appeared to be doing tests on the various aspects. They were looking through the viewfinders and adjusting the optical focus knobs while looking through the eyepiece.

"Time, gentlemen," he said. Everyone halted and took their seats. The gallery was full, as all the council was in attendance.

He carried out a thorough inspection of each instrument before making his announcement.

"There is one final test for these instruments to perform."

He instructed both teams to move the telescopes outside. He proceeded to use each one to find Venus in the daytime. Once he saw through both instruments a crystal-clear image of a silver ball floating in a sea of blue, it confirmed that the teams had successfully engineered them. After that, everyone was allowed to get their first taste of what these instruments could do.

With the demonstration complete, everyone went back inside, and he brought every student up, one by one, and graded them. He presented them with various certificates of honor. While he had determined that all of them deserved to pass, he felt he should reprimand several students who were lacking in certain areas.

"Congratulations, gentlemen! There shall be a gala held in your honor on Friday next. Gentlemen, dismissed."

IV: Star Party

JULIE stood before her floor-length mirror, taking in her newest gown that was commissioned specifically for this occasion. Made of the finest silks of turquoise and yellow, it felt luxurious on her skin.

One final inspection from head to toe, and Julie headed for the carriage.

When they came to a stop, just south of the labs, the telescopes had been placed on the Riverwalk, covered until their official unveiling.

Micheal took her hand as she stepped out of the carriage and led her through the entrance of the labs and into a section of the building that was decorated for the Science Gala.

The recognition ceremony included dinner and dancing, followed by the presentation of the telescopes. Micheal had made multi-observational eyepieces so six people at a time could look through each telescope.

She was amazed at the incredible views provided of all seven other planets, three different galaxies, a few star clusters and nebulae, and of course, views of the moon's surface.

"Julie, do you know why it looks so...pocked?" Cecily asked.

"Those are called craters."

"Like volcanoes?" Mary Rainsford cut in.

"Yes! Exactly. Also, when smaller objects crash into the moon at a high velocity, they leave marks—those craters," she explained. Julie surveyed the crowd of partygoers, then turned back to her friends. "Cecily, have you seen Alice this evening? I did not hear her arrival." Julie had not been looking forward to seeing Alice since she found out about her advances.

Cecily took Julie's hand, motioned at Mary to follow, and led them away from the group.

"You have not heard? Alice didst remain home to care for little Eleanor. Poor child came down with the chincough. Arthur's death has increased her duties and responsibilities, two-fold," Cecily explained in a whisper, trying to keep the gossip to a minimum for Alice's sake.

Julie's stomach felt heavy. In her pique, she hadn't considered how precarious Alice's situation was. She was alone. She didn't have a husband to care for and comfort her or provide for her and their children.

Julie turned her gaze to the second telescope and watched as Micheal seemed caught up explaining what could be seen. It wouldn't be easy, but Julie knew she cared for Alice too much to let jealousy come in the way of their friendship.

She excused herself from the company of the ladies and approached Micheal. The two of them wandered away from the crowds and to the edge of the river. "Wow! I didn't know we'd be able to see all of that. You're sure this isn't too big a pebble?"

"I checked and rechecked. It's not small, but the ripples are gone in something like five to seven years."

"How is that possible? Didn't you say that much of what we're showing them was unknown at this point in history?"

"I don't know how, but it will all get lost to history."

Julie wasn't convinced.

They were spending the night at the campus in MICHEAL'S private apartment, and they were sleeping in separate beds across the room from each other. He had stayed up a little while after Julie fell asleep. He found himself transfixed by her delicate complexion in the soft blue light of the moon. She had avoided him at night ever since he'd stopped her from making a mistake a couple of weeks earlier. If she were over her nightmares, then that would be one thing, but he thought it was out of embarrassment over the incident. After a few minutes of thinking in circles, he finally fell asleep.

A short while later, he awoke to Julie tossing about violently, apparently experiencing a bad episode. He threw his covers off and ran to her bedside, but as he leaned in, her fierce swings caught him in the face. Micheal was stunned. Then, a second hit came in. *I wish I hadn't taught her how to hit so well.* He thought.

He looked at Julie and realized she hadn't woken up. He came in more gently and brushed the hair out of her face. She seemed to respond to his touch. Once she was more relaxed, he picked her up and carried her to his bed.

He took her into his arms and held her until she calmed and relaxed into him. Then he fell asleep.

⸻ ⋈ ⸻

JULIE woke up and was surprised to find herself in Micheal's bed. She felt his body surround hers; she let out a deep sigh of relief. She was safe again. She turned into his chest and lost herself in his pleasant smell. She was thankful he had come to her without her asking and, after a moment, she drifted back to sleep.

When she awoke again and reached for his face, she was horrified to see he had a black eye; she jolted up with concern when a swollen lip revealed itself. She tried to gently feel his bruise, and he winced.

"Good morning, Jules."

"Micheal! What happened? Who did this to you?" Her mind was running wild.

He chuckled a little. "You have a good jab. I forgot to duck."

"You mean...I did this?"

"Don't even worry about it."

She leapt out of bed, wetted a rag, and wrapped it around some ice from his fridge. "Lay back," she said, returning to bed.

"Jules?" He touched her cheek.

"Yes, Micheal?" The pressure rapidly built in her chest. She feared what he might say next. She so badly wanted him to let her in again.

"Come here." He pulled her into him and whispered, "It's okay."

He seemed to read her mind. He ran his fingers through her hair and softly caressed her cheek. She looked into his eyes, rolled him over, laid his head on her chest, and ran her fingers through his hair. He fell asleep in her embrace. A while later, she followed.

The next morning, Julie went out for a late breakfast with her friends.

"Julie last night was so enchanting," Mary said, looking up at the sky, still entranced by the world above.

"I'm so pleased you enjoyed yourself." Julie turned to Alice and said, "It saddened me to have missed you. I do hope you'll attend next time."

"Of course I'll come next time, Julie." Alice looked down at the table, then back at Julie, making eye contact.

It had taken a little effort, but she really did like Alice.

"Can you believe the magic in the heavens? There are so many wonderous things above us." Cecily stared at the sky.

The ladies stood to greet Micheal as he approached. He was looking quite dashing, and his eye was only slightly noticeable.

"Ladies, how are you this blessed morning?" He removed his hat and gave a proper bow.

"Charmed. My lord." Alice smiled coquettishly as he took her hand and kissed it.

"Last night was captivating! My lord," Cecily beamed.

"My lord, it was a true pleasure," Mary added.

"My dear." Micheal leaned over and gave Julie a peck on the cheek.

This unusual public show of affection caused a stir amongst her friends.

"It's as if you're newly married!" Alice said. The jealousy in her voice was clear, matching her sidelong glance. Her other friends did as well.

Julie didn't hate the show Micheal was putting on for her benefit.

V: The Wall

Summer passed more quickly than expected, at least by MICHEAL'S reckoning. Over that time, they had made steady progress toward understanding temporal mechanics. They had successfully modified the neutrino scanner into a tachyon scanner but, by August's end, their steady progress had stalled. The months passed, the calendar flipped to 1694, and it felt like the stall was running into a wall.

"Happy anniversary, Micheal," Julie said as she entered the music studio. "And we *are* going to celebrate your birthday today. No arguments."

One look from Julie and he surrendered.

"Okay, Jules," he said, smiling. "So, are you going to join me today?"

"I don't know," there was doubt in her voice. He didn't know why. She sounded amazing.

"I know you had fun the last few times you did, and I'm doing Lady A! Unless you mean to watch and laugh at my impression. I most definitely make a poor Hillary Scott."

"I always do like your female vocals," she laughed. "Okay, but I will need to warm up first."

They sang a few songs, then Micheal turned to their favorite topic of conversation. "So, it's been a little while since we touched base on our progress or lack thereof in solving this time travel thing."

"I know what you mean. Based on all the tachyon readings we have up to this point, as well as our speculative projections pulled from the data, we are obviously missing something. Maybe we need a faster processor for the computer."

"We need to upgrade the micro assembly line to make the chip components any smaller. That would be the only way we could improve the processing speed of the computer. And we are already working on that as quickly as possible."

"I know. I used the data to open theoretical vortices, but the transfer conduit is unstable. It always ends up in a different time and place, even when using the same energy components to generate the transfer." Julie gripped her seat tightly.

"It feels like we've run into a wall after all that early progress." He searched his mind for answers.

"I'm sorry, Jules—"

"No, we're not doing this ag—"

"No! You put your trust in me and I'm failing you."

"You're not failing me. I knew the odds when I came here with you."

"Well, am I succeeding? No? Then, I'm failing."

Julie went quiet and Micheal knew that was tacit agreement and he looked away. He didn't want to fail the woman he loved. Then she broke the silence.

"On a different note, I have a gift for you. Birthday, remember? Follow me."

She led him to the lounge.

They were clearly paintings concealed by sheets. The first was about ten feet in length and five feet tall. She unveiled it.

"Wow, the Sun and all eight planets, beautifully detailed." Micheal was admiring the first when she unveiled the second.

"I decided on a more personal touch for the second one." It was an image of him holding Neptune in his hand.

"My favorite planet." He ran his fingers across the canvas.

"I know."

"This is incredible. Thank you so much. You didn't have to go to all this trouble."

"No, but I wanted to." She lifted her chin, smiling.

Micheal loved that Julie would put so much time and effort into a gift for him.

"This does remind me. I meant to inquire about the tablets I gave you last Christmas. Do you know what language it is yet?"

"Well...at least I've ruled out alien," he deadpanned. She laughed, then he joined her.

"But seriously, I'm not sure what language it is. I can say definitively that it is no known language." Micheal pulled up the image of the tablets in his mind.

"How do you know it's not alien?" This time, she sounded completely serious as she made eye contact.

"I suppose I can't completely rule out alien, but I tend to think not. After studying the cuneiform, I'm certain that it's Sumerian. I did detect some patterns in the unknown language, and I may be able to translate it. Whether it's alien or not, I can't say for sure.

I may need a larger sample size to fully translate the language. It may also help to have more samples of Sumerian cuneiform. After this year's Summerfest, I think we need to go to the Middle East to look for more examples of ancient languages."

"Do you think it's some form of Sumerian?"

"No, I think it's some lost ancient language. Maybe it's from Atlantis!" he joked, then he got more serious. "For those tablets to exist in such a form, the language itself would have to be much older. So, who knows?"

The months continued to pass with no further movement toward a temporal solution. They truly had hit a wall.

PART FOUR: THE TRIALS OF TIME

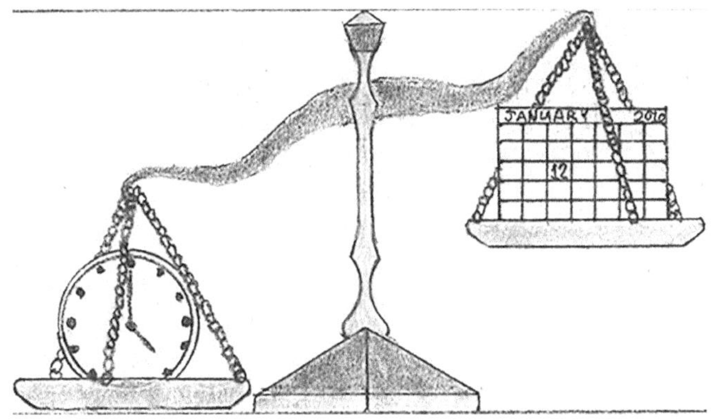

CHAPTER 18: LETTING GO

I: Two Years Later

*J*UNE *8, 1696*

As the months have turned into long years without any progress, writing in this journal is one thing that has been very therapeutic. In spite of this eventuality being put directly before me prior to coming to Boston, I had dared to hope that Micheal's calculations were wrong, and as our steady progress in those early months seemed to portend that miracle, the last three years of stubborn failure has sobered me to the realization that I will never see the twenty-first century again. That "home" is out of reach. But is there another home that I might see? My life has been unfulfilling since I arrived here. Never did I expect to fall in love again. My love for Aiden is still strong. I had expected it to fade, but they do say distance makes the heart grow fonder, but I fear that fondness will never be reciprocated again, centuries from reach. I think of Aiden every day and wonder if he's happy. I hope so. I continue in my efforts to remain true to him, but I must admit that having sex only twice in five years is very trying.

Then the unexpected love. When I first met Micheal, I never could have imagined he would be someone I could even fall in love with. He was physically unattractive and his piercingly negative attitude and "woe is me" antics were hard to deal with. But then his selfless nature and generosity started to show. He had no reason or obligation to help me, or to risk his life for me, to sacrifice a real life for me. No one was ever a match for me intellectually before. All those things and so much more are why I fell in love with him.

He's so difficult to read. On numerous occasions, he seemed to act as though he loved me as well, but most of the time, his walls were still standing. I don't think he truly realizes how strongly I feel about him. Of course, I have never actually said anything, and I can forget that despite his progress over the last four years, he's relatively oblivious when it comes to what is not said. Many times, when I have done things that any normal person would recognize as true interest, he reaffirms that he knows I would never be interested in him. He has likely built it up so much in his own mind that, should I decide to truly pursue a full relationship, it may take some convincing.

I also realize that I have still never said "thank you" to him for saving my life on multiple occasions, and particularly for Salem. I feel like such a terrible person. I never even thought to ask how he rescued me from the gallows surrounded by thousands.

"This one will be perfect for the festival ball." Cecily held the fabric up and admired herself in the mirror.

"Now, Cecily, already planning outfits?" JULIE enjoyed the excitement her friends placed on, the Summerfest Ball.

"Why, of course, Julie. It's only the social event of the year," Mary answered for her as she was being fitted for a new dress.

"Not everyone has a standing invite to the palace." Alice had an air of pride in her voice.

"And you, my dear Alice, you get to parade your charming new husband." Julie felt the texture of several threads.

"Charles is nervous for his first big formal." Alice had recently married Charles Lynde, a wealthy businessman.

"Charles has nothing to fear. Into your most capable hands shall he be." Mary said.

A few minutes later, Cecily approached with her purchases.

"I must be getting back. Matthew will expect supper. Are you coming Alice? Mary?" Cecily said.

"A pleasure." Alice moved to follow.

"Many thanks. Robert is occupied this evening." Mary seemed happy about the invitation.

"Julie?" Cecily turned to her with a raised brow.

"My apologies. I am otherwise engaged." She declined politely, as she was in the middle of putting in a special request for the seamstress to visit Bostonian.

Once she had selected the fabrics she wanted and scheduled the appointment for the next week, it was time to head home. She walked out of the shop.

"I'll be. It's the devil herself!"

Julie stopped in her tracks. She turned and Reverend Samuel Parris was staring at her.

"Beg pardon, sir?"

"If Mistress Buckingham hasn't learnt to speak all proper," he said with ire in his eyes.

"You mistake me, sir. Lady Whitaker, your servant." She feigned ignorance.

"I am no fool, Mistress Buckingham. And look, now you have gone and married into the House of Avalon," he said, glaring. "Do not think Avalon shall protect you. Do not think yourself safe. Since that devil come for you on the gallows, I did hope this day. The Lord delivereth, my lady." He sneered menacingly as he walked away.

"—apparatus that will rise into the sky—" MICHEAL was interrupted by the door opening abruptly. Julie ran into his arms with tears down her face.

Micheal didn't know what to think. She was clearly horrified by something.

He looked up and said, "Gentlemen..." but before he could finish his request, he saw his pupils rise immediately to give their professor privacy. The room cleared in seconds.

He led her into his office, and they sat down on the couch.

"What's wrong?" He gently wiped the tears from her cheeks.

"I ran into Samuel Parris in Boston. He knew it was me. He believes I'm the actual devil. He said that I wasn't safe and that the Lord will deliver me to him—"

"Whoa, whoa, slow down." She was speaking a mile a minute. "Samuel Parris? From the witch trials?" He quickly searched his mind for any records about Reverend Samuel Parris. His disgraced reputation following the witch trials saw him run out of Salem, and he disappeared. His current location was unknown to history.

"Yes! I tried to pretend I didn't know what he was talking about, but he knew. He knew who I was. He said Avalon couldn't protect me. I came out of the fabric shop, and he was there. He shouted and then told me..."

"It's okay. I won't let anything happen to you." He pulled her into him and held her for a while.

"I feel so stupid." She looked up at Micheal. "I should be stronger than this. I shouldn't fear him."

"Everything's going to be all right."

————◇◇◇————

June 15, 1696

I encountered Samuel Parris in Boston today. I had a bit of a meltdown. It's hard to imagine someone so self-righteous and despicably evil at the same time. What did Micheal do that day to make Parris call him the devil? Parris is truly mad and will not stop until he kills me! Of course, it was hours later before I remembered my martial training. I decided I should get him first. Micheal had to stop me. And why is Parris so sure the powerful House of Avalon can't stop him? My act didn't fool him.

After all this time, he still recognized me. I barely recognize myself. This role of the Lady of Avalon I have taken on has me disconnected from myself. I always feel like I'm pretending. I'm lonely. My husband is three hundred years from reach. My other 'husband' is honor-bound to keep his distance. I find myself asking questions. Will I ever fully connect again? Will I ever be truly happy again? I have found myself lost in melancholia more and more of late. I feel my connections growing further and further adrift.

II: Academic Review

"Professor Whitaker, may I introduce Master John Flamsteed and Thomas Willouby, Second Baronet of Middleton, both of the Royal Society," Brattle said in introduction.

"Your servant, Sirs," MICHEAL said, bowing. "What could bring men of such esteem to this quaint corner of the Empire?"

"Our associate, Master Isaac Newton, would be much honored if the Lord and Lady of Avalon would attend him in London," Flamsteed replied.

"I much appreciate Master Newton's invitation; however, I am vexed as to said interest."

"Word of my lord's exploits have been rampant throughout the colonies and have even reached across the Atlantic. It is not every day one hears word of a Lord of Avalon establishing themselves somewhere—or anywhere, for that matter," Willouby added.

"Sir Thomas, to which exploits do you refer?"

"Well, my lord. The astronomical telescopes, the great magnifying microscopes, the underwater dive instruments, those two bridges, and, of course, your estate, Bostonian."

"My lord, might I inquire as to the task at hand?" Flamsteed interjected.

"It is an apparatus intended to defy gravity."

The certification projects for the year were a hot-air balloon and an airship. Both teams were about halfway through construction.

"The apparatus on left shall use temperature differential to create lift, the apparatus on right shall use a low-density form of air for the same purpose."

"To soar with the birds?" Willouby indicated above them.

"Indeed, sir."

They followed him across the outdoor labs.

"Professor Rainsford. Might I present, Sir Thomas Willouby, Second Baronet of Middleton, as well as the esteemed astronomer John Flamsteed, both of the Royal Institute."

He'd made his former star student, and friend, his associate professor.

"Professor Rainsford, will you relieve me sir?" he said, passing the current review off to Rainsford. "Gentlemen, might I show you the science facilities?"

"My lord, forgive me. Did I confess to be an astronomer?" Flamsteed inquired.

"Sir, your reputation precedes you. Word of your stellar cartography abounds."

"I was unaware my exploits had traveled so prodigiously."

"My lady and I would be honored if you gentlemen would attend us at dinner. We are fond of hosting the university faculty of a Friday evening."

Micheal went to the art studio in Julie's tower to fill her in on the new arrivals.

"Isaac Newton sent them?" She didn't look up from the canvas.

"Apparently, our exploits have reached England. Newton just moved to London to take up a new post. I suppose his curiosity was piqued."

"So, are we going to London?"

"I suppose we are... is that your family?" Micheal studied Julie's current painting.

"I've been wanting to paint a family portrait for a while. I thought if I dressed them in period clothing, I could hang it in the Gallery."

"So, this is you with your parents and siblings?"

She proceeded to identify everyone. "In the middle looking very noble are my mother and father. To their right is my brother Jason, and my sister Jennifer. And to their left is me and, of course, Jessica." Micheal heard her catch her tears.

"It's beautiful." He touched her shoulder.

"Well, I should get cleaned up. We need to get ready for dinner." She set the brush down and exited the studio.

Micheal watched her leave, wondering if she would ever see them again.

They dressed as dinner was prepared, then went to receive their guests; the conversation flowed with the wine.

As the main course was served, Mary Rainsford returned to her favorite topic: science. "My lord, Robert talks nonstop of your next project—adventuring into the sky with the birds. It is possible?"

"To the sky indeed."

"A Lord of Avalon indeed," Flamsteed said, toasting the table.

"Was there cause for doubt?" Julie asked with a raised brow.

"My lady, men of the scientific arts are skeptical by nature. Had not I seen your husband in the flesh, I might be a skeptic still. But he might pass for His Grace, the Duke of Avalon himself."

"Master Flamsteed, have you met His Grace?" Julie asked.

"Ten years past had I the honor to attend Their Graces' farewell concert at Whitehall. It was a magnificent spectacle, my lady. Strangely enough, my lady, you bear a remarkable likeness to Her Grace."

"Her Grace would be my sister, Master Flamsteed," she said. Micheal was impressed with how well she improvised.

"I always understood your sister passed away, Julie," Alice said in confusion.

"Her Grace would be the eldest. Our mother passed many a year ago, then our younger sister and her husband became ill. I tended them until..." Tears streamed down her face.

Micheal finished for her.

"My lady wrote to me pleading assistance and upon my arrival in Virginia we were wed."

"What a terrible sorrow, Julie." Alice reached out a hand in comfort as Julie excused herself.

That evening in Julie's quarters, she and Micheal returned to what Flamsteed had told them.

"That is so odd," Julie began.

"What is?"

"Flamsteed is not the first person to remark on my resemblance to the Duchess of Avalon. That's what's odd. I mean, it's not unexpected that you would look like your ancestors, but it's weird that I would look like any of them."

Micheal didn't know what to think, so he just said, "Well, you covered it perfectly. That was brilliant improvisation."

"You don't think it's risky to make such a claim? What if the Duke and Duchess show up?"

"The Lords of Avalon are away from England at the moment, for around ten years, and they normally keep a low profile during their absences, so I think we are okay on that front, at least for a while."

"I guess time will tell."

III: Letting Go

Julie was exhausted from the long day. After a hot bath, she found her bed just in time for sleep to take her.

"What are you doing here?" JULIE asked.

"I came to find ya. I was feeling lonely," Aiden said.

"I was missing you, too."

He kissed her. "Let's go!"

"I have to work."

"Come, we're in Disney World. Work can wait!"

"All right."

They sat on a bench with Cinderella's Castle in the background.

"If only I could make your fantasy real," he said sadly.

"Dance with me."

They danced until the sun set. He cupped her face with his hands, then he kissed her deeply. Fireworks began exploding in the background.

"Now that you got me all hot and bothered. What are you going to do about it?" she raised and lowered her brows.

They couldn't keep their hands off each other in the hotel room. They made deep, passionate love, getting lost within one another.

As they lay in the pale blue light of the moon, she said, "I wish we could just stay like this forever."

Then the magic of the night faded into the dawn. Julie woke to the sight of Aiden staring out the window. "Good morning. Get back over here and we'll make a father out of you yet."

He just looked at her.

"What's wrong?" She climbed out of the bed, walked over, wrapped her arms around him from behind, and kissed him on the neck.

He turned around and looked at her for a moment, then said, "We have to talk."

She knew that was bad. That line is always bad. And the day passed in seconds.

"What do we need to talk about?"

"This isn't working anymore."

"What isn't?"

"Us... I've been trying to make it work, but you're so distant all the time."

"Do you think I want this? I have been trying everything I can to get back to you."

"I never said it was your fault. Sometimes things happen that are out of our control."

"I have been fighting for you—for us," she said, tears starting down her cheeks.

"I know you have, and I have moved heaven and earth trying to bring you back, but some things are not in our ability," he said with tears in his eyes now, too.

"But...I love you."

"I love you more than you know. If love was all it took to bring you back to me, you'd have only been gone a minute."

"We have so many plans. We're going to have a baby together."

"It was but a dream. A beautiful dream, but a dream. Out of reach."

"I've been fighting for us. Don't give up on me."

"We could wait a lifetime and never find each other again."

"I would wait, even a lifetime, if that's what it takes." Her heart was pounding.

"I know. That's one of the things that makes me love you so much. There never was a truer love than you, my dearest. But I don't want you pining away your days on my account. You have so much life to live and so much love to give."

"Love I give to you!"

"Julie... I am in no position to return that love. You deserve better than that. And I'd hope you'd want better for me as well."

"I do. All I want is for you to be happy—"

"Then you'll let me go."

"It's not fair!"

"I know. It's not fair for either of us. I will always love you. We will always be a part of each other, but I want you to be happy. That is all I want for you. You will find someone worthy to take

care of your heart for me. You will love again; you will live again."

"I'm not ready!"

"You are. I love you and—"

"I love you, too."

"Then let me go."

"But—"

"Just...let go," his eyes matched the setting sun behind him. She paused for a long while.

"I will." She pulled him into her. "In the morning. Just give me one more night?"

"Okay."

"I wish we could stay like this forever," an emptiness wanted to invade her chest. "I love you, Aiden."

"And I, you," he whispered back. Lost in the warm, familiar comfort, she drifted off to sleep.

She slowly opened her eyes, and the mellow light of her bed chamber made her realize it had all been a dream. She thought of Aiden, and she could feel the connection slipping away. She felt, in that moment, that Aiden was moving on, that her dream was him saying goodbye.

IV: Sky High

Julie had spent most of the week confined to her quarters. MICHEAL wasn't sure what had happened, but she assured him she was okay, so he gave her space. But it was his day to judge his class's final projects, and she hadn't missed one yet. He knocked on her door and she opened it a crack.

"Micheal? Is everything okay?"

"I was going to ask you the same thing."

"I'm fine. I've been dealing with...some thi—"

"You don't have to explain. You don't need to share everything with me. And if you need space to deal with whatever it is, I will give it to you. It's just that today is the final exam. I wanted to see if you wanted to come."

"Oh! I totally lost track of time. Give me an hour?"

As the carriage drove them toward Cambridge, Julie asked, "How have you been?"

"Busy, I've been dealing with the project and playing host to the emissaries from the society."

"I have been looking forward to going into the sky since you told me about this project."

"So am I. I've only been in a hot-air balloon once when I was in scouts, and it was tethered."

As they arrived at the labs, they saw crowds of people on the Riverwalk who had come to see the spectacle.

"My lady," Willouby said as Micheal helped Julie out of the carriage. "Does this occasion always inspire such fervor?"

"Indeed, many are often wonderstruck by the final projects, Sir Willouby."

A half-hour later, one team was filling the hot-air balloon and bringing it upright. A roar of excitement came from the crowd outside; it must have become visible over the roofline.

"How tall is that?" Julie whispered.

"One hundred feet tall, eighty across. And the blimp is one hundred and fifty feet long and forty in diameter."

"Lord and Lady of Avalon, what a sight to behold," Flamsteed said as he and most of the university staff entered the outdoor labs.

"Gentlemen, esteemed guests, the final inspection is complete. For purposes of safety, my lady and I shall perform the final test."

———⋈———

As they boarded the balloon, Micheal asked Julie, "you ready for this?"

"Let's go sky high," she said with a smile.

Micheal fired the burner, and the balloon began to lift from the ground, quickly clearing the buildings. As they came into sight of the crowd, it erupted again. They rapidly gained altitude, rising several thousand feet in a few minutes. A slight northwest breeze pushed the balloon toward Boston. A testing of the venting system caused them to drop about a thousand feet, and they drifted over the Back Bay.

"Whew, it's cold," Julie said, wrapping her arms around her body.

"We're nearly at 5,000 feet," Micheal said as he wrapped his coat around her. "It's so peaceful up here."

"It looks so desolate, nothing like what Boston should look like," she said, then she laid her head on his arm.

They had drifted northwest of Harvard. They vented their descent until they caught the northwesterly wind and moved toward the university. With some adjustments, they managed a perfect landing in the outdoor lab.

A week later, the balloons were featured at the firmly established Summerfest. Micheal and Julie boarded the balloon, the tether was let out, and they rose about one hundred feet above the ground.

"Ladies and gentlemen, esteemed guests, good people from far and wide. Allow myself and my lord to bid thee welcome our home," Julie said, giving her official welcome speech to the festival she had created.

Just then, a large gust of wind hit the balloon. It vibrated terribly against the mooring line. He was about to signal that they should retract the balloon when another gust hit and the mooring cable latch failed, sending the balloon adrift. He hit the burner just in time to clear the trees on Bunker Hill, and they rose into a stiff breeze that carried them over the Mystic River and out to the islands in Massachusetts Bay.

"Micheal! We are heading out to sea, fast!"

"We need to rise."

Julie turned the burner to high. They quickly climbed, and the balloon slowed, turning them west toward Boston. Micheal pulled a steering flap. The setting sun came into view as the balloon rotated them toward the western sky.

"We should stay on this heading for a while," he said as he came over to view the twilight sky. "I always love sunsets."

"I know, all the amazing colors. It's magical. While unintended, this balloon ride is so welcome." She sighed deeply.

They changed altitude a couple of times until they were drifting slowly southeast toward the palace. The temperature dropped further; night had fallen.

Micheal realized Julie might be cold, so he wrapped his coat around her.

"Thank you," she relaxed into him.

"Micheal?"

"Yes?"

"Are you happy? Living with me, I mean."

"I don't think I've ever been happier."

"Really?" She turned to face him.

She looked into his eyes, the mellow light illuminating her soft eyes like gems.

"It's like we're in a fairytale," she said with a sigh, as the palace was glowing in the background. "And this is the moment where we live happily ever after."

She pulled him into her and kissed him on the mouth.

His walls of resistance crumbled to the ground; he kissed her back. It was more amazing than he had ever imagined. Fireworks sparked between them. He got lost in the magic of the situation.

When he finally pulled back, actual fireworks were exploding in the sky.

She was staring up at him, her big doe eyes penetrating right through him. He felt lightheaded. He didn't know what to think. Then he didn't have time to think. He pulled her into him as they crashed down to earth. The basket tipped over on impact, and she landed on top of him.

"Are you all right?"

"I'm okay," she said, rising from his chest.

He didn't know what to say. She looked into his eyes for a moment, then looked away.

"I'm sorry," she said abruptly, then quickly walked away.

He shut his eyes and just lay there for a minute. Then he rose and went to find her. She was right where he expected, on the swing in the gardens. He sat down next to her.

She stared straight ahead. "I'm so embarrassed."

"Don't even worry about it. You got lost in the moment."

"No—"

"It's okay."

He hugged her for a second, pulling back as he took her hand.

"Happily ever after?" he said with a grin. She gave a slight smile back.

"Well, Princess Julie, we are late for the ball."

"Your loyal subjects await." She smiled at him, took his hand, and they headed toward the palace.

The doors were opened wide for their arrival. They made their way through the bowing crowds to the ballroom. Everyone stopped with the music. The center of the floor was cleared, the orchestra began to play, and they danced a magical dance. The whole thing reminded Micheal of a scene from a fairytale.

Then, like a villain in a story, Samuel Parris broke the magic.

"Ladies and gentlemen!" Everyone stopped.

"Your Queen of Hell and her heretical Avalonian stooge!" He couldn't believe this evil bastard was here.

"The Lord Almighty shall pass judgment on you presently. You shalt feel his wrath—soon!" A dark cloud descended over the festival.

V: Sea Change

A couple of days later, they departed on the *Liberty* for London with Yvette, Filipe, and ten more of their servants, Willouby and Flamsteed, and Darkness and Angel. JULIE was happy to put distance between her and Parris.

"How do our guests find the *Liberty*?" she asked as Micheal came to the sundeck.

"Blown away, as expected. I can't really blame them. Hardly anyone has ever seen anything like this."

"Who else has?"

"They spoke of Avalonian comforts being remarked upon by guests of my family."

"Oh yeah, I sometimes try to forget that to everyone else, we're practically royalty."

"People like celebrity regardless of what era they are from..." He stood up straighter and took a deep breath. "...Julie?"

"Yes?"

"I don't want this to turn into an argument, so if you could let me say what I want to say without interruption, I would appreciate it."

"Okay...." She didn't like where this was headed, but she decided to hear him out.

"I have been giving it some thought for a little while." He paused. "Are you happy with your life the way it is right now?"

This was more direct than he usually was.

"Well... I mean..." She wasn't sure how to answer that question.

"I believe that's a no. I am admittedly very much a novice when it comes to this kind of thing, but I think you are missing...." He stalled, seemingly trying to think how to explain himself. "Intimacy? I mean, I know it must be difficult to feel...fulfilled after such a long...dry spell."

"This is because of the kiss, isn't it? As I recall, you kissed me back."

"I didn't know what I was doing. But it's not just the kiss. There have been a number of incidents of a similar nature. I mean...it has been almost five years, that's a long time for anyone. I hope I'm not speaking out of turn here but, from everything you told me about Aiden, I don't think he would want you living only half alive on his account. I think he would want you to be happy. While we are in London, you might try to get familiar with it—see how you like the place."

"Why would I do that?"

"Back when we first met, I told you that if you ever wanted out of our arrangement, I would help set you up somewhere else, somewhere you could have a fresh start. I wish so much I would have been able to get you home, but I failed you, and in your attempt to fill that hole in your life, you're doing things you wouldn't normally do. I'm sorry I couldn't give you what you wanted. I just want you to be happy, and that will never happen if you stay in this situation."

"You think incidents like the kiss happened because I was desperate for fulfillment and nothing else? When will you stop presuming that you know my feelings better than I do?" she asked sharply. Then something occurred to her: "There's someone else, isn't there? That's why you want to get rid of me. You said there were dozens of women from society who were pursuing you. Have you fallen for one of them and I'm in the way?" Tears come to her eyes.

"Someone else? That's funny... And presume to know your feelings? I would never do that. But if I'm the subject of romantic interest? Then yes, I can say with certainty, I'm not worthy of any woman. So don't make presumptions on my account. Clearly, I'm a proxy. Excuse me," he said with a quiver in his voice and quickly left.

July 8, 1696

Today Michael reacted to the kiss from Friday night. I still don't know why I did it. I mean, everything is so confusing. Ever since the dream, it feels like Aiden moved on, and if the dream is to be believed, he wants me to. I don't know if I'm ready. And perhaps the moment did overcome me, but I don't regret it.

Julie paused from writing for a minute; she closed her eyes and replayed their kiss in her head.

The kiss was pure magic. Ever since I fell in love with Micheal, I had occasionally imagined what it would be like to kiss him.... It was everything and more. He kissed me back and, in that moment, I could've believed he loved me as well. Then we had our "discussion", and his words would say he didn't. Except his defensive statement was more emotional than he usually is. It felt like genuine emotion, like there might be something real behind that Great Wall around his heart. There might be love. But what if I'm wrong? If I expose my heart to him, what will be there to greet it? Should I tell him how I truly feel?

CHAPTER 19: LORDS OF AVALON

I: London 1696

MICHEAL COULDN'T DECIDE HOW to deal with Julie. Everything was confusing. He was more in love with her than ever before and it was painful to see her so unhappy. On top of all that, she was beginning to use him as a proxy. Someone like her was only tolerating him because of forced circumstances. Clinging to a fool's hope of getting home. The last four years had made that clear. He needed to convince her that the current arrangement was untenable. It would be better for both of them. He wasn't sure how much longer he could live like this.

On Friday evening, as promised, the *Liberty* approached London. Micheal heard people cheering. He looked out ahead and there were large crowds of people lining the Thames.

"Why are all these people cheering for us?" Julie asked.

Micheal shrugged. "I don't know."

"Lord and Lady Avalon, word of our arrival has spread across London. Well-wishers abound! We shall be expected at Westminster." Flamsteed answered Julie's query as he and Willouby joined them on the sundeck.

"Master Flamsteed, in what manner was word of our arrival sent?"

"My lord, the *Liberty* is clearly Avalonian. London is a large city, but in many ways, it is like a small town. It would take only one sighting of this ship for word to spread quickly and all who love and admire the Lords of Avalon to come out in greeting."

London Bridge was up for their passage. Julie was humming the song under her breath, causing Micheal to smile. Throngs of people waved flags and cheered. They were greeted by the harbormaster and directed to a special pier.

"What are we going to do?" Julie asked.

"Just go with it."

Finally, the Liberty drifted to a halt. As they exited the pier, the path was flanked by redcoats keeping the crowds at bay. JULIE swallowed her nerves and stepped into her role.

"Master Christopher Wren the second, at your servant," he showed deference, then helped Julie into the open-air carriage waiting to greet them. He was young, around twenty.

"My lord, we did not expect you for some months. Perhaps we should know better of Avalon." Master Wren said with a chuckle as he boarded after them.

As they passed Westminster Palace, the streets were lined with many people. Most bowed or curtsied; others stared in amazement. The whole scene was unnerving for Julie. She didn't know what to do, so she just smiled and waved.

The city thinned out, and they reached what appeared to be the countryside.

"Master Wren, where are you taking us?" Julie asked.

"My lady, Master Newton, desired your stay to be familiar and comfortable. We go to Château Le Belle."

The carriage was passing a large wall and she couldn't make out what was behind the trees that obscured it. They soon arrived at a large gatehouse that was decorated in the French style. As they drove down a large stone-paved driveway, the trees parted, and a massive French-style château stood before them. It was circular in the center, with rectangular wings flanking it.

Micheal whispered. "Now *that* is a palace."

The sun was setting and an orb atop the center glass dome was glowing. Flanking the curved driveway on either side of the glass portcullis were rows of people. They must be the service staff. There were more than one hundred of them, apparently come to greet their Lord and Lady.

"Lord and Lady Avalon, welcome to Château Le Belle! I am Mirielle, your hostess, at your service." The woman spoke with a strong French accent, and she possessed the irritatingly easy elegance that Julie was learning all Frenchwomen, regardless of the century, seemed to enjoy.

The inside of the palace was overwhelmingly grand and extraordinarily ornate.

"No wonder everyone thinks your family is superior. And this isn't even their main home, just their London residence," Julie said, rolling her eyes.

"Well, their money didn't trickle down to my family. We must have been the redheaded stepchildren of the bunch," Micheal said with a light chuckle.

That evening, after dinner, Julie went to Micheal's bed.

"Micheal?" she whispered, as he might be asleep.

"Yes, Jules?"

She paused for a second. She found the words almost impossible to say. "Is it still okay for me to share your bed?"

"Of course," he said, rolling over on his back.

She slipped under the sheet, laid her head on his shoulder, and felt his arms wrap around her. She had felt awkward since the kiss, but she really missed the warmth of his company.

"Crazy day, huh?" he said. She couldn't agree more.

"Do you ever think we're taking this too far?"

"In what way?"

"I mean, look where we are. This is the most spectacular palace I've ever seen—and I've been to Versailles. And here everyone bows to me like I'm royalty or something. I feel like such a fraud, and I'm about to be exposed."

He seemed to be considering something.

"Well, at first, I did feel like you just described, but then everyone who has ever met my ancestors says how similar we look, so I became convinced the family stories are true and I started to feel..." He paused for a second. "I don't know...like I belong, I guess?"

She had come to know when he needed more time to process his thoughts into words, so she waited.

"For the first time in my life, I feel like I might *not* be out of place." He looked at her.

"I wish I felt that way."

She laid her head down on his chest. He started running his fingers through her hair, and she drifted off to sleep.

"Mon seigneur ma dame, tu as trop dormi," Mirielle said, opening the bed curtains. "De'sole'e je ne savais pas!"

Julie was startled to consciousness.

"Oui, oui, nous sommes re'veille's Mirielle," Micheal replied.

"My lord, Master Newton will attend shortly."

He brushed the hair out of her face.

"Are you awake? Apparently, we slept in."

She laughed.

"I'm up. Who could sleep through that outburst?"

II: Sir Isaac Newton

As they sat in the West Pavilion overlooking the gardens behind the chateau, JULIE realized she was nervous. This would be the first truly famous historical figure she had ever met, not counting the despicable Samuel Parris who was more infamous than anything, and certainly not nearly as well-known as Sir Isaac Newton.

"Relax, he's just another person," Micheal whispered, interrupting her thoughts. "And remember, it's 'Master Newton,' not 'Sir.' He won't be knighted for another nine years."

When she was young, everyone around her compared her to the great Pantheon of genius: Da Vinci, Newton, and Einstein. When she entered Harvard, she began regular quarterly administrated IQ tests and her mean average score of 269 landed her in the 1995 Guinness Book of World Records as "the smartest person in the world". Everyone pushed her to go into science but was disappointed when the world of business caught her interest. Now she was about to meet one of the faces of Mount Genius. How would she compare?

"Lord and Lady Avalon, Master Isaac Newton," Wren said in introduction. They were flanked by Flamsteed and Willouby.

"Master Newton *Philosophiae Naturalis Principia Mathemati-*

ca made quite an impression upon me," Julie said in compliment.

"Domina mea latine loqueris?" Newton asked in interest.

"Dominus Newton, linguam latinum in juventute mea. '88 Inspiravit in Principiis scriberentur magni interest in naturalem mundum," she said in confirmation.

The conversation continued completely in Latin and the discussion of the principles put forth in the Principia went on for a few hours.

"My lord, it appears I have been distracted from my purpose," Newton said to Micheal.

"I have obligations. I do hope we might speak more on the morrow, my lord, my lady," Newton said, excusing himself.

The rest of the society members followed suit, and Micheal and Julie returned to their private suites.

"It seems you've made quite an impression on Newton," Micheal said raising an eyebrow, a little jealously, she thought.

"How could I have known of his interest in the Ladies of Avalon?"

"So much for being too nervous to meet Newton. What do you think now?"

"You were right. I guess I just...worked myself into a frenzy. It did also make me rethink something we discussed the other day."

"What's that?"

"You said that you felt like you belonged here. That's how I feel right now. Like perhaps maybe I belong here, too."

Later that evening, as they were finishing dinner, an emissary arrived. It seemed that Princess Anne wanted to see the new Lord and Lady of Avalon as well. They were to attend to her at Kensington Palace tomorrow.

"Now we're going before the Princess? What if they think we are the Duke and Duchess?" She asked Micheal as they returned to their quarters.

"So far, everyone is pretty sure we aren't them. I don't see why Princess Anne would think any differently."

"What do you know of the Contract of Avalon?"

"That it exists." He shrugged.

"One thing it says is that the Lord of Avalon, upon return to

England, must pay all taxes. I know we are rich, but it's usually a princely sum."

"I want you to stop worrying. We will be fine. Today was okay, right?" He paused. She nodded. "Everything will be okay."

III: Royal Court

"Their Graces, the Duke and Duchess of Avalon." Announced the herald as they entered the court. They walked up to the pedestal of the throne. They bowed and curtsied.

"Rise." Princess Anne instructed.

"Chancellor of the Exchequer Charles Montagu, questions your failure to appear."

"Highness, if I may?" MICHEAL asked. Anne indicated to proceed.

"Highness, Chancellor Montagu and your herald mistakes us. For we are not the Duke and Duchess."

"Indeed, My Lord Avalon. It is quite striking how much you resemble your brother. My advisor, the Lady of Marlborough, apprised me of your relationship. My Lady Avalon, you clearly are the sister of Her Grace." Anne examined Julie closely.

"Her Grace and I were well acquainted. My sadness saw her departure." Anne said with regret. "That His Grace's brother should marry Her Grace's sister, quite appropriate," Anne said with a smile.

"My Lord and Lady Avalon, welcome to court."

They were treated as guests of honor and seated next to Princess Anne at dinner.

"Lady Avalon, I have a request of you."

"Highness, anything." Julie smiled.

"Their Graces did occasionally perform a Queen's Concert. Might I request the same?"

"With pleasure."

After dinner and dancing, they retired to their guest quarters at Kensington for the night.

"Now, what have you gotten us into?" Micheal asked rubbing his face.

"What was I supposed to do? Say no?"

"Perhaps not... But now we need to put together a concert. Here I was thinking we would move from being big fish in a small pond to just another fish in a big pond. I didn't think we would have so many demands on us."

"So what songs could we possibly use for this concert?"

"Well, obviously no modern themes. It probably has to be slower paced, more vocal styles."

"My lord, Master Newton did send to inform you, he shall be occupied in his duties and unable to attend you," Mirielle said, interrupting them.

"Merci, Mirielle," Julie replied.

⎯⎯⎯◄※►⎯⎯⎯

The next morning, they returned to their château, which is where Micheal reminded Julie that he needed to visit the Cambridge library in order to backstop his forged degrees.

Over the next week, the château was abuzz with activity in preparations for the Queen's Concert. The grand ballroom was transformed into a concert hall and extra staff were brought in for the occasion. When the evening arrived, they stood in the entry hall, greeting an endless parade of courtiers from all over. Some came from Britain, others from France, and the low countries.

An emissary from King William III arrived from Holland, where the King was with the British Army.

"Lord and Lady Avalon, I am Lord Henry Gray of Kent. His Majesty, King William the Third, King of England, Scotland, France, and Ireland, Defender of the Faith, sends me on his behalf to bid thee welcome to London," Gray said with a bow.

"Lord Gray, many thanks to His Majesty," Micheal said.

The ball swirled around Micheal and Julie. It was clear that they—and their concert—were nothing but a success.

"Lord and Lady Avalon, magnifique!" one of the French courtiers said as they were leaving the stage. "I am Comte St. Pierre. I represent His Majesty King Louis of France. His Majesty sends an invitation to attend him at Versailles."

"Comte St. Pierre, that might be difficult. We have limited time—" Julie began saying.

Micheal interrupted. "Perhaps not. Comte St. Pierre, we have possession of an apparatus which flies through the air as the birds."

"Extraordinary!" St. Pierre exclaimed.

"Send word to His Majesty. A delegation from England shall

arrive a week after next via the air."

IV: Public Displays

MICHEAL departed early in the morning in the hot-air balloon with Princess Anne and ten others. Julie would pilot the airship to France with Isaac Newton, Comte St. Pierre, and nine others. He was guiding the balloon over the English Channel.

"Lord Avalon, will you sit for tea?" Princess Anne asked.

"A pleasure, Your Highness," Micheal said taking a seat. "How are you finding the journey?"

"Breathtaking."

"So peaceful, my lord," Lady Sarah Churchill added.

"Your Highness, I still question the wisdom of your attendance."

"My Lord Avalon, while true in current state of affairs, would I make a valuable hostage? I am a guest of Avalon on this visit. King Louis would never dare cross your family in such a fashion, and I would not miss this opportunity."

England and France were technically in a state of war. Princess Anne was first in the line of succession; she would inherit the throne of England upon the death of her Brother-in-Law, King William III.

Lady Sarah Churchill had been watching the water beneath them this whole time. They must have finished passing over the channel because her excited squeals could be heard. "Your Highness! We have arrived in France!"

As they arrived over Paris, Micheal descended to around one thousand feet altitude. The streets were packed; word must have gotten out and all of Paris had come for the airshow.

"Lord Avalon, we must be expected," Princess Anne said with a smile.

They continued over Versailles, then climbed a couple of thousand feet in order to backtrack for landing. As they rotated back to the east, the airship was clearly visible over Paris, the silver skin shining in the sun.

"Lady Avalon is very punctual," Sarah Churchill observed regarding the airship.

Micheal guided the balloon to a soft landing just south of the Bassin du Midi in the Gardens of Versailles.

Princess Anne led the landing party out of the basket door, and they stood in a line awaiting the King of France.

"Monseigneur Avalon, Marquis Alexandre Bontemps, Premier Valet. Sa Majeste le Roi Louis de France souhaite la bienvenue au Château de Versailles." The Marquis gave an elaborate bow.

Micheal responded in kind, then said, "Je remercie humblement votre Majeste' pour votre genereuse invitation. Permettez-moi maintenant de vous presenter une invitee tres honoree, Son Altesse Royale, la Princesse Anne de Danemark et de Norvege." He turned in a bow, allowing Louis and Anne to exchange formal courtesies. Then the rest of the delegation was presented before the King.

After that, the primary discussions continued in French.

She smiled at the compliment. "Your Majesty, I could not pass up the opportunity to see the world from above. Such a divine chance to come to Versailles, the most splendid of palaces, and meet Your Majesty."

"I am curious. Tell me about this flight."

"Indescribable, everything appears so small. And rivers shine like beautiful ribbons across the land."

As Anne was describing her sky-view, Julie's airship moved overhead. Louis led Micheal, Anne, and a crowd of courtiers over for her arrival. The blimp touched down, and the introductions began.

They were all asked to stand still for a while as King Louis' portrait artist sketched the occasion in order to make a painting of the event.

The conversation continued in French as they were given a tour of the gardens.

Later that evening, they retired to the King's chambers for a private audience.

"You very much remind me of your father," the King said. "And even more of your brother."

"Your Majesty knew my father and brother?"

"I knew your father only briefly. However, the Duke and Duchess paid a visit to Versailles not ten years past. Yours is a most fascinating family. It has been suspected for centuries that Bordemere Palace near Marseilles is of Avalon. However, we shall remain in happy ignorance."

"Well, Your Majesty—" Micheal began.

"It is our preference that it remain, a mystery. I always keep a special selection of Bordemere sparkling drinks." The King pulled out a large bottle.

"I believe it is called fruit of passion," he added, popping the top and pouring out three glasses of yellowish drink. The smell of passion fruit filled the air.

"I do envy your family. To explore the world amassing a great wealth of knowledge and resources."

"That lifestyle can begin to wear on you. That is why we chose to settle down for a while." Micheal had become a pro at playing the Lord of Avalon.

"So, Lady Julie, how is colonial life?"

"It is rather enjoyable, very relaxed, quaint."

"Much less bother than London I would imagine," Louis ventured, sipping his cider.

"Perhaps in scope, less so in fervor." She gave a slight smile.

"I have heard much of the goings on in Boston. I would expect nothing less. That is the destiny of Avalon."

After a lengthy discussion of the science projects, Louis stood and said, "A grand reception in your honor awaits in the Hall of Mirrors." And the King escorted them out of his chambers.

On their last full day in France following a week of non-stop displays and events all around Paris and Versailles. JULIE was being given a tour of the Gardens of Versailles by the king's wife and three daughters. They were all joined by Princess Anne and Sarah Churchill. Micheal and the men had all gone for a hunt with the King.

"Lady Avalon, do you have any children?" The Marquise de Maintenon inquired as they paused next to the Le char d'Apollon.

"Micheal and I have so far been unsuccessful." Julie pretended to be distressed by the fact.

"I know how difficult it can be. After so many pregnancies, I feel fortunate to have William." Princess Anne gave her a comforting touch on the arm.

"I understand. I never had children. And now I never will."

Princess Marie Anne dropped her head.

"I have five wonderful children myself. Please tell us you haven't given up." Sarah Churchill brought the conversation back to her.

"I certainly have no intention to stop trying."

At that moment, the King's hunting party came riding up the Grand Canal.

"No woman would stop trying with a man like that." Princess Marie Anne was admiring Micheal as he, Louis, and the rest of the hunting party returned.

Micheal and the King broke off and dismounted as the rest of the successful hunting party continued on toward the palace.

"Ladies." Micheal removed his hat and bowed elaborately before all the ladies present.

"Let's walk." Louis presented his elbow and Marquise de Maintenon stepped to his side.

Micheal followed the King's example. "My lady."

Julie took the cue.

She walked between Micheal and the King. "Your Majesty, how was the hunt?"

"Very successful, Lady Avalon. Your husband is quite the marksman. He took down a boar single-handed."

"Perhaps His Majesty's example inspired excellence." Julie served a deferential compliment.

"And how did you find the gardens?"

"A beautiful promenade. And the company was divine."

"We have one final farewell ball in your honor," Marquise de Maintenon declared as they reached the palace.

That evening Julie and Micheal took the King and some top dignitaries for a ride in their blimp, an event they called the Sky Ball.

They departed a few hours before sundown and headed straight for the Channel, explaining things about the airship along the way. A little before sunset, they reached Le Havre.

"Is that England?" The King seemed captivated by the white cliffs on the north horizon.

"It is, Your Majesty. At a distance of nearly one hundred miles." Micheal informed him.

"We will now trace the Seine back to Paris," Julie announced as they completed a circle around the port city.

The famous French river was a ribbon of gold, lighting the way back.

"Paris is quite fascinating from such heights." Louis' eyes were fixed over the side of the gondola as the sun sank below the horizon.

"The views from above are always so breathtaking," she agreed, observing how the golden Seine wended its way through the City of Light.

"As are the views up here." The King looked at her as he extended his hand. "Might I have this dance?"

"Majesty, with pleasure." Julie gave him her hand and music began to play.

"The Ladies of Avalon are always so mysterious. So unusual." Louis seemed to be examining her.

Julie wasn't sure what the King's angle was. She tried to evade the question. "I effort to be more than just an ornament on Micheal's arm. I also recognize that most men might be intimidated by such a woman." She dropped her head slightly while maintaining eye contact.

"A true statement, Lady Avalon. But perhaps less of a burden than you might expect." Louis spun her around.

"In my experience, even kings may be daunted, except Your Majesty, of course." She gracefully stepped back into a natural curtsy.

The music stopped; she stood back up. The king kissed her hand, and theirs, the first dance of the Sky Ball, was over.

All the men each took a turn dancing with all the women, while everyone else watched. The final dance was her and Micheal's.

"So, did you enjoy your time in France?" Julie broke the ice as he led her in a waltz.

"It's been interesting to see the extent of my family's influence." Micheal came close, and they turned faster.

"Where do you think the real lords are right now?"

"Look at how we've been treated. Perhaps this is due to our unusual circumstances, but would you want to deal with this all the time? Maybe my ancestors avoid Europe and its closest colonies to get a break from the spotlight." He did have a point.

Four years in Boston was one thing. Julie wasn't sure how she would feel under these bright lights for much longer.

Then, as if on cue, fireworks lit up the City of Light, bringing an end to their dance and signaling the end of the Sky Ball.

The next day, they returned to London. Julie met Micheal at the main fountain in front of their château after the balloon landed on the lawn.

"We went all the way to Paris, and I didn't even get to see the Eiffel Tower," Micheal said in feigned disappointment.

"Shut up," Julie said, laughing. "That was a different Versailles experience than my first one."

"But Jules, what about us?"

She understood the hint. "We'll always have Paris," she repeated the line from *Casablanca*.

He grabbed her chin. "Here's looking at you, kid."

She took the moment and kissed him.

V: Cambridge University

MICHEAL was preparing his lectures in his head as they took the airship, along with Newton, Flamsteed, Willouby, and Wren, on an academic tour. They brought the 1 m refractor telescope and a microscope as gifts for Cambridge University.

"Do you think the heads in Cambridge will feel insulted that we stopped off in Oxford first? I mean, there's a pretty fierce rivalry between them." Julie seemed to worry about academic scrutiny.

"How could they? We spent a few hours glad-handing, but we are spending several days in Cambridge. Now we find out how good my forgeries are," he whispered, still unsure how his trip to the Cambridge 'library' turned out.

He had made a side mission to plant documentation in Cambridge's Hall of Records to back up his false degree.

"When we first heard of your arrival, we failed to find your records. Then, upon further inspection, found they had been misplaced. My Lord, I inquired amongst the fellows, and none could recall your attendance. I found it odd that someone of such stature went unnoticed." Vice Chancellor Henry James was confused.

"I was late to grow to my full height. And with consideration to the distraction my family can bring, I efforted to keep a low profile." Micheal explained.

"Had we realized a member of House Avalon was in attendance, I think you would have garnered much attention." The Chancellor agreed. "I do hope we may now make a proud display of your association?"

"Quite all right."

Over the next three days Micheal gave lectures on a gamut of sciences, all demonstrated by his "famous antics." Nearly all significant academics in the region showed up. By the end, he was being offered a fellowship, which he politely declined.

"Lord Avalon, I must confess, this was a fascinating series of lectures. It is too bad you are here at Master Newton's behest." Robert Hooke said after Micheal's final presentation to the academics.

"Master Hooke, I have great respect for your many accomplishments. It pains me that these petty squabbles amongst great minds have squandered so much potential," Micheal said as they walked away, leaving Hooke speechless.

August 12, 1696

As our whirlwind trip to Europe approaches its conclusion, I'm feeling a bit trepidatious. It's been so hectic that we still haven't revisited our previous conversation. Micheal's reaction to me kissing him the other day appeared to get his wheels turning, which leads me to believe he will try to get me to stay in London.

I have decided not to express how I feel to him. I believe he would decide to leave one way or the other. And I don't think I can survive losing two loves so quickly.

A knock on the door led JULIE to cut off her journal entry. She quickly signed off and opened the door. "Micheal, what's up?"

"Can we walk?"

"Of course." They walked through the gardens of the manor house they were staying at in Cambridge.

"There's something we need to discuss."

"Oh great, here we go."

"What's that supposed to mean?"

"It means you want to discuss my future again, right? I knew this was coming," she shook her head. Julie felt her heart begin to beat more quickly. She crossed her arms as if to try to restrain it.

"Well, we haven't resolved anything yet."

"No! *You* haven't resolved anything yet," she faced him with a piercing glare.

"You're the one who's unhappy. I know you will never be truly happy as long as you're with me."

"I'm starting to think you're right about that." She turned her back to Micheal and stepped away.

"You resent me," his voice dropped.

Julie whipped back in disbelief at what she had just heard him say.

"Resent you? For what?!"

"For failing to get you home."

"Of course. I see it now. It's all about you." She was closing the distance between them. "You resent me because I remind you of your failure. That's why you want to get rid of me!"

"So, you *do* think I'm a failure!"

"There it is again, all about you." She kept pushing; she wanted to turn the tables.

"I just want you to be happy."

"No! You want me gone so you can be happy!"

"That's not true—"

"You're arrogant, self-important, and you let this whole 'Lord of Avalon' thing go to your head. The genius celebrity who looks down his nose at everyone else! And I'm just an inconvenience!"

"Why are you doing this?" He looked like he might cry.

"I was just responding. Why are *you* doing this?!"

"I just want you to be happy."

"There you go, again. You just want me to be happy! You just want me to be happy!" she mocked. "Well, you're doing a great job of it. I'm so happy right now! You don't care about my happiness."

"You're wrong!" he said, raising his voice.

"Just a self-centered, self-aggrandizing—" She started pushing again.

"I do care—"

"Sure, you do!" She couldn't stand to look at the man who held her heart in his hand. She could tell he was overwhelmingly frustrated, so she turned her back to him once more. Julie heard him pause for a second.

"I want you to be happy!" He yelled in frustration.

Julie pivoted back in rage and yelled, "Why the hell would you care so much about my happiness?"

"Because I'm in love with you!"

The words barely registered for a moment. She was stunned into silence. Before she could respond, he said, "I'm sorry, I shouldn't have said that." He seemed just as stunned as she was, then he quickly walked away. Julie was still too stunned to follow.

A moment passed before Micheal's words had sunk in. Then Julie went inside.

"Yvette, have you seen my lord?"

"Toward the stables, my lady."

Julie made haste, and, as she approached the stables, she saw Filipe.

"Filipe, where is my lord?"

"He took Darkness."

"To where did my lord depart?"

"My lord did not say, only that I need not care for Darkness."

She thought for a second. London. It had to be London.

As he rode south, MICHEAL kept going over and over the argument in his head.

"What am I going to do now?" he said aloud to himself.

After a few hours, he stopped at a river to water Darkness.

"Hey boy." He patted him on the neck.

"How can I possibly face her? Maybe I should just leave?"

"Maybe you shall start by handing over that pouch," a voice said behind him, and he felt a pistol push into his back.

He took a deep sigh.

"Sir, it is yours," he said as he turned around.

He gave up the pouch. He was surrounded by eight men.

"Gentlemen. Take all of this," he said, handing over all his other valuables. "Just leave the horse."

One of them hit him on the side of the head with a pistol. "We take what we want, Sir."

"Gentlemen, you don't want to do this."

He got hit in the side with the butt of a musket for his troubles. "Silence!"

Micheal was falling to the ground but, as the men began to converge on him, his total recall immediately took over.

"The key to Capoeira is all about keeping the momentum going through the attack...."

He rotated into a sweep, knocking three to the ground.

"...will be very effective against multiple foes, allowing you to be evasive and on the attack at the same time...."

Micheal used a hand thrust to jump to his feet then redirected his momentum into a cartwheel volley, scoring hits on all the others. As some were on the ground, he unleashed multiple kicks. Four were down for the count.

Others were back on their feet. One was raising his musket. Micheal grabbed the barrel directing the discharge away then used the musket as a staff, knocking out three more. The final man was running away.

Micheal mounted Darkness and ran him down. He bound all the men and planned to later notify the local sheriff.

JULIE bid an early farewell to their Cambridge hosts and took the airship to London.

During the one-hour flight, she considered what she might say to him. She'd spent most of the night awake with the memory of having said so many horrible things. Now, what if she told him of her feelings? Would he believe her?

The last half-hour to London felt like an eternity. She got to their château, and he was nowhere to be found. Her heart sank. She had missed him. As the tears streamed, she had one last desperate thought. The grove!

Julie saw Micheal sitting on the stairs of the gazebo. She noticed that his eye and nose were swollen. Her immediate urge was to go tend to him, but he held up a hand, signaling not to.

"What happened?" she asked softly.

"Highway robbers. But it's not important."

"Micheal..."

"Julie, there are things I have to say. Please let me finish before you say anything. Please?"

She paused for a moment. She just wanted to tell him. But: "Okay."

"I was going to leave. I was contemplating where to go—"

"What stopped you?" She couldn't help herself.

"Right when I was formulating a plan, the men attacked me. And I wasn't afraid. Even outnumbered, eight to one... It was you...you were right, Julie. I am selfish, and scared, and so many other things. Running away was a selfish thought, and in the middle of the attack, I wasn't thinking about the men attacking me, or whether I might die, or anything else. I was only thinking about you. And while I am all those things you said I was, I decided I couldn't run away anymore. You deserve better than that. After all these years, the truth is that you're the only thing that matters to me. And even if this is the last time I ever see you, I owe you an explanation." He paused for a moment.

"Most of those horrible things you said about me are true. But one of the things you were wrong about is that I resent you. I could never do that. I may be a smart man, but I didn't know what love was. Until you. When we first met I, of course, knew you were the most beautiful woman in the world. As I got to know you, I discovered you were also the most beautiful person in the world. How much you care about others. How brilliant your mind is. How loyal you are. I had never been in love before. I had all these confusing feelings. When you almost died..." He broke down for a second with tears coming to his eyes.

"When you almost died, it became clear to me. It had to be love. I did my best these last four years to hide it from you. I didn't want to complicate your life. I was sure I had revealed myself when I almost cried last month. I'm sorry Julie. I'm sorry I couldn't get you home. I'm sorry you got stuck with me. I'm sorry for all the horrible things I couldn't protect you from. I would give anything to get you home, to see you happy. I know I'm not worthy of you. That I need to let you go, but I don't know how..." He broke off.

She couldn't take it anymore. She went and kissed him. After a moment, he pulled back slightly.

"Don't let go," she said and kissed him again.

"I love you, Jules, and I'm sorry."

"Micheal. Don't be sorry. I love you, too." She kissed him again.

As she sat down with him, Mirielle came up the path. "My lord, my lady, Master Newton has arrived."

"Merci, Mirielle," Julie said.

"I think we should freshen up," Micheal said.

"Master Newton, how do you do?" Julie asked as he entered the colonnade.

"Very well, my lady, and a setting almost like Greece of old."

"Master Newton, that was the very idea," Micheal affirmed.

"To inspire philosophical debate," Newton reasoned.

And so they debated various philosophies for a good while.

"Indeed, I shall mourn the loss of such spirited debate with my lady," Newton finished.

"Master Newton, if we may, there is one more idea we would like to debate," Micheal said.

"What, my lord?"

"Waves."

And so they discussed all sorts of details about waves, their form, and their structure.

"What if one were trying to ride a wave, but the wave kept throwing them off? Can you conceive a way to ride without such consequence?" Julie asked.

"I went to a beach. As I watched the waves, they start as a ripple. On approach, they crest. A crest is violent, a ripple is calm. Ride the ripples."

"And if all are crests?" Micheal interjected.

"Waves always begin as a ripple, at a distance."

"How would one reach ripples through a multitude of crests?" Julie asked.

"Most waves roll inward towards the shore, however, small channels between waves lead away from shore."

"Of course!" Micheal's eyes widened. "Too close the forest... Master Newton, many thanks."

"My lord, my dearest lady, it has been a pleasure," Newton said as he rose to his feet.

"Master Newton, the pleasure was all ours," she said with a smile in farewell.

"Micheal? What did you realize?" Julie asked when they were alone.

"Remember how most of the vortices we could locate flowed to the past? What if we have to ride a riptide out past the waves to

the ripples so we can ride the waves to shore? If we went to the
past first, we might be able to find a wave to the future. We might
find a way home."

⸻◆⸻

August 18, 1696

  All of London came out to see us off today.
  *Micheal has seemed a little awkward since the grove. I can still
feel a sense of hesitation at my proclamation of love. But at least
he stayed. His laying his heart bare to me has given me a different
perspective on many of his actions toward me over the years. We
complement each other so well it feels like we are soulmates. I felt,
and to some degree still feel, that way about Aiden. Is it possible to
have more than one soulmate?*

CHAPTER 20:
A PHILADELPHIA
EXPERIMENT

A FEW HOURS AFTER departing London, MICHEAL was admiring the Cliffs of Dover, illuminated by the twilight. Julie joined him at the back of the sundeck and stood without speaking.

"A beautiful night, huh?" he said, breaking the silence.

"Most definitely."

He turned to face her.

"Julie, I'm sorry I've been...I don't know, awkward this past week or so. It's been a lot to deal with."

It was one thing to love her in secret, a whole other thing to be laid so bare, so vulnerable. He searched her face, but his struggle to believe that this perfect angel could possibly return his affection still persisted. She appeared to read him like an open book.

"Micheal, you are good enough. More than good enough. I do love you. I have for a long time. You do believe me, don't you?" Her head tilted, and she looked up at him.

He surrendered to her will. "Yes." Then, "I've never been in a place like this before. I need some time to...adjust. Please be patient with me? Can we take it slow?"

"Of course, whatever you need. I'm not going anywhere.... But there is something I need from you right now," she said, stepping up to him.

She looked up at him, and he understood. He locked hands, and, for the first time, initiated the kiss. After a minute, they broke off, and she slid inside his arms and laid her head on his shoulder.

Two days later, after unloading the *Liberty*, the two of them headed back out to run experiments in the Bermuda Triangle.

"The final summer, I'm sure," Micheal said.

"I'm glad to see your confidence is back. You really think we'll figure this out?"

"We do have a member of Mount Genius," he said with a smile.

"Looks like your arrogance is back as well."

"Oh! Not me, you!"

"Oh yeah, me." She rolled her eyes.

"Didn't you notice how much Newton gushed over you? It was like love-at-first-debate."

She sighed in exasperation. "I think you're jealous."

"Okay, we're approaching an energy vortex," he said, focusing on the task at hand.

"So, what are we looking for again?"

"An inverse well. Remember a couple of years ago when we encountered a particularly deep one? It probably has to be something like that."

They spent a few days cruising around the Triangle, running scans for any EM anomalies, but came up empty.

"Maybe an analysis of our past scan data could help predict frequency and likely locations," Julie suggested.

They spent the next few hours running computer simulations. Julie had gone to bed. After a few more hours, Micheal was becoming frustrated at the lack of results. Julie kissed his neck and said, "Come to bed. We'll pick it up in the morning."

He followed her into their cabin and prepared for bed.

"Are you sure you don't want to, you know, do anything yet?" She pressed her breasts into his back and wrapped her arms around his neck.

"Incredibly tempting, but..." She turned his head and kissed him. "You don't make it easy to say no but, I still think we should wait... Okay?"

"I will wait for you. Not too long, I hope," she said with a seductive wink.

After a few hours of sleep, an alarm went off. They rushed to see what set it off, but it was obvious.

"A hurricane!" Julie yelled.

"It must be a small one. It's bearing 285 degrees northwest, the center of circulation one hundred and twenty miles southeast, forward speed twenty-two knots. Bring the *Liberty* full speed north."

The sun began to rise, shining through the edge of the storm's umbrella. "We're almost clear!" he yelled to Julie.

"Micheal! There might be a problem!"

"What?!" He looked at the edge of the radar screen. A feeder band...

He hit the lockdown protocol. The band raced overhead but, as they ran toward the safety pod, a massive wave hit broadside. They had tethered themselves to the ship but still fought desperately to stay on board. The *Liberty* finally limped through the edge of the band.

Micheal crawled over to Julie.

"Are you all right?" he asked breathlessly.

"I'll live.... You?"

"Just need a little rest," he said, passing out from exhaustion.

Micheal woke to the setting sun and a pillow under his head.

"Good morning, sunshine. While you slept, I tracked and scanned an inverse vortex. I think it will be useful."

"Why didn't you wake me?"

"You said you needed the sleep," she said with a smirk.

"It's always an adventure when we come out here," he said, shaking his head. "I love Bermuda."

I: Sparring

"I saw that coming a mile away," JULIE said, deflecting Micheal's roundhouse kick. She was determined to win.

She countered with a spinning elbow, which he partially blocked. He tried to sweep her leg, but she immediately sprang into a back somersault to avoid it.

When they were back on their feet, Micheal patted his elbow and said, "You're still a little slow on the transition."

"Again!" She yelled as she began a new attack.

They went back and forth for a while until...

She flew at Micheal with a sidekick. He blocked it, sending her to the ground. She rolled up into a spinning back kick that put him off balance, then continued into a power chop kick that came down on his chest, sending him to the ground.

"Much better! Your speed is impressive," he said as he got to his feet.

The modest crowd of a couple of dozen cheered. It was a bit larger than usual, most likely because this was their first sparring session since they'd returned to Boston.

A portion of the service staff would get up early in order to watch their regular sessions.

One person who attended nearly every session was Master Liu, their primary martial arts instructor.

During the summer of 1693, they traveled to a Shaolin Monastery in Tibet so that Master Liu could take the trials to become an official Kung Fu Master.

Then, they took an expedition through the Middle East to search for more tablets containing cuneiform and, if possible, more of the unknown language.

At the end of summer, they returned to Tibet to retrieve Master Liu. He had been instrumental in helping them perfect their martial arts techniques.

After he got cleaned up, MICHEAL rode Darkness into Boston to see about a new artifact. He'd been working on the translations in the years since Julie first gave him the tablets.

"Lord of Satan!" some random man said with fire in his eyes.

What did he say?

"Professor from hell!" another woman yelled.

What?

"Good morrow, good people," Micheal replied with a nod.

"Go back ta hell!" another woman yelled.

What the hell is happening?

He dismounted and went into the rare procurement shop. He rarely went into Boston proper but, Master Oliver, the proprietor had sent word of something of interest.

As he came into the shop, he heard: "Devil's servant in flesh! The Lord of Satan come to blaspheme our Lord and Savior."

"Master Parris, what joy of your presence."

"Can you be so ignorant?" Parris scoffed. "Perhaps your family of mystery has made a devil's deal?"

"Why do you have such enmity for me?" Micheal glared.

"Your family is an abomination to God." Parris furrowed his brow. "Your wife, the devil's whore!"

Micheal thought he could see the flames of hell in the bastard's eyes.

"I would expect such scurrilous accusations. Your iniquitous reputation precedes you."

"Reputation?!"

"Your promotion of obscene claims of witchcraft put to death nineteen innocents. You are a murderer. I was there, one September day, when eight, all innocent, did hang—your accusation the cause."

"Innocent?! All were bewitched by your devil's whore of a wife!"

Micheal backhanded Parris, knocking him to the floor. "Your slander against my wife shall not stand! Of the devil you are! Blaspheming reverend, to hell shall you go!"

Parris rose to his feet. "I did the Lord's work when I hanged your wife five years ago. Would that she remained in hell." Parris walked to the door, then paused. "And the Lord's work I shall enact again."

The entire ride home was filled with thoughts of the threat Parris had made, as well as the reaction from the people of Boston.

"Micheal, did you get it?" JULIE asked as he entered her chambers. He didn't respond immediately, so she asked, "What's wrong?"

"I ran into Parris in Boston. He had all kinds of nasty things to say about you, me, and my family. It appears that, while we were in Europe, he started a campaign to turn the Puritans against us. Multiple people in the streets said horrible things to me."

"Damn! I hate him. Are you still against me going after him?"

"Unfortunately, yes. Anything you did to him would only give credence to his allegations. Even without thinking of what it could do to the timeline. Still, I got the tablets. This one has a sample of the unknown language—including a few elements I believe will help." He laid the parcel on the table. "These tablets, along with the other two we found in Mesopotamia, containing cross-sectional translations between Sumerian Cuneiform and Ancient Hebrew, should be enough to complete the puzzle."

"So finally, your Hebrew lessons and studies might become useful," she said with a hint of sarcasm.

He sighed.

"In our situation, knowing as many languages as possible could be vital. We don't know what the future—or the past—holds."

"Yeah, yeah, yeah." She rolled her eyes. "It just gets tedious sometimes."

II: A Philadelphia Experiment

"Are you sure about this? I mean, the government never confirmed that the Philadelphia Experiment ever actually happened." Julie seemed skeptical of MICHEAL'S latest plan to test temporal mechanics.

"They never completely denied it either. Like the government would ever admit such a colossal blunder. You kill half a battleship of sailors trying to turn the ship invisible. Would you admit it?"

"So you want to duplicate a colossal blunder?"

All his research into the Philadelphia Experiment had led him to believe the temporal elements were unexpected, so he was confident they were better informed. They had used all the scan data to predict which energy frequencies might open an artificial vortex.

"And what if you're wrong?" she asked with worry.

"Then we might be stuck in some new time or place, but we do have plenty of supplies on board. And, hey, you would get your wish to live on the *Liberty*," he said with a grin.

They fired up the generators. At first, nothing happened. They ramped up the power levels. A green light began glowing in the air above the boat. It expanded, then mist started emanating from the light.

"Increase the power quotient," he instructed. The mist was spiraling around the *Liberty*. A few miles south, the island of Martha's

Vineyard began fluctuating, shifting from solid to transparent and back to solid. The generators reached levels around the predicted necessary levels. Micheal was blinded by a bright flash splitting the air. A sudden dead stop caused him to lose his balance.

"Julie! Can you see anything?!" He yelled over the ringing in his ears.

"I can only make out colors!" she yelled. "My ears are ringing!"

As the ringing began to fade, he could hear the sound of cannon fire.

"What's going on?!"

"I think we jumped into a battle!" The bombardment was relentless, but he didn't think it was directed at them.

"Take us back!"

"We have no power! It must have overloaded the system." He looked out to the east and the closest ship was lowering one of their jolly boats filled with British redcoats. As they worked to restore power, the boat came closer and closer with another being lowered down.

As the first boat was about to reach them, the lights began flickering on and off. "Keep working on it. We're about to be boarded," he said as he ran off to meet the boarding party.

As several redcoats began climbing on the back deck, Micheal jumped from the second deck balcony, rolling underneath two, tripping them to the ground. As he rose to his feet, he counted about a dozen men. They had already been surrounding the Main Cabin of The *Liberty*.

He kicked two back onto the boat below, causing several to hasten up the stairs to the Sun Deck. As one of the remaining soldiers raised his musket, Micheal ducked past the end of the barrel, grabbing the musket in the process. He shoved the soldier to the edge of the ship, then swept his legs, sending him into the sea.

Micheal turned to see the others finish helping the first men back to their feet. But, as they began to raise their muskets again, several others flew overboard from the top deck, stopping them in their tracks.

Julie jumped from above, landing on two of the remaining soldiers. She spun and kicked the last man overboard.

"I got the power back on," Julie yelled as the generators fired up.

"Look out!" Two soldiers emerged from inside.

She tried to dodge the bayonets. The first one grazed her neck, the second one pierced her shoulder. She pulled it out, shoving the soldier in the process. She then swung it upward, sending him overboard.

Micheal caught the other musket as the other soldier was about to stab Julie. He threw it down, stepped in with a body check, and sent the man into the water.

Some Royal Marines attempted to reboard. Micheal and Julie threw the unconscious men down at them. Then a green orb of light flashed above the ship.

"Are you all right?!" he yelled to Julie. She had a gash in her neck and was bleeding from her shoulder.

"I'm fine. We need to get moving!"

They got clear of the boats, and the green mist began swirling around the ship.

Suddenly, another soldier emerged from inside the Main Cabin. He looked at Micheal, looked up at the glowing light, dropped his musket in fear, and jumped overboard.

A moment later, a bright flash split the sky. As the disorientation faded, he could see Martha's Vineyard to the south, and they were just off the coast of Cape Cod. He limped to the top deck.

"When are we?" he asked.

"We're back." Julie's blouse was open, and she was inspecting her shoulder wound.

"Where did we go?" she asked as he looked over the data.

"Looks like we were in the Delaware River, south of Philadelphia. Tachyon readings indicate the year was 1777." He thought about the American Revolution. "That had to be the bombardment of Fort Mifflin in November 1777, during the British Philadelphia campaign."

"A Philadelphia experiment indeed," Julie said, shaking her head.

III: The Last Thanksgiving

It was late November, the modern traditional time for Thanksgiving. JULIE was making sure everything was ready for the Massachusett. Typically, many of them would visit the palace for the occasion, but a couple of days earlier Thunder Hawk and Peaceful River had arrived to inform them that the entire tribe was coming to visit.

Despite several visits, most of the people still found Bostonian odd. Many questioned why anyone would go to such trouble to build something so unnecessary.

When the Massachusett arrived, they had brought everything they owned. The staff at the palace helped them assemble their longhouses on the grounds.

"Nightwolf, it's so good to see you again," Julie said, greeting the chief in Algonquian.

"Lady Whitaker, your speech is much improved," Nightwolf said with a smile.

The ballroom was turned into an enormous dining hall, accommodating the service staff, the Massachusett, and some of Julie and Micheal's closest friends, about three hundred in all. That night, Thanksgiving dinner was served.

Julie oversaw the menu. It consisted of the traditional turkey but in many styles—roasted, baked, fried, and deep-fried—along with all the modern classic fixings, as well as a variety of pies and ice cream for dessert.

After eating, chatting, and much drinking, they all discussed what they were thankful for in a mix of tongues. Regardless of the language spoken, Micheal would translate into Algonquian and Julie into English.

"I have been thankful for your friendship these many seasons," Micheal said to Nightwolf in Algonquian.

"Lord and Lady Whitaker have been valued members of the people. Regretfully, our time comes to an end in this place," Nightwolf's eyes dropped.

"You are leaving?" Julie asked.

"Our sister tribe in Quebec has invited us to join them permanently. We must make the journey before the snow," Nightwolf explained.

"You will be missed," Julie said with regret.

As dinner wound down, Micheal announced that was time for stories. Nearly everyone gathered around, and anyone could take the stage to tell a story.

The hour grew late, and Julie took the stage to close the evening. She told her story in Algonquin out of respect for the tradition.

"When I was aged 12, I was commencing from primary instruction. As the quest for enlightenment was of high value in my family, it was a cause for celebration. My mother put together a great feast in my honor, and I must admit I was quite proud of the achievement. My older sister Jessica had always been superior in every way, so I couldn't help but condescend to her. Finally, her jealousy overcame her, and she threw a spoonful of mashed potatoes that landed on my shoulder. I tried to retaliate, but I missed. My spoonful of potatoes hits my mother in the face. My father could not help but laugh. My mother became incensed and poured a bowl of soup over his head. Everyone laughed. I took the opportunity of the distraction. I stepped over and poured my drink down my sister's back. She tried to retaliate, but she missed, and her drink hit my brother instead. After that, the whole thing deteriorated into a family food fight. When it was all said and done, we were all covered head to toe with food and everyone was laughing with each other. A most memorable commencement." She finished and everyone in the room was laughing. She couldn't have asked for a better last Thanksgiving with the Massachussett.

Over the next few days, the audience for their morning sparring sessions steadily increased until most of the people were attending.

The tribe then requested that she and Micheal perform a ceremonial sparring match as a sendoff. They were honored by the request.

The Massachusett left that day with many extra supplies and blessings for their journey.

IV: The Waves of Time

"You really want to do this again?" JULIE'S stomach was filled with butterflies at the prospect of another Philadelphia Experiment.

"Jules, I know we're close. We are so close. Despite the negatives, we learned a lot from the experiment. I'm asking you to trust me."

She looked at him. Before she could say anything, he came over and took her hands.

"We don't have to do any of this if you don't want to. Of course I want to get back to the twenty-first century, but honestly, that is only secondary now. The twenty-first century is not my home anymore. My home is wherever you are. We could live out our lives in this century or any other, and I would be perfectly happy as long as you are with me." He kissed her.

After a long moment, he pulled back, looked her in the eyes and said, "You are my whole world. You're the only thing that matters to me."

"Micheal, I trust you, I love you..." She paused for a second. "Let's finish this."

"Jules, I love you," he kissed her again.

As they slowly separated, her desire for him nearly overwhelmed her. Her urge to grab him and take him was almost more than she could bear, but Micheal wanted to have his first time be on their true wedding night. He said that if she made any moves in that direction, he would be helpless to resist her. So she promised to be strong and to fight back any urge that might come.

"Here we go," she said as they fired up the generators.

They had taken the *Liberty* to the open ocean between Bermuda and the eastern seaboard. However, despite their preparations, the flash seared right through her closed eyelids. She was blinded and disoriented for a few minutes.

"When and where are we?" she asked when she got her wits about her.

"According to this, we are in New York Harbor, I think," he replied with uncertainty.

"Look!" she said, pointing to a ship inbound.

"It's flying a Dutch flag. And the tachyon readings are saying this is 1625.... This is the founding of New York City," he said with an air of certainty. They watched for a while until the *Liberty* was functional, then they returned to 1697.

Their second jump took them to a spot in the North Atlantic, at approximately forty-four and a half degrees north, sixty-one degrees west. As they observed the surrounding area, the blue sky began to darken. They realized a solar eclipse was beginning. The eclipse totality lasted nearly ten minutes. The tachyon scans indicated the date was January 26, 1656. When the eclipse was over, they returned to 1697.

Their third and final jump was the roughest one yet. Julie must have been out for a while. When they came around, the *Liberty* had been boarded by pirates and they were bound to the mast.

"Good day, sir. My lady." The captain tipped his cap. "The name is Teach, Captain Edward Teach. Some call me Blackbeard. Who might you be?" There was a sparkle in his eye.

"Whitaker, sir. And my lady," Micheal replied with a smile in his voice. "The infamous Blackbeard. Your reputation precedes you, sir."

Blackbeard looked around the ship, then back at them. "Your reputation as well, Your Grace," Blackbeard said with a smile. Clearly Teach believed he was the Duke of Avalon.

"Captain, I have a proposal. There is a secret compartment which contains two boxes of gold and precious stones. Take them with our compliments. And good fortune to you," Micheal offered.

"Your Grace is in no position to dictate terms."

Julie could hear the first power core firing up.

"Captain, five minutes further on and you shall wish to be elsewhere."

"A threat, Your Grace? I have always prized a ship of Avalon." Blackbeard was pacing the deck and seemed in a jovial mood.

"Captain, you do not understand the circumstances."

The vortex burst into the sky.

"Three minutes, Captain!" Micheal yelled over the noise of the vortex. Many of the pirates were rushing to get back to *Queen Anne's Revenge*.

"What happens?!"

"In two minutes you shalt find out! 'Twas an honor to meet you, Captain Teach. Now go! You need to be one hundred feet clear!" Micheal instructed.

Teach stared up at the swirl descending from the vortex, then he and his last few men hurried back to his ship. The sails had already unfurled, and the *Revenge* ripped away as rapidly as possible. As they pulled perhaps just over one hundred feet away, the flash split the air.

"Julie? Julie? Are you awake?"

"Yes."

"We need to untie ourselves."

She could feel him working on the ropes.

"Well, I guess the auto-restart was a smart idea. So when did we go this time?" she asked as they analyzed the data.

"January 18, 1718. Port Royal, in the Bahamas."

"Do you think it's possible to jump home?" she brought her hands together beneath her chin.

"I don't want to shatter your optimism, but that looks unlikely. All four jumps ranged between about twenty and eighty years in either direction. You can see on this chart. I've added the most recent jump. It is indicating that the temporal flow is circular. It's an eddy in between the regular flow waves. The eddy is approximately two hundred years wide in the fabric of subspace."

"So you think the artificially generated portals only tap into eddies? But the eddies are always trapped between the wave peaks, which means you would always just go around in circles within the eddy?"

"Yes, so the artificial portals can take us no more than a century in either direction. And never more than one jump in the same direction."

"Meaning they could never get us home."

"All hope is not lost. We still have the rip currents."

Three days of searching finally produced a deep rip current. The vortex echo scan showed a temporal depth of approximately five thousand years, which correlated with the only other deep rip current they had encountered. The data model clearly showed full confirmation of the structure of temporal waves.

"We'll have to see if any of this data is useful to us."

"It will be. I know it," she said with great confidence. "Do you have any idea why we had so many close calls in our Philadelphia Experiment jumps?"

"The only thing I can think of is that important events and people generate more 'wake' in the time stream, so the vortex is attracted to it."

"That makes sense...Want to jump again?"

"Let's not," he replied, laughing.

CHAPTER 21: THE PROPOSAL

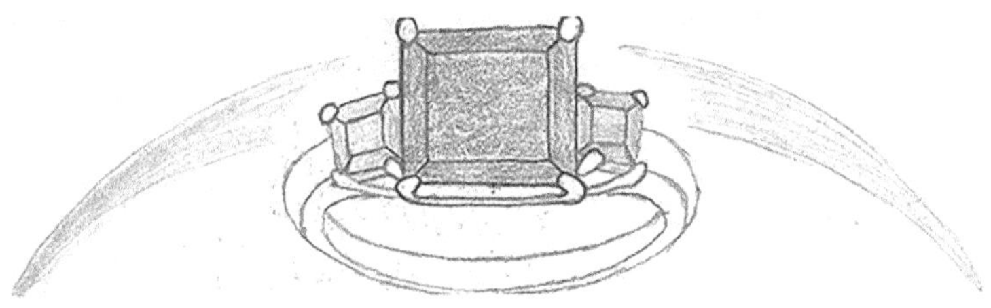

T HE HOLIDAYS PASSED INTO 1697 culminating with Micheal's birthday, and their fifth anniversary in the timeline. By the end of January, acting Governor William Stoughton summoned them.

"Lord and Lady Whitaker, problems with your operations have been expressed me." Governor Stoughton began.

"Your honor, to which operations do you refer?" Micheal already knew this might eventually come with the new governor.

"Primarily these...science displays. Perhaps the heathens in Avalon give high regard to such distortions of God's natural world, but many in the colony have come to disavow their heretical influence." The governor looked down his nose at them.

Governor Stoughton was no Sir William Phipps. Phipps was an open-minded reformer. Stoughton was as Puritanical as the wind-driven snow.

"Your honor, I fail to see how God Almighty might rejoice in the ignorance of man."

As they were about to leave, the governor added, "My lady, rumors abound that you be a witch, some say a demon. Were I in your shoes, I would be careful."

"Why do you think everyone is turning against us?" Julie asked as they pulled away from the governor's mansion.

"I suspect our friend, Samuel Parris, is behind it. It doesn't help that Stoughton is governor. He was the overseer of the witch trials back in '92 and '93."

"You never told me that."

"Since he replaced Phipps, we've only had one direct interaction with him before. I didn't want to needlessly alarm you."

"How about now?! It looks like those in power are all Puritans, and they are aligning against us. We both know Mather has been after you the whole time you've been at Harvard."

"And the board has always stopped him."

"But with the veto of Harvard's charter by the governor's council, Stoughton placed some of his own picks on the board. What if they're Puritans?"

He, of course, knew that was likely. The feeling throughout the colony was tense, almost as bad as in 1692.

A couple days later, JULIE returned to Boston. It had been a few weeks since she was able to visit the orphanage.

She always looked forward to the smiles on the children's faces when she would pass out candy.

"Martha, how fare the children?" She loved Martha's sweet, grandmother nature.

"Very well, my lady. Looking forward to seeing ya, they are."

"Lady Julie!" The children gathered around her.

She reached out in an embrace when Sister Mary, the overseer of the orphanage, broke through.

"My lady, might I have a word?"

"Pardon me, children." Julie followed Sister Mary into her office.

As Julie sat down, Sister Mary's disposition turned serious.

"My lady, it is with my deepest regrets that our arrangement must end."

"What? Why?"

"Lord Governor Stoughton issued decree this morning. My lady, I am sorry…" Sister Mary's voice broke. Through their shared love for the children under Sister Mary's care and Julie's patronage, the two women had formed a strong, if unlikely, friendship over the past four years. This was news was clearly difficult for her old friend.

"Say your final farewells. You shall not be welcome henceforth."

Julie rose from her seat and rushed out to see the children.

As she exited the building, a tear ran down her cheek. She thought about the special times she had spent playing with them, teaching them, and how much she would miss them.

"You shall corrupt these children no more."

She couldn't believe it. Samuel Parris stood in front of her with a self-righteous smirk. *That fucking bastard.*

"Would you let the children starve?"

"If it protects them from your unholy self." The malice in his voice turned her stomach. His voice disgusted her. "You shall hang again, quite soon." The hate in his eyes was heinous.

The commotion had drawn a small crowd. She decided not to press the matter further and began to untie Angel.

"Rejoice! For you shall reunite with your devil's whore of sister. Jessica, it was?"

She stopped in her tracks. She squeezed her fists with the heat rising in her face. She turned to see his evil grin widen.

Parris took a step closer, smiled and said, "Did the whore drown? Joyous must have been the day Satan reunited with—"

She could take it no longer. She brought her leg around and struck the side of his face with her foot, sending him tumbling into the street.

The men in the crowd looked at Parris, then at Julie, and began to rush at her.

She quickly mounted Angel and yelled, "Yah!"

Angel tried to gallop off, but the crowd surrounded them. Several men tried to pull Julie off. Angel reared up and the men in front dodged as she stomped down. Julie urged Angel to a gallop and saw people diving out of the way as they cleared the mob.

MICHEAL was running some numbers at the workstation in the lounge. "Dammit! All the models keep going so far back!" he said to himself in frustration.

"Micheal! Micheal!" Julie yelled as she ran down the stairs.

He stood up just in time to catch her in a hug. She was crying and rambling incoherently.

"It's okay. Everything is going to be okay," he said, trying to comfort her. She looked up at him, tears on her cheeks.

"He...He has to die..." she said through tears. Micheal had his suspicions but found himself asking anyway.

"Who?"

"Samuel Parris!"

"What happened?" He dreaded the answer.

"First, he had the governor order that I can no longer be associated with the orphanage. He was waiting outside to rub it in my face! Finally, he said the most horrible, awful things about Jessica. He knew how she died. He must've been listening to me when I was in the dungeon.... And there's one more thing."

"What's that?"

"I kicked him in the face."

"What happened then?"

"The crowd watching us came after me. Parris has turned the public against us." Her voice tremored.

"We can't kill Parris."

"Of course you would say that."

"It's not that. If we did, we would have to run."

February 28, 1697

Five years ago, I died. Not just died, I was executed. As a witch, how crazy it still sounds... It almost feels like some distant dream... If only that were true.

That horrifying feeling of helplessness. The shadow of death creeping towards me, agonizingly slow, has haunted my dreams these years past. Just when the light of love and joy was beginning to shine over that dreaded shadow, the devil who literally dragged me through hell has returned, intent to return me to that cold dark place. I feel I could truly kill him. I never thought I would feel such hatred. And feeling that way scares me...

... Micheal, we have been getting to know more and more of the secret sides of each other. The sides we rarely show to anyone else. It's been six months since everything came to a head in London. I still don't know what he's waiting for.

"It's not looking good," Micheal said, shaking his head.

"You mean we're at another dead end? No way home?" The results of their past scans had diminished JULIE'S hopes of finding a route back.

"Well, there might be, but I don't think you'll like it."

"Why?"

"I used all the data we've gathered over the years to model the wave formations in the time stream, and a pattern has become clear. The waves run in transactional sequences."

"You mean one wave perpetuates the next? Like in a linear sequence?"

"Yes, and, theoretically, we could ride a full sequence back to the twenty-first century. But..."

"What's the problem?"

"To begin with, all the rip current wells are extremely deep—about five thousand years, give or take a few hundred."

"But then we ride the waves all the way home, right?"

"During the perpetual transition, we would be stuck in a section of the timeline until the next crest arrives. Each of these transitional intermediate sections are an average of seven or eight years. I also was able to determine it would take between twenty and thirty waves to make it back..."

She did the math in horror.

"One hundred and fifty to two hundred and fifty years? We would never live long enough."

"We might. As far as I know, we haven't aged yet."

Over the next few months, Julie mapped out dozens of wave sequences.

"So one hundred and fifty years it is," Micheal said, shaking his head. "The shortest path home is just over one hundred and fifty years on twenty-one waves with twenty intermediate stops."

"Would we have to go to the Triangle each time?"

"No, the apex junctions in the Triangle send you to random points. The waves pass by without necessarily opening a vortex. We will be re-creating the event that brought us here. Take a look at this. I was able to calculate the fall event." He showed her the model. "This point is you. That one is me. Over there is the energy apex and these are our exit points." He indicated points on the other side of the apex. "So we will calculate our required positions to triangulate our temporal energy signatures to the requisite energy apex. It will generate a vortex, and we'll be transported through space and time just like when we fell."

She stared at the model. The cruel reality of "the event" boiled down to a simple diagram. Contemplating the variables that had to align for it to happen only emphasized the unfairness of how a one-in-a-trillion shot turned her life on its head.

———⋈———

June 12, 1697

So, it looks like we may get back to the twenty-first century after all... In one hundred and fifty years. If we survive the run through the timeline... I didn't want to accept this less-than-ideal outcome. I spent last month trying to find some other way, some kind of shortcut, and it only made matters worse. I discovered that if we miss a jump, we have to wait for the trailing wake to get a second chance. That wave is equidistant so our stay in that time doubles. If we miss the wake wave, we are stuck. Back at square one. And missing any jump adds additional stops in the timeline, extending our run even longer. This is apparently our only way home.

Where's Doc Brown or Alexander Hartigan when you need them?

Over the last few years, I've worked hard to prepare myself for whatever possibilities we might face. I've learned as many languages as possible and, particularly now, the ancient languages including Micheal's speculative translation of the unknown language. Although it's only a guess if he's right about the translation.

I find myself ambivalent toward this forthcoming quest. How likely is it we will survive centuries through some of the most dangerous times? Perhaps we should just stay in the here and now. As much as I miss my family and friends, how will they react to my return so many years later? And even if we make it through, who will we become in the process? I'm already not who I was that January day in 2010. Who will I be when I'm two hundred years old? The twenty-first century is not my home anymore, Micheal has become my home. I know as long as we are together, I will be happy. So maybe we should stay...

I: Darkness Falls

MICHEAL had been summoned by the new Head of the Board at Harvard to a meeting of the Overseers. He was in Master Richardson's office, seated in front of only seven of the twelve members, suspicious of their intent. Particularly since President Mather was here as well.

"Professor Whitaker. We are grateful of your presence this day," Master Richardson said.

"The honor is mine, gentlemen."

"Attention has been paid concerning your flamboyant public gestures. And questions of my lord's adherence to the ecclesiastical codes of norm have been raised," Master Elliott, the other new board member, said directly.

"Is not this university an institution of enlightenment also? Including the exploration of God Almighty's creation?"

"The original purpose of this institution was to ensure clergy for community worship. The grandiosity of my lord's displays are vanity projects for you," Richardson said.

"Professor Whitaker. Your distortions of our Lord God's wonders are at an end. Your current project ends. Professor Rainsford shall undertake a new process of review for pupils. Your tenure is revoked, your professorship shall pass to Professor Rainsford," President Mather said with a smirk.

"Magistrate Corwin requests further parley," Mather added, as the man entered the room, accompanied by two local inquisitors.

"Lord Avalon?" Corwin inquired.

"Yes, Your Honor?"

"My lord. May I present Father Jepson and Father Eldred. They shall be party to my inspection," Corwin added, signaling the two men to come inside.

"What source informs your unusual manipulations of God's natural law?" Master Jepson asked.

"Careful observation and study, Master Jepson."

"Many suspect your family is a cult of Satan," Master Eldred's voice pitched up.

"Preposterous!"

"Your knowledge be overly grand," Jepson accused.

Micheal abruptly turned the tables on the men. He said, "Master

Jepson? Do you know James 1:5?"

He could tell Jepson and Eldred were a bit flustered by his question, and immediate and exact knowledge of the Bible. Jepson stammered. He looked to Eldred who didn't seem to know.

"James 1:5: 'If any of you lack wisdom, let him ask of God, that giveth to all men liberally, and upbraideth not; and it shall be given him.' How is this different than what I have been doing here?" he said directly. They all exchanged looks.

"My lord, we shall speak again," Epson said, ending the interview.

Even though Micheal had clearly bested the inquisitors, a feeling of uneasiness lingered. As he rode to Bostonian, questions of what he and Julie would do about this new potential threat on top of the Puritan axis consumed his thoughts.

When he reached the palace, he stopped off at the Chapel of Heaven. It was one of his favorite features of Bostonian. It was located on the fourth floor in the center of the Gallery Tower. From outside, it appeared an orb suspended in the heart of the one-hundred-foot empty cylinder of art.

He entered the chapel and found it empty. Even dimmed, the light was calming. He lingered a moment then headed for his chambers.

"Don't you have the review? I thought you would be late," Julie said as he entered.

"The review has been canceled, and I am no longer the professor."

"They fired you?!"

"Not only that, but the magistrate and two inquisitors interrogated me, accusing me and my whole family of heresy and collusion with the devil."

"This is bad. Do you think they're going to charge you?"

"Maybe, but in these times, the wheels of 'justice' turn slowly. The status of my family also makes it harder for them to do it."

"They sure are turning the colony against us. Governor Stoughton sent word that the annual Summerfest was being taken over by the colonial government. Also, we're not invited. I was the one who made the festival to begin with!"

"We leave in just over two months. I was going to resign any-ways," he said, trying to rationalize away the turn things were taking in Boston.

The next day Micheal needed some time to think, so he went to the stables.

"Hey, old friend. Let's go for a ride." He patted Darkness on the neck and fed him an apple.

He rode Darkness north along the Mystic River toward Med-ford. It was like old times.

They spent most of the day gallivanting about the woods. He pulled his friend to a halt next to the Mystic, a couple of miles north of Bostonian.

"Hey, buddy. I need some advice." Micheal made eye contact and Darkness nodded as if prodding him to continue.

"It's been nearly a year and I still don't feel worthy of Julie. What do you think I should do?" Micheal stood by the river and his friend nickered in reply.

"I love her, too. But is that enough?"

Darkness then walked over and gave him a neck hug, as if to say yes.

A crack of thunder broke the silence and Darkness jolted back. Micheal saw blood on his hand. He looked up to see a crimson streak run down his friend's flank.

Micheal turned and drew his pistol. A small mob was coming from the west with muskets drawn. Before they could fire again, he unleashed a volley aimed at their feet, driving them back.

The majority of the mob turned and ran away, but a group of five men rushed at him with guns ready. Micheal was reloading his pistol when he heard the roar of gunfire.

There was a flash of black lightning. When the smoke cleared, the men were in full retreat and Darkness was standing in front of him.

Micheal saw blood streaming down his right leg.

"Darkness!" Micheal yelled as he ran to his side.

"No!" His hands began to shake, and his stomach became tight. "Why? Why did you do that?"

Darkness slowly stopped moving. His breathing, once mighty,

was shallow and miserly. In the end, Darkness nudged his friend in a final sign of loyalty. Micheal hugged Darkness one final time.

During the long walk back to Bostonian, he thought back on all the times he had spent with Darkness, his first friend in the seventeenth century, the one who had made everything else possible.

As he went over what had just happened, he pictured the men in his mind and his grief turned to rage. He came home, and he saw Julie talking to Yvette and he broke down. She came running over.

"Micheal! What happened?!"

Micheal immediately sought comfort in her arms. He had never felt so vulnerable.

"Darkness is dead."

She walked him inside to her chambers, and they mourned together.

The next morning, his noble friend was laid to rest next to the stables. And a few days later, a life-size statue was erected at the site. No horse was more worthy of such honor.

For the next couple of days, he decided to focus on all the good times with Darkness. Julie and Micheal shared their favorite stories of their giant friend late into the night.

A true light was Darkness.

II: The Proposal

MICHEAL stood at the edge of the deck, staring at the Mystic River, contemplating what he was about to do. Ever since the blowup in London, he had often wondered when or even if he would ever do this.

He still couldn't comprehend that someone as incredible as Julie felt for him what he felt for her.

He'd asked her for patience. He knew there had to be something influencing her feelings. She could never feel that way otherwise. The last ten months were spent waiting for her to come to her senses, to realize she had said she loved him by mistake. That entire time, he had also been trying to convince himself he was worthy of her. Even now, that conviction was failing him.

Over the last week, Micheal determined that he had to make a decision. He couldn't wait any longer. He had originally set a soft deadline of a year. If, by September, he couldn't convince himself of his worthiness, he would either just have to go for it or he would have to leave.

His instinctive urge was to run. He had done so his entire life. But that was the coward's way. He had been a coward his whole life, and he still felt like one.

The sacrifice Darkness made for Micheal showed him what it was to be brave. He decided this time he would follow his friend's example. He would push through the fear and doubt to the new horizons of their future together. He would risk everything and lay himself bare. He knew if she broke his vulnerable heart, he would never survive it. But he also knew he couldn't survive without her.

JULIE began dressing for a special dinner in the hot-air balloon. She had been feeling down since Summerfest had been taken from her.

Micheal planned this special dinner for the week of the festival to cheer her up. She always loved going up in the balloon, and he encouraged her to wear her festival dress for the occasion. It was made of satin. The royal purple colors ran all through the bodice. The black trim transitioned into a beautiful deep turquoise down by the skirt. She had curled her hair and tied it up with a matching turquoise lace band.

She took a diamond pendant choker and wrapped it around her neck.

"Goodness. You're beautiful!" She could see his eyes tracing the curves of her body, then he stepped in and kissed her.

"And you look amazing." His tuxedo matched her dress.

He ran his fingers down her cheek. "Shall we?" he said, giving her his elbow.

The balloon had been readied for them on the patio overlooking the Mystic River.

"My lady. My lord," Yvette curtsied as her husband, Filipe, opened the door to the basket.

As they stepped on board, she saw an ivory tablecloth setting with fancy silverware and a glowing orb in the center.

They climbed to five thousand feet. The air was calm, so they stalled out over the bay.

"Jules," Micheal pulled out a chair.

"Thank you."

"Now, my lady, allow me to present your dinner. Beef Wellington accompanied by crisp butter fried Brussels sprouts, asparagus with hollandaise sauce, and Dauphin's potatoes." His presentation was nothing short of spectacular.

"Wow, you sure went to a lot of trouble." Julie was constantly reminded why she loved him.

"And to drink, an assortment of sparkling, exotic fruit juices. Let's start with this one." The tropical smell of guava wafted off the foam.

As they ate, they shared stories of their past and talked of trivial things, which made her feel at home. The night went on with perfect serenity. Then it was time for dessert.

"An Avalon truffle, my lady." The flavors exploded in her mouth in a smooth satin texture.

"My god. This is to die for." She closed her eyes.

"Can you taste the subtle honeydew flavor?"

"Yes, it's magical."

"I added a light brine to bring out the flavor of the melon."

"You made this?!"

"I'm glad you like it."

"Like it? I love it, it's incredible," she took another bite.

They went to the west side of the basket. The sun was low over the horizon. They had drifted out over the Massachusetts Bay. The waters surrounding the islands in the bay were reflecting the amazing tapestry of colors in the sky. She felt like she was swimming in a painting. It was one of the most beautiful sights she'd ever seen.

Micheal stepped in behind and wrapped his arms around. She traced his arms and met his hands with hers and held him tightly.

"You have no idea how much I needed this," she said. He kissed the side of her neck.

"Jules, I have something I need to tell you," he said softly.

She turned to face him. He seemed nervous, and a pit formed in her stomach. She feared something bad had happened. Maybe he was being arrested.

"I have been afraid my whole life. Afraid of failure. Afraid I wasn't a good person. Afraid to let anyone get to know me and I mean all of me. Whenever things got tough, I chose the coward's way out."

She started to fear he was saying goodbye.

"Then, I met you. You wouldn't take my crap. You always encouraged me to keep trying. You taught me what real courage was. You're such a good person. You care so deeply for everyone around you. I know I'm not good enough for you—"

"That's—"

He put his finger to her lips to stop her. The butterflies were racing a million miles an hour.

"No, it's true. No man is. But you make me want to be a better person." He paused for a second.

"I love you more than you could possibly imagine. That you could love me in spite of my flaws, and there are many, means more than you will ever know. I know I'm not worthy of your love, but my life would end without it. I can't live without you, and whether it's one day or two hundred years, I want to spend the rest of my life with you." He went to one knee.

"Julie Alexandra Buckingham, I love you. Will you marry me?" He opened the ring box.

"Yes!" she said and dove to catch Micheal in her embrace. Their lips met and Julie felt the magic of the night come together in an explosive way.

Micheal took the ring and held her hand. Julie had to keep wiping the tears away. He slid the ring on her finger.

She cupped his face in her hands.

"Micheal William Hall, I love you, more than you could know." And they kissed again.

After a few minutes, they looked into each other's eyes. He brushed the tendrils from her face, tucking them behind her ears, then wrapped one arm around her. She did the same as they turned to see the last sliver of the golden sun slip below the horizon, leaving the beauty of the twilight canvas behind.

"A most perfect day," she said with a sigh.

"A most perfect day."

III: Arrested

July 1, 1697

Micheal surprised me with a proposal this evening during our balloon dinner. Thinking about it now, I should have suspected it. He did a great job of keeping me guessing. So finally, the boy becomes a man. I've dreamt of this outcome ever since London.

Most of the plans for our wedding are already set. In eleven days, the longest drought of my life will finally come to an end. I have fantasized about it so many times. Is it possible for reality to measure up? It will be his first time. In a way it feels like the first time for me. It's been six years, and the anticipation is making me nervous. I hope he studied, because my first time was a debacle.

Yeesh...I can only hope Micheal has a better first time than I did. But I will be a patient teacher.

***

"Well, you certainly move fast," Micheal said, seeing how fast all of JULIE'S preparations had seemed to come together.

"I put most of these plans together after London. I didn't realize you'd keep a girl waiting so long." Julie dipped her head and raised a brow.

"My apologies, my lady." He raised his arms in surrender.

"That's okay. We can make up for lost time. Just one more day then your"—she grabbed his ass—"is mine forever. Are you ready?"

He caressed her neck. "The anticipation is killing me."

Micheal started kissing her.

Then the doors flew open. It was Sheriff Gookin, followed by half a dozen redcoats.

"Lord Whitaker, you are under arrest for heresy."

Micheal looked at Julie. "Do not fret. I love you, Jules." They began escorting him out.

"Micheal!" Julie collapsed to the floor.

The emotions were swelling inside her. She'd been so happy, and now her world felt like it was crashing down around her. She was having trouble breathing.

As the tears began to stream, the devil himself appeared in the doorway.

"Lady of Darkness, your days are numbered without the protection of your husband. You shall swing from the gallows again soon."

She clenched her fists to steady herself. She could not afford to get arrested as well. She spent several hours watching redcoats ransack Bostonian, looking for evidence. She felt helpless.

That night she hardly slept and when she did, it was to lucid nightmares of being hung from the gallows.

July 12, 1697

Today was supposed to be my wedding day; now it's a day of misery. I feel like I'm in suspended animation. My life has screeched to a halt. How many times can I take this? Every time I think my life is beginning to go well, some horrible event comes to tear it all down.

The noose tightens once more as the world falls away below me. This time I fear I will end up a corpse at the end of a rope.

CHAPTER 22: THE TRIAL OF AVALON

"MICHEAL!" Julie entered, ran to him, and kissed him. "How are they treating you?"

"I have been well treated. The magistrate insisted on the shackles, but they deferred to my social status on accommodation."

"We should escape, run away—"

He shook his head. "I can't run away."

"I know you don't want to run away anymore. But we both know this is a complete sham. We can get out of here—"

"I can't, even if I had that in mind. I gave my word."

"You don't owe them anything," her head and shoulder slouched, knowing when he gave his word, he would never go back on it.

"These charges aren't just about me. They intend to put my family on trial."

"The Lords of Avalon? But you're *not* a Lord of Avalon!"

"Yes, I am. The same blood flows through my veins. My family's honor is at stake. I will not have their legacy, the legacy of Camelot, sullied by my fear."

"What about us? You would give up our happiness for some distant ancestors who you don't even know?!"

"I'm not. It's not a binary choice. I can defend my family's honor and then I will marry you. I promise."

Micheal hoped his words resonated with conviction, but Julie lowered her head, and he could see that she wasn't convinced.

"Don't make promises you can't keep."

"I never do. I know I can win this." Micheal took her hands in his and said, "You once asked me to trust you. I'm glad I did. Now, I need you to trust me. Do you trust me, Jules?"

She stared at him with tears in her eyes.

"Always," Julie said as she fell into his arms. "You better keep your promise. I can't live without you."

He was interrogated numerous times over the next few days. Due to the high-profile nature of the case, the governor and Supreme Court Chief Justice Stoughton ordered the proceedings to be moved from Cambridge to Boston.

Julie visited as often as possible during the three weeks they kept him for questioning. It was what he most looked forward to. Her soft touch was vital to help him handle the situation.

On the last visit, Julie informed him she had rescheduled the wedding for August 12. He hoped the trial would be over by then. She expressed extreme dissatisfaction at the trial's tentatively scheduled court dates. They'd been changed again for some time between August 5 and 8.

JULIE sat by the South Cascade, worrying about Micheal. Then the world broke open once again.

A mob of twenty or thirty men rushed her. She fled into the Tier Gardens, but they surrounded her. She attempted to fight her way through, taking out a few before they tackled her. She was hit hard in the face, and everything went dark.

"Whore of Satan!" she heard as she began to come around. She felt the noose tighten as she was lifted off the ground.

"No! Not yet!" A log was placed below her, and they stood her up on top of it. She began coughing as the rope loosened, then she nearly passed out as the blood drained out of her head.

"Why not?!" one man said.

"Not till he come," another man replied.

She tested the bindings. They had bound her ankles and tied her arms behind her back. She overlooked the crowd, a veritable lynch mob of about thirty men. Perhaps this was what Parris had meant with his threat.

"We do *this* before he comes," another man said, then came over and ripped her corset open, fully exposing her to the combined horror and delight of the crowd.

"That will be quite enough," Parris said as the crowd parted for him. "This is not the way!"

"Let the demon's whore hang!" a man yelled. The crowd roared.

"Good people, that is not justice. Let us leave her so," Parris said as he moved closer, pointing to her naked body. "She most likely will die. Should some devil deliver her from this, swing aside her plaything, she surely will." The mob begrudgingly agreed, and they left her precariously on the log.

One wrong move would be her last.

I: Day 1

As MICHEAL walked into the courtroom, his stomach dropped. Julie was absent and, following her failure to visit in the past two days, he feared the worst.

Magistrate Hathorne entered and sat on the pulpit.

"Lord Whitaker, you are accused of heresy in sight of the Lord our God. What say you?"

"The Lord our God is my keeper. I serve no other."

"Master Parris, what say you?"

"Ladies. Gentlemen. Good people. There has been a devil in our midst. I shall prove that devil's influence upon Lord Avalon."

While he spoke, Micheal observed the entire room. Of course, most of the audience was against him. At least eight of the jury members, he knew, were Puritans. The trial was obviously supposed to be just a formality. But he still felt that he had a chance—if he could get through to the hearts of the jury.

"My Lord Avalon, many wondrous achievements have you done since arriving in Massachusetts these five years past. First of which is your palace. 'Bostonian' is it not called?" Parris asked.

"Sir, it is."

"Many marveled at how quickly it was built. Is such a thing possible absent an unseen hand?"

"With understanding, all things are possible. Through God does understanding come."

"How, my lord, did you receive such understanding? Are you a prophet?"

"Through God's grace, does he grant all men understanding? In his mercy, did he allow me the gift for greater understanding of his creations?"

"A gift? Should such a gift sanction promotion of vanity?"

"Vanity is of no desire—"

"A palace fit for a Prince of Europe yet no want of vanity?" Parris said with an incredulous laugh. He walked up to the jury box with his bible held tightly, slammed his hand down the rail, saying, "Clearly there is some unseen hand in the darkness."

Parris turned his head and glared at Micheal. He held his bible close to his heart and began approaching him.

"Shall I suppose you will argue the same in the matters of the university and the bridges?" Parris asked rhetorically. "Gentlemen," Parris continued, addressing the jury. "The Lord our God never could assent to such vanity projects. They most surely are of the devil." He turned to Micheal once more.

"My lord, each year did you not conspire wondrous distortions of our Lord's creation for your instructive review?"

"Do you refer to the final examinations devised with intent of discovering enlightenment through discourse?"

"You admit freely the evidence of your unholy influence on your pupils," Parris said, attempting to place his admission in the worst way possible. Parris turned to the jury. "An apparatus for breathing beneath the sea, an eye for observation of the underworld, another eye for a distorted view of heavens. My lord, might you explain of what understanding do you entertain for such a device?"

"Master Parris, means of operation of said eye for heaven tis a telescope, a larger version of a sailor's glass. The apparatus captures light to focus, thereby magnifying objects of distance," Micheal explained to the jury.

Some on the jury seemed to understand, to Parris' dismay, so he moved on.

"What of these flying contraptions? What devilry allows such to fly with birds? 'twas witnessed as recently as one month past."

"Have any of you gentlemen witnessed air bubbles rising from the water?" Micheal inquired of the jury. All assented.

"Within the balloon apparatus, we create such a bubble by heating the air beneath the canopy. Both the air bubble in water and the heated air bubble within the canopy are less heavy than that which surrounds them. By such circumstances do they rise." Micheal could tell that at least a few of the jury members seemed to understand.

This appeared to annoy Parris further. He walked to a table and retrieved a satchel. Upon lifting the flap, he revealed one of the palace lights.

"Gentlemen," Parris said, showing the light to the jury. "No flame, yet light there is. Truly devil's magic. My Lord Avalon, might you explain this?"

Micheal gave a pedestrian explanation of friction and static electricity. However, failing a live demonstration, the jury was clearly unconvinced.

"Lord Avalon, might we know the source of your family's wealth through which Avalon does purchase obedience or inspires fear amongst prince and priest alike, a shield against disobedience to the teaching of the Lord?" Parris began his attack on Micheal's family.

"Through contract with His Majesty, shall I not speak," Micheal replied. One thing he knew about the Contract of Avalon was that the crown would not be privy to the source of his family's wealth or their whereabouts when not in England.

Parris knew he couldn't legally pursue the question further.

"Your family goes absent from the realm for decades upon end. To where do they abscond?"

"Through contract with His Majesty, shall I not speak."

"My lord, of course, your family's shield against challenge," Parris smiled as he bowed.

"Your house are as shadow monarchs. The House of Arthur of Camelot? From where do such claims arise?"

"My forefather Arthur, first King of Britain, brought light to a very dark age, unifying the whole of Britain. Power, however, corrupts even the most valiant amongst us. So it did to Lancelot, subject King from Mercia. He did conspire treason against his sovereign and friend, King Arthur. Queen Guinevere sought refuge with the Prince and Princess in Warwickshire and did take the name of White Acre, Whitaker, as token to the white shores of Avalon, the final resting place of Arthur. This ring..." He pulled out the Ring of Destiny.

Micheal heard a collective gasp of surprise from the audience and the jury all exchanged looks with one another.

"...has passed through eight-one generations, from King Arthur down the line to me. Delivered by divine providence and signifying divine right to rule." He told the story his grandmother had told him when he was eight, the day she gave him the ring.

"Children's tales! My lord would have you believe stories for children." Parris laughed.

Micheal wasn't sure what the jury thought, but Parris clearly felt he was winning and the court was adjourned.

JULIE woke up to a jolt, like the falling sensation that wakes you up from sleeping. This was different. This was the end. Her throat tightened and her wrists seared with pain.

No...no...no...this can't be happening again...

Her head began to clear, and her eyes filled with tears.

She had spent the night struggling against her bindings, to no avail. She fought to stay awake when a cramp brought new panic to her situation.

Fuck! Oh, God, no!

Her legs felt like they were going to give out on her. She tried to breathe, but the rope gave no mercy. After a moment, she was able to steady herself as she was forced to tolerate the pain or die.

As she caught her breath, her panic turned to anger, and her thoughts turned to Micheal.

Why *didn't you let me kill him?! Why, goddammit?! Parris deserves to die! We shouldn't have let him do this to us.*

Her tears ran dry as the sun rose. She felt guilty for blaming Micheal for this. His decision to leave Parris unharmed was for their benefit. She reminded herself that Micheal would always put her before any and all things.

The light of the morning helped her better assess her situation. She looked all around to see what she could use to set herself free.

The tree branch was too thick to break. She would likely not live long enough to work through her bindings. But the rock they had tied at the other end of the rope just might be light enough to jar loose.

That's limestone! About two feet across. What's its density?

She approximated a weight anywhere between six hundred and one thousand pounds.

She took a deep breath, flexed her neck, and kicked off the log toward the tree behind her, but she didn't get as much swing as she had hoped.

She continued to kick her legs forward and back until she finally made contact with the tree and got a good kick-off of it. She swung higher out, swung back, got another good kick, swung herself high, then quickly whipped her legs. The jolt budged the rock, but not far enough.

Goddammit! Come on!

Pressure began to build in her head and chest. Julie knew she was running out of time.

As she swung back and forth, her toes brushed the ground. She was able to time when it would happen again. She kicked off to get momentum going and repeated the process.

The jolt moved the rock far enough that her feet fully touched the ground, but the rope had wrenched and twisted from all the swinging, so the noose didn't loosen.

Julie closed her eyes tightly, fighting the pain. When she opened them...

Who are you?

A young woman in a flowing white gown with silky, strawberry blond hair and beautiful emerald eyes was approaching.

Are you an angel?

Everything will be okay, the angel said simply.

Was that your thought?

I'm here for you. You are very special.

This is all too much. I'm going to die! That's why you're here...

The woman came over and touched her cheek and tucked her hair behind her ear. Julie felt a calming sensation wash over her.

No, Julie. Be brave, believe in yourself. It was an honor to meet you. You're so much like her. The woman smiled at her.

What is your name?

The woman disappeared in a flash.

Where did she go? Julie, focus on the problem at hand. What can I do...? Okay, I need to pull my arms around my legs...

Julie tried several times.

Everything was going blurry, and the world became distant.

She tried again, her whole body going numb.

She finally got her arms around her legs, but she could feel everything slipping away. Julie knew she only had seconds to live. She fought against the noose with all her strength and finally wrenched it open, throwing off the vile thing.

Air! Thank you, my angel...

Her thoughts turned to Micheal, but they were quickly flooded by a rush to her head, and everything faded to black.

MICHEAL was escorted back to his cell by Samuel Parris and two other men.

"My lord, what a shame your lady be absent. I pray no malfeasance befell her," Parris said with a hint of a smile. "The devil abandons you at your moment of most need."

Rage was boiling beneath his forced, calm exterior. He was surer than ever that something terrible had happened to Julie. If it had, he would never forgive himself for not running away with her.

"Reverend Parris," he began as calmly as possible. "For all the evil acts committed against my lady at your hand, I would kill you where you stand. I do solemnly swear, if my lady be dead when this farce is over, I shall kill you and all who had hand in my lady's torment these five years past. Never do I make a promise I cannot keep," he threatened, staring down Parris with a look that could kill.

Micheal had developed a pure and utter hatred for this man. If only his tachyon scanner could prove Parris' death wouldn't alter the timeline, he would kill him where he stood.

"My lord. It would be a shame if your wife from hell hath suffered same fate as your devil horse." Parris departed quickly.

Micheal couldn't sleep that night; his stomach was in knots.

Then it was time for round two.

II: Day 2

"My Lord Avalon, perhaps you were not always so astray of the teachings of God, until you were bedeviled by a woman. Lady Whitaker of Avalon. Our God-fearing community has been deceived. My lady's true name be Buckingham. She beguiled Lord Avalon into darkness. Where is she now? What cause, if she should be innocent, could keep her from support of husband? She is possessed of the devil. Only one month past did she commit unprovoked assault upon my person, as these sworn statements attest," Parris said, handing Hathorne a stack of parchment.

"Tis known that woman be the weaker sex, as is demonstrable in Genesis 3:13. Lord Avalon, it please this court?" Parris finally pivoted from his sermonizing bullshit.

"'And the Lord God said unto the woman, what is this thou hast done? And the woman said the serpent beguiled me, and I did eat.'"

"Revealed in Eve's original sin is the weakness of woman towards Satan's influence."

"Reverend Parris, Genesis 1:27-28, if you please?"

"'Tis not I on trial."

"Perhaps, reverend, you are not so knowledgeable of God's word?"

Reverend Parris indignantly took the bait. "So God created man in his own image, in the image of God created he him: male and female created he them. And God blessed them, and God said unto them, be fruitful and multiply, and replenish the earth, subdue it; and have dominion over—"

"Reverend Parris. Of what did God command them?"

Parris glared at him, but his pride prevented him from relenting. "Be fruitful and multiply and replenish the earth."

"And what did God mean by that?"

"In simple terms," Hathorne instructed Parris, trying to turn him away from this avenue, but Parris couldn't help himself.

"To have many children!" Parris raised his voice.

"Does God give such instruction prior to his instruction of forbidden fruit?"

"He did!"

"To which obedience should the woman, Eve, have obliged? Did they not understand their nakedness prior to eating of the fruit? Without such carnal knowledge, obedience to God's first command would have been impossible?"

"Evil is the weakness of women!" Parris yelled.

"Order!" Hathorne yelled. "My Lord Avalon, your line of question is not relevant."

"Your Honor, Reverend Parris carries particular enmity towards women, including a personal distaste of my lady, which has inspired such argument be made against my person," Micheal argued, then turned to the jury. "Had not Eve chosen knowledge, she and Adam would have violated God Almighty's first commandment. Therefore, the condemnation of women on Eve's account would be casting false aspersion."

"Master Parris, what next?" Hathorne ordered.

Parris stewed and glared fire at Micheal.

"Lord Avalon, the vanity of your family shines bright."

Over the next hour, Micheal and Parris sparred over the accused pride and vanity supposedly inherent in The House of Avalon, using bible passages as weapons. Micheal came out victorious as Parris fumbled for several passages.

Back in his cell, he went over all the proceedings so far. He felt he was currently losing this battle, but then his thoughts became dark. Julie's absence for the second day, along with Parris' repeated insinuations, convinced him she was dead.

That evening Yvette entered his cell, trembling. "My lord? My lady went missing three days past. Rose said a mob stormed the gardens that night. They would not allow me to visit sooner."

JULIE, exhausted by the events of the last day too, spent the night near a stream. When she knew she was strong enough, she began walking south, towards Bostonian.

A sudden headache pulsed; she stumbled and tripped over a root. She rinsed her face in the stream and the throbbing of the bruise around her neck became more evident. As she dabbed the cool water on her neck, her reflection came into focus. She almost didn't recognize herself.

Then a thought struck her. It had been about four days since Micheal had seen her. He probably assumed the worst. If he didn't think it mattered anymore, he might turn his vengeance on those he held responsible. She had to get back as soon as possible.

After walking the rest of the day, she could see Bostonian ahead. Exhaustion overtook her and all faded to black once more.

III: Day 3

MICHEAL entered the courtroom. His focus wasn't on what the day's proceedings would be, it was on finalizing his plan to escape and rain vengeance down on all those who took Julie away from him.

"President Mather. Explain if you would the bastardization of reason introduced by Lord Avalon," Parris began. Mather laid down a litany of supposed distortions of the holy search for enlightenment.

"President Mather, would you say His Majesty's sanctioned institutions in Oxford or Cambridge be heretical? And by way of reason, would not our sovereign himself be a heretic?" Micheal asked directly.

"How dare you!"

"My instruction at Harvard is no different than at King's College or Trinity. If my curriculum be heresy, then so are they. Do they not enjoy sponsorship of His Majesty?"

Mather was stewing.

"Will you not answer?"

"You cast aspersions!"

"No aspersion that is not well-deserved. You have been jealous of the adulation espoused me. Have you not?"

"I am not!"

"Upon your return from England, you showed disdain for me. If not jealousy, what cause was there?"

"Your arrogant house came to look down on we common folk from on high!" Mather exploded.

"So you are jealous?!"

"Aye! Your family takes all light on themselves, throwing shade on all else!" Mather took a step toward Micheal as if to charge him and some spittle was visible on his chin.

JULIE woke in her bed.

"My lady!" Rose said, seeing her awake.

"Ready Angel, I must go to Boston!"

Micheal. Please, please don't make a terrible mistake...

"Yes, my lady!" Rose said as she hurried out.

Julie hoped she wouldn't be too late.

The next witness was Mistress Katherine Talmage. MICHEAL

knew her testimony would be used to attack Julie over the incident in the woods.

"Mistress Talmage, what say you in this matter?" Parris asked.

"Four years past, that devil woman, Lady Avalon, did take my husband's life. 'Twas as a devil inside her. She did strike my husband's head with unnatural force, causing embolism."

"Mistress Talmage, how did this affect you?"

"We were trying for a child. That lady of darkness ruined my life." Tears came to her eyes.

"Many sorrows." Parris finished.

"Mistress Talmage, was not Master Talmage engaged in a vengeful plot against my wife on behalf of one Master Nash?" Micheal said coldly.

"My husband did aid in a quest for justice for Master Nash." She sneered.

"Justice? Is it justice to lynch an innocent accused of no wrong?"

"The lady was not innocent."

"You surely knew of your husband's plot with Master Nash. What offense did my lady commit against Master Nash?"

Mistress Talmage stammered.

"You knew my lady had committed no trespass against Master Nash but was a convenient proxy for some alleged trespass by my sister, the Duchess of Avalon. Was she not? Mistress Talmage, you are sworn before God the Almighty," Micheal reminded her.

Mistress Talmage broke down. "My lord, she was."

"Mistress, my apologies most sincere for your loss. We do forgive your husband his trespass," Micheal finished.

JULIE entered Boston proper; it was like a ghost town. Evidently, this was the trial of the century. She wasn't sure how anyone would react to seeing her. She came around the corner and saw two nooses hanging from the gallows. Of course. She knew this was just a show trial.

She approached the courthouse and saw a large crowd. Angel made her way through the sea of people and Julie could see them staring at her as if she was a ghost.

Samuel Parris took the stand. MICHEAL had secretly released his shackles. When he felt the moment was right, he would pounce.

"Ladies. Gentlemen. Good people, unusual it may be that I should testify. Were my sworn account not so vital, I would forbear. Many witnesses did see Lady Avalon commit an assault upon my person, then abscond. I swore that, should she a devil be, I would prove it.

"All remember the tragedy which befell our God-fearing communities these five years past. Brother turned against brother. Great is my shame for the part I played. Even more is my shame that I covered up its terrible cause. In January, the year of our Lord 1692, did my daughter and niece fall to fits of hysteria? I sought the cause. A witch, said they, a witch in the north of the woods. Not a week should pass, but a strange woman did appear from north, wearing naught but a shift, speaking with a strange tongue. She did inspire fear in my daughters. Upon inquiry and inspection, a witch's mark I did find on her inner leg. She failed the Lord's prayer. She cursed and threatened us throughout her inspection and trial. She professed her name to be Julie Buckingham. Many a witness did so testify of the deleterious effect of her witch's curse. Through fair trial was she convicted. In pure justice was she executed by hanging from the neck until dead."

Micheal could take no more. He readied himself but, as he began to stand, a commotion stirred behind him. Parris had abruptly stopped, wearing a confused and horrified look on his face.

He turned and Julie was standing there, a rope bruise around her neck and a fierce look on her face. Hathorne called the room to order, then called a recess.

"Thank goodness I got here in time," JULIE said once they were in private.

"You have no idea how close that was. I had just stood to begin my revenge the moment you entered the room. What happened?"

"A lynch mob came to Bostonian and attacked me. I tried to fight, but there were too many of them. They knocked me out and took me into the woods and strung me up. Obviously, I got out of it, but at great pain," she said, rubbing her neck.

Tears came to his eyes. "I thought I lost you," he said, searching her face.

"You'll never lose me. I promise." She kissed him.

A knock came from the door. The marshal entered and said, "Lord and Lady Avalon, we convene."

"Reverend Parris, you shall continue with your testimony," Hathorne said.

"On Gallows Hill did she," Parris pointed at Julie, "hang until dead. I was witness, as was Sheriff Corwin with his brother, and your honorable self, Magistrate Hathorne. As she hung without life, a demon rider did appear. Our musket shots had no effect. It was the demon Effbeeye, we presumed, that once she did curse us, now come to claim his bride. We did hope this was the end of the witch's scourge. We feared incitement of further strife, so we did pledge silence of this account. We did not know she had her minions living amongst us. They did inspire the fervor of '92. Not one year ago did I encounter the demon's bride, Julie Buckingham." Parris pointed at her again. "This time she portrayed herself as one of House Avalon. When Lord Avalon refused to heed my warning, he was clearly under her spell. She is an instrument of the devil. I must protect this community, for the devil's whore, Julie Buckingham, does return a second time from death."

Micheal rose in argument. "Return from death? You and your lynch mob did abduct and leave my lady for dead. But for God's grace, did she survive your murderous attempt upon her life?"

"Were it God's grace, she would be dead."

"She is innocent of any murderous offense. In bearing false witness, Reverend Parris did contribute to the death of nineteen innocents, not to mention the many others who perished in jail. Calling Master Parris 'Reverend' blasphemes the title," Micheal's eyes flared.

"Your devil's whore caused the loss of communal faith in me!" Parris yelled, standing up. Judge Hathorne shut down Parris' testimony at that point.

"It would appear your lady did return twice from death. I myself did pass judgement of Lady Avalon. I was witness to her first execution."

"You are mistaken, your honor. For my lady hath never passed unto death. Might I explain?" Micheal looked at Julie and she assented.

Hathorne gestured to continue.

"As many know, my lady was in Virginia, tending her sister and her sister's husband. Both were ill. Following their deaths, my lady did write me requesting assistance. I came to care for her. We did wed. After having tended to matters in Virginia, my lady did desire a new start and so did we set sail from Virginia. Caught in a storm, did I go overboard into the sea and wash up outside of Weymouth. Our ship crashed on the rocks east of Salem. My lady, her decent clothes at the bottom of the ocean, was lost in the woods north of Salem Village and, by unfortunate mischance, fell into the hands of Master Parris' hysteria. In my need, in desperation, did I borrow assistance from a farm outside Weymouth, to which later did I repay many fold. After which I did spend a month searching for my lady. Upon entry into Salem did I see my lady being executed as a witch. With no time to waste, I did pull my cape over my head and rode through the crowd and cut my lady down. I did nurse her back to health."

"You were the horseman?!" Hathorne asked in surprise.

"Indeed, your honor. My lady never passed unto death."

"And her odd speech?" Hathorne said, confused.

"Under Parris' duress, hysteria did she suffer."

"And the horseman who was immune to musket fire?" Parris interjected.

Micheal proceeded to lift up his shirt, revealing his scars. The revelation stunned Hathorne and Parris. The jury also seemed confused. Hathorne decided to adjourn the session.

"Are you sure that was a good idea," Julie asked as they entered Micheal's cell.

"I didn't have a choice. It became obvious to me that their stories were convincing the jury. I needed to short-circuit that. The one risk is admitting to interceding in an official execution. But if I'm believed, then the rest of Parris' case becomes tenuous."

"This is just a show trial. They already have the gallows set up."

"They might want it to be a show trial, but I realized something on day one. There is a potent fear of my family. The only way they could convict and execute a Lord of Avalon is for the trial to at least seem to be fair, which gives us a chance."

"I sure hope you're right."

IV: Day 4

"Due to an unforeseen development on the day prior, this day may run long," Hathorne announced. "Master Parris."

"This witness shall give an unusual tale of devilry at hands of Lord and Lady Avalon. It is in that context that I call said witness. Gentlemen of the jury, free your judgment to hear him."

MICHEAL was shocked when the last red coat from the *Liberty* walked into the room.

"State your name," Parris said.

"Major Lord George Henry William Cavendish, fourth son of the Fourth Duke of Devonshire," his chin raised.

He was dressed in full military regalia. "My lord, on which day were you born?"

"The sixth of June in the year of our Lord 1754."

"I do beg pardon. Did you say the year 1754?" Parris' eyes went wide.

"Indeed, I did, sir."

"Lord Cavendish, please explain this to me. This year is 1697. If you be of some year not yet reached, how have you come to abide here?"

Micheal felt terrible, but also nervous. Cavendish obviously did not clear the *Liberty* far enough and had come through with them. Micheal would have to play this perfectly.

"In the year 1777 I was fighting against rebellion in the waters south of the city of Philadelphia in the Pennsylvania Colony when a ship did appear out of nowhere. I commanded the boarding party in an attempt to assess the threat. Lord and Lady Avalon did proceed to resist our efforts with physical force, expelling my entire boarding party. As I searched the interior, a strange sound began vibrating throughout the vessel. Upon my reentry to aft deck did I see Lord Avalon. A bright light above the ship attracted my attention. Erie green in color, it did appear to rotate. It shames me to admit, it inspired fear in me. I did jump into the river. Upon return to the surface, I was blinded by a bright flash. I could not see. There was a ringing in my ear as if by cannon fire. When finally I did get my wits about me again, I swam for shore. I come into a village. Falmouth did the people call it. In Massachusetts Bay

Colony. Some weeks did it take to fully convince my mind of the truth of it. The year was said to be 1696. What sorcery, I thought, brought me into this place, this year? Lord and Lady Avalon, it had to be some sorcery of theirs," Cavendish glared at Micheal.

"Your situation is most regrettable, Lord Cavendish," Parris shook his head.

"Lord Cavendish, quite a tale you tell—" Micheal began.

"'Tis all true, Lord Avalon. You canst deny it, surely."

"Much detail of said situation is correct. However, much also askew."

Cavendish's proud composure seemed to tense at his insinuation. "Before the Lord our God, I speak truth."

"My lord, I cast no aspersions. Confusion and ignorance, I believe, caused your distortion of the facts."

The jury had clearly been impressed by Cavendish. Micheal had to show he wasn't worried. He knew the story involving time travel would be difficult for the jury to believe. He needed to make Cavendish look the fool.

"Ignorant am I not—"

"No? Then do tell of what we were doing that day?" Micheal challenged. Cavendish stuttered, at a loss for words. "Many a seaman claims the sighting of green light. Our endeavor was to understand its cause. That is what you were a party to, one year ago. Our effort to remove you from our ship was for your protection, my lord. I fear you have allowed fear to distort your memory of that day."

"My memory serves just fine, my lord." Cavendish sat up straighter, eyes narrowing.

Micheal decided to press Cavendish's arrogance. "Our families have been neighbors for centuries. Is it not true that your family, that yourself in fact, harbor jealous enmity towards my family, and myself thereby?"

"There could be no cause for jealousy."

"Is there, no?"

"Nay!"

"Nay?! Of your noble superiors?"

"House Cavendish are superior to all! Including Avalon!" Cavendish slammed his fist on the rail.

"Royalty then? I do beg pardon, your Highness, Prince George," Micheal bowed extravagantly. Many in the courtroom laughed.

"House Avalon feel superior to all, bloody petulant bastards!"

"Lord Cavendish, is it not possible that your deep-seated jealousy, as well as the confusion brought on by our encounter, has affected your memory?"

"My memory serves, Lord Avalon, I testify truth."

"Temporary madness is of no shame," Micheal said in closing. Cavendish stewed but kept silent.

Hathorne was about to call final arguments. "No more witnesses?" Both Micheal and Parris affirmed.

He was interrupted by a commotion in the audience. "Would please the court? Your honor, would that I could speak?" It was Master Nathaniel Billington, the man Micheal had stolen from the first day he was in the seventeenth century.

"To what do you intend?"

"On the goodness of Lord and Lady Avalon. I be well acquainted with their kindness and generosity."

"Master Parris?" Hathorne inquired.

"We do not object," Parris replied, unconcerned.

"Master Billington."

"'Twas January, year of our Lord, 1692. Set o' my clothes did go missing, to where, I did not know. A week or so later an unfamiliar man did stand on ma porch. He said he represent Master Whitaker who in desperate need did borrow a set o ma clothes. That he did come a set things aright. Three new sets o clothes did he deliver, with a letter expressing sorrow for unfortunate trespass. As well, he did give a bag o silver. My family were a starved. Silver did preserve us the winter. Little more an a year later did we attend Summerfest at Bostonian Palace. I did realize it was Lord Avalon who did repay multitude over that day. A thousand blessings, Lord and Lady Avalon," Billington said, nodding to Julie. "Two years later our crops failed. The generosity of House Avalon is well known. Remembering my lord's generosity, I did seek charitable assistance. Unto Bostonian did I go. My lord was away on business. My Lady Avalon heard my plight and gave generously to fill our need." Tears came to his eyes. "In my occasional travels around the colony did I hear tales abundant of others. Lord and Lady Avalon been a godsend to our colony."

Hathorne cut in, "We appreciate your testimony, Master Billington. Master Parris, you may close."

"Ladies. Gentlemen. Honorable gentlemen of the jury. Heresy, distortions, blaspheming the Lord our God's holy teachings. Through vanity, Lord and Lady Avalon do aspire to too lofty a height for any man, believing themselves as God's equals. Their prideful excesses are clear for all to see. My lord, in his arrogance, tries high-sounding rhetoric to obfuscate you and call it an explanation. I was a firsthand witness to evidence that Lady Avalon indeed be a demon in league of Satan. She did inspire witchcraft in our God-fearing village. Enmity did she create between neighbors, the cause of the death of a multitude. My lord bears false in his attempted defense of his demon lady. The demon Effbeeye, headless, did ride to claim his bride. Let not the testimony of a meager mind impede your clarity. For all their charity, Lord and Lady Avalon are but a wolf in sheep's clothing. They use subversive good acts for evil's sake. Were it not evident to you, as yet, that they be guilty? And even if you believe Lord Avalon did pursue heretical understanding with good intention. That is vanity which breeds pride. Through pride, this becomes blasphemous of God's teachings. The very definition of heresy." Parris said in closing.

It was Micheal's turn to address the jury. "Gentlemen. 'Tis but one question you must ask: Does God want us to live in ignorance, or seek enlightenment for the betterment of all God's children? God blesses us all with gifts and abilities. One might have a gift of music. One might have a gift of the sword. Another might have a gift of oratory, as Master Parris certainly does. Gifts we all have, of God they all are. The gift that God in his benevolence did grant myself and my family is the ability of understanding God's creations. God has blessed us, as he has many others, ever since Adam and Eve. First god gave understanding of fire, then of the wheel. My flying balloon demonstrates understanding of the sky. My light demonstrates understanding of the power of lightning. Would God have us living in the wilderness, lacking clothing to cover our nakedness, eating uncooked food? Nay, do I say. God grants understanding of fire that we might cook our food, grants understanding of knitting that we might cover our shame. Understanding of the wheel that we might more easily transport ourselves and our goods. Understanding of smithing that useful tools we might make. Where does God say that be enough, you have reached the limit of understanding? Some would say the exploration of God's creation be at odds with God himself. God himself created the heavens and the earth. How then are they at odds? Some argue it hubris to seek such understanding in attempt to rise to God's level. In quest for enlightenment, clear does it become how grand is God's creation. Humble does it make you to discover that should you live a thousand lifetimes in avid study would you but scratch the surface of the grandness of God's creation. Never could we aspire to the grandness of understanding of God. Finally, I ask you: Is the fire maker a heretic? Is the wheel maker a heretic? Is the seamstress a heretic? Is the blacksmith a heretic? Or the watchmaker? If none of them be heretic, then how does the meager understanding of my family qualify as heretical? If seeking understanding of God's creation be heresy, then heretics we all are. Understanding God's creation be not against God. We are judged by how we use such understanding. For good or evil. My family, the House of Avalon, be not perfect, but we do strive for such, for we believe most of God's children are good. To all we give generously of the blessings God hath given us. Titles we have, but superior we are not in God's eyes. Trust your fair judgment we do. Many thanks for your service," Micheal said in closing.

"Gentlemen of the jury, this case I give unto you, we are adjourned." Hathorne said.

"Remand Lord and Lady Avalon till final judgment," he added. Julie was taken into custody with Micheal. They would share the same fate. In two days either they would get married or be executed.

V: Day 5

"Lord and Lady Avalon. The jury renders verdict," The court marshal said, waking them up.

"Gentlemen of the jury on guilt of heresy of Lord and Lady Avalon, what sayst you?" Hathorne asked.

One by one, they responded.

"Aye."

"Aye."

"Aye."

"Nay."

"Nay."

"Aye."

"Aye."

JULIE'S heart sank. Only two more would mean death.

"Nay."

"Nay."

"Nay."

"Nay."

"Nay."

Just as Julie was about to celebrate, Hathorne said. "The ayes are five, the nays seven. Gentlemen of the jury, I do beseech you to reconsider your judgment. This court will reconvene this day after the noon hour." Hathorne ordered an adjournment.

"This is total bullshit!" Julie said as they entered the cell. "We're acquitted! That bastard Hathorne, orders them to reconsider."

"He's trying it again. It worked for him before."

"What do you mean?"

"During the witch trials, a jury acquitted the accused and Hathorne ordered them to reconsider, and they came back and convicted them. Typically, if the judge insists, the jury more or less give him the verdict he wants. Only a unanimous acquittal will likely stop him from ordering them to reconsider until he gets his conviction. I'm sorry, Jules, I shouldn't have made promises I can't keep. I should have expected the fix was in. I don't know how much time we have left, and I want to tell you in case I don't have another chance." He took her hands, looked her in the eyes, and said, "I love you, Julie Buckingham. These years that I've spent with you have been the best of my life. I wouldn't be the man I am today without you. You saw the good in me. You helped me find myself. And though we may die tomorrow, it would be worth it for the privilege of loving you," Micheal kissed her.

"There is no one more deserving of love than you. I am honored by your love for me. I would be dead if it wasn't for you, and I don't just mean literally dead in body. I would have died in spirit, soul, and sanity if you hadn't been the rock I can lean on. I give my heart to you without shade knowing fully that it's safe in your loving hands. I love you. I regret for nothing that we found one another. I will never stop loving you, no matter what happens," Julie kissed him.

They were interrupted by a knock on the door. "Lord and Lady Avalon, the jury returns."

"Gentlemen of the jury, what say you?" Hathorne said.

The jury once again responded, one at a time.

"Nay."

"Nay."
"Nay."
"Nay."
"Nay."
Julie was hopeful...
"Nay."
"Nay."
"Nay."
"Nay."
"Nay."
"Nay."
"Nay."
The jury was unanimous.

Parris looked as if he might boil over with rage. Hathorne studied the jury.

"Gentlemen of the jury, are you firm in decision?" Hathorne asked, his irritation clear to see.

"Aye." They all said in unison.

Hathorne paused for a moment, in obvious anger.

"Lord and Lady Avalon, you are free to go. Gentlemen, the Lord our God and His Majesty thanks you for your service."

Micheal stood, Julie took his elbow, and they walked out of the courtroom. A large crowd greeted them. Many were jeering, others cheering. Micheal raised his hand, and everyone went quiet.

"Ladies. Gentlemen. Good people, might you hear me?!" he said loudly.

When everyone remained quiet, he began: "Five years past, an unexpected storm at sea washed us upon these shores. We decided we would stay. To our ever gratitude, the good people of Massachusetts did embrace us. A joy it was to become a part of your community and sorrow does it bring to leave behind our home—the only home we have had together. As is known of House Avalon, rarely do we linger a place. It has become apparent our continued presence doth inspire enmity between peoples of this colony. Our gratitude to those who did support us at this trial. I know some may harbor disappointment or anger for favorable verdict. No enmity do we hold for you. We beseech you to be satisfied by our self-banishment, for never shall we return. We bid farewell of you, good people of Boston, good people of Massachusetts. Good day to all," Micheal finished.

The crowd parted to let them through. Yvette and Filipe had

brought a carriage, just in case.

As they reached the edge of the crowd, they were surrounded by a mob led by Samuel Parris.

"Proper justice shall be served, one way or the other," Parris' eyes narrowed.

The mob closed in from all sides. Micheal and Julie looked at each other. They had practiced multiple strategies for countering long odds like these.

Come and get it, you bastards!

Julie ran a circle around Micheal to gain momentum, then, as they locked arms, sprung into the air and Micheal carried her into a full circle swing around him. As he rotated, she connected kicks to nearly half of their attackers.

She then thought of something. "Micheal! Throw me!"

And with that command she felt Micheal first swing her low, then up and into the air, towards a small group that remained. She tucked her body into a ball and crashed into them with great force.

You fucking bastards!

She locked in on one man; she dove and knocked him out with a punch. She turned and saw two others getting up. Julie stepped and swung her right leg, striking each man in the face and putting them down for the count.

"Seize that devil's whore!" Parris yelled and Julie saw two men rise and charge her.

Not today, assholes!

The first man tried swinging a staff, but Julie ducked and struck the second man with an uppercut under the chin, rendering him unconscious. She turned just in time to duck another attack. Julie grabbed the man's staff, kicked his knee in, and connected with a backhand, subduing him immediately.

She had neutralized more than a dozen of the mob when she saw Parris turn and run.

She chased him down.

You motherfucker! You'll pay for what you did.

Julie struck him hard in the back and heard him scream in pain. He spun around and held his arms out to defend himself.

You tortured me!

She rotated and swung the staff low to sweep his legs. Parris went down but tried to crawl away. She struck him twice more in the back. Parris was on his knees; his left hand was nursing his injured back.

You tried to kill me. You hung me, twice!

Julie planted the end of the staff on the ground, kicked up, then cartwheeled down, striking his face with her heel. Parris went down hard. The rest of the mob fled.

She walked over to Parris and said, "Justice, indeed, be served."

Julie laid several more strikes to his side as he wriggled on the ground like a worm.

Micheal came up from behind her and said, "For my lady!" And kicked Parris in the side.

"For Darkness!" Micheal kicked him again.

Julie looked at Micheal and smiled. She had never felt so good. She turned to face the crowd and found them stunned at the spectacle.

She straightened her bodice and brushed her hair off her face. She poised herself as a Lady of Avalon would to address, cleared her throat, and said, "Our apologies, ladies and gentlemen."

They boarded the carriage and headed for home.

CHAPTER 23: 'TILL THE END OF TIME

JULIE GAZED ACROSS THE waters of the North Atlantic to Hay Island off the coast of Nova Scotia. They had erected a launch pad with an empty test rocket.

"So we finally finished the orbital rocket," Julie said as Micheal ran diagnostics.

"One-inch diameter satellites were a pain in the ass. Working through the scaling sequences required to make the components that small was a bitch." He explained.

"Tell me about it. You know, it would've been useful to have a satellite network during our time here, but I know we couldn't just build whatever we wanted and launch it into space willy-nilly." She examined one of the micro-sats.

"It's never simple, is it?"

"I hate time travel."

"How long will they remain in orbit?" She had found it a little hard to believe the resonance field would be strong enough to maintain the sky network.

"The micro-satellites generate an EM field that resonates with the others. The fields combine to form a net of sorts around the planet that should also maintain their altitude indefinitely. Well, I think we're ready for liftoff. Start the launch sequence at sixty seconds."

Julie couldn't help herself and sang, "It's the final countdown!"

They both had a good laugh.

"Okay: five, four, three, two, and liftoff!" he finished as the rocket rose from the launchpad.

After some time, the telemetry indicated an altitude of more than sixty miles.

"Drop the stage one rocket case into the atmosphere. So it's not floating around up there somewhere." Micheal instructed.

"We still have to see if the second stage will get it into orbit." Julie knew things could still go wrong.

"It will make it. Just a little bit longer."

"Hopefully not too long. It's about to go into blackout on the night side."

Julie watched the screen for some time as the probe went ever higher, then finally, "Stable orbit achieved. Altitude 180 miles."

"A successful test launch. I think we'll be okay for the thirty-third century B.C.," Micheal said confidently as the images and data confirmed the rocket had achieved orbit.

A few hours later, they transmitted the kill command to plunge the test rocket into the Pacific, then turned the *Liberty* for home.

That night, they held a special dinner for their friends and all of the service staff.

"All in this room are true friends. On this evening of our vow renewal. Our true wedding pain does it bring to notify all of our impending departure. We are to leave Massachusetts permanently two weeks hence. All of you have meant so much..." Julie could hardly stop the tears. "You have become family, and in our hearts shall you remain. To our devout and loyal staff, Bostonian shall pass to you. Mistress Rose and her husband, Haider, shall be named principal stakeholders in the property. We have set up a trust to ease the transition of ownership and sponsor management of the property for years to come. In Rose's capable hands, you shall all be prosperous," she said, forcing a smile.

In spite of all the horrible things she had gone through over the last five years, the staff had been one of her great joys. They truly felt like family.

"Cecily Penn, you have been a true friend and I will miss you greatly. Alice Windsor, Mary Rainsford, you are such kindred spirits, as sisters to me. The kindness of each and every one of you did fill a piece of my heart that was missing," she said, tearing up again. "The legacy of Avalon seemed an insurmountable mountain to climb. Unworthy, did I feel whence first we arrived. The peak of that mountain have I reached. Because of you, all of you, do I feel worthy of Avalon."

Micheal delivered a supplemental farewell speech.

Then, unasked, Professor Rainsford stood. "With heavy heart I bid you farewell. Whence first did I meet you 'twas most terrifying. That a Lord of Avalon should instruct me. I would never hope to uphold such a lofty standard. And how much more intimidating you are, my lady. The mind of a philosopher of old, as well as the beauty of the angels. As personal tutors did you bring light to my eyes of the wonders of God's creations, and through such process did I discover incredible genuine souls. With trepidation, did I accept your rightful professorship. Intimidated, I am to follow you. True friends are you both. Joy and grief shall tomorrow bring. Joy of the celebration of your love for one another, grief in our parting thereafter. So honor do I, Lord and Lady Avalon." Rainsford finished his toast and there was a cheer from the entire room.

Following the dinner party, they separated and spent the remaining evening with their friends. The ladies, including Colette and Rose, joined Julie in her private suite as they talked of casual things, played various games, and, of course, discussed love.

Just before midnight, there was a knock on the door. Micheal was on the other side. She decided to improvise a Shakespeare-an-style scene.

"Fair prince, how late doest thou call," she began.

"Mine eyes doth fear the night lacking thy rays of light so fair," he picked it up immediately.

"What sorrow mine for lack of same light thine?" Cecily tiptoed over and hid behind the door. The other ladies followed.

"Fair princess, a taste of lips so sweet shall bide until the light."

Alice was swooning, and the others were fawning over their exchange.

"Then bide"—she kissed him—"fair prince lips so divine." Cecily let out an audible sigh.

Micheal couldn't help but let out a light giggle, then composed himself and continued.

"Thy lips"—he kissed her—"do taste of such sweet sorrow. Alas, that I shall bide until tomorrow," he kissed her again.

"'Tis a sonnet to my heart..." Cecily said as the crowd of ladies giggled and swooned.

Julie smiled. Micheal mirrored her.

"I love thee," she kissed him.

"And I thee," he kissed her one last time.

I: The Wedding

August 12, 1697

Today is the first day of the rest of my life. Cliché, I know. My old life feels more like a dream than a memory. I feel born anew. As I prepare to take that walk into a new reality, my only desire is to give myself fully to him—mind, body, and spirit—and receive the same from him in return. I feel we are two halves of a single soul about to become one. I have been celibate for nearly six years and, while that hardly compares to his thirty-two years the virgin, I myself feel a virgin again. After so long, the anticipation is killing me.

It's fitting that this is the final page of the journal Micheal gave me nearly five years ago. This one book documents everything that's happened during our time in the 1690s. Everything that made me—no, us—feel worthy of the legacy I am about to officially become a part of. This is Julie Alexandra Buckingham, signing off for the last time. By tomorrow, I will be Julie Alexandra Buckingham Hall, Lady of House Avalon, the legacy of Arthur King of the Britons.

This is my chronicle: The Book of Avalon, Volume One

MICHEAL woke from what little sleep he could snatch. Anticipation had made sleep difficult. He hoped it would see him through this, the most important day of his life. It did grieve him that his family and friends couldn't be here to celebrate with him, but Julie was his family now, and he couldn't wait to start his life with her.

"My lord, it is time."

"Merci, Yvette." He closed his eyes and took a deep breath. He was ready.

JULIE was having final touches put on. Mary was applying flesh-tone concealer to the rope bruise under her chin; it was still sore. Cecily tied the choker around her neck. Alice fastened her veil as the final touch.

"You are as an angel, Julie," Alice swooned.

"You look a princess," Cecily added with a smile.

"You are as Guinevere to his Arthur," Mary gushed.

She arrived at the bridge to the Chapel of Heaven in the central tower of Bostonian.

She had to fight back tears that her father wasn't here to walk her down the aisle.

"My lady, abide one moment," Yvette said. Julie sighed deeply to settle her stomach.

"My Lady Avalon, you are the very definition of grace and beauty," Isaac Newton said as he walked up.

"Master Newton, what are you doing here?" She couldn't believe that her mentor was here.

"Lord Avalon sent for me. Your father be absent. Should that I in his stead?"

"Most welcome, Master Newton."

"My lady," Newton said, giving his elbow. She took his arm and breathed in deeply as the doors opened to a magical scene.

It was entirely made out of white marble. There were crystal chandeliers and more crystals adorning the walls. The circular chapel had a dome forty feet high; inside you truly felt enveloped by light.

Julie heard the music start up and her attendants began the processional down the aisle, wearing the colors of Avalon.

"Ah," Newton sighed, "*The Canon* by Johann Pachelbel?"

"Indeed, in D major," Julie added. "One of my favorites."

As they entered the chapel, she got her first look at Micheal. He was an incredible image of elegance. His tuxedo was white from head to toe with white velvet shoes. It all sat splendidly on his broad shoulders. His light brown hair was slicked back in a short pompadour. His hazel eyes seem to illuminate the room. And they were transfixed on her.

To MICHEAL, it was as if the doors to heaven had just opened. He was utterly mesmerized. Time seemed to slow down, and he studied every aspect of her.

She wore a white dress embroidered with lace flowers and the corset had diamond-encrusted borders. Her dark brown hair was up in a braided crown capped with a diamond-cut tiara with a long veil flowing out from it. She wore large diamond stud earrings and a white lace choker. Her shoes appeared to be made of glass. And she was carrying a white calla lily bouquet.

He thought his heart might stop. Her deep turquoise eyes were locked on his. He felt lost in the tides.

She came to a halt, and the minister asked, "Who brings this woman to be married to this man?"

"I do," Newton answered, snapping Micheal momentarily out of his trance.

"Never have I witnessed such incomparable beauty," Micheal whispered to Julie as he led her up the stairs.

JULIE'S nerves and excitement caused the proceedings to pass by in a daze.

"Julie Alexandra Buckingham, will you give yourself to Micheal William Hall, to be his wife, to live with him according to God's word? Will you love him, comfort him, honor and protect him, and, forsaking all others, be faithful to him so long as you both shall live?"

"I will," she replied. Then the minister requested consent from Micheal.

Following consent of the congregation, she took Micheal's hands facing him.

"Julie, love hath no other name, for love thou hast become in me. Nothing there was before thee, nothing there shall be after."

She was lost in his eyes, enveloped by his words of love. They were one soul.

"Thou art the night and the day, the heavens and the earth. Thou art everything. Thou art the air I breathe, the water I drink, which springs forth a fountain of life within me. Thou art the very blood in my veins, for thou art everything. Our souls are one. I love thee now and till the end of time."

She could feel the power of his love for her radiating out of his entire being. Then it was her turn.

MICHEAL had never felt anything like this before. Energy from her was pulsing right through him. It had to be the power of love. Then she spoke.

"Micheal. I was dead. Day had turned to night. Thou art the dawn's first light, which breathed new life into this heart of mine. Thou chased away the dark with the light of thy love. I fear nothing for thou art with me."

As she spoke, he had a flash of their every moment together, which in the light of love meant so much more.

"Our love spans time and space, from the most distant star to the end of eternity. I am for thee and thou art mine forever and ever. I love thee now and till the end of time."

They shared a smile at the last line, for they spoke with one mind.

"Micheal, will you speak your vows?" The minister asked.

"I will. I, Micheal William Hall, in the presence of God, take you, Julie Alexandra Buckingham, to be my wife, to have and to hold, from this day forward, for better, for worse, for richer, for poorer, in sickness and in health, to love and to cherish, so long as we both shall live. All this I vow and promise," he proclaimed with all his heart.

He could see tears welling in the ocean of her eyes. Micheal lost himself in her eyes as she recited her vows.

"The rings?"

Rainsford, his best man, produced the rings.

They were single-piece cut diamond. Designed to capture and emanate light, they nearly glowed. They were both engraved with

the same inscription: "Micheal and Julie for all time and eternity."
It would be difficult to believe that they weren't magical.

Then Micheal took her hand and said, "I give you this ring as
a symbol of our marriage. May God enable us to grow in love
together."

Then she replied, "I receive this ring as a symbol of our marriage."

"You may kiss your bride." Some lines are timeless.

Micheal took her in his arms and kissed her deeply.

II: Eternal Love

"Have you waited long enough?" Julie whispered in MICHEAL'S
ear as the reception wound down.

"A day would've been too long."

"Then let's not wait any longer."

"Ladies and gentlemen. Honored guests. What pleasure of your
company on this special day, alas we have urgent business to
attend."

Most of the people let out an embarrassed laugh.

"Good evening and farewell," he led Julie out of the ballroom.

"I was this close to tearing your dress off and taking you right
there in the ballroom," Micheal joked, trying to settle his nerves.

"What stopped you?"

"Self-control. It is the true measure of a gentleman."

"At least you proved your intellect."

"Oh?"

"You didn't read that study from Yale? Where they proved a link
between delayed gratification and intelligence? You disappoint
me," she teased.

"My apologies, my lady," he said as he picked her up. He carried
her over the threshold into his chambers, then set her down.

"Goodness, you're beautiful." He felt as if he had just seen her
for the first time. They climbed to his bed chamber. "I've dreamt
of this night for so long."

"And still you kept me waiting a year."

"I—"

"I know, but at least you got a preview," she smiled, referring to
their *almost* night in bed.

He felt the heat rise in his cheeks.

"Honestly, that made it worse, in a way."

"I'm sure it did." Julie raised a brow. "Well, now it's my turn." She slid his coat off, tracing his form.

Micheal felt her pulse penetrate his flesh causing his heart to flutter.

"You are such a gorgeous man. My prince in white." She kissed him.

As she removed his shirt, he began tasting her neck with his lips. Her scent filling each breath. She ran her fingers gently over his chest and down his stomach, kissing him along the way. She came back up and ran her hands along his arms and shoulders as they locked lips.

JULIE had imagined this night for the last year, but to her, the reality so far already surpassed her fantasies. He was the perfect man.

She unbuttoned his pants and slipped them off. He stood in only his underwear. This was as much as she had ever seen. She rose to meet his penetrating gaze.

"I could get lost forever in your eyes," he said.

He ran his hands down her neck, then traced the curves of her body as he went to one knee.

"May I?" he asked, taking her foot in his hands.

"You may."

He gently removed her slippers, then ran his hands up her legs and under her skirt. His touch was like fire on her inner thighs. His kiss on her feet sent shockwaves through her. He stood and circled behind her. He kissed her neck passionately as he began loosening her corset.

The last tie came loose, and her dress slid down a little. He slowly slid it the rest of the way down. He was on his knees and began tasting her thighs as his hands moved up her backside. He gently kissed his way to her neck again. His hands traced her hips to her waist, then to her breasts. As he outlined them with his fingers, the heat was building to a boil.

His mouth was soft and warm on her neck, then he came around to face her.

"How is this possible?" he searched her face.

"What?"

"That anyone so beautiful could possibly exist." he shook his head slightly.

She looked him up and down, then said, "I was thinking the same thing."

Julie kissed MICHEAL and pushed him to sit on the bed. She stood for a moment, just staring at him. He took the opportunity to admire her perfection.

Her long, silky-smooth legs. The supple curve of her hips. Her slender, soft stomach. Her porcelain white breasts. The delicate and perfect vee at the base of her neck, accentuated by the lace choker.

She removed her tiara, then came over and pressed her lips into his. She began exploring his entire body with her mouth, finally removing his last item of clothing. Micheal stroked her hair as she went down on him. His head was swimming.

When JULIE finished, she came up, and they locked lips again. It was now her turn.

He slowly removed her panties and kissed her inner thighs. After a minute, he laid her down on the bed with her legs over his shoulders. He wrapped his arms around her thighs, securing himself between them. His head dove and immersed itself in her wet lips. His moans sent chills up her spine. She had never felt such desire, such intensity, from anyone before. Micheal slid his hands up her body and to her breasts, causing the tension to build. He was licking her clit, sending her into ecstasy. He brought her to the point of climax, then settled her down, only to bring her to pleasure again.

His care and attention to her every desire was more than she could have asked for. Her mind was filled by Micheal.

MICHEAL slowed everything down for a little while. He kissed and caressed her.

"Are you ready?" Julie whispered.

He had been thoroughly enjoying every aspect of her. It was beyond his greatest fantasies.

"You have no idea."

Micheal entered through the final gateway. Their eyes were locked, and he felt completely connected to her. He could not have imagined anything more perfect. He was finally able to express his love for her in a complete and intimate way. The energy was vibrating.

He felt her legs wrap around his hips. She was holding him tight, her nails digging into his back. Micheal began to thrust more deeply. Waves of sparks pulsed between them. Julie's back arched as he moved in faster and faster still. She took him by his hair and guided his lips to hers.

"Jules," he whispered.

"Micheal, I love you."

"I love you," he said. His head dove to her neck, and as he kissed her, he felt her hips tremble and her body tighten around him, bringing him to climax. He never thought love would find him. Now, he was face to face with it and felt all boundaries that separated them disappear. It took a few minutes for him to recognize himself individually again.

Micheal had collapsed on JULIE, his head rested on her chest. She was running her fingers through his hair. "Are you all right?"

After a moment, he rose up, looked at her, and said, "I'm in heaven." He then rolled off and pulled her into his embrace.

"Do you feel any different?" She wasn't sure what he was thinking. She only hoped he had felt the same level of beauty and pleasure she had.

"At thirty-two years old, I finally feel like a complete man. That sounds pathetic, I know."

"No. There's no one who deserves to live fully more than you." She stroked his cheek.

"Was I any good?"

"Do you even have to ask? Let's just say I'm glad you studied."

She laughed. "You were perfection."

"As were you... I hope you're ready for more." he raised his brows.

He dove into her being without hesitation. She welcomed him with open arms for several more intense rounds deep into the night.

"How do you have so much stamina?"

"I did some research on the topic."

"Of course you did," she said with a smile. "How much more do *you* have left?"

"Is that a challenge?"

"Show me," she said as he took her into his arms.

They made up for lost time over the next two days; he certainly put her to the test. They left for their honeymoon on the *Liberty* the next day.

"So where are we going?" Julie asked.

"Only your favorite location."

"Bermuda?"

"I prepared it specifically for this purpose. So we can make new, better memories there."

They arrived in the evening on the secluded west side of the island. There was a newly built bungalow right on the beach. It was a week of sun, beach, and "fun." It was the perfect honeymoon.

As they lay on the beach, watching the sunset on their last day in Bermuda, Julie said, "I wish we could stay here forever."

"Do you want to?"

She thought about it for a moment.

"No, we have to go home."

"We'll leave tomorrow. We have a few things left to prepare."

"Let's just enjoy this night."

"Absolutely."

They kissed as the sun finally set on their honeymoon.

III: From Time to Time

JULIE began a new volume of *The Book of Avalon*.

September 1, 1697

The day is finally here. Five and a half years ago, I fell through time. I have lived all that time here in the seventeenth century and we are about to embark on an uncertain adventure. It will take one hundred and fifty years through twenty time stops to get back to the twenty-first century. I still feel ambivalent. The most important reason for my desire to get home has changed. I knew in my heart over a year ago that Aiden moved on, and now I am married to Micheal, and I am completely happy. In that light, I almost feel the risk and uncertainty might not be worth it to get back to my family and friends. I could spend the rest of my life here in the seventeenth and eighteenth centuries and be perfectly happy in my life with Micheal. Together, we have become so much more than I could have ever imagined. When we first came together, I felt unworthy to be considered noble. Now, I feel not just worthy, but a sense of belonging in the most noble House of Avalon, the legacy of King Arthur. I understand now why Micheal was willing to risk his life, everything, to defend his family's honor. As his wife, I'm a Lady of Avalon. His Guinevere. No matter where we go, no matter what we face, I know we will persevere. As long as we're together, there's nothing we can't do.

They returned from Bermuda and began final preparations for their jump. They ferried their supply modules to the jump site on the Massachusetts coast between Plymouth and Weymouth. They spent the better part of the week gathering all the necessary supplies and getting everything properly positioned so as to be pulled through the portal with them. They also brought the launch systems for the sky network or sky-net for short.

It was still theoretical, but Julie sure hoped their calculations were correct. It would be so much easier to get accustomed to the thirty-third century B.C. if they didn't have to start over completely from scratch. "Anything else?" Micheal asked her.

She took one last look at her chambers, then said, "No, I think we have everything."

They headed down to the entry hall.

"Living here was incredible. Not because it's a palace, but because it was your vision," she explained as they entered the gallery.

"I hope you felt it became *our* vision. These galleries are a chronicle of our lives here at Bostonian, painted in your hand."

"It certainly came to be my home—our home." Julie looked up at the paintings on the wall. She had put the art studio to full use to decorate their home.

When they walked out onto the patio deck, Angel was there to say goodbye.

"Hey girl!" she said, patting Angel on the neck and feeding her an apple.

"A most trusted friend and companion. I'm going to miss you. Take good care of her," she instructed.

"Lady Avalon, we will, I promise." Filipe bowed.

The entire staff was lined up to see them off for the final time. They made sure to say goodbye and thank each and every one of them, particularly Rose, Yvette, and Master Liu.

Then, her three best friends were last to see her off.

"Cecily. Alice. Mary. You are as sisters. Shall I miss you most of all," she said, and they all hugged.

"Farewell, Julie," Cecily said with a smile.

"Shall I mourn your leaving?" Alice said with tears in her eyes.

"I don't want to say goodbye." Mary shook her head.

As the *Liberty* pulled away, tears began to flow. She felt such love from all of them, and such loss in the leaving.

"Are you all right?" Micheal came up from behind and kissed the side of her neck, wrapping his arms around her.

"I hate goodbyes."

A couple of hours later, they had hidden the *Liberty* in a secret location and made their way to the departure site. MICHEAL was double-checking his calculations.

"Five minutes," he informed Julie.

"Micheal?"

"Yes, Jules?"

"I don't know if I can do this," she was fidgeting. They were about twenty feet apart.

"We don't have to go. You are my life. I would follow you anywhere, anytime. Your love is all I need."

"What about your family? Your friends?"

He walked over to her.

"Jules, I'm not worried about anyone else. I will be perfectly happy no matter where or when we are, so long as you're with me. What do you want? That's the only thing that matters."

"I...I'm not sure."

"One minute."

He pulled her in and kissed her passionately and deep.

"It's okay, we'll stay." He tucked her hair behind her ear.

She looked deep into his eyes for a moment.

"No. Micheal, let's go." She kissed him again. He looked at the clock.

"Ten seconds!" He hurried to the spot.

A few seconds later, two tunnels opened in front of them like swirling vortexes. Green mist began spiraling around them.

He looked over and yelled, "I love you."

"I love you!"

Suddenly, at the edge of the mist swirling around her, he saw Lord Cavendish.

Micheal yelled, "No!"

But at that moment Micheal was sucked into the tunnel.

Micheal broke through the wall of green mist into a tunnel of light. He could see a palette of colors rushing past. Heat was building around him and everything was accelerating. It felt like jumping to warp speed. Or perhaps passing through a star-gate.

His whole body felt like it was on fire. He seemed to be flying through space. Stars were racing past. The darkness closed in around him and became a tunnel, the light at the end rapidly approaching.

As he reached the end, there was a bright flash and everything went dark.

WELCOME TO ATLANTIS

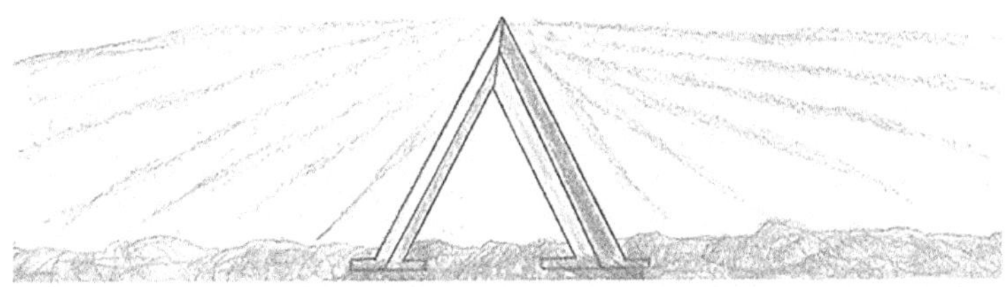

T HE LAST THING LORD GEORGE CAVENDISH could remember was seeing the Lord and Lady Avalon doing yet another trick of sorcery. Then he was pulled into some vortex.

"Bloody Lords of Avalon," he said spitefully as he got to his feet. "What have they done to me now?"

He made his way to a clearing; he could not comprehend what his eyes were seeing.

An unbelievably large city was surrounded by water. There were concentric rings of water and land. Large pyramids were everywhere, with edges that glowed purple in the twilight, culminating in brilliant lavender beams radiating into the sky.

Then he noticed all kinds of strange objects floating or flying through the sky. He made his way down the hill from the overlook. He was approaching an incredibly long bridge leading into the city when he was surrounded by about a dozen men holding what looked like some version of muskets.

A man who appeared to be in charge stepped forward and began addressing him in a strange tongue, one he had never heard before.

He had no idea what they said, so he just responded with, "I am a soldier in His Majesty's Navy.

The man responded with, "............................... English."

He understood "English."

They said it again: "............................... English."

After that, they held him at musket point for what felt like hours.

Finally, a very beautiful woman walked up to him. She had reddish-brown hair and green eyes. She was wearing clothing that clung to her body.

She stared at him for a moment, a slightly confused look on her face. Then she said, "Lord George Cavendish, welcome to Atlantis."

<<<<>>>>

IN MEMORIUM

T HE SALEM WITCH TRIALS were one of the most terrible episodes in American history. In memory of the victims of the trials.

BRIDGET BISHOP
SARAH GOOD
REBECCA NURSE
SUSANNAH MARTIN
ELIZABETH HOWE
SARAH WILDES
GEORGE BURROUGHS
MARTHA CARRIER
JOHN WILLARD
GEORGE JACOBS, SR.
JOHN PROCTOR
MARTHA COREY
MARY EASTY
ANN PUDEATOR
ALICE PARKER
MARY PARKER
WILMOTT REDD
MARGARET SCOTT
SAMUEL WARDELL
GILES COREY
SARAH OSBORN
ROGER TOOTHAKER
LYNDIA DUSTIN
ANN FOSTER

RECOGNITION

IN RECOGNITION OF THE NATIVE PEOPLES OF AMERICA

The effect of contact with Europeans was tragic for the people who were already living in the Americas. The forcing of people from their homelands, combined with the exposure to new diseases to which they had no defense, led to the death of 90% of the original population.

I would like to recognize the original people living in Massachusetts.

MASSACHUSETT
WAMPANOAG
PENNACOOK
NIPMUC
POCOMTUC
MAHICAN
NAUSET

ACKNOWLEDGMENTS

VICTOR TORRICO – My brother from another mother.

MAREN JENSEN – For all your help and insights.

CLAIRE EVANS, LINE EDITOR – Your helpful insights greatly improved my book.

KATHARINE FRANCIS, COPY EDITOR/ PROOFREADER/ CRITIQUE – For your keen eye to correct my many grammatical mistakes and your insights into my characters.

BYRON PIXTON – For your help with my beautiful cover.

MY BETA READERS – KJYRSTEN ASHDOWN, DIANA TINGEY, LINDSAY FINDLAYSON, MICHEAL JENSEN, TAMARA WARD, DANIEL CLUBB and NATHAN MITCHELL.

LISA JENSEN – For your beautiful art.

And of course, my parents – RALPH, CAROL and CHARLOTTE JENSEN. Without your love and guidance I could not have completed this work.

ABOUT THE AUTHOR

STEPHEN JENSEN grew up fascinated by the world around him. He spent his childhood studying science and history. In his youth, he became interested in the stories and worlds of sci-fi and fantasy. As an adult, he's spent the last couple decades traveling the world to see the history and cultures firsthand. All of this fostered his imagination to create his own fantasies and world in his head. The last few years he's put pen to page to bring some of these stories to life. The Avalon series is the culmination of this life journey. He lives in Salt Lake City, Utah.